LOST
IN THE
CRAZIES

A RICK MORRAND MYSTERY

BOOK TWO

PETER J. RYAN

In memory of my mother, Frances C. Ryan

Man's law changes with his understanding of man.
Only the laws of the Spirit remain the same.

—Crow Indian proverb

CHAPTER 1

Bartenders tend to notice things, and the first thing Jesse Lone Wolf noticed was the blood.

Too much blood.

The larger man, the one with *Boone* scripted along the inside of his dirt-encrusted forearm, wrapped the coarse flesh of his right hand around his fourth bottle of Moose Drool, having instructed Jesse to serve him two beers at a time. His teeth were yellow, gums rimmed with the residue of tobacco, eyes bloodshot from alcohol. He carried the odor of a bedroll left in the pouring rain.

The crimson color beneath his fingernails was understandable for someone who had field-dressed an elk, but the broad stains that had dried like hardpan on the front of his T-shirt were curious at best, even for the most careless of bow hunters.

Boone and another hunter had drifted in shortly after one o'clock. The Gold Bar was dead, just as it was every Wednesday afternoon. The only drinking establishment in Mariah, Montana, population 237, was lightless and sad, seemingly by design. A filthy rectangular window delivered a sliver of light from behind the bar, iron security rods casting a shadow found only in a prison cell. Two tables with wooden chairs had been placed along the wall, separated by a jukebox with a light that sporadically flickered, the round puncture in its glass cover matching the butt of a pool cue. An opaque plastic film covered the front door, protecting the dour setting from any hope that sunshine might bring. "The Gold," as it was called, was not a place for conviviality and pleasure. Its existence emphasized function, with most of those in attendance primarily interested in the immediate medicinal benefits of a sturdy drink.

Boone's mood appeared uneven at best, likely due to the restless sleep that accompanies several nights in the backcountry. Or perhaps he was just an asshole—Jesse couldn't be sure. He studied Boone's grizzled face, noticing a pinkish crescent along the rim of his receding hairline. The scar was the perfect match for the base of a beer bottle, likely one that had shattered against Boone's forehead.

Boone's friend, shorter and rail-thin, was somewhat more congenial, if not a bit restless.

"We really should call his house, Boone," the smaller guy said.

"Relax, Kyle," Boone answered. "I'm sure he made it out just fine."

Kyle shook his head slowly. "We still should call him."

Jesse's eyes roved between the two men, considering their conversation. *Call whom?* He popped the cap off a Moose Drool and put it in front of Kyle, figuring it might calm him. Kyle waved it off. Jesse shrugged, took a sip from the bottle, and looked through the rust-caked shafts covering the murky window. The Crazy Mountains glistened in the distance, untamed and free, their upper peaks teased by a sprinkle of early snow.

"You guys bow-hunting in the Crazies?" Jesse asked as he turned toward them. Both men nodded their heads. "Where you from?" He'd never seen them before. He figured maybe they lived in Riverton, twenty-five miles to the south.

"Three Forks," Boone grumbled with disinterest. He drained the last half of his beer.

Jesse looked back out the window toward the parking lot, spotting a charcoal Ford one-ton with a white three-horse slant trailer hooked to the back. The horses took turns poking their noses out of slits in the side. Jesse's eyes drifted to the bed of the truck, where the head of a bull elk with a six-point rack streamed blood down a side panel.

"Nice bull," Jesse said. "That the only one you got?"

"You the warden?" Boone snapped.

"Just askin'," Jesse answered. Yep, he was an asshole, all right.

"A guy who was with us got a nice cow elk," Kyle said. "We already field-dressed it and put it on ice in the Yedi." Boone shot a glare at Kyle, who swallowed hard, color leaving his face.

"Where's the other guy now?" Jesse asked.

"We really need to call him, Boone," Kyle muttered. His eyes were sad and watery, his face carrying the look of a mistreated mongrel accustomed to perpetual blame. "We need to do it *now*."

"Go right ahead," Boone huffed.

"My phone's dead. Can I use yours?"

Boone stared straight ahead. "Mine died two days ago."

Jesse grabbed a rotary phone from next to the register. It made a dinging sound as he placed it on the bar. Kyle flashed a tight smile of gratitude and dialed. His eyes blinked rapidly. Sweat beaded on his forehead. "Amber, it's Kyle Ricketts," he said, tightly gripping the receiver. "Has Garrett come home?" He listened. "No, we're in Mariah, at the Gold Bar. He's not with us. We haven't heard from him since Saturday. We thought maybe—"

The voice on the phone became loud and animated. Jesse thought he heard the word *bar*. Kyle waved an open palm. "Amber, calm down," he said. "I realize it's been a few days, but ... Hello?"

Kyle dejectedly returned the receiver to its cradle. Boone chuckled. "That went well," he said as he pushed his empty bottle toward Jesse. "How about another couple of beers? And a shot of Jack."

Jesse picked up the empty and used a tattered gray bar rag to wipe the wet spot beneath it. "You might want to slow down."

Boone's eyebrows tightened. "I've been in the mountains almost a week. Why would I want to slow down?" Flicking a ten from the bills scattered in front of him, he sharpened his tone. "Two beers and a shot—just like I asked."

Jesse shook his head. "Not if you're drivin'." He popped the cap on a single bottle and put it on the bar. "The new sheriff over here has really cracked down on drunk drivers. I don't need you killin' someone and have them track it back here."

Boone's jaw muscles pulsed as he held his eyes on Jesse. The bartender returned the ire, a rush of blood warming his face.

Kyle studied the two men. "New sheriff?" he asked uneasily. "What happened to the old one—the young guy?"

Jesse kept staring at Boone. "Caleb Tidwell? He's dead. Shot through the neck with an arrow. Happened about a year ago."

Kyle nodded rapidly. "Yeah, now I remember. The new sheriff killed him, right?"

Jesse turned toward him. "No, it was another guy who killed Tidwell," he said, folding what was left of his bar rag. "But the new sheriff was there when it happened."

"What's the new sheriff's name?"

"Morrand ... Rick Morrand. Used to be a lawyer ... I guess he still is. But his main job now is sheriff." He glanced at Boone. "For some reason, he really don't like drunk driving."

Boone's nostrils flared, eyes widening. "I ordered a shot," he said with bite.

"Not a good idea," Jesse said without looking at him.

Boone took a long swig of beer, then slammed his bottle onto the bar. "I'm not asking for your opinion," he growled.

"I can drive," Kyle meekly offered.

"You ain't drivin' my truck," Boone said without looking at Kyle. "And I don't need no Indian—or, should I say, *Native American*—telling me how much I should drink!"

Jesse's body tensed at the sound of Boone's mocking tone, a flame igniting inside him. *Native American*—the white man's designation. An elixir for white guilt, perhaps, but how had that term and changing the name of football teams ever benefitted the Indian? Jesse's soul—his *spirit*—belonged to the Crow Nation, his veins coursing with the fiery blood of his ancestors, brave and determined warriors who had defended their people and heritage. Their sacred land had been taken from them, stolen without conscience by men devoid of the Spirit and filled only with greed and arrogance.

Men like Boone.

"Boone, maybe you've had enough," Kyle stammered. "Garrett hasn't shown up. We need to—"

"Shut up, Kyle," Boone snapped, his face reddening with rage. "I ain't leaving until I get my shot."

Jesse leaned forward, placing both hands on the bar. "You need to listen to your friend," he said through gritted teeth. "You've had enough."

Boone cocked his head. "What ya gonna do? Call 911?"

Jesse drew a deep breath, eyes fastened on Boone. His right hand dropped behind the bar, and he produced a sawed-off shotgun. He held it inches from Boone's forehead. "I don't believe in 911," he said. "Takes too long."

Boone's eyes bulged, his face turning pale. "I …. Isn't that thing illegal?" he asked meekly.

Jesse nodded. "I would imagine it is."

Kyle was off his barstool, backtracking several steps as he stared at the shotgun. "C'mon, Boone. Let's get out of here."

Boone pushed himself away from the bar, his stool scraping across the weathered wooden floor. "You and me, we're not done," he said, his tremorous finger pointing at Jesse.

The shotgun barrel followed Boone and Kyle as they headed out the door. Jesse lowered his weapon, still thinking about the blood.

CHAPTER 2

Rick Morrand stepped quietly onto the porch of his fiancée's house, careful not to announce his arrival. His lips curled into a mischievous grin as he rang the doorbell and waited.

Sage Fontenot appeared, her eyebrows collapsing into a quizzical frown as she pushed open the storm door. "What are you doing standing out there?" she said with a half-chuckle. "The door's open."

Rick didn't budge. He removed his Stetson hat and held it waist-high, his thumb and forefinger tracing the crease. "It's my understanding, ma'am, that you were in need of the sheriff," he said in a level tone.

Sage paused and studied him, suppressing a grin. "Well, yes, that's correct, *Sheriff*," she said. "Please … please come in."

Rick stepped inside, remaining in character, his eyes methodically inspecting the interior of a home he'd seen hundreds of times. A bulky sliced turkey sandwich rested on the kitchen table, accompanied by a generous scoop of potato salad. An inviting glass of iced tea glistened nearby.

Sage took two steps toward him, close enough for him to inhale the warmth of her breath. "They sure are makin' sheriffs handsome these days," she said, her fingers stroking the top of his open-collared uniform shirt. They held their eyes on each other momentarily before desire pushed their lips forcefully together, intense passion interrupted by spontaneous bursts of joyful laughter.

Rick feverishly unbuttoned Sage and she unbuttoned him, their hands flailing about as they fought desperately to keep their mouths joined together. Rick removed his duty belt and holster, his arm extending in a blind attempt to place the gear on a chair. He wasn't close. A loud thud rose from the wooden floor. More gleeful laughter.

They awkwardly edged their way to the table. Sage swept the sandwich aside with a brush of her hand, knocking the iced tea onto the tablecloth.

Rick glanced at the spill for an instant before she directed his face back toward her. "I've got more," she said.

He leaned over her, savoring her emerald eyes framed in flowing cinnamon hair. Her forehead glimmered. She pulled him closer, the tips of her fingers pressed hard against his shoulder blades. He kissed her full lips again, surrendering to her invitation to be inside her. The table began to make a rhythmic creak. They giggled.

His cell phone rang.

"No!" Sage shouted.

"But—"

"No!"

She held his face between her soft hands. "Look at me," she said.

"I am looking at you."

"No, I mean *really* look at me. I need you here—with me. I need all of you here with me."

"I'm here with you," he whispered as his lips wandered down her neck.

Was he here with her? Rick knew what she meant. Sage had been there four years earlier, when Rick had lost his wife and soul mate, Christine. Sage was well aware that he was approaching the first anniversary of the death of his daughter, Chloe, murdered by the troubled Tessie Lou Hunter in the Montana backcountry.

Rick had suffered devastating traumas of the heart. Sage surely couldn't blame him for his hesitation to splash headfirst into a new, perilous sea of vulnerability. They were engaged to be married, but they hadn't set a date. Plans had been discussed, and at times she appeared to hesitate as well, her luckless history with men perhaps cautioning her against riding roughshod into the sunset with a man still nurturing festering wounds.

He lifted his head and stared into her pleading eyes. Their lips danced as they traded each other's essence.

Rick had no doubt of his love for Sage. He desired badly to give her—in her words—"all of him." But perhaps that was his quandary—he had a deep desire, but something tugged at him, holding him back.

His phone rang again. "No!" Sage repeated.

Rick's head collapsed next to hers, his face sliding down the damp, warm skin of her cheek. He inhaled the sweetness of her hair, which captured the distinct and pleasant scent of her perfume. He stayed there a moment, basking in the aroma as if lying in a sun-drenched mountain meadow. Tuberose was what she called it. *Tuberose.* His mind trailed to the time he walked into

Darcy Landon's Flower Shop, requesting a bouquet of this special flower called tuberose. Darcy shot him a look as though he was buck naked with his hair on fire. She explained that tuberose was a tropical plant native to the warmth of southern Mexico. Not much tuberose to be found in Montana, even in summer.

After several rings, his phone lay quiet for a beat, only to start ringing again. It likely was the sheriff's office. Rick lifted his head and gently kissed Sage on the lips. "I have to answer it," he whispered. "I'm the sheriff. Remember?"

He slid down into a chair next to the table and hitched up his khaki uniform pants. Releasing a deep sigh, he fished his phone from a side pocket. "Morrand," he said, his voice slightly labored.

"Thank God you picked up," said Helen Prichard, the office dispatcher. "Why didn't you answer your radio?"

"It's in my truck," he said. "I was having lunch."

"You really should carry your radio."

Helen was right, of course. Rick was as unripe as a sheriff could be. He'd been pressed into public service by the death of Caleb Tidwell. Helen was gently schooling him on the nuances of law enforcement, and he wasn't always a willing student. A fully equipped duty belt felt a bit on the bulky side, weighted down with extraneous items such as a flashlight, handcuffs, and radio. He often would lighten the load.

"I'll be sure to wear my radio," he said, his voice soft with appeasement. "What's up?"

"We have a situation up in the Crazies. Lost bow hunter."

"Give me details."

"His name is Garrett McRae. His wife is here, and she's beside herself, to say the least. According to his hunting buddies, they haven't heard from him since Saturday morning."

"It's Wednesday."

"Affirmative."

"When did the hunters report him?"

"They didn't. She did."

Sage sat on the table behind Rick, affectionately massaging the back of his neck. He looked up to see her pinched eyebrows ask, "Who is it?" He lifted his chin. "Helen," he mouthed back. He buckled his belt and retrieved his uniform shirt off the floor. He held it in the air, flicking it with his wrist to straighten the wrinkles.

"Where are these hunters now?" he asked as he placed an arm into a sleeve.

"They told the guy's wife they were at the Gold Bar in Mariah," Helen said. "They're from Three Forks, so they're probably heading our way."

Rick began buttoning his shirt. "Is Jack Kelly around?" he asked, referring to his friend and undersheriff. "Get a vehicle description from the wife and ask him to track these guys down on Highway 89. They'll need to come in so we can talk to them. You also should put a call out to Ben Westfall, see if he can start putting together a search-and-rescue team." He glanced at Sage and winked. "I'll be there in fifteen to twenty minutes."

"Where are you?" Helen asked.

"I'm on my way."

Rick stuffed his cell phone in his pocket, rose to his feet, and tucked in his shirt. "A guy is missing in the Crazies. No one has talked to him since Saturday."

The word *missing* echoed in his head. He remembered how Chloe, under the torment of drugs and mental illness, would suddenly vanish. The last time she went missing he was worried sick about her, but she was already dead.

The Crazy Mountains were wild and treacherous, home to merciless underbrush, hidden ravines, and unsociable grizzlies. Rick hoped Garrett McRae wasn't already gone.

Rick glanced toward Sage. She had dressed and was using a yellow dish towel to mop up the spilled tea. "I'll wrap this sandwich," she said flatly. "You can take it with you."

"Thanks," Rick said as he picked his gun belt off the floor. He stopped and leaned toward her, waiting until she looked at him. "You okay?"

Sage stopped sponging the tea. "When are we getting married?" she asked. "This sneaking around is getting kind of silly, don't you think?" She shrugged. "It's not like Abby doesn't know that adults have sex."

Rick's granddaughter, Abby, was a month away from turning ten years old. Following Chloe's death, Rick became her guardian, and he and Sage were raising her. Abby likely did know that adults had sex, and she knew a lot of other things, thanks to the internet. Still, as much as he wanted to wake up each morning with Sage Fontenot, he insisted that they not live together until after they were married. "Keeping up appearances," is what he called it, the phrase that often caused Sage to wince.

Rick laid his belt and holster on the table and walked toward her. "I'd get married tomorrow at the courthouse if you wanted to, Sage," he said.

"We both want a nice wedding, a reception with music, a happy occasion, right?" He smiled and hiked his eyebrows. "And don't forget the honeymoon."

She pressed her head against his chest. "You sure?"

He lifted her chin and stared far into her eyes. "I'm sure."

She buried her head again. "I love you, Rick Morrand," she whispered. He placed a long, gentle kiss on the top of her head, breathing in the scent of her skin. "I love you too," he said, keeping his voice steady as he mouthed the words that seemed to have invited so much pain.

As he turned the knob of the front door, he looked at Sage one last time, saying nothing. Her eyes beamed confidence, saying she believed in him—no hint of worry. He wondered if that was true. Her fingers combed thick hair over her ear, once again revealing her sensuous eyes. He wanted to stay, finish what they'd started.

"Rick," she said softly, her eyes now pleading. "Be careful."

CHAPTER 3

Helen was on the phone when Rick walked in, her lips pursed and forehead tightened. "I'll tell the sheriff, sir," she said with resignation. "Just do the best you can."

She hung up the receiver and looked toward Rick. "That was Ben Westfall. As you probably already know, half the search-and-rescue volunteers are firemen. With all the wildland activity we've had this summer, they're either out on campaigns or dog tired 'cause they just got back."

Helen's hair was the color of flint, pulled back to reveal thin streaks of white, her brown eyes focused and businesslike. The uniform she wore was clean, pressed, and meticulously creased, much like her approach to her job. Now in her early sixties, she'd been divorced for two decades. Though she'd never been seen with a new beau, there were rumors she'd carried on with former deputy and widower Billy Renfro, but both parties had scoffed at such talk, correctly claiming that Riverton could be a petri dish for innuendo. The daughters she'd raised were both married and living in Seattle. The Dexter County Sheriff's Office was her life, and Rick considered her indispensable.

He exhaled, propped his hands on his hips, and scanned the small lobby. "Is Mrs. McRae still here?"

Helen lifted her brow, eyes opening wide. "Oh yeah, she's here all right. I have her sitting in your office. She's still pretty upset. In addition to her husband being missing, I guess she has a disabled child at home. A neighbor is watching him. She says he doesn't do well when she leaves him behind."

Rick removed his hat and pushed back his thick hair as he approached his office. He opened the door slowly, uncertain what he might find inside. A petite woman, strawberry blonde, maybe twenty-nine or thirty, sat slumped on a wooden chair in front of his desk, her forearms crossed on her lap, palms cupping her elbows. The corner of her bottom lip was curled beneath her upper teeth, her gaze fixed on the floor. She turned toward Rick, eyes sunken and face drawn.

"Mrs. McRae, my name is Rick Morrand. I'm—"

She jumped from her chair as if she'd been splashed with ice water. "Thank God you're here, Sheriff," she stammered. "You've got to find my husband. This isn't like him. Something has happened."

Rick waved open palms toward her. "Try to remain calm, Mrs. McRae. I'm sure he—"

"Amber."

"Excuse me?"

"Amber," she said. "My name's Amber."

She spoke at the speed of a seventy-eight-rpm vinyl record, eyes blinking as she stared at Rick expectantly. "Okay … Amber … Please tell me when you last spoke to your husband," he said, leading her back to the chair. She settled into her seat. Rick folded his arms and perched on the corner of his desk.

"I spoke to Garrett last Thursday, before they headed into the Crazies," she said. "There's no cell service back there, so I pretty much have to wait until I hear from him. He said he planned to come out Monday night, or Tuesday at the latest."

"Does he go hunting every year?"

"Since we were kids," Amber said. "He's experienced, but he's a bow hunter. It's a lot more dangerous than hunting with a rifle."

"I tried bow hunting myself once," Rick mused. "I wasn't very good at it." He studied Amber's face. She had almond-shaped eyes, a button nose, and full pink lips. She wore no lipstick or makeup and required neither.

"Can I get you something? A soda, or a glass of water maybe?"

"No, thank you," Amber said. "Someone just needs to—"

She stopped talking as loud shouting erupted outside Rick's office. He strode toward the door and looked into the lobby, where his undersheriff, Jack Kelly, was nose to nose with a burly man in camo pants and a red flannel shirt. "You need to stand down, sir," Jack said, his scowl remaining steadfast as the hunter flailed his arms in protest. A smaller, slightly built man stood quietly nearby, lips flattened as he shook his head.

Amber appeared behind Rick and burst right past him, heading straight for the hunter sparring with Jack. The man easily outweighed her by one hundred pounds, but that didn't stop her from delivering a shove that nearly knocked him off his feet. "You bastard!" she shouted. "You left him out there?" She lunged toward him, pushing him and getting in his face. "What the hell is the matter with you, Boone?"

Boone appeared prepared to retaliate, but Jack stepped in front of him. "Whoa!" Rick shouted as he placed a firm grip on Amber's biceps and ushered her back into his office. After a moment, he emerged, closing the door behind him.

"Where'd you find these guys, Jack?"

"Highway 89, just north of town," Jack said. He nodded toward Boone. "This guy's loaded—mainly alcohol, as far as I can tell. Luckily, the other guy was driving. They probably realized we'd be looking for them."

Rick squared his stance, folded his arms, and looked at Boone. "What's your name, sir?"

"Boone."

"I already gathered that. I meant your *full* name."

"Randall Boone."

Rick turned toward the other hunter. "And you?"

"Ricketts, sir," he answered. "Kyle Ricketts."

Rick studied the men. Boone's lips were twisted into a defiant snarl, his thumbs plunged into the front of his pants, head cocked sideways, and boots squared with his shoulders. Kyle resembled a frightened rabbit, his scrawny frame drooping like a timid third-grader on the first day of school. "It's my understanding that you lost contact with Mr. McRae on Saturday," Rick said. "Any particular reason you waited until now to mention that he's missing?"

"Elk season only comes once a year," Boone said without emotion, "and Kyle hadn't punched his tag."

Kyle began to speak, perhaps in protest, but Boone's glare quieted him. Rick raised his chin. "Were you going to say something, Mr. Ricketts?" he asked. Kyle wagged his head briskly. "He's right … I still had my tag."

"Besides," Boone said, "there was no reason for us to worry about Garrett. He knows those mountains better than anybody. We figured he'd come out before we did."

"Thing is, you guys have his horse," Jack said. He turned toward Rick. "They're pulling a trailer," Jack said. "Three horses in the back. One of the horses belongs to Garrett McRae."

"Who's vehicle is it, gentlemen?" Rick asked.

"Mine," Boone said.

"Is it open? With your permission, we'd like to take a look—the horse trailer mainly, but also the truck."

"Suit yourself," Boone mumbled, "but don't give me shit about the empties on the floor. We drank those at the trailhead before we went in. We didn't want to litter."

"Right," Rick huffed. "You guys strike me as civic-minded." He walked toward the window, where he saw Boone's dark-gray Ford one-ton, a trailer snaked behind it. He glanced toward Jack, who headed out the door.

Rick turned toward Kyle. "So, you went in ... when was it—Thursday?" he asked. "What trailhead?"

"Granite Peak," Boone interjected. Rick turned and frowned. "I wasn't speaking to you, son," he said. "I'm talking to Mr. Ricketts."

"Granite Peak, sir," Kyle said softly.

"And when was the last time you spoke to Garrett McRae?"

Kyle threw a nervous glance at Boone. "Late Saturday morning," he said. "He radioed me, saying he had just left Campfire Lake and was headed east."

"Where were you guys?"

Another glance at Boone, as though seeking permission to answer. "I was at our base camp—maybe four or five miles from the trailhead," Kyle said. "Boone had already left to go hunting."

"Did Garrett say when or where he would meet up with you?"

Kyle shook his head. "The radio signal went dead."

"Where'd you find his horse?"

Kyle hesitated again, so Rick turned toward Boone. "I found his horse wandering a trail," Boone mumbled, "coming from the east side of the mountains."

"When?"

"Early Monday morning."

"And it didn't occur to you that your friend might be in some kind of trouble?"

Boone shrugged. Rick studied him. The hunter's right hand appeared swollen, his knuckles flecked with red craters of missing skin.

"What happened to your hand?"

Boone glanced down with nonchalance, implying his precious time was being squandered. "My knife was dull," he grunted dismissively. "My other hand must have slipped when I was dressing my elk."

Rick felt his jaw tightening, Boone's demeanor hardly agreeing with him. Staring at the smirk on his face, Rick resisted a sudden urge to deliver a solid smack upside his head. He'd just met the man, but he already didn't like him, and he suspected others didn't either. He was as pleasant as biting into cold steak.

Boone's flannel shirt was buttoned unevenly, perhaps done with haste. His upper chest was exposed, his white skin gleaming beneath his tanned neck. Random red blotches were visible, along with scratches beneath his throat.

"You mind unbuttoning your shirt?" Rick asked.

Boone frowned. "What for?"

"It looks like you have some scratches on the top of your chest," Rick said. He whirled his finger in a circular motion. "C'mon, let's have a look."

"Are you accusing me of somethin'?"

Rick shook his head. "Let's just say I'm curious," he said. "I'm trying to reconcile why you guys would stay in the backcountry for three whole days when your friend was missing." He squinted at Boone. "You know what reconcile means, don't you?"

Boone's eyes seethed as he unbuttoned his shirt. A pair of scratches trailed beneath his rib cage, deep red before fading to pink. An ugly purple bruise splashed across the right side of his hardened stomach. He didn't wait for Rick to request an explanation.

"I've been sleeping on the ground for almost a week," he said as he buttoned his shirt. "I've been climbing over rocks and all kinds of crap. What do you expect?"

Rick shook his head and released a sigh. "Did you shoot an elk or wrestle it?"

They turned toward the door, where Jack Kelly was walking in. "Who owns the Red Dun?" he asked, his thick voice sounding displeased. Though he'd reached his fifties, Jack had retained his build of thick muscle. With his chiseled features and deep-set eyes, his face look like it belonged on Mount Rushmore. His skin, the color of powdered cocoa, made the beads of sweat on his forehead glisten like pearls under the florescent lights.

"It's mine," Boone said.

Jack's eyes narrowed. "You sure as hell don't know how to take care of a horse, do you? When's the last time that animal was shoed?"

"None of your business," Boone snarled.

Jack got in his face. "Hell yes, it's my business," he shouted. "That poor horse has two split hooves. And when the last time you watered him? I pinched the skin on his neck—he's seriously dehydrated."

Rick looked curiously at his friend and deputy, wondering when the former detective from New Jersey had become a horse whisperer. "You see anything else, Jack?" he asked.

Jack glared once more at Boone and turned toward Rick. "No," he said. "Both elk in the truck bed have tags. Their gear's piled in the backseat. That's about it."

"I'm sorry to interrupt, Sheriff," Helen said as she came over to Rick. "Ben just called back, and he has a team headed for the Crazies. He's wondering when you and Jack will be there—they need all hands on deck."

Rick nodded. "Tell him we're on our way."

Boone threw a look of contempt toward Jack and edged forward. "Are we free to go?"

"Yeah, you can go," Rick said. "But leave your contact information with our dispatcher. We may have some more questions as we conduct the search."

As they headed for the door, Jack glared at Boone. "And, dammit, take care of that horse," he hissed through clenched teeth. "If you don't, I'll be coming for it." He took a step closer, standing inches from Boone's face. "And I'll be comin' for *you*."

CHAPTER 4

After turning off Highway 89 north of Mariah, Rick and Jack wound their way on dusty gravel through fifteen miles of sprawling ranch land, the surrounding amber hills dotted by occasional herds of grazing cattle. When they finally descended into the forest, they jostled haphazardly along a narrow road littered with rocks and pocked by bucket-sized chuckholes.

"Tough to make it through here with a horse trailer," Jack said.

Rick shrugged. "It can be done. My father and I used to ride up here when I was a kid. You just need to take it slow."

"I doubt those two hunters took it slow. Those horses were in bad shape."

Rick nodded. "My dad used to say that any man who was mean to a horse probably treated people even worse." He paused. "Likely his wife. Maybe even his kids."

"I don't care much for anyone who mistreats horses *or* people," Jack said, staring out the window.

Rick glanced toward his friend. "So when did you become such an expert on horses? Newark never struck me as an equestrian hotbed."

Jack shrugged. "I've been studying 'em. Taking riding lessons." He poked the front brim of his hat upward and flashed a toothy smile. "Thinking of getting me a *hawse* of my own."

Rick smiled. "Sounds like you're starting to wrap your arms around this whole Montana thing. I'll bet you're even listening to Country. George Strait, maybe? John Conlee? Keith Whitley?"

"You're not going to mention Charlie Pride?"

"Hadn't planned on it. You listen to Charlie Pride?"

Jack turned toward him and cocked his head. "Now why would you *assume* that?"

The cab echoed with uproarious laughter. Between them, political incorrectness did not exist. They'd met as college athletes from separate universities, their friendship spanning decades. More recently they had become like brothers, primarily because they shared the permanent anguish of having lost a child.

It was Jack who had braved the elements beneath Sawtooth Rock, nearly freezing to death as he stood sentry over the corpse of Chloe Morrand. Jack had lost his only daughter, Shaina, six years earlier in New Jersey. Only seventeen, she went missing for several days until her body was discovered in a Newark tenement, sexually assaulted and brutally murdered. The man responsible was found three days later, the victim of what authorities termed an "assassination." Internal Affairs investigated, but their findings were inconclusive. Only two months passed before Jack was invited to retire.

After he moved to Montana, Jack would barely even mention Shaina's name, the mere act akin to extracting a serrated blade from his chest. When Chloe died, that all changed. Perhaps Jack could sense the torment that would rumble like a freight train through Rick's soul. He likely noticed the scattered thoughts, fits of anger, flashes of guilt. The memory of a deceased child haunts the grieving parent like the needle of a record that had finished playing and continues to scratch the label. It's the end, but it's not. There's that ongoing numbing realization that you've lost part of your very being that you can never, ever replace.

Jack had something to offer his friend, and that's what he did. In the months following Chloe's death, he would check on Rick incessantly, keeping him engaged in life while sharing his own experience. The arrangement proved to benefit Jack as well. If he had become Rick's rock, perhaps Rick became his refuge.

"Charley Pride is pretty damn good," Rick said. "*Do* you listen to him?"

"Hell no," Jack bellowed.

"Any country music?"

"Nope."

"What then?"

"Springsteen."

"Right," Rick said. "Jersey."

He steadied the truck after its left front tire plunged into a rut. Peering through the top of the windshield, he winced as he watched low-hanging spruce branches scrape the light bar on the roof of the cab. "So much for our new trucks," he mumbled.

Jack nestled into his seat, the brown leather still smelling showroom fresh. He stroked his middle finger across the dash, as if removing a speck of dust from the pristine surface. "Looks like you made a pretty good choice, if you ask me."

When he became sheriff, Rick learned the Dexter County Commission had budgeted funds to update the department's vehicles. He proposed that he and his two full-time deputies switch from SUVs to crew-cab trucks, given the latter's utility in everyday duties, such as removing a deer carcass from the highway. It represented his most meaningful decision in what had been a sleepy first year of his tenure.

Now he was in search of a missing hunter who was lost in the merciless Crazies, a jagged spine of Montana Rockies cresting across the upper reaches of Rick's jurisdiction. The impending search marked the first imposing challenge on his watch. Rick suddenly felt that the fate of Garrett McRae rested in his hands.

"Finally," Jack grunted as they rounded a bend to see a small assembly of trucks and SUVs gathered at the Granite Peak Trailhead. "Only problem with a new truck is that the shocks are stiff. I feel like someone's been whacking my lower back with a Louisville Slugger."

"It's probably a good idea for you to stay with the truck, Jack," Rick said.

Jack's face crinkled, his eyes turning into slits. "Excuse me? I didn't become your undersheriff to sit in no truck. Relax—I got Advil."

Unless one had actually observed the thin seam down the center of Jack's chest, it was difficult to fathom he'd had open-heart surgery. Against his wife's protests, he was as active as ever, routinely splitting wood and hammering through lengthy hikes in the backcountry. After he nearly lost his life at the Sawtooth, Jack's wife, Tamara, made him promise he would never hike alone—under any circumstances. He agreed, and his latest challenge was finding a hiking partner who could keep up with him.

Securing his wife's permission to become Rick's deputy proved a more daunting task, but she finally relented once they assured her Jack would be kept on light duty.

"I promised Tamara that I primarily wanted to lean on your expertise," Rick reminded him. "I told her I'd keep you out of the line of fire."

Jack huffed. "Trust me, Cowboy—you get your ass in the line of fire, you'll want my expertise."

Rick turned off the engine. "So you're gonna buy a horse, huh?" he said with a smile. "Bet Tamara loves that idea."

Jack released a grunt. "Not so much."

• • •

Ben Westfall peered through a pair of half-rim reading glasses as his leathery hands tried to steady a wilderness map against persistent gusts of wind. He was surrounded by half-dozen or so volunteers—men and women of various ages, shapes, and sizes, all carrying backpacks, eager intensity in their eyes.

"Sheriff Morrand!" Ben said as he looked up from the map sprawled on the hood of his rig. His tanned cheeks had the texture of sandpaper, words spilling out of a nutcracker jaw that dropped open beneath a smoke-colored walrus moustache. "And this must be Deputy Kelly?"

Sheriff Morrand. The title still sounded odd to Rick, somewhat like an ill-fitting suit, even though he'd worn it for over ten months. He watched Jack and Ben exchange a warm handshake before Ben turned back toward him. "So I guess Billy Renfro finally decided to call it quits?"

Rick nodded. "Yep, Billy's retired. Turns out he has COPD—or CPOD, as he calls it."

"CPOD?"

"Coughing Pissed-Off Deputy."

"Guess the Chesterfields caught up with him," Ben said, casting a sympathetic frown. "Is he able to get around?"

"Oh, sure—he's got medication," Rick said. "Once he pulls on his waders and gets a few feet into the Yellowstone, he seems to do just fine."

Ben smiled. "As long as he can still fish, that's all that matters."

Rick looked skyward at the burning September daylight. Ben took the cue to turn the conversation to the task at hand. "From what Helen said, the last contact from Garrett McRae was when he'd just left Campfire Lake, correct?"

Rick nodded. "And one of the other hunters supposedly found his horse to the east, close to Lupine County."

Ben shook his head as he perused his map. "That's a lot of territory, and we have limited personnel. The search dogs are on a call outside Great Falls, and they won't be back to Bozeman until late tonight. We'll start with a hasty search, teams of two. We'll head toward their base camp then split up from there. I'm thinking we should concentrate our efforts to the east, where his horse was found."

The radio in Ben's truck crackled to life. "SAR Command, this is Lupine County Six-Oh-One," a voice said, the search-and-rescue acronym rhyming with *czar*. Ben reached inside and snared the receiver from a silver clip on the side of the console. "Go ahead Six-Oh-One."

Rick thought he heard the word *fire* buried beneath a storm of static. When he and Jack had stepped out of their vehicle, he could swear he smelled smoke. He'd dismissed it—the way Montana had been burning all summer, the entire state carried the odor of a smoldering fireplace.

Ben plugged an ear with his finger and listened. "Copy, Six-Oh-One," he said. "We're going to use a hasty for now … Keep us posted."

Ben slammed the door of his truck, his eyebrows collapsed as though he'd just discovered a flat tire. "That was Lupine Rural," he said, referring to the fire department of the adjacent county. "A brush fire broke out on Sunday morning on the east slope of the Crazies. They thought they had a handle on it, but by late Monday it got away and made it to the trees. Now the wind's picked up, and it's moving west pretty fast."

"In other words, we don't have much time," Rick said.

"Exactly."

Rick and Jack hustled to the truck, where they had emergency packs and hiking boots. As he opened the door of the crew cab, Rick turned to his friend. "You sure about this?" he asked. "I told Tamara—"

Jack pressed his forefinger against his lips, telling Rick, "Shhh …" Rick nodded and handed him a pack.

"You just take care of yourself, my friend," Jack said, replacing his cowboy hat with a weathered Rutgers ball cap. "And don't forget your damn radio."

CHAPTER 5

Amber McRae had this dream. It had come to her more than once, and it was always the same. She sees her four-year-old son, Gabe, running gleefully through an open field, the warm summer sun glistening off his blond hair, blue eyes aglow among the bright yellow arrowleaf flowers and dancing native grass. He always has a gleaming smile, his open mouth lined with his tiny white teeth, head jostling as he runs toward her. She reaches out, her lips curling into a broad smile as she prepares to gather him into her arms. He gets closer, and closer, and then—

"Mommy, do I really have to take a bath?"

Amber gently tugged a striped cotton shirt off her son, his head stuck for a moment before popping through the crew neck. As was their routine, Gabe lay back on his bed, thin arms at his sides, as she pulled the ankles of his blue jeans. She turned to her right, reaching for his pediatric wheelchair.

"No, Mommy! I want you to carry me!" he pleaded. "You promised!"

Amber drew a deep breath and stared at the chair. She remembered when Garrett had brought it home, after they had finally saved enough money to buy it. They were excited that Gabe would have some degree of mobility, if you wanted to call it that, but their joy quickly faded into a dense fog of gloom. Gabe would never be able to have a childhood like other kids. He wouldn't play or jump or run. Her dream would forever remain a dream.

She gave the chair a forceful shove, casting aside its evil spirit. *No child should ever be in one of these.*

"Okay, Tiger, you win," Amber said as she removed Gabe's Ninja Turtle underpants and folded them with his other clothes. Her back strained as she lifted her naked son into her arms and walked across the hall to the bathroom, his lifeless legs bouncing off her right arm. She reached down to check the temperature of the water before lowering him into the sloped yellow bathing chair inside the clawfoot tub.

"No!" Gabe protested.

"Now what?"

"I don't want the chair. It's for babies!"

Amber rolled her lips inward and paused. Damn, she missed Garrett. He was better at this. Much more patient.

"No chair, Mommy!" Gabe said again. She slid the chair out from under him, allowing him to sink lower into the tub. Gabe smiled.

Her phone rang.

Amber placed Gabe's tiny hands on either side of the tub. She gripped his fingers. "Now, if you don't have the chair, you have to promise you will hold on tight. You promise?"

Her phone rang again. Gabe began to giggle and splash. She stepped away from the tub, answering her phone without looking at it.

"That was quite a show you put on at the sheriff's office," Randall Boone said.

Amber felt her jaw tighten as she walked out of the bathroom. "You have a lot of balls calling me," she whispered loudly, wishing she'd chosen better words. Surprisingly, Boone let her comment slide.

"When can I see you?" he asked.

"How about never?"

A long sigh. "C'mon now. You don't want to be that way."

"Uh, yes, I do," Amber snapped as she stormed down the hallway. "I told you to never call me again."

"But we had a good thing going—"

"We had *nothing* going."

"I want to see you."

"Damn it, Boone. No!"

The line was silent for several seconds. Standing in the living room, Amber suddenly froze. *Gabe!* Her chest pounded as she hustled down the hallway. When she reached the bathroom door, she couldn't see Gabe's head. Tossing her phone behind her like a spent cigarette, she rushed toward the bathtub, her knees slamming hard onto the black-and-white octagons that tiled the bathroom floor. Gabe's terrified eyes were wide-open beneath the water's surface, hands flailing at the sides of the tub, trying to grip the slick acrylic surface.

"Gabe!" Amber shouted, tears welling in her eyes she plunged her hands into the water. She yanked him above the surface, where his small heaving chest gasped for oxygen before he broke into a deafening wail.

"I'm so sorry! I'm so sorry!" she stammered as she turned off the water cascading into the tub.

Her trembling hands snatched the towel that lay folded over the side of the bath. She blinked rapidly as she swaddled her frightened child, warm tears falling onto her cheeks. "You're just frightened," she said, trying to persuade herself as much as Gabe. "This is why we use the bath chair."

"The chair is for babies!" Gabe screamed before breaking into more sobs.

Amber held him tighter, her face buried in the ruffled towel that shrouded Gabe's head. "You're okay, Gabe," she whispered. "Mommy's got you now." She clamped her eyes shut as she rocked him. *Haven't we suffered enough?*

Gradually, Gabe's whimpers subsided. Amber turned and leaned her back against the side of the tub, crossing her legs to form a cradle for her son. Her motherly instincts told her she needed to hold Gabe for a while, nurture him, somehow spirit him far away from his sudden, unsettling brush with danger.

Gabe fixed his eyes on his mother, blinking eyes the color of the sky. "Mommy?" he asked. "When will Daddy be home?"

Amber pulled her child closer to her breast, her nostrils flaring as she filled her lungs with air. She stared out toward the hallway, where her phone lay quiet on top of the gray shag carpet. The visage of Randall Boone flashed inside her head like a single frame of film footage, the duration just long enough for her to wish they'd never met. *Bastard.*

"Daddy will be home soon," she whispered to Gabe as she adjusted the towel surrounding his cherubic face.

"I miss him," he said softly.

"I do too, Gabe. I do too." Her precious child lowered his eyelids and soon succumbed to sleep.

CHAPTER 6

The trek to the hunters' base camp was relatively flat, easily covered in less than an hour. Led by Ben Westfall, the searchers pounded down the trail, Rick and Jack following at the rear. Three miles in, Rick flicked a couple of fingers off Jack's bicep.

"I'm going *that* way," he said definitively. He pointed to a trail sign that read "Campfire Lake," its letters charred into gray barnwood. Jack's brow furrowed as he volleyed glances between Rick and the sign.

"We're headed toward the area where his horse was found," Jack said.

Rick shook his head. "When they last talked to him, he said he was leaving Campfire Lake. That would be the point of last known contact."

"That was Saturday. Garrett said on the radio he was leaving and headed east. There's no reason to believe—"

"What if he got injured?" Rick asked. "Maybe his horse got spooked somehow, threw him off and bolted on him."

"Why didn't Garrett radio?"

Rick shrugged. "Radio contact in these mountains is sporadic at best. Or maybe his battery died."

Jack looked up the trail. The search crew was vanishing behind a stand of dense aspens. "We have limited resources, Rick."

"You have enough people for three teams, plus you and Ben," Rick said. "You guys cover the trails around the base camp. I'll make a run this way."

"By yourself?"

"It's been a while, but I know these mountains," he said. "Trust me on this one. I got this."

Jack's dark-brown eyes argued against the plan. He paused a beat, using his sleeve to wipe beads of sweat off his forehead. "You got your radio?"

"Very funny," Rick broke into a smile as he tapped the handheld on his duty belt.

"Flashlight?"

Rick nodded again. "How are *you* holding up?" he asked, gently reminding his friend which man was sheriff. "Those SAR folks are moving at a good clip."

"I'm fine," Jack turned and headed briskly up the trail, his long strides defending his fitness. "Keep in touch."

• • •

"I'm hungry, Auntie Sage."

Sage Fontenot awoke with a sudden frightened jolt, blinking her eyes rapidly as her head rose from her pillow on the couch. The living room was dim, lit by a narrow shaft of light from the kitchen. Open blinds revealed only darkness. She released a relieved sigh when she saw Abby standing beside her, the child's hand gently caressing Sage's shoulder.

Abby's teeth were clamped together, a pained expression on her face. "I didn't mean to scare you, Auntie Sage. You've been asleep since we got home from school."

Sage sat up. "It's okay, sweetie." She brushed her hand across Abby's cheek. "What time is it?"

"Eight o'clock."

"Oh my God! You must be starving!"

Abby shrugged. "I'm okay. I was going to have some cereal, but—"

Sage wagged her head with disdain and wrestled her way off the couch. "Like hell—heck—you're going to have some cereal. You go get cleaned up, and I'll make you a proper dinner."

Abby disappeared into the hallway as Sage trudged toward the kitchen, her thighs feeling like concrete. Her jaw cracked as her mouth opened wide with a lengthy yawn. She could go to bed right now and easily sleep until dawn. Rubbing her eyes, she peered into one of the lacquered pine cabinets, selecting a box of Tuna Helper. No one would confuse her with Julia Child, but it was better than cereal. At least it was *dinner*.

Sage had never been a mother, and now she was one. The sudden and heart-wrenching murder of Chloe Morrand saw to that. Sage had barely begun to grieve Chloe's death when she and her fiancé were awarded custody of Abby. The learning curve had been steep.

As she cranked a can opener through a can of tuna, Sage's eyes wandered to the screen of her cell phone lying on the counter. She had a missed call—it could be Rick. She dialed voice mail, punched in her password, and hit the symbol for speaker.

"Hi Sage, this is Beth from Dr. Tillotson's office," the scripted voice said. "I'm just calling to confirm your appointment tomorrow at two thirty. No need to call us back unless you have to cancel."

"Why are you going to the doctor, Auntie Sage? Are you sick?"

Abby had startled her again, quietly slipping into the kitchen after washing her hands. Shaking her head, Sage deleted the message and began spooning tuna into a pot on the stove. "It's just a regular doctor's appointment," she said as she picked up a fork to stab at the tuna.

Her eyes were averted lest she lie to Abby's face. To be sure, Sage was on edge as of late, her mood uneven, her patience narrow. There also were the hot flashes. At first, she'd chalked the symptoms up to menopause, which for her had been relatively mild. After all, she'd considered murdering Rick only on a couple of occasions, both for reasonable cause.

The fatigue had come about more recently, in doses both sporadic and sudden, and that had drawn Sage's concern. As much as she dreaded doctor visits, Sage had spent enough time in her body to acknowledge that all was not quite sound.

"Is that Tuna Helper?" Abby asked.

"Yep."

"Your special recipe?"

Sage grinned. Her *special recipe* involved the adding cheddar cheese to the dish. "You bet," she said.

"Cool."

Abby walked closer to Sage, staring at the stove as Sage poured water into the pot. "Auntie Sage, can I ask you something?"

"Of course, sweetheart."

"Corrine Lipsack told everyone that after you and Pa-Pa get married, you'll actually be my grandma, since Pa-Pa is my grandfather. I guess that's true, huh?"

"Yes, that's true," Sage answered, feeling a slight cringe as she let the "grandma" part sink in. "Corrine Lipsack has a lot of time on her hands, doesn't she?"

"So, I guess I won't call you Auntie Sage anymore," Abby continued, her forehead tightening in thought. "But it seems kind of weird for me to call you Grandma."

"Tell me about it."

Abby watched Sage stir the pot. "So when are you and Pa-Pa getting married?"

Sage paused. Rick had proposed shortly after Chloe's death, but they agreed to wait at least a year, allowing themselves—and Abby—time to grieve. "It will be soon, I'm sure," Sage said, even though she wasn't sure at all.

"Can I stay here tonight?"

"If your grandpa doesn't show up soon, you may have to."

"Where is Pa-Pa?"

"He had to go up to the Crazies."

"Isn't that far away?"

"It's a bit of a drive."

"Why did he have to go?"

"Someone—a hunter—got lost."

"I bet Pa-Pa will find him."

"I bet he will too."

Abby paused a moment in thought. "Why do they call them the Crazy Mountains?"

"It's a long story," Sage said.

"Tell me."

Sage turned toward the refrigerator, emerging with a brick of cheddar and a carton of milk. Using a silver grater, she dropped flakes of cheese into the pot. She handed Abby a couple of glasses from the cabinet. "Can you pour us a couple of glasses of milk?" Sage asked, hoping Abby might forget the Crazy Mountains.

"*Please* tell me the story," Abby said.

Sage released a long breath, trying to ignore the soreness radiating through her entire body. "Okay, so there was this pioneer family that had a cabin on the east side of the mountains. According to the legend, the mother went for a walk one day while the other family members stayed behind."

"Why did they stay behind?"

Sage rolled her eyes but maintained her patience. "I … I guess she wanted to be alone."

Abby nodded, the answer plausible, and Sage resumed. "Anyway, when the mother came back, her husband and four children had been attacked by Indians, and their cabin had been burned to the ground."

"Was everybody dead?"

"Yes," Sage said, blowing out a breath. "Everybody was dead."

"Cool."

"Cool?"

"I mean, it's a cool story."

Sage shook her head as she reached into the cabinet, retrieving a couple of plates and laying them on the counter. She spotted a bottle of Advil. She generally avoided ibuprofen, figuring her years as a musician and saloon keeper had tortured her liver enough. After a moment of indecision, she shook two gel caps from the bottle and cupped her hand beneath the kitchen faucet.

"So what happened next?" Abby asked as she focused on pouring the milk.

"Well, a week later, the Indians returned to kill the woman. When she saw them, she grabbed a tomahawk that had been used to kill one of her sons. She started swinging it wildly, killing a few of the Indians and chasing the others away. When she was done, she ran into the mountains, never to be seen again. At first, people called them the Crazy Woman Mountains, and then it was shortened to the Crazy Mountains."

"Wow," Abby said in wonder. "Pa-Pa would have *never* told me that story."

"I know." Sage chuckled. "I probably shouldn't have either."

"Why not?"

"The story makes Indians look bad."

Sage scooped Tuna Helper onto a couple of plates. She hadn't eaten all day, but she wasn't hungry, which struck her as odd. She dismissed the thought with a shrug.

They walked to the dining room table, Sage allowing herself a sly snicker as she considered her interlude with Rick earlier in the day. Maybe *that* was why she was so tired, she mused. Doubtful, since things hadn't lasted as long as she had hoped. Another snicker.

"What's so funny?" Abby asked. Sage shook her head and didn't answer, her smile vanishing as she was overcome with nausea. Maybe it was the smell of the Tuna Helper. Or perhaps the Advil. She gingerly lowered herself into her chair, using her napkin to brush perspiration from her forehead.

"Are you okay, Auntie Sage?"

Sage nodded as persuasively as she could, but Abby's question had merit. Was she okay? She couldn't tell. It had been like this for a couple of weeks, maybe more. One minute she would feel fine, the next minute …

"Let's pray," Sage said, taking Abby's hand. The request seemed strange as the words tumbled from her mouth, but Rick had insisted that they introduce Abby to prayer. While he and God had experienced their fair share of discord, Rick figured it was only right and just to provide Abby with some raw concept of a deity before she could eventually fashion her own. Sage was warming to the newfound ritual, recognizing its ability to deliver a measure of nurturing peacefulness in times of turbulence.

She nodded toward Abby, indicating for her to proceed. Abby looked toward the ceiling, as if trying to remember the words. "Bless us, O Lord, and these Thy gifts, which we are about to receive … from Thy bounty … through Christ our Lord, Amen."

Sage kept her eyes pinched shut, fear raking through her body. *Please, Lord, let me be okay. They need me …*

Abby squeezed Sage's hand. "Dear Jesus, please bless Pa-Pa in the Crazy Mountains," she said. "We pray that he is okay."

"Yes," Sage whispered. "We do."

CHAPTER 7

Whenever he was alone, Rick couldn't help thinking of Chloe.

His daughter's memory would drift into his brain with subtlety, somewhat like slow-burning incense winding its way into his senses. The recollections could be pleasant at first, allowing him to crack a gentle smile as he recalled her exceptional intelligence—or perhaps her quick wit born from a masterful sense of humor.

Other thoughts drowned him with torment, hurling him into an unannounced state of fathomless grief. He would recall their arguments—shouting matches, actually—their twin Irish tempers clashing like fierce swords as the decibel level quickly escalated. He'd said things he wished he could take back. And he hadn't said things he wished he'd told her.

His radio made a loud sputter, jarring him from his thoughts. He stopped on the trail, drawing oxygen into his stinging lungs. He heard a faint voice drowning in static before the radio went quiet.

Hands on hips, chest heaving, Rick scanned the terrain. He found himself on a stretch of trail climbing upward through a narrow canyon, a fast-flowing creek below hidden from the last vestiges of sunlight. "Garrett!" he shouted, his cupped hands framing his mouth. "Garrett!" His words created a fleeting echo that vanished into nothingness. He resumed walking. If he went a little farther, achieving higher ground, he could make radio contact with either his undersheriff or the SAR team.

He had seen occasional footprints on the trail, belonging to both man and beast. Without sufficient study, it was difficult to determine whether the horseshoe imprints were made by the chestnut gelding belonging to Garrett McRae. While Rick saw no prints leading back toward the trailhead, it was always possible that either Garrett, his horse, or both had traveled east by another route.

His boots made a rhythmic grinding sound as the trail gradually lifted him out of the canyon. He blinked flecks of dirt from his eyes, noticing that the wind had picked up considerably. The air temperature had dropped with nightfall fast approaching, but the wind felt warm and dry.

He smelled smoke. Looking to the east, he saw thick white billows rising just behind the distant crest of the Crazies. His radio sputtered again before Ben Westfall's voice came through loud and clear.

"Dexter One, this is SAR Command," Ben said. "You copy?"

Rick wrestled his radio off of his duty belt. "Go ahead, Ben."

"What's your location?"

Rick's eyes traced up the trail that was barely visible in the twilight as it climbed the high ridge that rimmed Campfire Lake. He knew the journey well from his childhood. The full trek required reaching the ridge before descending nearly one thousand feet down to the lake, a breath-taking strip of emerald-colored water resting serenely on the floor of a verdant valley, its shores dotted with stands of lush conifers. Rick recalled the terrain as steep and treacherous, requiring his father and him to walk their skittish horses.

"I'm still about two miles out from the lake," he told Ben. "I saw some horseshoe tracks, but no sign of the hunter. Any luck on your end?"

"Negative. Jack's here with me, and we're almost back to the trailhead. That fire that started in Lupine County is moving fast. Dexter Rural is sending two engines, possibly three. You should start heading back down."

Rick drew a deep breath, the smell of burning timber continuing to waft into his nostrils. "Garrett!" he shouted again. Was the missing hunter just over the ridge at Campfire Lake? Was he alive? Injured? God only knew. His mind flickered to the face of Amber McRae, her sleep-deprived eyes filled with panic as she had begged him to find her husband, the father of her child. His chest grew thick, the visage of Chloe appearing from nowhere, speeding past on the highway within his head.

Rick looked once again toward the peaks to the east. Plumes of smoke continued to rise, joined now by angry orange flames that danced atop the crest, piercing the sky like tongues of a serpent. The pace of the fire might slow, he reasoned, as it backed down the western slope. That was *usually* the case, anyway.

He squinted at the sea of green tumbling from the crest down to the forest floor. His eyes widened. Embers had ignited three spot fires below. From his vantage point six miles away they looked like campfires. It wouldn't be long before they would unite and chase back up the ridge, gorging on the abundance of dry fuel.

If the wind failed to shift, the fire crews from Dexter Rural would be powerless to stop the carnage. This would end up being another campaign fire begging for resources from across a state stretched thin by blazes that had been burning all summer. Thousands of acres in the Crazies would turn into moonscape.

Rick exhaled, dreading the notion of informing Amber McRae that the forest was ablaze, her husband likely consumed in the flames.

"Rick, you there?" Ben's voice asked.

"Yeah … I'm here," Rick muttered into the radio. "I'm on my way."

"Copy," Ben said. "See you at the trailhead."

Rick tucked his radio back into his duty belt. He retrieved his flashlight and turned it on, cursing himself when he realized the batteries were low. He shook his head, knowing he needed to take better care of his gear. He sometimes wondered if the whole sheriff thing had him wading beyond his depth. It had been Billy Renfro's idea for him to replace Caleb Tidwell, a *reward* of sorts for Rick's efforts in solving Chloe's murder and uncovering Tidwell's involvement in a conspiracy. Rick embraced the call to serve, and the citizenry of Dexter County welcomed him with open arms. His only requirement from the county commission was to get his certificate from the Police Officer Standards and Training Course, a relatively low hurdle to clear. Skeptics could argue that the local folks had traded one green sheriff for another.

Clouds and white smoke shrouded the Montana sky, dimming the faint, hazy glow of a crescent moon. Rick aimed his flashlight at the ground immediately in front of him, the shale-strewn trail much more difficult to navigate coming down.

He stopped. *What was that?* He listened. Wind whispered through the branches of giant spruce trees, causing distant deadfall to creak. He dropped into the forest, the narrow trail turning to silky dirt as it tunneled through blackness. The faint rumbling of a creek was heard to his left, the water wandering far below along the base of a timber-covered ravine. He continued walking, hearing the sound of his measured steps as his feet slid along the trail.

He stopped again. Another sound. His heart pounded, his breathing labored. Up ahead, he heard a plaintive whimper, like a dog snared in a trap. A lone wolf maybe? Rick eased forward, raising the rust-colored beam of his flashlight further up the trail. Two gleaming eyes peered back at him.

He released a sigh, embarrassed by his anxiety. It was a small bear cub, likely born the previous winter. Its coat was deep brown, its snout a light tan. Likely a grizzly, Rick reasoned. The cub's eyes pleaded to him like a rescue puppy yearning for adoption. Rick allowed himself a smile before a cold chill climbed the length of his spine.

A grizzly cub? What was he thinking? It wasn't like cubs go out for an evening stroll by their lonesome. A sow had to be nearby. Rick drew a deep breath, slowly moving his flashlight away from the baby bear and into the thick underbrush of the forest. His heart thumped as he deemed the right side of the trail to be clear. He turned the light to his left, passing the cub's face. He jumped backward as the baby bear released a loud barking sound followed by a lengthy howl. "Easy, little guy," Rick whispered as he scanned the left side of the trail.

Rick sensed that someone—*something*—was behind him. Adrenaline flooded his veins, his body screaming that he was in grave danger. He whirled, gripping his flashlight tight enough to crush it. A raging grizzly sow, jaws open wide and towering well above seven feet, stood on its haunches only twenty-five yards away. He felt certain that the ground shook and his bones rattled as the mammoth beast clacked its jaws and unleashed a deafening roar.

Rick staggered backward. He had seen a grand total of three grizzlies in the wild, the closest one perhaps one hundred yards out. The animal had been on a hillside, dragging its powerful claw through the soil like a backhoe as it foraged for insects. Rick remembered how effortlessly the bear had brushed aside ten-inch rocks as if they were pebbles. He had followed standard backcountry protocol on that occasion, averting his eyes and acting submissive in an effort to allow the bear to absorb his presence. The animal ignored him, focusing instead on its search for food. Like most grizzlies, the bear wanted absolutely nothing to do with a human being.

This was different. *Much different.* Grizzly attacks usually occurred for one of two reasons—either the bear was guarding a fresh kill or protecting its young.

Rick's trembling hand instinctively reached for the front strap of his backpack, accustomed to years of carrying bear spray he'd never needed to use. In his haste, he'd left the canister in the truck. Drawing a deep breath, he pawed at the side of his duty belt, fingering the grip of the Sig Sauer semi-automatic that had been issued to him. He was no fan of the firearm—it had jammed on him on the practice range more than once when it failed to eject spent shell casings.

He began to remove the weapon from its holster, then shook his head. Even if the Sig fired properly, he probably would need to empty it on the animal, and his shots would have to be near-perfect. But that was beside the point. He didn't *want* to kill a bear. He could see the headline now: "Dumb-Ass Sheriff Panics, Shoots Sow Grizzly."

He released the grip of his gun, pushing it back into the holster. Tilting his head and pointing his fading flashlight toward the ground, he cast his eyes forward, trying to assess the bear's movements through the darkness. Her shoulders swayed as she stared at her frozen adversary.

Rick braced for an attack. The bear reared up again, belting out another bone-chilling bellow that rumbled through the trees. He considered the animal's hesitation, wondering whether the grizzly was granting him an opportunity to step aside. Slowly inching backward, he used a murmuring voice to assure the bear he meant no harm. A few more feet and he could offer the sow a clear path to her cub.

A final roar, the sound enveloped Rick like a heat from a blast furnace. He swore he felt the grizzly's breath. His quaking legs took two rapid steps backward—one too many. His ankle curled off the edge of the trail.

He hurtled backward, flashlight sailing through the smoky September air. As his head whiplashed off the hard ground, he saw his hiking boots trace across the night sky, his body making a backward somersault down the steep ravine. Air vanished from his lungs. He thumped onto his stomach, a runaway train crashing through the underbrush. The strap of his backpack snagged on something, ripping it off his shoulders. Arms flailing, his hands grabbed fistfuls of soil as he clutched for something— *anything*—that might prevent him from vanishing into the darkness. The stream grew louder, its pounding waters cascading over boulders and fallen timber.

Rick managed to grasp the base of a spruce seedling, the prickly surface tacky with sap. His body swung below the tree as he hung on for dear life. He heaved two quick breaths, cherishing his respite, before the roots began to loosen like tearing fabric, the seedling breaking free from the soil and sending Rick rolling sideways down the ravine. He grunted loudly as his hip rolled over what he guessed was a small tree stump.

Bark, branches, granite, stars, and sky whirled around him. He fell farther into darkness. The sound of water drew closer. Sage's voice played in his head. "*Rick … be careful.*"

The last thing he heard was a sickening thud.

CHAPTER 8

When Jack Kelly informed his wife that he wanted to become Rick Morrand's deputy, he may as well have been introducing her to his new mistress.

"Deputy! *Deputy?* Are you crazy?" Tamara had shouted.

"Actually the title would be undersheriff."

"That's even worse! Jack Kelly, have you lost your mind?"

Having completed her oral evaluation of his mental fitness, Tamara pressed the button on the audiotape of Jack's police career, taking special care to mention the questionable kill of notorious drug dealer Marvin Moore, the incident prompting Internal Affairs to suggest that it might be best for Jack to take his pension while he could. The incident had been preceded by all the classic symptoms of burnout—fatigue, irritability, even depression. Then there was the triple bypass, performed one month after Jack's retirement party, even though Jack had deemed it "unnecessary."

Tamara's synopsis was delivered at high volume and was followed by a weeklong Ice Age. Dinners were consumed in silence, provided there were dinners at all. The mattress they shared may as well have been a frozen hockey rink, both of them ready to drop the gloves had they ever decided to venture into conversation.

Jack argued that the new job would be without danger, Dexter County being quiet and uneventful. The hypothesis was flawed, of course, considering there had been a murder, attempted murder, domestic violence, suicide and assault of a peace officer, not to mention the death of a sheriff whose actions had spawned an investigation by the Securities and Exchange Commission.

Eventually, Tamara relented, perhaps tired of watching Jack mope around the house like a teenager who'd misplaced his iPhone. She knew deep down that not only was being part of the action built into Jack's DNA, he also was the kind of man who genuinely wanted to be of service to his good friend Rick Morrand.

Upon issuing approval, Tamara's only caveat was that Jack promise to always come home safely, her emphasis on the part about "coming home." Their pact was sealed with some of the best makeup sex in the history of Western civilization.

"Dexter County One, Kelly on Purple," Jack said into his portable radio as he and the team reached the trailhead. "Rick, are you there?" He turned to Ben Westfall, who was starting the engine of his rig. "How powerful is the radio in the truck? Fifty watts?"

"Hundred."

"Maybe this handheld isn't reaching him."

Ben blew out a breath. "Help yourself," he said with attitude, stepping out of the cab. He paused a beat. "What was Morrand thinking?" he grumbled. "Why'd he take off on his own?"

Jack sat in the driver's seat squinting at the radio receiver to confirm the channel. "Rick likes to blaze his own trail. Some folks like that about him."

Ben huffed. "Yeah, well, that wasn't the plan. Next time he wants to go cowboy—"

"Hey, Ben?" Jack interrupted. "Spare me the lecture."

Ben did have a point, of course. Rick should have never taken off solo. He had good *intentions*—the same ones used to pave the road to hell. Jack gazed at the night sky and its approaching amber glow. Hell was on the way.

He pumped out a few short breaths as he keyed the mic. "Rick, it's Jack. We're back at the trailhead. The fire is moving fast. Do you copy?" He stared with desperation at the roof of the truck. "Rick! It's Jack. Do. You. Copy?"

Ben dropped his chin as he watched Jack return the mic to its cradle and step out of the truck. "I'm going to have to get my people out of here," he said, his tone more conciliatory. "I'm responsible for their safety."

Jack nodded. "I get it, Ben," he answered with resignation.

The radio crackled. "SAR Command, Dexter Rural," a voice said. Ben grabbed the mic. There had been no word from the fire detail. "Go ahead, Rural."

"We're turning this over to the Forest Service and DNRC," a voice said, the latter a reference to the Department of Natural Resources and Conservation. "They instructed us to fall back. They've already called in helicopters and slurry bombers from out of state to slow it down. You guys need to get out of there."

"Copy," Ben said. He draped his wrist over the top of the truck's door, intently staring at the blazing horizon, eyes blinking in disbelief as he stood on the doorstep of what seemed like Armageddon. "You're letting it burn?"

"We have no choice," the voice said. "You guys need to leave—now."

Ben returned the mic to its cradle. He raised his eyebrows and swung his pursed lips to one side, his moustache brushing the bottom of his nose. "We shouldn't be here, Jack," he said rapidly.

"You go on ahead, Ben—keep your people safe," Jack answered, squinting into the glare of Ben's light bar. "I'm staying here."

Ben swept his hand across his surroundings. "We're in a trap. There's one road out of this canyon, and it ain't no interstate. If a spot fire ignites behind us, you're toast. *Literally*."

"I understand," Jack said. "Thing is, we still have Sheriff Morrand—not to mention Garrett McRae—stuck out there somewhere." He stared at his handheld radio, eyebrows furrowed, then cast his chin toward the mobile inside Ben's truck. "Mind if I try one more time?"

• • •

Rick awoke to the piercing tone of the Emergency Broadcast System screaming inside his head. At least, that's what it sounded like. He wasn't sure how long he'd been out. *A minute? An hour?* All he knew was that his head throbbed and he couldn't breathe.

He lay on his stomach, his body wedged against the broad base of a sturdy tree, its bark feeling like shrapnel buried in his side. He would have screamed in agony had he possessed the oxygen to generate a sound. Instead, he remained motionless, his mouth fluttering like a trout lying on the riverbank. Starting with a high-pitched wheezing sound, he slowly drew air into his lungs. His eyes moistened with agony as he pushed out breaths into the dirt and dried leaves that surrounded his lips.

He touched the back of his head. His hair was soaked with a thick, syrupy substance. The side of his torso stabbed with pain. The cracked ribs he had suffered when his truck flipped a year earlier might have fractured again. He could hear the creek rumble past beneath him. The tree had shielded him from falling off a sheer edge and plummeting perhaps twenty-five feet into the fast-moving water. He could have easily hit a boulder, impaled himself on a broken tree limb, or found himself snagged beneath the brush and drowned. Maybe a bump on the head and couple of broken ribs weren't such a bad bargain.

His fingers traced along the side of his duty belt, searching for his radio. It was gone. Gingerly raising his head, his eyes scanned the landscape. He could see the detail of the ravine, trunks of mammoth fir and spruce glimmering in the light of the approaching fire, the yellow-orange hue reminding him of the glow a blazing hearth might cast on a Christmas tree. A thick haze hung in the air. Smoke felt sharp in his nostrils. His face streamed with sweat in the intense heat. The fire was drawing near.

Rick rolled onto his left side, away from his wounded ribs. Face pinched in a grimace, he lifted his ankles, checking to see if his legs were intact. He felt wetness midway up the front of his thigh, where his finger traced a quarter-sized puncture. His skull continued to pound mercilessly, strangely reminding him of those woebegone all-nighters when his head had swelled with booze and cocaine.

He paused and listened, treasuring short breaths. The steady rhythm of the creek calmed him. He just needed to rest a few moments before—

A rustling sound chased down the hillside, perhaps fifty yards away. Someone—*or something*—was coming, drawing closer by the second. An icy chill shot up his spine as he heard an unmistakable sound. A deep-throated growl rumbled through the trees. He thought he felt the ground vibrate.

The bear wasn't done.

* * *

Jack Kelly walked across the parking lot, gazing over his shoulder to see taillights vanish into the darkening haze as Ben Westfall's crew evacuated the Granite Peak Trailhead. He keyed his portable radio. "Rick! It's Jack. Do you copy?"

Eyes stinging from smoke, Jack shook his head and clipped his handheld to his belt. Ben's hundred-watt radio hadn't reached Rick, and now Jack was left with his six-watt portable. With no repeater towers within miles, his best hope of transmission was line of sight, without obstructions. The harsh terrain of the Crazies argued against that possibility.

He heaved breaths short and labored as he pointed his flashlight toward the trail. Entering the canopy of the forest, he was met with the same foreboding feeling he had ignored so many times before.

• • •

The grizzly crashed through the brush. Rick figured he had two seconds, maybe three. His brain screamed for his gun, telling him he could put a slug down the sow's throat, animal activists be damned. His hand slapped down on his holster—once, twice, three times. A sick feeling filled his stomach. His weapon was gone.

The bear's face appeared in the firelight, its eyes aflame. Rick had only one choice.

Play dead.

He pressed his wrists against his ears, interlocking his hands behind his neck, spreading his legs so the bear couldn't roll him. He tried to lie still, the muscles in his body a maze of twisted cords. *Stay calm? Yeah, right.* The thought flashed that playing dead was just a rehearsal for the real thing.

Rick buried a muffled scream into the soil as the irate grizzly swiped a paw across his scalp and then down his back, its iron claw tearing through his shirt like wet tissue. Next was a bite on the back of his thigh, the bear's teeth stabbing through his skin. He froze. By some miracle, the sow removed its jaws without tearing away a chunk of flesh.

Play dead. Just play dead.

The bear hovered over him, its thick breathing sounding like a rumbling death rattle. A foul odor assaulted Rick's nostrils, the smell of a wet dumpster. Rick lay rigid, his mouth drawing short gasps as his face pushed against the earth.

He felt the bear's wet nose press against the back of his leg. A texture like fine sandpaper stroked his wounds, a warm sensation filling his veins. There was a brief pause before the process was repeated on the claw marks that streaked across his back.

Rick's muddled brain tried to process what was happening. After a beat, a thought hit him like a bag of hammers connecting with the back of his skull. The bear was licking Rick's wounds, sampling the taste, like a keg-bellied guest torn between the buffalo wings and fried mushrooms at a Super Bowl Party.

This bear is predatory. Play dead, my ass.

Rick slowly removed his grip from behind his neck, his fingers crabbing their way through the dirt beyond his head. He discovered a half-buried rock, perhaps five inches in diameter. In a single motion, he flipped over onto his back, ignoring the razors of pain firing inside his rib cage. The sow tilted its head, staring at him curiously, affording him the second that he needed.

Clutching the rock firmly, Rick delivered a solid blow to the bear's snout. Its teeth clacked, dropping saliva onto his face, bursts of breath smelling like the decay of a corpse. He struck the sow again, delivering two rapid-fire blows to the side of its head, this time adding a deafening barbaric scream.

He found himself in a strange blur, his fear replaced by the brazen ruthlessness of a crazed beast. It was anger—*unbridled, glorious anger*! As a child, he'd lost his favorite uncle, Phil, to a self-inflicted gunshot wound. Christine, his beloved wife, had fallen victim to cancer. He'd watched his daughter overcome addiction and mental illness, only to be murdered. Rick decided the Morrand clan had taken enough bites from their shit sandwich. This bear happened to be in the wrong place at the wrong time.

Another shot, this one cracking the bone above the bear's eye socket. And another, scraping its nose as its head jerked away.

The grizzly stepped back, beyond the reach of his primitive weapon, staring into his eyes, stunned by the attack. It looked over its shoulder as if it heard something. Returning its glare toward Rick, it seemed to wonder whether the prey was worth it. Rick drew frenzied breaths through clenched teeth, eyes opened wide. Raising the rock above his head, he unleashed another bloodcurdling roar.

The bear looked up the ravine. Chest heaving, Rick watched and listened. A barking sound echoed through the forest. It was the cub. The sow walked a few steps before breaking into a run, effortlessly zigzagging its way upward through the trees.

Rick dropped the rock and exhaled, his shoulders curling forward with relief. He had survived—for now.

Bracing himself against the side of the tree, he staggered to his feet. Warm rivulets of blood flowed from the wounds on his head down the nape of his neck. He winced in agony as his soaked shirt ripped away from the gashes on his back.

Gasping for air, he turned his eyes to the east. White smoke billowed into the air, the sky now a brilliant orange. Through the forest he could see flames chasing up the trunks of trees, the fire rapaciously devouring the abundant and limitless bounty of rain-starved timber.

Rick whirled back toward the ravine behind him. He'd heard a sound. He stepped away from the creek and listened. It was a voice. *Jack Kelly's voice.*

"Rick, can you hear me?" Jack said, followed by a crackle and static. "Rick, do you copy?"

The radio. Rick followed the sound, gripping the trunks and branches of trees as he climbed up the hillside. "Rick, it's Jack," he heard again. "Key your radio if you can hear me."

Rick spotted his handheld resting against a boulder on a shallow bed of leaves. He keyed the mic. "Dexter County Two, I copy," he said. "I'm on my way."

"Thank God," Jack whispered to himself, his voice coated with relief. "How far out are you?"

"Two miles, maybe a little more," Rick said. "Where's Ben? Any luck finding the hunter?"

"Negative," Jack said. "Everyone's heading out, Rick. This fire is moving fast. If we don't—"

"Got it. On my way."

Rick placed his radio on his duty belt and began to climb on all fours up toward the trail, his entire body seizing in agony with every movement. As he curled around a stump near the top, he spotted his Stetson. It stung his bleeding scalp when he fastened it on his head. He allowed himself a pained smile as he wondered if finding his treasured hat meant that the pendulum of good fortune might now be swinging his way. He considered that the bear could still be in the area. He wasn't out of the woods just yet.

He hobbled along the trail, favoring his injured thigh. Reaching down to feel the wound, his fingers felt only a trickle of warm blood, assuring him the puncture had missed his artery. His calf stung where the bear had bit him, but he was relieved it hadn't been treated like a drumstick. He winced when he tugged the back of his shirt glued to his spine by dried blood.

He drew short, shallow breaths, trying to ward off the dense smoke that choked the forest. Sweat continued to pour down his face, the fast-moving fire intensifying in heat. The bear and its cub were long gone, Rick thought, as were any other creatures with a half-lick of sense.

He crossed a long meadow and entered another stretch of dense forest. A light twinkled through the trees, perhaps a quarter-mile up the trail. Rick blinked his eyes rapidly, praying it wasn't an apparition. He quickened his pace, sensing deliverance from the fast-approaching inferno.

"Damn!" Jack Kelly said. His voice sounded like someone who had just arrived at the scene of a car wreck. He scanned Rick from head to toe and back again. "What in the hell happened to you?"

"I was ... detained."

Jack's eyebrows pinched. "*Detained?* What's that supposed to mean?"

"Let's get out of here," Rick said, casting a nod down the trail. "What's the status of this fire?"

"DNRC and the Forest Service have it," Jack said.

"You heard any chatter?"

"Not in a while."

They hustled down the trail, Jack's flashlight beam reflecting off the thick silver smoke that layered the forest floor like an eerie harbor fog. "For a while there I thought you were a goner, my friend," Jack said in a funereal voice.

"You and me both."

"Care to talk about it?"

"Bear attack," Rick said without breaking stride. "I got between a sow and her cub."

"Did you kill her?"

"Nope."

"You play dead?"

"Not dead enough." Rick stopped suddenly. "Jack, wait. Listen."

Jack turned toward him, chest heaving, hand on a hip, flashlight pointed toward the ground. The massive fire continued to rumble, sounding like an approaching locomotive. It crawled without pity through the underbrush, its flames exploding into devilish tongues that chased up the trunks of trees and ignited the forest canopy.

"It'd be a good time for a couple of those fire shelters," Jack said through labored breaths.

"Did you have them with you?"

Jack shook his head. "Negative. But I saw two of them in the storage shed behind the sheriff's office."

"Good to know."

They continued to lumber along the footpath. Heat seared the back of his neck like an invisible blowtorch. He drew rapid breaths of smoke-filled air, wincing from the agonizing daggers of pain pulsing from his injured ribs. "Wait!"

Jack turned toward him, face colored with exhaustion, head slumped forward as though he were hanging from a meat hook.

"Listen," Rick said, eyes scanning the tops of the trees. "Hear that?"

"What now?" Jack said with an edge.

Rick lurched toward his friend and snared his flashlight. "A plane."

Jack squinted skyward. A white aircraft passed over them at a low altitude, its wings illuminated by the flames below. "Wonder what he's doing here," he said.

"It's a spotter," Rick answered, his voice filled with panic. "There will be a bomber carrying slurry right behind him. I doubt they even know we're down here."

Rick snared Jack's flashlight and waved it into the trees. He spotted a granite outcrop jutting from the hillside like a precious stone, perhaps twenty yards off the trail. It promised cover. He grabbed a fistful of Jack's sleeve, dragging his giant friend behind him as if closing a reluctant barn door.

"Slurry?" Jack muttered as he staggered behind Rick. "Is that—"

"Fire retardant," Rick said. "Ever have a sidewalk fall on you?"

On cue, the roar of the DC-8's engine filled the air. Rick and Jack dove toward the base of the rock, which shielded them from the sky. The plane started dropping its load on the exact spot where they had been standing, the slurry crashing through the tree branches like a tsunami. Rick shielded his face with his bicep as the plane trailed into the distance.

He reached for his radio. The screen was dark. It was dead. "Jack, you have any juice left in your radio?" Jack was staring at the stretch of forest drenched in red retardant, eyes opened wide and mouth agape. "Jack!" Rick repeated. "You have a radio?"

The ex-detective handed him the radio without speaking. Rick stared at the screen. It was cracked, looking like fissured ice on a frozen lake. He started fumbling with the channels until he heard voices. "Granite Peak Command, Dexter County One," he shouted. "Do you copy?"

After a beat, the radio sputtered. "Sheriff, this is air-to-land," a voice said. "We been trying to contact you. What's your location?"

Rick's jaw tightened. "We're about thirty feet from where you just dropped that slurry," he grunted through his teeth.

"My bad, Sheriff," the voice said. "We normally don't fly when it's this dark. I was about to turn back, but command told me to make the drop. This fire ain't showing much quit."

"Any choppers in the area?" Rick asked.

"None, sir," came the reply. "We're done for the night. But you have spot fires kicking up around you. I'd recommend—"

"Trust me, we're leaving." He tossed the radio toward Jack. "We'd better hustle, my friend. With some luck, we'll still have a truck."

CHAPTER 9

There were plenty of times when Meredith Hart figured she should just march into her mother's bedroom, snag that idiotic My Pillow that the old woman was so damned proud of, and press it hard and fast against her toothless, wrinkled face, relieving Meredith of ceaseless misery while sparing the rest of the humanity from any further collateral damage.

The task would be tidy and quick, of course, what with her mother currently sucking minimal oxygen from the tubes tracing into her nose. In less than a minute, the world would be rid of Patricia Celeste Hart and the suitcase of selfishness, self-centeredness, cruelty, and myriad other malignant character defects imbedded within her being.

"Meredith?" Patricia Hart said from the next room. "Can you hear me, Meredith?"

"I heard you, Mother," Meredith said as she tapped on the keyboard of her laptop. "What do you need?"

"Bring me a cigarette, will you, dear?"

Meredith rolled her eyes. "Mother, you have emphysema," she said, her voice littered with derision. "You use an oxygen tank, remember?"

"Don't get smart with me. I know damn well I have an oxygen tank."

"Then why would you want a cigarette?"

"Because I like to smoke, dammit!" Patricia's voice sounded as though she had a throat coated with road mix. "I quit drinking, for God's sake, so I should at least get to smoke." She paused to allow herself to explode into a violent series of mucus-laden hacks. "Besides, I've only had one today."

Right, Meredith thought. The woman had quit drinking. Big deal. Meredith actually *preferred* her drunk. At least Patricia would eventually pass out, providing an occasional reprieve from her jagged moods, nonstop petulance, and overall ill humor.

"Have you finished the meatloaf I made?" Meredith asked.

"I don't really care for it."

Meredith stared at the screen, which now displayed a sketch of a male standing in the anatomical position, his various bones and organs labeled by an orbit of words surrounding his body. Closing her eyes and nervously tapping a ballpoint pen on the table, she would whisper a half-dozen or so terms to herself, then open her eyes to gauge her progress. The medical memorization process had been slow-going, especially with the constant interruptions from her mother.

"C'mere, Tango," Patricia said from the other room. "Here, boy."

"Don't give him any food, Mother!" Meredith shouted.

"Why not?"

Meredith pursed her lips, nostrils flared. "Do we have to do this again?"

"Do what?"

Meredith sat hunched in her chair, measuring her breaths in an effort to arrest her temper. "Come here, Tango," she called. The dog didn't respond. "Tango?"

As she rose from her chair, she could hear a smacking sound, Tango clacking his jaws as he devoured a sizeable chunk of food. She threw her pen onto the desk and stormed toward the bedroom, where she saw her Shepherd Collie mix staring innocently at her, fragments of meatloaf falling from the sides of his mouth. He couldn't have come to her if he wanted to—her mother had a tight grip on his collar as she tried to shove a dog biscuit into his mouth.

"What in the hell is the matter with you?" Meredith shouted. She removed her mother's boney blue-veined hand from the dog's collar.

"He looked hungry," Patricia said with a half-snicker.

"He's a search dog, Mother!" Meredith said. "He is only supposed to get special rewards when he's on the job."

"He looks thin."

"He's not thin! He's the perfect weight."

"You pay way too much attention to that dog."

Meredith shook her head. "C'mon, Tango," she said. Liberated from Patricia's grasp, the dog obediently trotted out the bedroom door. Meredith glared at her mother, whose hands clutched the sheets on her bed as her face shriveled in apparent pain. It was a ploy she often used—feigning discomfort as a means to garner sympathy. The two women languished in silence, the only sound coming from the intermittent click of Patricia's oxygen machine.

"Can you *please* allow me some time without distraction so I can study?"

Patricia furrowed her brow. "Study what?"

"My EMT course."

"EMT. What's that stand for again?"

"Emergency Medical Technician," Meredith said. "I'm trying to get my certification."

"What for?"

"To advance my career."

"What *career*?" Patricia huffed. "You need to stop wasting your time with this nonsense and get married."

Meredith raised her hands, pushing her palms forward. In a perfect world, she would be shoving her mother off a cliff. "Can we please not talk about my personal life?"

"Sure … not a whole lot to talk about anyway."

Meredith abruptly turned and left the room, the sting of her mother's words feeling like a dagger buried between her shoulder blades. She plopped into her chair and stared at the sketch of the naked man on her computer screen. Releasing a sigh, she closed the laptop, her mind far too disquieted for her to study.

It would be easy to blame her situation on her mother, her duties as a caretaker constricting the amount of time she would be able to date. But dating wasn't the problem. She had already found the one she admired and adored, a man with whom she wanted to spend the rest of her days. She dreamt of him incessantly. They would get married, start a family, maybe even buy a home someday. When she was with him, she delighted in his being. He was her first thought upon waking, her final thought before retiring at night. In her mind, he was *perfect*.

There was only one small problem. He was taken.

She had wanted more than anything to change that.

CHAPTER 10

Four hours and forty-three stitches after leaving the trailhead, Rick's truck murmured up the crushed gravel road leading to Sage's house. He rolled to a stop, pushed open his door, and gingerly eased his body from the cab. Waddling like a journeyman bull rider, he staggered toward the cream-colored glow of the porch, every part of his body aching, save perhaps his eyebrows.

He could hear the gentle rustling of the Yellowstone River steadily meandering nearby in the darkness. The temperature had dropped—a good sign, since colder air and humidity would quiet the fire in the Crazies. Flames would awaken again at mid-morning, likely resuming their march of destruction.

Garrett McRae was still out there, a consideration anchored in Rick's mind. He would need to update the man's wife, a chore best done in person. Perhaps he could catch a few hours' sleep on Sage's couch. Such an arrangement would do little to aid his convalescence, but at least he could get an early start.

He winced in pain as he pushed his hand into his pocket, his index and middle fingers trying to pinch the ring of his keys. Mercifully, Sage was awake. She opened the door and leaned toward him. "I was worried about you!" she said as she thrust her arms around his neck.

"Don't!" Rick said as gently as possible, his body feeling as brittle as late-autumn leaves.

Sage stepped back. "What's wrong? Are you okay?"

"Well, they say only a couple of my ribs are cracked this time," Rick answered. "Besides that—"

"What happened?"

"It's a long story."

As he stepped through the doorway into the light, Sage scanned the dirt and grime on his tattered uniform. Her nose twitched a couple of times before she fanned her hand sideways in front of her face. "What *is* that?" she asked. "You smell like a salad that's been sittin' in someone's trunk."

"Yeah, I guess I may have a bit of an odor," Rick said. "They could only clean me up so much at the hospital."

"Hospital?"

"Let me take a hot shower, and I'll tell you all about it," Rick said. "Do you have any Advil?"

Sage frowned. "They didn't give you any meds?"

Rick shook his head. "I don't do well with meds."

• • •

Sage stood at the kitchen counter, waiting for a kettle of water to boil. She pressed the back of her hand over her mouth, attempting to stifle a lengthy yawn. Despite her hours of sleep, fatigue draped over her like a suffocating shroud.

The water in the shower stopped. Sage walked down the hall with a T-shirt and pair of gym shorts Rick had left behind during the summer. After a couple of soft knocks on the door, her fiancé emerged from the steamy bathroom with a white towel wrapped around his waist. She had seen his body plenty of times when they'd been intimate, but that didn't stop her from taking a moment to assess the goods. She was impressed at the way he had maintained his athletic physique at his age, right down to the acute definition of his abs. Ranch work could do that for a man.

His shoulders and chest were covered with abrasions, as if he'd rolled out of a fast-moving pickup. She stepped closer to him, gently passing a finger over a wound on his shoulder. "What in the—"

"I was wondering where this was," Rick said as he pulled the threadbare San Diego State T-shirt from her grasp. He gingerly tried to pull the neckline over his head.

"Let me help you," Sage said. She stepped into the bathroom and turned him around, where she saw the stitched lacerations on his back and scalp and sucked in a breath. "Are you going to tell me what happened or not?"

"I was attacked by a grizzly," Rick said. His tone was as flat as if he were informing Sage that he'd stopped in for an oil change.

"A grizzly? Where?"

"The Crazies?"

"Did you kill him?"

"Her—she was a sow," Rick answered. "I got between her and her cub."

"Okay, did you kill *her*?"

"Not quite."

"Did you play dead?"

Rick chuckled uneasily. "For a while, I guess."

Sage wagged her head in disbelief. "How did you end up running into a bear?"

Rick turned toward her, his face tightening into a grimace as he pulled the shirt over his back. "How about we talk about something else—it's been a long night." He drew closer, her senses filling with the scent of his clean skin. "I've been thinking a lot about a wedding date," he said. "How about Valentine's Day? We can get married, then go on a honeymoon someplace warm?"

Sage lightly put her hands around his waist and gazed into his eyes, a sliver of light between their lips. "That sounds perfect."

He placed his hands along her jaw line, pressing his lips to hers. She loved when he kissed her that way. Firm and virile, yet sensuous. Their kiss grew more intense, sending ripples of arousal through her body.

He stopped.

"What's wrong?" she asked.

Rick's fingers gently stroked the back of her neck. "There's something back here. A bump or something." He paused and touched her neck again. "Actually, it feels like there are two of them."

Sage felt a queasy sensation in her stomach, heat roving across her face. She slid her hand beneath his until she reached the back of her neck. He was right.

"I'm sure it's nothing," Sage said, even though she feared it must be *something*.

Rick lowered his head, eyes fixed on hers. "Have you been the doctor lately?"

Sage's throat tightened. "Actually, I have an appointment tomorrow with Dr. Tillotson." Her voice quivered. "My regular checkup."

Rick's brow wrinkled, leaving her unsure whether he was buying her story. "What time is your appointment? I can come—"

"Hi, Pa-Pa. Are you okay?"

Rick looked over Sage's shoulder to see Abby standing outside the doorway, her balled fist rubbing sleep from one of her eyes. "Hi, sweetheart," he said.

"Are you all right, Pa-Pa? We were worried about you."

"I'm fine, Abby," Rick said. "I was just—"

"Pa-Pa got attacked by a bear," Sage said.

Rick winced. Sage didn't believe in treating children like … well … *children*. It wasn't the way she was raised. While she and Rick were synchronized on the majority of their parenting techniques, they diverged on that one—that, and not "shacking up," an expression Sage considered prehistoric.

"You got attacked by a bear, Pa-Pa?" Abby asked. "Was it a grizzly?"

"Yes, it was a grizzly."

"Did you play dead?"

Rick's chin dipped toward his chest. He blew out a breath. "Tell you what," he said. "Let me finish getting dressed, and I'll come in to say good night. Fair enough?"

Abby nodded, hugging Sage's waist before disappearing into the bedroom. Sage turned toward Rick. He smiled briefly before tilting his head, his eyes drifting toward the back of her neck.

CHAPTER 11

The opening of the new Starlight Coffee on Central Avenue in Great Falls was hailed as a seminal event, somewhat akin to a large metropolitan area landing a major sports team. Having the popular coffee franchise in town made younger folks believe their drowsy hamlet had finally arrived, the establishment serving up mochas and macchiatos just like the ones in faraway sprawls like Seattle and San Francisco.

After watching white cups with exotic logos start popping up all over town, Spencer Bible figured it was high time he discovered what he was missing. He was sensitive that way, always feeling like he was on the outside looking in, a hole in a donut, the perennial last player picked whenever they were choosing up sides in life.

The door jingled as he stepped into the coffee shop on Thursday morning, Spencer feeling self-conscious as a half-dozen people in line turned to witness the latest lemming joining the local java crusade. He faked a cough and dropped his eyes toward the floor, his forefinger plunging beneath the knot of his necktie in a vain effort to loosen the grip of his buttoned collar, a ritual repeated unsuccessfully numerous times a day. He could have used the drive-through, he thought, had he not walked over from his office located one block away.

Mimicking the twenty-somethings standing in line, Spencer stared at the screen of his iPhone, sifting through SPAM in his in-box with the intensity of a man expecting an urgent communique from a foreign dignitary. It wasn't until after he was invited to order that he realized that he hadn't yet looked at the menu.

"May I help you, sir?" a young woman asked, her voice as soft and gentle as a hymn from the heavens. Spencer lifted his eyes and found himself unable to speak. The barista who stood before him was unlike any woman he had ever seen, a goddess in a green apron, her large blue eyes sparkling like precious sapphires, dark-brown hair bursting with thick flowing curls that tumbled carefree across her shoulders. Luscious lips, the color of cabernet, opened to showcase two rows of perfect teeth glistening like deep-sea pearls.

"Uh, I'll have …," Spencer managed to mumble, warmth flowing into his face. He squinted at the menu, a complex mosaic of selections hanging on the back wall.

"A lot to choose from, huh?" the woman offered sympathetically. He glanced at her briefly, his palms growing sweaty as he found himself pressured by some artificial clock. His eyes lingered long enough to notice a name badge that hung to one side of her open-collared white blouse. The homemade tag read "Lizzie," two tiny hearts floating above the i's.

Lizzie. He repeated the name to himself, caressing its perfection. He wouldn't dare attempt to say it aloud, reluctant to venture to such levels of familiarity when he hadn't mastered the chore of establishing simple eye contact.

"Skinny caramel macchiato for Stephanie!" a young male shouted from behind an intricate coffee contraption. "Extra whipped cream!" A woman who wasn't skinny at all gleefully shuffled forward, grasping a drink that looked more like a malted milkshake than a cup of coffee.

"I … I'll take one of those," Spencer said. "Please."

Lizzie chuckled for reasons he didn't understand. He cast a brief uneasy smile toward her before averting his eyes, tugging at his necktie once again. Spencer was convinced he was the only Montanan under thirty years old who wore a tie. The discipline was introduced by his father, Cyrus Augustus Bible, who had drafted Spencer into the insurance industry. "If you are going to be a successful businessman, you need to look the part," Cyrus would declare. It was one of many dictums his father had offered him, along with the oft-repeated "There are two ways—the wrong way and the Bible way," a statement that left Spencer somewhat vexed since he wasn't quite sure whether his father was referring to his family, the Good Book, or some curious amalgamation of both.

He gazed back toward Lizzie, hoping to steal another glance at her fairness. His heart pounded when he realized her eyes had never left him. Her head tilted as she studied him, a perfectly manicured hand resting on one hip, her smile more subtle now, perhaps designed to allure.

"You're that insurance guy, aren't you?" Lizzie asked. Her words floated toward him as though transported on billowy clouds. Spencer took a quick glance over his shoulder before awkwardly pointing at himself. He was the only person there, and she was staring right at him.

"Yes," he croaked. "How … how did you know?"

"I have a friend who works at the flower shop on Main," she said. "I saw you walking into your office a couple of times." Spencer nodded as Lizzie stepped toward the cash register. "That will be three ninety-five."

Spencer quickly plunged a hand into his pocket, trying to disguise the notion that the cost of his drink had to be some kind of mistake. He'd never recalled paying four bucks for a cup of coffee before. He pushed a five-dollar bill toward Lizzie, using the counter to calm the nervous quiver in his fingers. She offered him change, but he declined. He was rewarded with another smile.

"You know, my uncle was in the insurance business," Lizzie said, dropping Spencer's change in a glass tip jar. "He seemed to really enjoy it."

Spencer chuckled. "I find it kind of dull."

Lizzie folded her arms, her fashion-model eyebrows furrowed. "Then why do it?"

He shrugged. "It gives me an opportunity to help people," he said matter-of-factly. He cringed as the words spilled from his mouth like toothpaste he couldn't force back in the tube. It was another old adage belonging to his father. Coming from Cyrus, whom Spencer revered, the sentence was always delivered with deep sincerity, but Spencer somehow managed to make it sound pretentious.

"Skinny caramel macchiato for … *Spencer?*" the male server shouted, curiously staring at the name on the clear plastic glass. "Extra whipped cream!"

Spencer nodded at the barista and collected his drink. He offered a taut smile as he raised his glass toward Lizzie. Picking up speed as he headed toward the door, he wondered when he might ever marshal the courage to enter Starlight Coffee again.

• • •

Razors of pain shot through Rick's body as he walked stiffly into the Dexter County Sheriff's Office, the pair of ibuprofen he'd consumed feeling about as potent as jelly beans. Helen was talking on the phone, but her eyes were glued to her boss, studying him as though they'd never met. Adjusting his hat to cover the stitches cresting his forehead, Rick did his best to disguise his troubled gait lest Helen become overly curious.

It didn't work.

"How are you feeling today, Sheriff?" Helen asked as she finished her call.

"Doin' fine, Helen," Rick said. "Yourself?" He picked up a small stack of messages that lay in a plastic tray at the corner of her desk. He started to read them but quickly felt a wave of dizziness, his vision briefly losing focus. The ER doc at Riverton Memorial had said he might have suffered a concussion, and the theory certainly had merit, considering Rick's head had hit a variety of objects during his plunge down the ravine.

"You sure you're okay, Sheriff?" Helen asked. "I didn't even expect you to come in today, given what happened."

"What exactly happened, Helen?" Rick asked, feeling somewhat piqued. He liked Helen well enough, though she leaned toward the nosy side. Then again, given the size of Riverton—population 6,742, give or take—not much happened without other folks knowing about it. The moccasin telegraph was alive and well, with news spreading like a brushfire on cured cheatgrass.

"I understand you had a bear encounter," Helen said.

"Where'd you hear that?"

"I have my sources."

Rick sighed. "Yes, I did have a bear encounter, Helen, if that's what you want to call it."

"You're lucky to be alive."

"I suppose I am."

"How did you survive?" Helen asked. "Did you play dead?"

Rick put his hands on his hips and stared at Helen, his tongue sweeping across the inside of his cheek. She raised her eyebrows expectantly, as though she were talking to a coma patient who'd returned from the other side.

"How are they doing with that fire in the Crazies?" he asked.

Helen paused, disappointed for not gleaning more details. "Not good," she answered. "Right now they're saying it's about five percent contained."

Rick pursed his lips with disappointment. "That hunter is still out there. I plan to go out to see his wife, give her an update. Maybe I can get some more information. I'll need an address."

Helen nodded as Rick gripped the knob of his office door.

"So, did you, Sheriff?" she asked.

Rick stopped. "Did I what?"

"You know … play dead?"

"The address, Helen," Rick said. "Get me the address."

• • •

"Does that hurt?"

Dr. Janice Tillotson was palpating Sage's neck, her forefinger rubbing back and forth across a bump below Sage's left earlobe. Sage said nothing, shaking her head slowly. The exam room was deathly silent. An antique clock ticked ominously on the wall, as if to remind patients that precious seconds of their lives were rapidly fading away. Sage's heart thumped in her chest as she studied Dr. Tillotson's expressionless face, suddenly expecting a death sentence from a one-person jury.

"Have you experienced any fever or perhaps night sweats?" the physician asked. She tossed her latex gloves into a trash bin and picked up a manila folder from the black Formica counter. "I see here in your chart that you've lost some weight—over ten pounds."

"I figured the fever I had was the flu," Sage said glumly. "As for the weight, I tend not to weigh myself."

"Well, you look thin," Dr. Tillotson said. She laid the folder on the counter and stared at Sage, arms folded across her chest. "Have you talked to Rick about this?"

Asking about Rick was well within bounds. Janice and Sage had been friends since childhood, when they sat next to each other in Miss Adams's homeroom at Riverton Elementary School. Their paths diverged when Janice headed to Missoula for college and then to med school in Oregon. Sage stayed in Riverton, eschewing higher education for gifted vocal chords and a twelve-string guitar.

Janice never married, unable to find the right guy. Sage had married twice, adept at finding the wrong one. In addition to being doctor and patient, they were confidantes, Janice even an occasional visitor to Sage's establishment, The Spur, where the physician would heal herself with a cool glass of wine, never once complaining the beverage flowed from a cardboard box.

"Rick didn't really notice anything until last night," Sage said. "He doesn't know I came to see you three weeks ago."

"You need to tell him," Janice said.

Sage studied her friend's features. Janice had declined to color her long black hair as she had aged, but the gray had an attractive appeal. Her face was smooth and youthful, seductive without makeup, making her a worthy catch by anyone's measure. It was no surprise she'd had her share of suitors, though most of them shied away when they realized she was married to her patients.

"I don't want to worry Rick—he's got a lot on his plate." Sage was staring out the window, watching lifeless curled leaves tumble off the branches of a cottonwood tree.

Janice's face grew somber. "Sage," she said. "Your condition has gotten worse."

Sage's body twitched as she felt a sudden chill. Her entire being flooded with dread, drowning her with the same foreboding gloom she'd felt as a child when her mother entered her bedroom with news that her father was dead. Janice's lips appeared to move in slow motion, stripping away Sage's cowgirl toughness in an instant, ripping away defenses that had taken a lifetime to build.

Her throat felt thick. "Uh … well," she stammered, "would you mind telling me exactly *what* condition you think I have?"

"I have some suspicions, but I want to do a biopsy."

"I don't want surgery."

"It's not surgery—it's a procedure," Janice said. "I need to take some tissue from one of the lumps on your neck."

Sage bit the side of her lip. "When are you going to do it?"

"Immediately."

"Immediately? Like right now?"

"It'll only take a minute."

* * *

Meredith Hart's phone buzzed on the console of her Toyota truck. She was about a mile out from her job in Bozeman, where she worked for a district office of the US Forest Service.

It was a text. Trading glances between her phone and the road ahead, she saw the message was from Brian Scott, team leader for Big Sky Search Dogs. "BOW HUNTER MISSING IN CRAZIES," the text read. "STAND BY FOR FURTHER DETAILS."

Meredith felt a flash flood of adrenaline thunder through her veins. She and Tango hadn't been on a search in more than a month, when they had recovered a drowning victim outside Butte. They were in desperate need of another opportunity, one that might provide a brighter ending.

Meredith went into her contacts and punched Brian's cell. The call went to voice mail. "Shit," she said, teeth grinding. She Googled the number for the Dexter County Sheriff's Office. A woman who introduced herself as Helen answered.

"This is Meredith Hart calling," Meredith said excitedly, convinced her name might hold some significance. "Is Sheriff …"

"Morrand?" Helen asked.

"Yes, that's it. Is he available?"

"Sheriff Morrand isn't here at the moment. Is there some way I can help?"

"Yes, there is," Meredith said. "I received an alert that there is a missing hunter up in the Crazies. I was wondering when our search dogs will be needed."

Helen drew a deep breath. "There's not a lot of searching going on at the moment, Miss … What did you say your name was?"

"Hart. Meredith Hart," she answered. "I'm a member of the search dog team over in Gallatin County."

"Search dogs," Helen repeated. "We usually deal with Brian Scott over there."

"Yes," Meredith said impatiently. "Brian is the team leader. I was just—"

"Oh, I don't think you understand, Miss. There's a huge wildland fire up there. It's already burned twenty-seven-hundred acres. Nobody's gonna be able to search for anything until they get things under control."

"But there *is* a hunter up there?"

"Yes."

"Is he local?"

"He's from Montana, if that's what you mean," Helen answered. "Three Forks."

A cool shudder climbed Meredith's spine. "Three Forks?" she asked. "That's right near me. Can you tell me his name?"

"His name is Garrett McRae," Helen said. "Do you know him?"

Helen's words came across the line in slow motion, as if they were part of a horrifying dream. Meredith's lips quivered as air left her lungs. She didn't answer.

CHAPTER 12

Shortly before noon, Amber McRae finally got Gabe down for a nap, even though he probably didn't require one. It was Amber who needed a break, perhaps some time to think.

She'd barely sat down on her weathered velour couch when she heard the sound of tires grinding on the gravel drive leading to their two-bedroom home. Rubbing her temples as she blew out a breath, she dragged herself toward the kitchen window. Randall Boone's truck was rolling to a stop, horse trailer in tow. He pushed his hat down on his head as he exited the vehicle, girding himself against a gust. The morning had been sunless, thick clouds forming a low ceiling of clay. Despite the brisk weather, Boone wore only a black T-shirt, faded and stretched tight by his bulging biceps and sculpted chest. Amber pursed her lips as she watched him draw a lengthy drag from a cigarette and casually flick it toward the ground.

Glancing toward Gabe's room, Amber headed out the front door. She rubbed her bare arms vigorously while she strutted across the courtyard toward her frail and faded metal barn, its flaking brown paint having fallen well shy of its lifetime guarantee. Steady morning winds had ushered in the acrid scent of cattle dung from a nearby ranch. The odor hung in the air, perhaps heralding Boone's arrival.

She could sense Boone's eyes watching her—or perhaps some *part* of her—as her boots kicked up clouds of dust. She shot her best glare of disgust toward him, only to see Boone flash a wry smile as he led Garrett's horse from the trailer, the animal still carrying a saddle. She continued to stomp forward, walking straight toward a dust devil that whirled in front of the barn entrance. The dervish danced out of her way, as though wary of her present demeanor.

Amber threw open the sliding door, its deteriorated metal rattling like a fast freight on rusted rails. She could feel Boone's presence behind her. The uneven sound of the horse's gait suggested it had thrown a shoe. After opening the entrance of a stall, she stepped forward and snared the bridle.

Garrett's horse, named Ronan, normally wore a gleaming coat of reddish-brown. Garrett had purchased him right after he and Amber first married, back when their love was seamless, life seemed effortless, the future without limits. It felt like a lifetime ago. After Gabe's accident, Garrett wanted to sell the horse, giving the family more money for medical bills. Amber refused. She watched her husband, eternally hopeful and upbeat, suddenly staggering through life as if it was something he loathed, a torturous daily death march that he fought to endure without consent. It seemed he was perpetually clinging to the edge of a precipitous cliff, bloodless fingertips barely maintaining a grip.

The brief moments he spent alone in the barn with Ronan seemed to offer Garrett some degree of solace, a time to grieve at his own pace and on his own terms. Some moments were better than others. She had approached the barn on one occasion to find him crying uncontrollably, his face buried in the soft glistening hair of Ronan's thick neck. She slipped away without disturbing him, her own tears warming her cheeks as she hastened back toward the house.

When she walked Ronan into the stall on this Thursday morning, the horse's movements were slow and labored, his eyes dull and expressionless. "When is the last time you fed him?" Amber asked as the back of her fingers stroked the horse's face. "Did you bother to feed him at all?"

"I fed him," Boone grumbled. "Of course I fed him."

"Right."

Fueled by anger, Amber lifted Ronan's saddle off his back as though it were a sofa pillow, then slung it over a side rail. Tucking his blanket beneath her arm, she examined the cinch marks on the horse's girth, her finger touching the fluid that oozed from sores as red as raspberries.

"You're such an asshole," she grumbled toward Boone. "You couldn't take off his saddle?"

Boone shrugged his shoulders, lips downturned in mock sadness, the painted face of a rodeo clown. He shifted his weight to one side and locked his sinewy tattooed arms across his chest. "You really ripped me a new one yesterday," he said. "What was that act all about?"

"Like I told you, it wasn't an act," Amber shot back. "You shouldn't have come here."

"I had to bring back the horse."

"Kyle could have brought him back."

Amber continued to caress the weakened horse. Ronan dipped his head into some hay. When he lifted up, half of the strands fell from his mouth. He appeared too exhausted to eat.

"You shouldn't be here," she repeated. Peering beneath Ronan's girth, Amber bent over in search of more wounds.

She heard Boone move closer. "C'mon, baby, why are you behaving like this?" he said. Amber rose, her eyes opening wide as she felt him place his hands around her waist, pressing his aroused midsection against her backside, the coarseness of his unshaven face feeling like sandpaper on her neck.

Amber whirled and shoved him backward, Boone's brawny shoulders cracking a slat of wood on the side of the stall, his hat tumbling from his head. His mouth fell open, seemingly dismayed that Amber's five-foot-four frame could deliver such force.

"Get the hell off me!" she screamed. "What the hell do you think you're doing?"

Boone's eyes narrowed. "What's with you?" he asked, palms held open as he wagged his head. "I thought we—"

"You thought *we* what?" Amber snapped. "There is no *we*. Never was. Got it?"

Boone huffed a breath smelling of stale alcohol. "So now all of a sudden you care about your husband?"

"I've *always* cared about my husband," Amber said through clenched teeth. "And my husband is *missing*. What part don't you understand?"

Boone's eyes softened, his lips curling into a gentle, patient smile, the same one that had lured her when she had been vulnerable, too drained and filled with heartbreak to know any better. She studied his features. His long oily hair was combed straight back, exposing a forehead broad and thick. Faded acne scars pocked his rugged skin, partially shadowed by his grizzle. He wasn't even all that handsome, she thought. Not like Garrett, anyway. Just the wrong guy at the right time.

He moved toward her again, this time more slowly, his steel hands resting on her shoulders.

Her arms violently flailed at the inside of his forearms, rebuffing him once more. She retreated to a corner of the stall, where she snatched a shovel caked with horse dung. Jaw muscles taut as wire, Amber jerked the tool above her head, the bleached and splintered wooden handle vibrating in her shaking hands.

"I said get the fuck away from me," she hissed. Her heart quaked within her chest, her breaths short and potent.

Boone lifted his chin, his darkened eyes reserving reprisal for a later date. He took a few measured steps backward.

"Hello? Anybody home?"

Amber lowered the shovel. She and Boone both turned toward the door of the barn. A man in a cowboy hat stepped inside, his hand resting comfortably on his sidearm as he walked toward them through layers of the barn's uneven light.

It was that sheriff. The one from Dexter County. Amber wondered what he had seen. Or heard.

"Everything okay here?" Sheriff Morrand asked. His steel eyes lasered toward Boone from beneath his hat. Amber sensed the sheriff didn't consider things to be okay at all.

Amber leaned the shovel against the side of the stall, wiping her hands on the front of her thighs. She inhaled deeply, trying to slow her breathing. Squaring her stance, she buried her fingers in the back of her jeans, hoping the lawman would overlook her trembling hands.

"Hello, Sheriff," Amber said uneasily. "Mr. Boone here was just returning Garrett's horse and some of his gear."

Morrand's eyes followed Boone, who was picking up his hat from the floor of the stall. He appeared more irritated than unnerved by the sheriff's presence.

"I was just leaving," he said as he walked past Morrand. He cast a final eerie glance toward Amber, one that sent a river of ice down her spine.

CHAPTER 13

Rick paused on the porch of the McRae family's century-old farmhouse, watching Boone's tires spew crushed rock as his truck reached the end of the drive and sped away. On infrequent occasions, Rick had encountered men who simply rubbed him the wrong way from the get-go—whether it be by manner or speech—and Randall Boone certainly fell comfortably within that class.

Amber held the screen door open, eyes downcast while waiting for him to come inside. "We'll have to speak quietly, Sheriff," she whispered without looking at him. "My son is sleeping."

The inside of the McRae home was small but cozy. The low textured ceiling, built for the shorter men of its era, was patched in certain places yet meticulously painted. Original wallpaper adorned the living room, colored light gray and sprinkled with large faded pink flowers that resembled cotton candy. A bead-board wainscot rose halfway up the walls, its surface shimmering with layers of oil-based white enamel.

Amber hustled ahead of Rick, quickly turning off the murmur of the TV and placing the remote meticulously on the end table. "Can I get you something, Sheriff?" she asked, her voice rapid and unsteady. "Coffee?"

Rick waved an open palm and wagged his head, the minor movements sending shock waves rumbling down to his injured ribs. No, he didn't want coffee. More Advil, perhaps. Or, better yet, a couple of Vicodin, were they not taboo.

"I wanted to give you an update, Mrs. McRae," he said. "I'm sorry to say that our search efforts have been … delayed. There's a fire going through the Crazies, and it might be a while before they get it under control."

She didn't look at him as she walked toward a small kitchen area, its rose-colored walls folded in the corner of the house, the room seemingly conceived as an afterthought. Small printed photos checkered the refrigerator. One of them captured Amber and Garrett standing on top of a mountain peak, their smiles joyful as she snuggled against the side of his chest. Another showed a hunter—likely Garrett—holding a compound bow and wearing blue camouflage as he stood behind the carcass of a massive eight-point elk. Despite his conquest, his flat lips and vacant eyes were devoid of elation, the photo closer to resembling a mug shot than recording a memorable event.

Taking a moist towel from the sink, Amber began wiping the kitchen counter, which already appeared spotless. "You're saying Garrett got caught in the middle of a wildfire?"

"No, ma'am, I didn't' say that at all. I said that the fire has hampered our search efforts. It might be a day or so before we can resume looking for him."

Amber slowly folded the towel in the sink and turned toward him, arms crossed as she leaned against the kitchen counter. Her eyes scanned the black-and-white tiled floor. "They're not going to find him, are they?" she said, a shiver in her voice.

"Please, Mrs. McRae, you don't want to jump to any conclusions," Rick said. "You just need to have a little … faith." He regretted the words as soon as they fell from his mouth, not wishing to encourage false hope. Sadness draped over him as thoughts of his daughter roamed through his mind. He drew a breath. "Do you mind if I ask you a few questions, ma'am?"

"Please call me Amber," she said. "The ma'am thing makes me feel kind of old." She flashed a smile, her eyes showing the brief flicker of a match before it quickly dies out. Rick understood why a man would be attracted to her. Her full lips, smooth skin, and high cheekbones gave her an appearance that invited the gaze to linger, like taking in a flowered mountain meadow or watching a lavender summer sunset.

She nodded toward a small wooden table pressed against the kitchen wall. "Please … sit down. Are you sure I can't get you some coffee? I can make a fresh pot."

"No coffee, thank you," he said. He slid a chair out from the table and lowered himself into it, his movements appearing as if his limbs were attached to cables. "Water could be good, though."

Amber brought him a plastic tumbler of water and retreated toward the kitchen sink. Her movements were slower now, more measured, as she appeared to contemplate the news Rick had delivered.

"How long has your husband known Randall Boone?" he asked. The presence of Boone on the McRae property had surprised Rick, especially since Amber had seemed intent on scratching the man's eyes out only hours prior. He thought he'd heard arguing when he approached the barn, but he couldn't be sure due to the whip of the wind. When he entered, his arrival had appeared to make Boone and Amber ill at ease.

"Garrett has known Boone about two years," Amber said quietly.

"How did the two men meet?"

"They worked construction together."

"And how about the quieter one? What about him?"

"Kyle? He and Garrett have known each other since grade school." She paused a beat. "Why do you ask?"

Rick took a sip of water, turning his eyes toward a picture hanging on the wall beside the refrigerator. It was an eight-by-ten canvas print, the kind they'd begun selling at Costco. It showed Amber and Garrett, smiles wide and faces aglow, flanking a baby that Rick assumed to be their child. Rick looked back at Amber. Her eyes were much different than the picture. They appeared unhappy and bleak, her ability to experience joy somehow ransomed.

"I just want to know how well Garrett knows them—you know, what kind of friends they are," Rick said. "I'm having trouble reconciling the fact that they would lose contact with Garrett on a Saturday and wait more than three full days before reporting him missing."

Amber nodded. "It bothers me as well, Sheriff, and that's why I was so upset last night," she said. "Garrett is fairly skilled in the backcountry— believe me, he's a *survivor*—but they should have called earlier for help."

A sound came from down the hallway, muffled at first before growing louder. A young child was crying. "Excuse me," Amber said. "It sounds like my son is waking up from his nap."

Rick took another sip of water as Amber left the room. He decided to get up from the table before his injured body became too stiff and left him unable to rise. Teeth clenched and eyebrows pinched shut, he guided himself from the chair.

He tried to stretch his neck muscles as he wandered from the kitchen. The living room was immaculate, as though it was cleaned several times a day. The carpet had been vacuumed, the furniture void of the slightest speck of dust. A collection of magazines lay on the coffee table. Rick reached for one of them before spotting an array of trifold brochures for cruises and vacation destinations. He picked up the stack. Several locations in Mexico were represented, as well as cruises in the Caribbean. He began thumbing through the brochures before hearing a clatter behind him. He turned to see Amber coming down the hallway, pushing a smiling young child seated in a wheelchair. Rick guessed the towheaded boy was three or four years old.

"Gabe, this is Sheriff Morrand," Amber said. "Can you say hello?"

Gabe offered a shy wave of his hand. "Hi, Sheriff Rand," he said quietly.

Rick walked toward Gabe and extended his hand, but Amber flashed a tight smile as she pushed the chair past him. She positioned the child in front of the TV, turning on the remote and switching the channel from CNN to Disney. As she turned back to Rick, her smile dissipated when she noticed the brochures he clutched in his hand.

"I'm sorry, but I couldn't help but notice these," he said as he glanced down toward his hand. "I'm engaged to be married, and my fiancée has been talking about places she'd like to honeymoon. She mentioned Mexico, among a few others."

"Congratulations," Amber said flatly. "I'm not even sure why we kept those. Garrett brought them home, saying that we could go on a vacation at some point, maybe a second honeymoon." She shook her head and laughed uneasily. "He's always been a bit of a dreamer. With Gabe's medical bills, we can't go to a Mexican restaurant, let alone Mexico or the Caribbean."

She took the brochures from Rick's hand and walked into the kitchen. Using the towel in the sink, she wiped down them down before placing them with precision back on the coffee table. Rick's eyes traced her movements as he wondered why Amber was acting like the second coming of Howard Hughes.

"I'm sorry," she said. "Gabe's condition leaves him susceptible to infection. It's important for me to—"

"No explanation needed, Mrs. McRae," Rick said. He adjusted his hat, the tug on his rib muscles making him wish he hadn't. "I'd best head back toward Riverton. I will certainly keep you apprised of any developments." He walked toward the door before turning to look back at Gabe.

"Good-bye Gabe," he said. "Nice to meet you, son."

The child turned toward him, eyes bright and hopeful. He waved again. "Bye, Sheriff Rand."

Amber followed Rick outside. The wind had died, the white sun trying to push through a thin veil of clouds. "Thank you for coming all the way out here, Sheriff," Amber said. She appeared more relaxed, perhaps because he was leaving. "If you need anything else—"

"You have one heck of a sweet boy there, Mrs. McRae," Rick said. "If you don't mind me asking, can you tell me how Gabe became injured?"

Amber cast her eyes toward the horizon, contemplating the question. Anguish drifted across her face. Rick swallowed, sensing he had sliced open a wound.

"I'm sorry, ma'am, I—"

"No, it's fine," Amber said. She waved her hand rapidly in front of her face, fanning away her emotion as if shooing a persistent insect. She drew a slow, deep breath. "Gabe was two years old—in fact, it was his second birthday," she said. "We went camping in the Beartooth Mountains, down near Cooke City. Garrett got off late from work, and it was almost dark when we arrived at the campground. Garrett had his gun, of course, since it had only been a couple of years since grizzlies had attacked those campers …"

Rick nodded as he recalled the incident. A mother and two cubs had invaded a campsite, dragged a man from his tent, and mauled him to death. Two other campers were critically injured. Rick swallowed hard, a shiver laddering up his vertebrae, the horror of his own grizzly attack suddenly hitting home.

"We were in a hurry to set up camp," Amber said. "Garrett placed his gun inside the cooler as he went to pitch the tent." She shifted her weight, stroking her fingers through her long, thick hair, eyes fixed on the ground, head shaking, doubting her own words. "Gabe somehow got into that cooler and—"

"Mrs. McRae, you don't have to—" He gingerly reached toward her shoulder but pulled his hand back.

"We're lucky Gabe is alive," she said. "The bullet went through the cooler, ricocheted off his pelvis, and hit his spinal cord, paralyzing him from the waist down. It was a miracle he didn't bleed to death." She looked up at Rick, her eyes filling with tears.

"I would imagine that was hard on you—both of you," he said.

Amber wet her lips, eyebrows pinched in distress. "It affected Garrett the most," she said. "He couldn't forgive himself. He wandered around in a daze for over a year. He got rid of all of his guns, sold every last one of them. He *hates* guns. But he loves hunting, and the grief counselor said he should go again. She thought it might help him. It took a while, but finally he agreed." Amber stared once again at the horizon. "That's when he became a bow hunter," she said.

The words *bow hunter* hung in the air like thick smoke. Rick stepped from the porch, nodding toward Amber. "As I mentioned, we'll let you know of any developments," he said and turned to walk away.

"Sheriff?" Amber asked. "How long do they typically look for someone … you know, when they're missing?"

Rick paused, considering her question. "We look until we find 'em," he said.

Amber rested her hands on her hips and stared at Rick, her sad eyes squinting with sympathy. "I guess that was pretty hard what you went through."

"Ma'am?"

"With your daughter. I mean, she was missing before …"

Her words caught him off guard, as though Chloe's death was some closely held family secret. In truth, the murder had been a national news story. Still, he wasn't prepared to talk about it with just anyone. Sage, maybe, or even Jack. But certainly not someone he'd just met.

He studied her weary face. She couldn't be much older than his daughter would have been. Amber's eyes were lacerated with anguish, the same hopeless desperation he felt when Chloe had gone missing. Further darkening the skies of her circumstances was her child, Gabe, an innocent who'd received a merciless sentence for the crime of toddler curiosity. Rick wondered why life dealt cards like this, leaving a trail of wounded souls with lonely burdens to bear, each tortured individual issued their own burlap sack chock-full of rusted hammers.

"I'm so sorry, Sheriff Morrand," Amber said. "I didn't mean to pry."

Her question was not totally out of line, especially when one considered the information she had just shared about her husband and child. *You show me yours, I'll show you mine.*

Rick shook his head. "No, you're fine," he said, awakening from his lethargy. "It's just …"

They stood in an awkward silence. "Is there anything else you need at this time?" Amber asked.

Rick exhaled. "Do you have a photo of your husband I can take with me? Also, maybe one or two articles of clothing?"

"Why clothing?"

"For the search dogs."

"Right."

Amber opened the screen and went inside. Rick stood in the doorway, watching her rifle through a stack of pictures in a drawer next to the sink.

Choosing two and holding one in each hand, she studied them briefly before returning one to the drawer and handing the other to the sheriff. She then disappeared down the hall, emerging moments later with a pair of T-shirts. "I hadn't gotten around to washing these just yet," she said, her voice unsteady as moisture formed in her eyes. "I suppose they should work."

Rick pressed his lips together and nodded while Amber quickly folded the shirts. He studied the photo in his hand. Garrett was standing in front of the barn door, his eyes joyless as he held Ronan's lead. The photo was black and white, which only added to the gloom.

"Pardon me for asking," Rick said, "but given how deeply your son's injury affected your husband, do you think he'd ever be capable of taking his own life?" The words barely left his mouth before he received a reply.

"*Never*," Amber said definitively, her bottom lip pausing beneath her upper teeth for emphasis. "He would *never* leave Gabriel, and he would *never* leave me."

Rick tugged the brim of his hat, the sweatband stretching the skin on his scalp and stinging his stitches. Masking his pain with a tight smile, he offered a quick polite nod. "I'll stay in touch, Amber."

CHAPTER 14

As his truck meandered through Bozeman Pass and descended into Dexter County, Rick dialed Sage's cell phone again, the third time in less than an hour. It was odd that she wouldn't pick up—or at least call him back when she saw his number. Ever since he had requested her hand in marriage, their relationship had kicked into a blissful overdrive. They shared a deep intimacy that was celebrated with glorious lust, their moments apart almost painful. Her query about a wedding date disquieted him somewhat, since it was the first hint that her patience might be wearing thin. He had considered her concern and dismissed it, persuading himself that marrying Sage was destiny.

"Hey, beautiful, it's me," he said gently, his voice slightly beyond a whisper. "I'm headed out to Mariah, to talk to the guy who works at the Gold Bar—see if he can give me some more information about those two hunters." Glancing out the window, he watched a small herd of elk peacefully grazing in a bronze-colored cattle field. He allowed himself a half smile, knowing that once hunting season entered full swing, the animals would magically vanish, seeking refuge in the high mountain forests. "Give me a call, will you? I want to know how it went at the doctor's office." He considered telling Sage he was worried about her but decided it would serve no helpful purpose. "I love you," he finally said. The phrase felt mechanical as it exited his lips.

The scent of burnt timber wandered into his senses. Looking into the distance, he could see Riverton blanketed in an ashen haze, one more suited for a sprawling coastal metropolis. The Granite Peak Fire, so christened in honor of the Crazy Mountain trailhead it had ravaged so effortlessly, would be delivering smoke and soot to distant states before it could be successfully brought under control.

The weather offered no reprieve. Overcast skies in the morning had departed without delivering much-needed moisture. Local winds had been both powerful and fickle, sending the wildland blaze careening in untamed random directions, its flames eagerly devouring new sources of fuel.

It would be at least a few days before the search for Garrett McRae could resume.

Returning his phone to his top pocket, Rick's fingers rapidly tapped the top of his steering wheel as he exited the interstate and turned north on Highway 89 toward the Shields River Valley. He crossed the Yellowstone, where aspen-lined September shores would normally sparkle like bullion as they nurtured the river's rippling flow of jade. Beneath the suffocating ceiling of smoke, an iconic fall portrait had turned a dreary black and white.

Rick took out his phone and dialed his fiancée's number again.

• • •

Sage sat in front of Washington Elementary School, brushing away the tears streaking down her cheekbones. Within minutes, Abby would be spilling out of the school's entrance with a host of other children, and it was critical that Sage get her emotions under control.

Her phone vibrated on the console. Rick had been calling incessantly. She moved her hand toward the phone, then pulled back.

Not now. Not yet.

She had been crying intermittently ever since she had left Janice Tillotson's office, where the physician had suggested a biopsy as a precaution. The tips of Sage's fingers felt the bandage at the base of her neck where Dr. Tillotson had made an incision and removed a portion of the tumor just beneath the surface of her skin. The local anesthesia had worn off, and her neck was now sore, but that was not Sage's chief concern. She tugged at the neckline of her sweater, careful to conceal the dressing from view.

Results would not be available for a few days. While Dr. Tillotson prescribed that she remain calm and focus on the present, Sage found herself in total disarray, her brain replaying an infomercial forecasting certain doom. She stared through her windshield as a young mother stepped out of an SUV, arms outstretched as her child exited the school and ran to her, life appearing abundant and limitless. Sage's head throbbed. A shiver climbed her neck, causing her shoulders to twitch. She'd been charged and convicted—she was sure of it—and now she was awaiting her sentence.

Rick would surely want to know what is happening with her. He would want to support her, let her know that she is loved. A nauseating feeling filled her stomach. How could she tell him? Only a few years after losing his wife, he had lost a daughter. Now his fiancée? She told herself she should have never agreed to marry him, convinced she had been selfish.

Nothing made sense.

Sage put on the pair of sunglasses sitting on the dash, then glanced in the rearview mirror. "Buck up, Cowgirl," she whispered to herself. Abby waved eagerly and sprinted toward the truck.

• • •

The sky to the north looked like cast iron, dense smoke hovering above a layer the color and texture of brown mustard. A fierce wind blew to the west, where tongues of orange flame flickered for miles across the horizon, the seemingly omnipotent Granite Peak Fire jeering at the mere mortals attempting to tame it. Rick saw flashing lights appear out of the darkness in front of him as if spit directly from hell. Two ambulances blazed past him in succession, sirens blaring as they raced toward Riverton.

Listening to his scanner, Rick heard the familiar voice of Mike Greer, chief of the Dexter County Fire Department. Switching his radio channel to GOLD, he lifted the mic.

"Incident Command, Dexter County One," he said. "Do you copy?"

"Got you, Rick," Greer said, dispensing with radio formalities. "It's Greer."

"I'm on 89, just south of Mariah," Rick said. "Looks pretty bad from here."

"Don't worry. It's a lot worse that it looks," Greer deadpanned. His voice was coarse from smoke and threaded with exhaustion. "The wind has this thing rip-sawing all over the place. We've already had two men injured."

"Just saw them, Mike," Rick said. "I'm sure you've heard by now. We have a hunter lost—"

"Forget it," Greer answered. "You can't get a SAR team anywhere near this—at least, not now."

Rick lowered the mic onto his chest, pursing his lips as the forlorn faces of Amber and Gabe McRae flashed in his mind. "Looks like the fire is headed west?"

"For now, but that could change," Greer said. "Where was your guy last seen?"

"Campfire Lake," Rick answered. "*Maybe*."

"You're not sure?"

"Like I said—maybe. And if he was there and left, we're not sure which way he went."

"Copy that. We'll try to clear you to get a team in there as soon as possible."

"Thanks, Mike," Rick said, relaxing his grip on the mic. Smoke stung his nostrils as he entered the town of Mariah. Squinting to his left, he could barely see the Gold Bar through the haze. One hundred yards ahead, two yellow DNRC engines had arrived and blocked Highway 89, lights flashing and noses angling south to form an arrowhead. He squeezed the microphone. "Do we need to evacuate the area around Mariah?" he asked Greer. "I'm guessing the locals won't be overly amenable to that."

"Given the direction of the fire, not just yet," the chief answered. "We've had some looky-loos up this way, and that's just plain dangerous. Perhaps a little law enforcement presence in Mariah wouldn't hurt."

"Got you covered," Rick said. He flicked on his light bar and pulled his truck in front of the DNRC rigs. Two firefighters, perhaps in their early twenties, leaned against one of the vehicles, thumbs hooked beneath the belt loops of their forest-green pants. Charcoal streaks scarred their yellow Nomex shirts, their faces oily with grime. They probably signed up to fight fires for glory or maybe to impress women. Buried deep in a twenty-four-hour shift, eyes burning and bloodshot, they likely were reconsidering their decision.

Rick waved at them, but they appeared too exhausted to gesture in kind. Leaving his engine running, he exited his vehicle and began walking toward the Gold Bar.

• • •

Rick disliked barrooms, and he tended to avoid them, although his new-found occupation dictated otherwise. No one breaks up fistfights at the Riverton Public Library.

The Gold Bar mimicked some of the establishments he had frequented during the final demoralizing days of his personal Pompeii. When he opened the front door of the saloon, his senses were assaulted by an odor that resembled a saddle soaked in urine. He felt a slight tug on the soles of his feet, his boots sticking to spilled beer that had dried on the warped wooden floor. The vinyl stools lining the bar were torn, their padding held in check with slices of silver duct tape. Ceiling panels were missing, exposing electrical wires. A lonely corner jukebox was lightless, its glass face smashed, a defeated plug resting at its side.

The dolorous darkness of the place wanted to welcome him, like a murmured greeting from a long-lost friend. A fleeting feeling of warmth and comfort drifted in, the call of a seductive siren. His vigilant sober brain quickly snapped awake, filling his chest with a feeling of dense gloom as his mind was ushered through a nickel tour of his one-time life of despair.

Rick thought the place was empty, but it was not. A cracked mirror along the wall held the reflection of a man standing behind the bar, his frozen silhouette lit by the murky light allowed by the bar's only window.

"Looks like things are a little quiet this afternoon," Rick said as he approached the bar.

The man remained silent, his face devoid of expression. He was a Native American. His shoulder-length hair was as shiny and dark as the wet feathers of a raven. Black jeans were matched by a collarless black shirt buttoned to the top, his high and sculpted cheekbones appearing to be carved from wood. His skin was the color of deep caramel, smooth and hairless, marked only by the thin scars hidden beneath each of his brows. He slowly raised his eyes, which looked like dark gemstones. His glare was filled with the fire of a deep resentment for which there could be no amends. He looked at Rick as though they were mortal enemies.

Rick studied his face but paid him no mind. He looked at his watch. One thirty, roughly the same time the two hunters would have been in the bar. "Is it always this dead, or is it because of the fire?" he asked, rephrasing his earlier question.

The man looked toward the far end of the bar, where three longneck beer bottles were evenly spaced in front of empty stools as if being enjoyed by ghosts. "There were a few people in here, but a rancher hired them to wet down the roof of his house—protect it from embers," he mumbled. "I guess they needed the money."

"You're Jesse, right?" Rick asked. "Jesse …"

"Lone Wolf."

Rick nodded and took a seat at the bar. "Right," he said. "You were here yesterday when the two hunters came in."

"I already told the sheriff's office everything I know," Jesse said. "Some woman named—"

"Helen," Rick said. "Helen is my dispatcher. But I'm the sheriff. I like to hear things for myself."

Jesse ran his fingers through his hair. "Like I said, I told her what I know. So, unless you want a drink—"

"I don't drink," Rick shot back. He felt warmth flow into his face, a signal his patience was quickly beginning to wane. His head throbbed, his ribs feeling like loose daggers rattling around inside him, piercing his sides every time he moved. "Got any Advil?"

Jesse shook his head.

"Aspirin? Tylenol?"

"Nope."

"What kind of bar doesn't have aspirin?"

Jesse shrugged.

Rick drew a breath that was cut short by the pain in his rib cage. He massaged his temples. First, Randall Boone. Now this guy.

"You have some kind of problem with law enforcement, son?"

"*Son?*"

"Yeah, *son.*"

Jesse's eyes flared. Rick had pricked a nerve. "Maybe I do," he said. "My father was *murdered* by law enforcement."

"*Murdered?*" Rick asked as he cocked his head. "What was your father's name?"

"Justin Spotted Bear."

"Different than yours."

"I took my mother's name."

Rick stared at the bottles of alcohol lining the shelves behind the bar. He recognized the names, most of them rotgut. A small black-and-white photo leaned against a post next to the cash register. It showed what looked like a mixed-martial-arts contest, one man connecting with a roundhouse kick that sent a mouth guard and saliva soaring from his opponent's jaw. The man delivering the blow, his body rippling with muscle and hair pulled into a ponytail, looked like a younger version of Jesse.

"Justin Spotted Bear doesn't sound familiar," Rick said flatly. "All the same, I'm sorry for your loss."

Jesse cast a dismissive glance. "I can tell." He scanned the empty saloon. "Look, I have things to do. So, if you're not—"

Rick dipped two fingers into the top pocket of his uniform shirt and pulled out the photo given to him by Amber McRae. "I understand that this gentleman wasn't here with the other two hunters yesterday, but I was wondering whether you might have seen him before," he said, laying the picture on the bar. "Maybe he stopped in with these guys before they headed into the backcountry? Or maybe he had hunted this area before?"

Jesse stared at the photo, paused a beat, and then shook his head. "I've never seen that guy before—here or anywhere else."

Rick stared into Jesse's black-pearl eyes. "You're sure?"

"I'm sure."

The sheriff picked the photo up and returned it to his pocket, trying to gauge why the bartender was being so uncooperative. Was it only because Rick was law enforcement? Because he was white? Or was there something else?

"I understand you have a sawed-off twelve gauge you keep behind the bar."

Jesse squinted innocently. "Sawed-off?" he asked. "Those are illegal, aren't they?"

"I doubt it's behind there now, but it might be around here somewhere," Rick said. "I suppose we could get a warrant and find out. Who knows? Maybe you got rid of it?"

Jesse squared his stance and folded his arms across his chest. "What is it that you wanted to know?"

"When these hunters came in, how did they act?" Rick asked. "What was their demeanor?"

"*Demeanor* ...," Jesse repeated, mockingly rubbing his chin.

"Right," Rick said. "How were they behaving?"

"I know what demeanor means," Jesse said. His words were robotic, delivered from lips that formed a flat line across his jaw, his mouth appearing physically incapable of a smile. Drawing a breath through his nostrils, he picked up three overripe limes and began cutting the first one with a dull paring knife, the blade creating a furrow before finally breaking the skin and sending a shower of juice onto the bar. The sorrowful wedges were tossed into a filthy cocktail glass. "Basically, the bigger guy was acting like a total asshole, and the other guy pretty much seemed like a pussy."

"Did they talk about the missing hunter?" Rick asked. "A guy named Garrett McRae?"

Jesse shook his head. "They didn't mention a name," he said. "The smaller guy kept saying how they should call the missing hunter's house, see if he made it out of the Crazies okay. The asshole didn't seem all that interested."

"His name's Boone."

"Who?"

"The guy you called an asshole. His name is Boone."

"Right," Jesse said with a smirk. "Boone."

"Anything else?"

Jesse paused. "The asshole—*Boone*—had a lot of blood on him."

Rick shrugged. "That wouldn't be completely unusual if he'd field-dressed an elk."

Jesse held up his paring knife, pressing his thumb hard against the blade. "I guess it wouldn't be unusual if he used a blade like this," he said. "It was all over his T-shirt."

Rick's mind flashed back to his discussion with Boone at the sheriff's office. He recalled Boone wearing a flannel over his bare chest. "You sure it was a T-shirt?"

"Positive."

Rick lifted his eyebrows. "That it?"

"Nope," Jesse said, wiping off the knife with a dirty rag. "The smaller dude finally called the missing guy's house. The guy's wife starts screaming at him—loud enough for me to hear. Sounded like a total bitch. That's when they took off."

"After you pointed a shotgun at him," Rick said.

"Not sure what you are referring to, Sheriff."

Rick stood from his stool and patted his fingers on the bar, adjourning their meeting. "Thank you for your time, Mr. Lone Wolf," he said. "If you happen to remember anything else, I would appreciate it if you gave me a call." Straightening his hat, he began to walk toward the front door.

"Hey, Sheriff?" Jesse said. "I would *never* get rid of my shotgun. It was a gift—from my father."

The Indian's face remained as rigid as stone. Rick stared at him but didn't speak. Deep-seated anger, rooted in perceived injustice, could build its nest in any man. If anyone knew that, it was Rick.

He turned and headed out the door, his mind focused on Randall Boone.

• • •

Rick was relieved in Mariah by Clint Roswell, the gawky beanpole of a deputy who remained as green as a springtime field of alfalfa. Though Clint was gentle in heart and possessed a deep desire to advance, Rick feared the rookie's learning curve might well resemble the Milky Way.

Clint's arrival did free the sheriff to return to Riverton, where he answered a report of a truck stalled on railroad tracks on the edge of town. The truck's owner, ninety-four-year-old Winifred Haynes, had attempted to push the vehicle, but her four-foot-eleven frame would have better luck moving a tree stump. Rick arrived just in time to nudge the truck off the tracks, preventing it from being decimated by a thundering freight traveling westbound with crude from the Bakken.

Rick also mediated a border conflict between Evan Earley and Chance Ralston, Riverton's answer to the Hatfields and McCoys. The neighboring ranchers and one-time friends were engaged in a perennial dispute over whose livestock destroyed whose fence. Rick managed to intercede before a verbal altercation escalated into a shooting war.

Hank Morgan, chafed at both his wife and horse, then decided to torch a pile of dead cottonwood without a burn permit, the raging flames causing widespread panic in a burg already resting beneath a canopy of thick smoke. Two volunteer firefighters were able to douse the flames with their one remaining engine, and Hank was issued a citation and choice words from Rick, the sheriff's language sprinkled with generous splashes of color.

A yawn turned into a grimace when Rick finally exited his vehicle in front of Sage's house, his sore ribs and various other wounds stealing his breath. Intermittent raindrops pecked at the brim of his hat, more of a tease than anything that might affect the Granite Peak Fire. Moonlit clouds drifted lazily across a sky the color of graphite.

If nothing else, the hint of rain might bring an increase in relative humidity, tempering the arid winds that blew the mountains and valley floor like air from an incinerator. The gusts had ebbed slightly for the evening, putting the blaze at rest while fire crews marshalled additional resources. Without more moisture, the flames would be raging again by mid-morning, advancing through the mountain forests like an invading army. The good news was that the wind was blowing to the north, meaning the Granite Peak Trailhead and surrounding area would be in the black. It was possible that the resumption of the search for Garrett McRae was only a few days away.

As he slipped through the front door, he removed his boots and tread lightly on the aging wooden floor, hoping not to cause it to creak. The television in the living room was on, turned to the Lifetime channel, the volume reduced to a murmur.

Rick eased his way down the hall and looked into Sage's bedroom, where she and Abby appeared to be asleep. "Sage, you awake?" he said in a loud whisper. He needed to rouse her gently lest she bolt upright in bed. The reaction was a souvenir from her childhood. When her father would go off gambling, her mother would get drunk and wake her daughter by shaking her violently. No wonder Sage's first marriage commenced at age seventeen. Rick marveled that she was as level-headed as she was.

"Hi, hon," she said in a drowsy voice, extending her hand toward him. "You smell like smoke."

Rick sat on the edge of the bed. "Hard to avoid."

"Do they have the fire contained?"

"Not even close," Rick answered. "The wind is blowing pretty hard up there."

Sage propped herself on her elbows. "When do you expect to resume your search?"

"Maybe a few days—if we're lucky."

"You think you'll find him?"

"If he's even still alive, his chances are getting worse by the day."

They both were silent, the only sound coming from Abby's deep rhythmic breathing. Rick could swear his daughter was in the room, hovering above the bed. Rick caressed Sage's forearm. "You okay?" he asked. "I was trying to call you all day, but I kept getting voice mail."

"My phone went dead," Sage said, stroking Abby's hair. "I wasn't able to charge it until I got home."

Rick nodded. "How did it go at the doctor?"

"Fine. They're running some tests."

"What kind of tests?" Rick asked, his voice louder.

"Shhh …," Sage said, glancing at him before turning her eyes back toward Abby. "It's routine stuff. They check my blood … things like that." She looked into his eyes and patted his thigh. "Don't borrow problems from tomorrow, okay? I'm sure it's *nothing*."

Rick nodded. She was hiding something; he was sure of it. He'd experienced more than his share of secrets and surprises, and he was fond of neither. He preferred guarantees, of which there were few. Rick looked over at Abby, who made a gurgling sound as she burrowed her head deeper into her pillow. He leaned closer to Sage. "I brought you some brochures," he whispered.

"What kind of brochures?"

"Mexico. You said you wanted to go to Mexico."

Sage offered a half smile. "You're sweet," she said. The back of her fingers stroked his cheek, but her eyes turned away, finding a hidden place. He reached for her hand. It was warm, her palm moist. He paused a moment, preparing to speak, but he said nothing. He kissed Sage and stood up from the bed.

"You want to put Abby in the other room?" she asked.

"No, let's leave her be. I'll sleep on the couch."

"You sure?"

Rick nodded. He leaned over and kissed her again, his lips lingering on hers, the lush scent of her hair and skin filling him. He held his gaze on her as he eased toward the bedroom door.

Running tests? Why?

CHAPTER 15

Henry and Eleanor Gustafson sat in front of Spencer Bible's desk on Friday morning, squinting at the tables and pie charts he had laid out in front of them.

"What did you say all this was?" Henry asked as he looked at Spencer over the top of his oval wire-rimmed glasses. His snowy-white hair, parted just above his left ear, looked like an orderly field of corn as it climbed over the top of his head. His wrinkled skin was flecked with liver spots, the natural result of spending long hours ranching beneath a blistering sun.

"It's called diversification, Mr. Gustafson," Spencer explained. "You already have three insurance policies that are whole life. What I'm suggesting is that you diversify. If you are intent on investing more money, there are other options with a higher return."

Henry stroked his chin with long boney fingers that looked like twisted roots. "My daddy always told me there was no such thing as a quick buck."

"There are plenty of conservative mutual funds out there," Spencer said. "You don't necessarily have to do something that is high-risk. All I am saying is that you have other options besides a whole life policy."

Henry looked briefly at Eleanor. She didn't speak, freeing him to make the final decision for the both of them, just as he had done for the previous sixty years. "I wonder what your father would say."

Eleanor patted her husband's forearm. "Come now, Henry," she said. "You're not being fair." She turned toward Spencer, her hopeful eyes like tiny violets. "How is your father doing, Spencer? Is he getting better?"

"Thanks for asking, Mrs. Gustafson," Spencer answered politely, "but my father will never get better."

Awkward silence hung over the room like a harbor haze. Eleanor's finger stabbed at a print on the wall behind Spencer.

"Did you do that drawing?" she asked, mercifully changing topics. "What building is that? I don't recognize it. Is it somewhere in Great Falls?"

"It doesn't exist," Spencer said. "It's a design of a multipurpose event center that hasn't been built—and probably never will be. I drew it as a school project when I went to MSU."

"It's beautiful," Eleanor said. She tilted her head as her eyes roamed the drawing, admiring it as she would a piece of fine art. "What kind of events would be held there?"

Spencer swiveled his chair toward the drawing. "All across the board. Concerts, conventions, sports … even an indoor rodeo."

Henry let out a snort, adjusting the contents of his nasal cavity. "Something about an *indoor* rodeo doesn't ring right with me," he said as he dabbed the tip of his nose.

Eleanor pursed her lips and glared at her husband. She turned back toward Spencer. "So you were a Bobcat?"

Spencer forced a smile and exhaled a wistful sigh. "Indeed I was."

"At the School of Architecture?"

"Yes."

"That's a good program. Did you get your degree?"

"Yes it is, and no I didn't. I was a junior when my father got sick."

Awkward silence returned. "Well, you're a damn good insurance man," Henry offered.

"Thank you," Spencer answered without conviction.

Spencer's eyes drifted toward a wood-framed wedding portrait on the corner of his desk. His father, Cyrus Augustus Bible, then forty-three with streaks of silver slicked across his temples, stood stoically beside his young bride, Katherine, the mother Spencer never knew. He was two years old when Katherine died from a seizure, leaving his father to raise him alone. Cyrus stood six foot five and was a giant in the community in ways that extended far beyond physical stature. In addition to establishing the highly respected Western Montana Insurance Company, he served on an array of local corporate boards and philanthropic committees. Urged on numerous occasions to run for mayor of Great Falls and perhaps beyond, he politely declined.

Though he would have preferred that Spencer enter the insurance business, Cyrus supported his son's choice to pursue architecture at Montana State. A diagnosis of early onset Alzheimer's had already been a tightly held secret for several years. Spencer noticed subtle differences when he would return home to visit, but his father would insist that his forgetfulness and lack of concentration were simple signs of advancing age. Then the disease suddenly worsened. Spencer realized that if he didn't leave school and return to Great Falls, his father's business would surely perish. Cyrus offered gentle guidance for as long as he could. Spencer worked tirelessly, his desire to please born not from a fear of disappointing his father but simply because he worshipped him.

Once Cyrus required full-time care, Spencer was left to fend for himself. His father would eventually have difficulty remembering his son's name, let alone weigh in on the complexities of the insurance trade.

The intercom on Spencer's desk emitted a shrill tone before he heard the voice of his secretary, Rachel. "I'm sorry to interrupt, Spencer, but I'll be leaving for lunch soon. You wanted me to remind you that you wanted to go see your daddy before one o'clock." Spencer felt his face grow warm. He'd requested Rachel not refer to his father as "daddy," but it was a habit from her native Tennessee that she'd never quite shaken.

"Thank you, Rachel," Spencer said. Henry Gustafson rose stiffly from his chair, his sluggish movement clear evidence that his horses had issued the final word. He shook Spencer's hand with a grip as sturdy and firm as a pipe wrench, then gently cupped his fingers beneath his wife's elbow, tenderly raising Eleanor to her feet. "Let us think about your recommendations, Spencer," Henry said. "Like I said, you're a damn good insurance man. Your father would be proud."

Spencer smiled and nodded. The intercom crackled again. "Sorry to interrupt again, Spencer," Rachel said, "but you have a visitor."

* * *

Tamara Kelly wrapped her arms around her husband's waist and pressed her smooth, soft lips against his. Her thick golden hair was pulled tight, making her indigo eyes sparkle as she gazed at him.

"Are you going to be late again tonight?" she asked, her breath warm and pleasing. "You never know what you might be *missing*."

"Yeah?" Jack Kelly asked, the corners of his mouth curling into a smile. "What have I been missing?"

Tamara lowered her eyes playfully, her manicured finger circling a button on his uniform shirt. "I guess you need to come home and find out."

After more than two decades of marriage, Jack was more attracted to Tamara than ever. It never took much—the caress of her hand, the touch of her mouth, the smell of her skin—for him to desire more of her. His eyes roamed the cream-colored kitchen in which they were standing. In his mind, it was as good a place as any.

"Tonight," she whispered, reading his thoughts. "Don't be late."

When he signed on as Rick Morrand's undersheriff against her spirited protests, he promised Tamara that his position would not have an adverse effect on their home life. He would work normal hours and stop home often. He assured her he would only take the job for one year, and that year was just about up.

"That missing hunter has us pressed pretty thin," Jack said softly. "The fire in the Crazies hasn't helped."

Tamara brushed her tongue across her lips and drew a deep breath, her go-to expression of discontent. "I need to talk to you about something," she said as she walked toward the refrigerator.

Jack's stomach churned as though he'd swallowed a river rock. Throughout his life, whenever he'd heard a woman mouth the words, "I need to talk to you about something," the ensuing discussion never held great promise.

She's going to ask me when I plan to quit.

"Is Sage okay?" Tamara asked. She was standing in front on the refrigerator, the door ajar, her head tilted, awaiting his answer. Late-afternoon sunshine poured through the window, glistening off her tanned cheek.

"Uh, yeah, Sage is fine, as far as I know," Jack answered, relieved he'd temporarily spit the hook. "What makes you ask?"

Tamara began pulling cold cuts out of the fridge. "I saw her yesterday at Town and Country," she said. "She nearly doubled over with abdominal pain. I offered to take her to the doctor, but she said she'd already gone to one. She claimed it was some kind of food poisoning."

"Food poisoning?" Jack asked. "From what?"

"I have no idea," Tamara answered. "I told her I could drive her home, but she said she needed to pick up Abby."

Jack shook his head. "I'll ask Rick about it."

Tamara was opening packages of sandwich meats and placing the meat on slices of wheat bread. "I guess this missing hunter situation must be strange for Rick."

"How so?"

"A person missing. Kind of a déjà vu?"

"I suppose," Jack murmured. "Maybe."

Jack and Tamara had never talked much about the death of Chloe Morrand. Perhaps they realized that discussing Rick's tragedy might cause them to wander into one of their own.

Tamara sealed a sandwich in a Ziploc and placed it along with an apple in a brown paper bag. She handed it to Jack and moved closer to him, her face inches from his. "Be careful, will you?" she asked. "Especially if you happen to be around that fire."

He had arrived home two nights earlier reeking of smoke, claiming that he had viewed the Granite Peak Fire from a DNRC truck parked in the distance. Little did she know that he had nearly perished, a wall of flame half a football field away, dense smoke drawing into his lungs and invading his surgically repaired arteries.

"I'll be safe," he said, kissing her lips, some things better left unsaid.

* * *

Before good fortune had steered Spencer Bible into Starlight Coffee a day earlier, Lizzie had only seen him on a couple of occasions, and both were from a distance. Up close, he was far better looking than she'd thought, enough so that she found herself willing to cast aside his obsolete attire and puzzled demeanor.

A large fiftyish woman with the chestnut-toned nameplate "Rachel" on her gray metal desk alerted him that he had a visitor. Lizzie watched through a large pane of glass as Spencer exchanged pleasantries with an elderly couple in his office. When he glanced toward Lizzie, he appeared momentarily stunned, his eyes as frozen as a deer facing high beams on a pitch-dark country road. The couple left his office, nodding briefly at Lizzie as they passed. Spencer then emerged, his hands nervously brushing the length of his paisley tie before he buried them deep in the pockets of his double-knit slacks.

"Hi, M-Miss ..." he stuttered.

"Lizzie."

"Yes, right. Lizzie. I'm sorry, I—"

Lizzie stepped closer, seeming to startle him. His nose twitched, perhaps reacting to the Chanel she'd applied during the walk to his office. Color flowed into his cheeks, his face contorted as though he was underwater, far out of his depth.

The woman named Rachel clutched a small purse as she abruptly rose from her desk. "I'm going to lunch," she announced. "If I don't get to Lorraine's at noon, they run out of the Friday Special."

Spencer didn't answer, his eyes pleading toward Rachel as if witnessing a final lifeboat leave the *Titanic*. The secretary brushed past Lizzie and waddled briskly toward the door. Lizzie smirked to herself, judging Rachel was fond of Friday Specials.

"You left so quickly yesterday, I didn't get a chance to give you one of these," Lizzie said, handing Spencer a small laminated card. "It's our rewards program. Every fifth coffee drink you buy is free."

Spencer studied the card. It had five circles along the bottom, two of which had already been punched. He looked at her and nodded rapidly. "Thank you," he managed.

Lizzie tilted her head and smiled. "You do plan to come again, don't you?" she asked. "I mean, we'd *love* to see you again."

The word *love* seemed to momentarily buckle his knees. "Sure," he said. "I'm sure I'll—"

"Great!" she said as she turned toward the door.

"Wait!" Spencer said. His fingers fumbled over one of two business card holders on Rachel's desk. "Here's my card," he said, his hand shaking. "You know … in case you need insurance? We handle auto, health—"

Lizzie smiled brightly. "Thank you. So, we'll see you soon?"

"Yes," he said with an innocent shrug. "Sure."

Lizzie nodded and went out the door, her lips curling into a broad smile.

CHAPTER 16

Rick awoke with his teeth clamped in pain, the forest-green velour couch in Sage's living room having done no favors for his ailing back and tender ribs. It had taken him nearly three hours to fall asleep, his mind sampling a wide array of explanations for Sage's peculiar behavior.

Was it something he said? Something he did or *didn't* do? If that was the case, Sage surely would have told him about it. When she had something on her mind, she wouldn't hesitate to tell you how the cow ate the cabbage. He often thought of her as a shotgun with a hair trigger and no safety, always more than willing to send the contents of her brain spilling from her lips like buckshot, come what may. In an odd sense, it was a quality of hers that Rick deeply admired.

No, it wasn't anything Rick had said or done. His instincts told him that something serious had occurred during her Thursday visit to the doctor. They would need to have a talk. The sooner, the better.

He exhaled and stared at the pine-covered ceiling, the back of his hand resting on his forehead. He would have much preferred to have slept with Sage. Whenever they'd been alone, they would lie next to each other with bodies intertwined, their chests heaving from the exhilaration of their lovemaking. On some occasions they would drift off to sleep, foreheads touching, their lungs filling with each other's breath, eyes pressed closed like dozing lion cubs. Sage would rise from the bed with no intention of donning a robe, prancing around in the nude, treating the invention of clothing as an unnecessary nuisance. His eyes would follow her movements, soaking in the perfect features of her ageless body. Before long, he would urge her back to the bed, craving her once again with the virility of a man half his age.

The house was quiet. He reached for his phone on the coffee table, checking the time. Nine forty. He sat up quickly, his ribs paying a price.

Sage was already gone, having taken Abby to school. He found her number but hesitated, his thumb hovering above the screen. Setting the phone back on the table, he ran his fingers through his hair. He needed coffee, then a shower.

The cell phone rang. Rick snared it, hoping it was Sage. No such luck.

"You coming in today, Boss?" Helen asked. "We're kind of busy—at least, for us."

Rick rubbed his temples. "What's going on, Helen?"

"We had a rollover on Highway 89 this morning just before daylight. The hospital says he blew three times the legal limit. He has some significant injuries, but I guess he's trying to leave."

"Where's Jack?"

"He's standing in front of me. He was saying that you might want him to pay a visit to that hunter with the attitude." She paused. "Let's see. What was his name—"

"Boone," Rick said. "Randall Boone."

"Right. Boone. You want to discuss it with Jack?"

"No," Rick answered. "I want to talk to Boone myself. Have Jack go out to the hospital and cuff the drunk driver to his bed. I'll call him from the road." Rick stood up from the couch, cradling his phone beneath his chin as he gently massaged his rib cage. "What's going on with the fire?"

"Mike Greer called, looking for you. The fire is still going strong, but he seemed to think they were getting a handle on it."

"When can we resume the search?"

"He said Monday—possibly. The wind is blowing northwest right now. If that holds, SAR teams can get in there early next week."

"It has to be Monday at the latest."

"Just relaying what he said, Sheriff. He has guys mopping on the east side of the Crazies, but it's a pretty small crew. Mike sounded like he hasn't slept in days."

"Text me the address of Eagle Ridge Construction," Rick said. "It's my understanding that's the place Boone worked with Garrett McRae. I plan to go straight there."

"Copy that, Sheriff," Helen said. "You'll have it shortly."

Rick laid his phone on the kitchen counter and took a black ceramic mug from the cupboard. The scent of burnt coffee filled his nostrils. He poured the half-full pot into the sink, lifted the lid of the coffee maker, and reached through the hot stream to tug out the paper filter filled with spent grounds. Pressing his foot on the plastic pedal on the bottom of the stainless steel garbage pail, he tossed the filter and pulled a coffee can toward him.

Suddenly, he froze. He tilted his head in curiosity, as though his brain had photographed a Polaroid image but hesitated delivering the print. Removing his hands from the coffee can, he stepped closer to the garbage pail and lifted the lid with his fingers. A stack of glossy brochures were partially buried beneath the coffee grounds. The skin on his head tensed as he stared at the photo of a tranquil beach in Cancun, its coconut trees tarnished by deep-brown stains. The garbage lid fell from his grasp. Swallowing hard, he picked up his phone and called Sage's number.

It went to voice mail.

CHAPTER 17

The understanding of the Crow word *Awaxaawapìa* to mean "Crazy Mountains" was a loose interpretation at best. A slightly more accurate translation was "Ominous Mountains." The latter certainly would be far more appropriate for the circumstances that had befallen Garrett McRae.

Provided Randall Boone and Kyle Ricketts were being truthful—which remained open to serious debate—it had been nearly a week since Garrett was last seen. Assuming he wasn't seriously injured, it was doubtful he had enough food to last more than twenty-four hours. The Crazies were legendary for their rugged terrain, unpredictable weather, and wildlife that ranged from bears to wolverines. Then there was the small matter of the ruthless fast-moving Granite Peak Fire. By the time SAR teams would be able to reenter the mountains, Garrett would be missing for nine days. It wouldn't be long before the mission would transition from a search to a recovery.

The Hemi engine of Rick's truck engine purred as he climbed Bozeman Pass. Resting his elbow on the console, he propped his chin between his thumb and forefinger, studying the surrounding foothills draped in a gunmetal haze. Rick had numerous questions about the two hunters who had left Garrett behind. First, there was the casual manner in which they delayed notifying authorities that their companion was missing. Second, they were in possession of Garrett's horse, as well as a cow elk bearing his tag, but Garrett was nowhere to be found. Finally, and perhaps most significant, Randall Boone was wearing a bloody shirt that had vanished somewhere between the Gold Bar and the Dexter County Sheriff's Office. With wildland firefighters still a few days away from harnessing the Granite Peak blaze, it was worth paying Boone a visit.

Rick's phone rang. It was Janice Tillotson, Sage's physician and dear friend. Rick and Janice had experienced some small run-ins—the doctor sometimes tilting toward the bossy side—but they generally got along. Or so he hoped.

"Janice, how are you?" Rick said in a gentle tone. "Thank you for calling me back."

"Sure," Dr. Tillotson said abruptly. "What's up?"

"I was wondering if you could help me with something. Ever since Sage went to see you yesterday, she's been acting a little odd. She's—"

"You mean physically?"

"Uh, no, not really," Rick said. "Something seems to be going on that she doesn't seem to want to talk about. She said that you were running some tests. I'm wondering whether—"

"You need to discuss it with Sage, Rick."

"I understand," he said. "I was just wondering—"

"Ever hear of the Health Insurance Portability and Accountability Act?"

"Of course. But—"

"HIPAA has a lot to do with patient privacy. You should check it out."

Rick's temples began to throb. "Janice," he said, trying to remain calm. "She's my fiancée."

"I'm well aware of that."

"Well, then?"

"You need to talk to her, Rick. I'm sorry I can't help you."

Rick drew a breath as he lowered his phone and rested it on his thigh, his head feeling like a boiling thermal pot. His brain offered a flash flood of sentiments, most of them unproductive, some of them plain childish. He lifted his phone to his cheek.

"Thank you for your help, Janice," he managed to utter through gritted teeth. "I'll speak with Sage."

CHAPTER 18

Randall Boone took a deep drag of his cigarette as he stood on the second floor of a half-framed townhouse, staring at the smooth, rounded peaks of the distant Bridger Mountains. He pulled out his phone, glanced at the screen a moment, then returned it to his pocket, a ritual he had repeated with nervous obsession at least a half-dozen times.

"You okay, man?" Boone heard a voice say. It was Jackie Wyatt, a journeyman carpenter who was working with him at the site on Bozeman's west side. "You seem kind of out of it. We need to get this floor done before the weekend, or the boss will be all over our asses."

"I'm good," Boone said without looking at Jackie, drawing again on his cigarette. "I'm gonna take a break."

Jackie stood five foot eight, a human tree stump whose rust-colored Carhartt overalls barely snapped over his bulging barrel chest. He had a round mouth surrounded by a scraggly goatee, his ungroomed mustache often capturing unpleasant remnants of his lunch. His pinpoint pupils, which appeared to dance around aimlessly, looked like a pair of black-eyed peas. "You're shittin' me, right?" he asked.

Boone's head swiveled sharply. He glared at Jackie, who swallowed hard as he retreated a few steps and returned to work. Boone hustled down a flight of bare wooden steps and went out back, flicking sawdust off the screen of his phone. He called Amber McRae's number and put the phone to his ear.

Voice mail.

"It's me," he said. "Not sure what's going on. We need to talk."

He slid the phone into his pocket and flicked his cigarette, feeling weak and exposed. He knew that his triumph in bedding Amber was tainted by her vulnerability, her marriage to Garrett severely fractured by the tragic injury to their innocent son. Still, Boone believed that his affair with her had been genuine, or at least as authentic as things in his world could be. His upbringing by a mother who was either reluctant—or perhaps incapable—of requiting his love surely justified his view that women were chattel meant strictly for utility. This was how he had kept himself safe and protected. In the case of Amber McRae, he had made a solitary and dangerous exception. He would do just about anything in the world for her.

In his estimation, he believed he had.

"Hey, Boone!" he heard Jackie say. He looked toward the second floor, his eyes fighting the sun as he saw Jackie's silhouette protruding from a framed window.

"I thought I told you I was taking a break," Boone scowled.

"Just wanted to give you a heads up," Jackie said. "A sheriff's rig just pulled up, and I'm pretty sure he ain't here for me."

* * *

After dry-mouthing a couple of Advil, Rick stepped gingerly out of his vehicle. He stood with hands on hips as he was approached by a burly foreman wearing a weathered yellow hard hat and holding a scroll of engineering drawings in his gloved left hand. The man's face was as red as a baboon's rump, a river delta of blue blood vessels flowing beneath his cheeks. Air puffed forcefully from his nostrils, suggesting his next breath might well be his last.

"Can I help you, Deputy?" the man said. His voice reminded Rick of broken glass crushed beneath a boot heel.

"It's *Sheriff*," Rick answered. "I'm looking for Randall Boone."

"Yeah, well, he's pretty tied up at the moment," the man said, throwing a glance over the collar of an open coat that exposed his expansive girth. "Can you tell me what it concerns?"

"No."

"Excuse me?"

"What it concerns is none of your concern," Rick said, his head suddenly throbbing again. "Tell me where I can find Randall Boone."

The man pointed Rick toward a two-story skeleton of two-by-fours. "He's over there." The foreman shook his head as trudged back toward the metal steps of a white trailer, a placard with "Eagle Ridge Construction" attached to its side.

Rick walked toward the structure, gravel crunching beneath the soles of his boots. He passed a pair of pickups, one of which he recognized as belonging to Randall Boone. Shielding his eyes from the sun, he peered into the backseat of the crew cab. A backpack and compound bow were lying among a pile of scattered clothes.

""I could get fired for this," a voice said. Rick turned to see Boone standing in a framed doorway, his work boot squashing his cigarette on the plywood floor of the townhome. A steel-claw hammer dangled from his left hand.

"Let's not be dramatic, Mr. Boone," Rick said. "They're not going to fire you when there's not enough help around here to replace you."

"I already told you everything I know. I need to get back to work."

Rick adjusted his hat, careful not to disturb the rows of stitches on the back of his head. Boone's right hand was taped across the knuckles. It was the same hand that was cut and bruised at the sheriff's office. "You break your hand?" Rick asked.

Boone glanced at the hand, flexing it in and out of a fist. "Hairline fracture," he said, sounding rehearsed. "I must have whacked it on a rock or something. I taped it so I wouldn't miss work."

Rick looked at his own hand, flexing it in and out of a fist. "I had a hairline fracture once," he said. "Happened in a bar fight just after I left college." He traced his forefinger across the metacarpal bone above his right pinky. "Doctor said I broke it 'cause I was punching incorrectly. Imagine that."

Boone's expression remained unchanged. "Like I said, I had a dull knife. I must have hit it on a rock."

Rick nodded. "The guy at the bar in Mariah said you were wearing a bloody T-shirt when you were there. I didn't notice you wearing a T-shirt at the sheriff's office."

"I took it off. I was hot."

"Where is the shirt now?"

Boone stared at his steel-toed boots, flecked with loose sawdust over speckles of paint. "Can't be sure," he mumbled. "Might have thrown it away."

"It wouldn't be in the back of your truck, would it?"

"Nope," Boone said. "But you're more than welcome to look." Boone raised his eyes and cocked his head. "What's this all about, anyway?"

Rick glanced at the truck, which Boone seemed all too willing to have him examine. "How long have you been hunting?"

Boone shifted his weight and stuffed his hands in his back pockets. "I really need to get back to work," he said, throwing a glance at the foreman's trailer.

"How long?"

"I shot my first deer when I was nine, using a Marlin thirty-five. Got into bow hunting later on."

"You've been hunting a long time, then?"

Boone nodded.

"Field-dressed a lot of deer and elk?"

He nodded again.

"A skilled hunter might get some blood on his wrists, maybe the forearms," Rick said. "But according to the bartender, you looked like you crawled inside that animal's belly. Now, how could that be, considering you've been hunting your whole life and all?"

Boone shrugged. "Like I said—"

"Right," Rick interrupted. "You had a dull knife."

Boone leaned against the side of the doorway, stroking his thumb along the top of the hammer. "Am I being accused of something here?"

"Not just yet," Rick answered. "As soon as they get that fire under control, we'll be looking for your friend." He paused a beat. "Garrett is your friend, is he not?"

"I'm not big on friends," Boone said, "but I suppose."

Rick studied Boone. The man's defiance suggested he didn't care much about Garrett McRae or anyone else. "I can't figure why you and Kyle Ricketts would come out of the backcountry without even looking for a guy who'd been missing three days."

"Garrett was a search-and-rescue guy and a trained EMT," Boone said.

"*Was?*"

Boone huffed a breath. "Manner of speaking," he said. "Point is, he knew the Crazies better than anybody. We figured he could fend for himself."

"I guess we'll find out soon enough," Rick said.

● ● ●

Sage's stomach churned as she sat in the waiting room of Janice Tillotson's office, her brain painting a collage of grim scenarios. Janice had called an hour earlier, saying that she needed to see Sage in person to discuss her test results. Sage told her friend that if she had something to say, she should spit it out, but Janice demurred.

A young mother was seated near her, quietly reading a story to her young child. Sage watched them with remorse, lamenting that a hysterectomy as a young woman had robbed her of the opportunity to ever have children. She wondered whether life was about to issue her another unfortunate tiding.

The door across the room opened, revealing a young medical assistant in green scrubs. "Miss Fontenot?" the girl said, eyes rising from the chart she held in her hand. "Dr. Tillotson is ready to see you."

Sage pointed toward the mother and child. "I believe these people were here first," she said, hoping to somehow delay her date with destiny.

The medical assistant offered a tight smile. "Dr. Tillotson is expecting you, and she's ready for you now."

Sage slowly rose from her chair, trudging forward at the pace of a pupil bound for the principal's office. The nurse led her halfway down a hallway, where she stopped next to a scale. "Let's go ahead and get your weight," she said.

"Nope," Sage snapped. "You weighed me yesterday. I'm losing weight. I get it. Where's Janice?"

The assistant drew air into her nose and rolled her eyes. Without speaking, she led Sage into a room at the end of the hall. Sage stepped past the examination table and plopped into a chair, suddenly feeling exhausted. Her illness, whatever it was, had been like that. At one moment, she was awake and alert. Seconds later, she was Dorothy overcome by poppies en route to the Emerald City.

The medical assistant gingerly approached her with a temporal thermometer, her other hand clutching a blood-pressure cuff. Sage glared at her, causing the assistant to recoil. The young woman set the items on a speckled white counter and backed out of the door as though retreating from a poisonous snake. "Dr. Tillotson will be with you shortly," she murmured.

The door clicked shut, leaving Sage shipwrecked on the island of her mind. The temperature in the room seemed to plummet, the antiseptic scent in the air making it a sterile tomb. She folded her arms across her breasts, her hands rubbing her shoulders to ward off the sudden chill. She wished Rick was there, his tender embrace wrapped around her. She cursed herself for pushing away the person she needed most, something she had done since she was a young child. She had been dishonest with Rick, just as she had been with so many men before him, the natural impulse of someone dreadfully unacquainted with the concept of trust.

Three minutes' worth of forever passed. Janice Tillotson finally walked through the door, her eyes glued to a chart in front of her as if she had never seen it before. Sage figured that staring at a chart was a technique all doctors were trained to use, allowing them to avoid eye contact when delivering grim news to Dead Patient Walking.

"How are you doing?" Janice asked gently.

"How am I *doing*? Uh, not good," Sage huffed. "We could have done this over the phone. You're supposed to be my friend."

Janice plopped onto a wheeled stool, the instep of her left foot tucked behind her opposite calf. Resting Sage's chart on top of her thigh, she released a lengthy sigh. "The fact that you are my friend is the reason you are here. Results for these tests normally take up to a week. I didn't want you to have to wait."

Sage rolled her eyes and tightened her jaw. "So let's have it," she said with an edge. She was acting tough, which meant she was scared to death.

"You have Non-Hodgkin's lymphoma," Dr. Tillotson said, her dark eyes unflinching. "It's a form of cancer."

"A *form* of cancer?" Sage asked, voice rising. "What the hell is that supposed to mean? It's either cancer or it isn't."

Janice crossed her arms, one hand still clinging to Sage's chart. She frowned at her patient with an expression a parent might deliver to a rebellious child. "Okay, it's cancer, period—and you're not the first person to have it," she said. "It's treatable."

Sage's shoulders slumped, head tilting forward as her hands clutched her knees. Her eyelids clamped shut to dam the tide of warm tears that had begun to fall onto the thighs of her jeans. Janice reached for a yellow-flowered box of Kleenex on the counter. Sage tugged out two tissues and clenched them in her fist. "How did this happen?" she asked, her voice quivering. "I mean ... How is it *caused*?"

Janice shrugged. "There's a big class-action suit that claims it's caused by weed killer. So, if you've been exposed—"

"In rural Montana?" Sage huffed. "Yeah, I'd say I've been *exposed*."

Janice offered a half smile and nodded. "Or, it could be stress over an extended period of time." She paused a beat. "You know, you've been through a lot in the last year or so. When you lose someone close to you, there's a grieving period that needs to take place."

Sage's eyes roamed the doctor's face. The death of Chloe Morrand had created a bond between Rick and Sage that felt coiled in steel wire, perhaps one that was wound too tight. In their efforts to support each other, presenting an impenetrable front against the outside world, perhaps they had not allowed each other to properly mourn the loss. The immediate obligation to care for Abby offered no pause, no opportunity to experience—or even acknowledge—the crippling devastation that had crashed through their lives. They buried their emotions, perhaps fearful that any vulnerability might be seen as an act of betrayal to each other. Somewhere along the line they may have lost the simple ability to cry.

Sage forced an uneasy laugh. "I was under stress from the day I exited the womb," she said dismissively. "I'm not sure if you recall, but I wasn't exactly raised by June and Ward Cleaver."

Janice didn't answer, curling her lips inward in thought. She leaned closer to Sage. "I wouldn't say we caught this early, but we caught it early enough," Her voice settled into a tender whisper. "We just need to develop the right plan."

Sage's brain flashed with images of Rick, Abby ... even Chloe. She extended the fingers of her left hand, staring at the diamond Rick had placed on her finger. She had accepted his proposal instantly, no previous decision in her life having arrived with such certainty. Now, she wondered.

"Why?" she muttered aloud as she tried to compose herself. "I mean ... Why now?"

"There's never a good time for this kind of diagnosis—trust me," Janice said. She sat upright, pushing a gray-streaked strand of hair from her forehead. "You know, I talked to Rick briefly this morning. He was trying to find out what was going on."

Sage looked up, eyes opened wide. "You didn't tell him anything, did you?"

"No, I didn't," Janice answered, shaking her head. "My question is, why haven't you?"

Sage stared at the tissues in her hand, using her fingers to straighten the wrinkles. "There wasn't anything to tell," she said. "At least, not until now."

"You need to tell him. He needs to know."

Sage shook her head slowly. "He doesn't need this—not after all he's been through."

"He might not need it, but here it is," Janice said. "You'll need his support."

Sage reached for the side of her head, burying her fingers in her thick cascading hair. "What is the treatment? Chemotherapy?"

Janice nodded.

"Will I lose my hair?" she asked, clutching a fistful of curls.

"Probably. The good news is it's temporary."

"Great," Sage said, flicking her hair behind her shoulder. "Guess I won't need it anymore after I'm dead."

Janice rose from her chair. "You're not going to die—at least, not if I can help it. Go home, take a hot bath, have a glass of wine. Enjoy your weekend. First thing Monday morning, we start kicking cancer's ass."

CHAPTER 19

Rick picked up his phone to follow up with Jack Kelly, but he was interrupted by an incoming call. "We found a backpack," Mike Greer's hoarse voice said.

He paused, allowing Mike's words to sink in. "A backpack? Where?"

"Eastern slope of the Crazies, quite a ways into the trees," the Dexter County fire chief answered. "It could belong to a bow hunter, but it's hard to tell. It got burned in the fire."

"Well, don't touch it," Rick said. "Close off as wide an area you can with tape."

"Too late for that—it's already been moved," Mike said. "The girl who found it. She didn't know—"

"What girl? A firefighter?"

"Negative," Mike answered. "She's a member of Big Sky Search Dogs."

"I thought you said it wasn't safe to search until Monday."

"It isn't," Mike said. "She just showed up, and she wouldn't take no for an answer. I sent one of my guys with her, but he couldn't keep up." He paused, releasing a long sigh. "To be honest with you, Rick, a dog might be the best chance we got at this point."

"So, she ditches your guy and shows up with a backpack?"

"Pretty much."

"Do we at least know *where* she found it?"

"She can probably give us a good indication of where she picked it up," Mike said. "For what it's worth, she feels pretty bad. She says she knows Garrett and recognized the backpack as his. Got excited, I guess."

Rick saw himself wag his head in his rearview, eyebrows furrowed. "You say you found it on the eastern side? How far out are you guys from the Granite Peak Trailhead?"

"Twelve miles, maybe more. We came in from Lupine County, up from Big Timber. I wanted to get a read on how this fire started."

Rick paused. Campfire Lake was several miles north of the hunters' base camp, which would have meant Garrett McRae had traveled nearly fifteen miles to reach Greer's location.

"Rick, are you there?" the fire chief said.

"Just a backpack, huh?" Rick muttered.

"Just a backpack."

"Color?"

"Looks like camo—blue camo."

Rick's mind flashed to a photo he saw at the home of Amber McRae. "I'm thinking it belongs to Garrett."

"Do you want me to look for ID?"

"No," Rick said quickly. "Hang tight. I'll be there as soon as I can." He paused a beat. "What is this woman's name? You know, the one with the dog?"

"Meredith," Mike answered. "Meredith Hart."

• • •

Sage went directly from Janice Tillotson's office to Abby's school, where she asked Mildred Wentworth to pull Abby out of the final class period of the day. Millie's eyes squinted curiously from behind her horn-rimmed glasses, making her look like a gopher rising on its hind legs to pick up a scent. In addition to her duties at the school, Millie played the organ at the Sunday services Rick and Sage attended.

"There's only about fifteen minutes left before the students all get out," Millie said. "You sure you just don't want to wait? I have some coffee—"

"I don't want to wait," Sage snapped. "And I don't want coffee."

"Everything okay?"

Sage blew out a breath and shifted her weight from one boot heel to the other, hand jammed into the right rear pocket of her Wranglers. *Would people please stop asking whether everything is okay?*

"Dammit, Millie!" she shouted. "Will you just go *get* her?"

Millie's jaw fell, reminding Sage they shared the same church. She glared coldly while rising from her desk, her frown suggesting Sage's use of a profanity had single-handedly severed the tabernacle. Sage didn't really care what Millie thought. "*Please*," she managed to mutter.

Moments later, Millie reappeared. Abby stood at her side, arms outstretched, palms facing upward, head wagging back and forth in a tremor. "What are you doing here?" Abby said. "I have basketball practice."

"Get in the truck, Abby. I'm not in the mood."

"What did I do?" Abby huffed.

"Get. In. The. Truck."

Abby stormed toward the exit doors of the school, Sage stalking behind her. They jumped into the truck without saying a word. The engine hesitated a beat before coughing to life, the ignition making a grinding sound when Sage held the key in place too long.

"Are we going to your house or the ranch?" Abby asked, her voice as delicate as someone stepping past a coiled rattler.

"The ranch," Sage said as she sped down the street. "Just like every Friday."

Sage pulled onto Highway 89 and headed south. Abby glared out front windshield of the truck. After a moment, her eyes trailed to the speedometer, causing Sage to slow from eighty to seventy. Sage blinked, trying to hide the wetness welling in her eyes.

They traveled through miles of silence. Sage glanced toward Abby, who had her chin resting on her cupped hand. Their trips home from school, usually following basketball practice, were often filled with joy and laughter. Girl time, they called it. Not today.

The tires of Sage's truck slid on the gravel on the road leading to the ranch, her front bumper narrowly missing one of the foot-thick timbers that framed the entrance.

"You have homework?"

"Not really," Abby answered.

"What does that mean?"

Abby shrugged. "I mean, no, I don't."

"Then maybe you can read a book."

Abby thought a moment, then brightened. "Can I ride Big Sky?"

Sage wagged her head. "No. I need some rest."

Abby sighed and rolled her eyes. "What's the use of having a horse if I can't ride it?"

"Good question," Sage shot back. "It was your grandfather's idea to get that horse—not mine."

"But—"

"Stop it!" Sage shouted. "I said no!"

"Auntie Sage, what's wrong?"

"Nothing," Sage grumbled as she slammed on the brakes next to the ranch house. "I'm *fine*." She turned off the engine, slammed the door, and headed up onto the wooden front porch, leaving Abby sitting in the truck.

• • •

Rick trotted down the three steps leading into the basement of Memorial Hospital, heading for Charlie Duchesne's office. The coroner was seated at his desk, his hand reaching for a Styrofoam cup of coffee as he perused the *Riverton Herald*. He raised his overgrown brow as his eyes peered at Rick over the rims of his silver reading glasses.

"You busy?" Rick blurted out. He stared at the newspaper and Charlie's coffee. "Guess not."

Charlie offered a glare, apparently not amused. "I was taking a late lunch. What's up?"

"Are you in the loop on that missing bow hunter?"

"Is he dead?"

"No," Rick said. "I mean, I don't know if he is or not. But I need your help."

Charlie took a last sip of his coffee and tossed the cup in a wastebasket beneath his gray metal desk. "I usually deal with the dead," he grumbled. "But please … proceed."

It was a numb response, even from a crusty old coot like Charlie. Rick ignored the remark, aware that Charlie's crankiness appeared to be growing exponentially with age. "They found a backpack on the eastern slope of the Crazies," he said. "No positive ID yet, but I believe it belongs to the missing hunter, Garrett McRae. I'd like you to head up there with me, secure the scene, see what forensics we might find."

Charlie looked at his watch. "That's quite a ride," he said. "By the time we get there, we'll be losing daylight."

Rick nodded, stone-faced. "That means we'd better get going."

The coroner stared at his watch again as though the time may have changed drastically in the previous ten seconds. He picked up the moldy bread off his desk, looked at it with disdain, then returned it to a troubled wrinkle of cellophane. The sandwich wasn't made by Charlie's wife, Dora, who would always wrap his meals in wax paper, as he preferred. This one looked like it came from the filling station. Charlie crumbled the plastic wrapper in his fist and threw the remains in his wastebasket.

"Dora is expecting me," he said. "I might have to sit this one out."

Rick cocked his head. "Sit this one out? We don't have enough people around here for you to sit one out." He paused a beat to gather himself. "What's going on?"

Charlie rolled his tongue around the inside of his mouth. His sad eyes slowly rose toward Rick. "Dora thinks I'm gambling again."

"Are you?"

"Hell no, I'm not gambling," he croaked. "They were repairing the sidewalk outside the front door of the Town Pump, so I left the store through the Indian casino. Apparently, someone told someone to tell someone to tell Dora."

Rick suppressed a chuckle. "Did you explain to Dora what happened?"

"I tried, but she didn't seem interested. Even after all these years she still has some scar tissue, I guess."

Charlie shook his head, lips downturned. Rick removed his hat, studying it as his fingers gently stroked the crown. The men were silent for a moment, mourning Charlie's circumstance. The coroner folded the newspaper that was on his desk and placed it on top of a file cabinet.

"I would guess a missing person case might hold special significance for you," he said softly. "Am I right on that?"

Charlie couldn't have been more accurate. Rick's visit to Amber McRae had him reliving the excruciating torment he felt when Chloe went missing only a year earlier. If there was a God—and, as of late, Rick believed there was—why would this Supreme Being put people through the anguish of a missing loved one? The pain was like stage-four bone cancer without morphine, relentless and throbbing. It was cruel sport—scores of innocent, powerless humans needlessly tortured before receiving the inevitable crushing blow that came in the form of news that a deceased body had been found.

That's when they say you have closure. *Closure?* Of what? Your windpipe maybe, as you feel an iron grip wrap around your throat, robbing you of oxygen and emptying the contents of your soul, a tidal wave of hopelessness and doom washing over you. Your next breath becomes impossible to draw, every step like walking through dense sludge, the mere act of putting together cogent thoughts an impossible task.

"I'm not sure if the guy is even alive," Rick said. "Chances aren't good, I would think. Thing is, he has a wife and a young son. I'm just—"

"Say no more—I get it," Charlie said, raising an open palm. He rose from his chair and reached for his ancient Carhartt jacket. "I'll be out in a moment. Let me call Dora and tell her I'll be late. If I tell her I'm with you, maybe she'll believe me."

Rick turned and walked outside to his truck. The Indian summer afternoon had grown warm, the temperature rising near eighty as the Granite Peak Fire to the north served as a furnace. The air tasted like smoke, making Rick's mouth bone dry. He started his ignition, the fan of his air conditioner roaring to life. He fumbled for a Thermos he kept behind his seat and unscrewed the cap. Taking a long draw of water, he glanced at his watch, figuring Abby would be in the middle of basketball practice. He smiled as he imagined her out on the wooden floor, arms flailing above her head as she waited for someone to pass her the ball. If she scored a basket, she would look up into the stands, where Rick or Sage would be sitting. Rick would smile broadly and sneak a wave at her. Then his heart would sink as Abby's eyes traveled to the opposite end of the stands, to an empty area where her mother used to sit. Rick and Sage couldn't bear to sit in that spot anymore. It only gouged the wound. In his mind, he could still see Chloe there. They all could see her there.

He stared at the door opening carved out of the faded red bricks of Memorial Hospital, the rusted brown-and-white awning above the entrance ready to blow away with the next powerful wind. He felt sympathy for Charlie consigned to a windowless office in a subterranean workplace that sometimes resembled the catacombs.

Rick wondered whether Charlie was lying about his gambling. As he knew all too well from his own experience, honesty was not a strong suit for those who wandered through the gates of addiction. Whether it was done out of fear or for mere convenience, an aptitude for elaborate insincerity and deceit was a routine, essential element of the overall package.

Rick prayed Charlie was telling the truth. Being fond of Dora, he mourned the thought of anything ever coming between them and the life they had built in Riverton. He took another sip from his Thermos, wiping his mouth with the back of his hand. Drawing a deep breath, he shook his head. To him, gambling simply made no sense. Rick wasn't a gambler, nor did he have any desire to be. It was a tedious waste of time and treasure. Of course, that was the same way Charlie likely viewed alcohol or cocaine. Rick chuckled at the thought. As they had become friends, Rick had resigned himself to the fact that Charlie experienced the same exhilaration in rolling a pair of dice onto a green felt table that Rick had encountered when using his AMEX card to carve out a fresh line of blow. Addiction was addiction, and united they could beat it.

He placed the Thermos behind his seat. His vehicle had cooled some-what, so he lowered the fan and turned on the mobile radio inside his rig. Within moments, he heard Helen's voice crackle on the dispatch channel.

"Riverton Ambulance, please respond to 714 Cottonwood Road. We have a report of a school-age female who has fallen from a horse. Unknown injuries at this time."

Rick sat stunned as he listened to the response. "Riverton Medic One en route with two on board," a male voice said. "Confirming address as 714 Cottonwood Road."

"Affirmative," Helen said.

Rick blinked in disbelief as he heard Helen confirm the address of his ranch over the radio. *School-age girl.* His heart pounded, his pulse rising through his jaw and into his temples, his face feeling on fire. *Unknown injuries at this time.* He snared the mic from its cradle.

"Dispatch, Dexter One," he shouted. "I'm en route."

"Copy, Dexter One," Helen said.

Rick's tires burned as his foot slammed on the accelerator. Flipping on the light bar above his cab, he barely glanced at Charlie, who had exited the hospital. The coroner backpedaled out of Rick's path, his head doing a quick swivel as the truck roared past him. Rick returned his mic to the cradle and grabbed his cell phone. He speed-dialed the sheriff's office, eager for Helen to supply more details, ones he didn't wish to share with locals tuned in on police scanners.

"Dexter County Sheriff," Helen said.

"Helen, it's Abby, isn't it?" Rick blurted into the phone. "Do you have more details?"

Helen paused, seemingly uncertain which question she should answer first. "We don't know for a *fact* that it's Abby," she said. "We don't have anyone on scene just yet."

"Where's Sage?" Rick repeated.

"I'm not sure," she said. "It was your propane guy who called it in. He had dropped by to top off the tank and saw … *a girl* … lying in the corral. He said it looked like she was unconscious. We told him not to move her. We have—"

A voice came over the radio in Rick's truck. "Dispatch, this is Medic One. Please contact Life Flight to check on the availability of a bird. We may need to transport to Bozeman or Billings."

"Copy, Medic One," Helen said. "Contacting Life Flight."

"Life Flight? What the hell for?" Rick shouted into his phone. "They haven't even seen her yet. Shouldn't—"

"It's just a precaution, Sheriff," Helen said in a soft tone. "Riverton Ambulance asked us to put Life Flight on alert when we have a horse accident. A lot of things can happen."

Rick bristled, jaw clenched shut. He tossed his cell phone on the console. He knew damn well what could happen when someone—*anyone*—fell off a horse. *Broken ankle. Cracked ribs. Punctured lung. Dislocated shoulder. Brain bleed. Shattered vertebrae.* The list went far and wide. Rick had been thrown plenty of times himself. In most cases, you pick up your hat, dust off your jeans, and make sure you have Advil in the medicine cabinet. Other times, you break a bone. Conk your noggin. Get *stomped.* When something sends a horse into deep fear, the safety of its rider is of peripheral consequence to it.

Rick's truck roared south on Highway 89, pushing ninety miles per hour as he swerved past vehicles scurrying to the side of the road. Two whitetail deer, barely visible in the late-afternoon light, rose gingerly from a gully and stepped onto the pavement, an adolescent trailing a few yards behind a doe. Rick's hands wrapped tightly around the steering wheel. Hitting the brakes was futile. He laid on the horn, freezing the second whitetail in place, his truck slicing between the animals with only inches to spare.

His breath came in bursts, his heart hammering in his tightened chest. His brain shot back to the previous autumn, when his daughter had gone missing and he learned that a body had been found at the base of the jagged rock formation called the Sawtooth. That night was lightless and unsparing, its howling winds random and violent, an icy driving rain blowing sideways as it turned to snow. Rick remembered his truck being enveloped in the darkness, disappearing into a black hole from which there would be no return. In many ways, there had been no return, nor would there ever be.

Days after losing Chloe, Rick had purchased Big Sky, a mammoth majestic chestnut standing nearly eighteen hands high. Rick's muddled mind had told him to buy the horse for Abby, thinking perhaps the animal might somehow seamlessly mend the heart of a child whose life had been shattered into oblivion by the sudden, violent death of her mother. Sage had scoffed at the purchase, wondering aloud why Rick hadn't just handed Abby the keys to a tractor trailer. She was right, of course, as she often was. Rick was an expert at trying to fix things that couldn't be fixed.

Abby had been strictly instructed that she could never enter the corral—nor, God forbid, get on Big Sky's back—without close adult supervision. As she approached her tenth birthday, she was a few years away from riding alone. It had little to do with Big Sky's temperament, of course, the animal being a gentle giant. It had more to do with Big Sky being a *horse*. Rick knew from his own experience the abilities of a horse to provide much more to humans than a mode of transportation. In the aftermath of the death of his wife, Christine, Rick had spent countless hours in the presence of his paint horse, Rescue, who proffered no hint of judgment as his master stood crumpling in front of him, tears flowing like rivulets through dust on his cheeks. Rescue would draw closer to him, eyes blinking and ears swiveling with interest, his peacefulness tumbling like silken ocean waves onto the shore of Rick's wounded soul.

Yet, the keen senses of a horse presented a double-edged sword. In addition to comforting human sadness, they can perceive when a rider lacks confidence or is given to fear or indecision. This can quickly sever the connection between man and beast—or, as the case may be, horse and little girl. At other times, horses are just plain spooked, whether by a barking dog or something as innocuous as a plastic bag blowing in the wind.

Rick nearly skidded past the entrance of his ranch, the truck bounding through potholes as it climbed the two-track up toward the house and barn. He spotted the flashing emergency lights of the Riverton ambulance, its rear doors flung open as an EMT dropped the wheels of a gurney onto the gravel. He thought once again about Chloe—everything reminded him of Chloe.

Sage was on her knees in the dirt, her face riddled with anguish as she clutched Abby's right hand. An EMT cradled Abby's head and the blue cervical collar fastened around her neck while another medic positioned a yellow plastic backboard next to her tiny body. A small blue splint extended from her left wrist to her elbow. Rick jumped out of his truck, leaving the engine running and door flung open, his adrenaline and fear pushing him past any hope of remaining calm. Abby's eyes turned sideways toward him, tears streaming down the side of her face.

"Please don't kill him, Pa-Pa," she shouted, her voice trembling. "I swear— it wasn't his fault."

Rick's heart sank, ashamed at hearing the dread in Abby's voice, the child uncertain what extremes her grandfather might employ to remedy damage done to a Morrand family member. Rick dropped to the ground, taking Abby's hand from Sage's grasp. "Nobody's going to kill anything, Abby," he said in a soothing voice. "I promise."

Rick turned to the medic positioning the backboard, a new man he didn't recognize. "What do we got?" he asked, his pounding chest signaling his uncertainty about receiving the answer.

"Vitals are good, Sheriff," he replied quickly. "No indication of head trauma. She has feeling in all of her extremities. It looks like her only injury at this point is a fracture of the distal radius, which likely occurred when she tried to brace herself from the fall."

Rick released a long exhale and gently stroked the top of Abby's hand. "What happened, Baby?"

"All I wanted to do was sit on his back, Pa-Pa."

"Without a saddle?"

"He was *fine!*" Abby pleaded, a teardrop trickling from the corner of her eye. "The wind slammed the gate of the corral shut. I think it scared him." Her voice quivered. "Please promise you won't put him down. It wasn't his fault!"

Rick swallowed hard and shook his head. "I promise," he said with a raspy voice, his throat coarse and dry. He looked toward Sage, his steely eyes piercing her with blame, righteous anger seething within. She received his message, her eyes filled with hurt and shame.

"We're going to get on a backboard as a precaution, Sheriff," the medic said. "We have room in the ambulance if someone would like to ride with her."

Abby's eyes turned quickly toward her right shoulder. "Will you come with me, Sage? Please?"

"Of course I will," Sage said, gently stroking Abby's forehead with the back of her fingers. "Of course I will." Rick swallowed hard, looking at Abby and then toward Sage.

"We're going to roll her on my count of three," one of the EMTs said. With Rick's help, the medics gently turned Abby on her side, briefly checking her back for contusions. After strapping her onto the backboard, they lifted her onto the gurney and loaded her into the ambulance. Rick offered his hand to Sage in an effort to help her in. She ignored him, preferring to clutch a shiny metal handle on the inside of the door.

"I guess I'll see you at the hospital," Rick said. Sage flicked a glance at him but didn't reply. *What had happened? What was wrong?* Rick took a step back, allowing a medic to close the ambulance, its heavy doors sealing in a vacuum.

He blew out a hard breath as he watched the taillights ease down the two-track. Abby would be okay, but something about Sage was not.

He felt strangely alone.

CHAPTER 20

Charlie Duchesne had always been drawn to the Crazy Mountains.

From the moment he and Dora had settled in the Shields River Valley, the physician from Western Pennsylvania found himself captured under the spell of the range's razor-sharp peaks, their edges looking like they'd been carved out of the rich blue skyline with a scalpel's blade. On warm summer Sundays, following church services and breakfast, Charlie would hike deep into the Crazies and fish beside a turquoise lake, closing his eyes as his face was teased by cool breezes, his senses bathed in the aroma of conifers and clear mountain air.

On many occasions Dora would come along, having packed a lunch that they would share along the grassy shore. He would gaze at her adoringly, at times causing her to blush and turn away. When she wasn't with him, he couldn't get her off his mind.

As he drove his SUV up Highway 191 on the eastern edge of the Crazies, he considered how nothing had changed. He still adored his wife, and for that reason he was deeply pained by her belief that he had relapsed into gambling, a vice he had shunned for more than two decades. Her suspicions were predicated on rumor, which Dexter County had in abundance. Despite his denials, Dora was barely speaking to him. "Once burned, twice shy, I guess," Charlie mumbled to himself as he turned west onto a gravel road leading into the mountains.

What troubled him more was that the temptation to gamble had returned. As he drifted into his late sixties, he found himself swirling in an eddy of complacency, confronted by a sudden emptiness that he somehow needed to fill. Ever since the death of Chloe Morrand, he had doubted his role as Dexter County coroner. While he was lauded for helping solve Chloe's murder, he questioned a calling that had made him far too acquainted with death. In his mind, he didn't *solve* anything. Instead, he was a witness to the misery of others, his job many times involving nothing more than a detailed explanation of how their lives had been suddenly and irreversibly shattered.

Charlie looked at the digital clock beneath the cracked gray leather of his dashboard. Five thirty. He had maybe a couple of hours of daylight left at best. Rick Morrand was leaning on his friend's expertise, the coroner's ability to gather forensics in an effort to trace the movements of Garrett McRae. Helen, the dispatcher, had informed him that Rick's granddaughter had suffered an accident, but she would be okay. Charlie was determined to carry out his duties with loyalty and diligence.

He spotted a collection of vehicles up ahead, where the long grasses of the foothills were abruptly swallowed into a sea of smoldering black. Firefighters in yellow wildland helmets and grime-covered Nomex shirts dotted the terrain, carrying out the unenviable task of mop-up, a seemingly endless whack-a-mole endeavor that involved extinguishing buried embers that had the potential to reignite. Chainsaws whirred as charred trees fell, firefighters stabbing the trunks with Pulaski axes and other tools in search of orange sparks hidden beneath the burnt, crusted bark.

Garrett McRae's backpack was discovered somewhere in the depths of what had once been a vibrant forest. By all accounts, the fire had started in the brush, its twenty-five-foot-tall flames likely rushing toward the bow hunter as he tried to escape the trees. Charlie turned off his ignition, breathing a plaintive sigh as he shook his head.

He feared he would deliver more bad news. In fact, he could almost bet on it.

• • •

Rick stormed into the side entrance of Memorial Hospital, a forceful nod of his head ordering the front desk nurse to unlock the doors of the Emergency Department. He poked his head into the first room, where an elderly woman, jaw dropped and mouth wide open, had either dozed off or expired. Abby was in the second room, her arm still wrapped with a splint and ACE bandage. His granddaughter brightened when she saw him.

"Pa-Pa!" she shouted. "They're going to give me a cast! I get my choice of color, so I picked bright green. They told me everyone at school will get to sign it."

Rick had endured his share of casts, most of them resulting from injuries on the football field. Itched like hell, as he recalled. "Green's a good color," he managed to mutter. Abby beamed at his approval.

Sage was seated close to the bed, a few feet in front of him yet a million miles away. He looked at her and offered a smile. She stared at him without emotion before turning her attention back to Abby. "The nurse says she can get her hands on some ice cream, if you happen to be interested," Sage said. Abby smiled broadly, nodding her head with vigor.

A nurse appeared at the door. "Okay, young lady, are you ready?" Her eyes danced between Rick and Sage. "We shouldn't be too long. We'll take X-rays to make sure the bone is set properly and then apply the cast."

Rick nodded. "Is it true this brave girl will be having some ice cream?"

"I believe that is being arranged."

Abby smiled again as the nurse released the brakes on the gurney and wheeled her from the room.

Sage rose from her chair, smoothing the wrinkles from her flowered cotton dress. Rick noticed how thin she looked. He watched as her hands, tremoring slightly, traced across her boney hips, their gentle curvature now having the sharpness of a rock ledge. "I think I'll go have a cup of coffee," she said.

Rick stepped toward her, removing his hat and stroking the hair on the back of his head. "You think maybe we can talk?" he asked nervously, gently reaching for her thin, frail wrist. She nodded, reluctance followed by surrender, and slowly sat back down.

Rick took her hand in his. Her skin was cold, her eyes distant. His heart raced and his stomach churned, vulnerability hardly his forte. "I … I want to apologize," he said. "I was way out of line at the ranch. I just—"

"It's fine," Sage said without looking at him. "It was my fault Abby got hurt."

"No, it wasn't your fault. It was an accident." He gently caressed the back of her hand, noticing that her engagement ring was missing. He waited for her to look at him. "Can you *please* tell me what is going on?"

Sage's eyes began to fill with tears. "You don't want to marry me, Rick," she said, her voice shaking. "I'm bad luck."

Rick felt a sick twist in his lower abdomen, the skin covering his skull feeling as though it were shrinking. "What are you talking about?" he stammered.

"I'm bad luck," Sage repeated. "It runs in the family. Look what bad luck at cards did to Daddy. Got him killed."

Rick shook his head. "Bad luck at cards didn't get your father killed," he said. "He failed to pay up when he lost—*that's* what got him killed."

"Still," she whimpered, "bad luck just seems to follow the Fontenots, especially me. I've been married twice. Both decent men, but I left them both."

Rick chuckled. "Neither of those 'decent' fellas understood that being married means you're only supposed to sleep with your wife."

Sage released a sigh. "I don't seem to be wife material."

"If I didn't want to marry you, I wouldn't have asked."

Sage stood and placed her hand on the side of his neck, burying her face into his uniform shirt. "You don't understand," she said, her face trembling with more tears.

"Understand what?"

She didn't answer immediately. He watched her head rise and fall with the heaving of his chest. After several seconds, he gently placed his hands on her thin shoulders. "Sage, look at me," he said. "Understand *what?*"

She lifted reddened eyes flooded with weariness and pain. "Rick, I have cancer."

Breath emptied from his lungs, his lips beginning to quiver. "You have what?" The question was senseless. He'd heard Sage loud and clear. She easily could have spoken over the hospital's PA system. *Cancer. Cancer. Cancer.* The word seemed to be echoing off the walls.

"I can't do this to you," Sage said. "Not after what you went through with Christine."

Christine, the love of Rick's life, woman of his dreams, had been diagnosed with breast cancer. It went into remission for a period, teasing them with hope, before returning for a second time. Sage had been there through the entire ordeal, including the final, dreadful days, when the disease spread to the bones, liver, and lungs. Always so graceful and stoic, so full of life, Christine was left vomiting and incontinent, crushed beneath her insurmountable pain, finally surrendering to—if not welcoming—the patient and merciful gates of death.

Rick had known *something* was wrong. How could he not, given Sage's odd behavior? But he didn't expect this. More precisely, he hadn't known what to expect. What were the odds that he could fall in love with two women who developed cancer? Maybe Sage was right—what kind of luck was that? If lightning hadn't struck twice, a second bolt was certainly in the vicinity.

He tried to steady himself, standing on the deck of a ship rocked by stormy seas. "Is this what those tests were about?"

Sage nodded. "I have non-Hodgkin's lymphoma. It's the reason I've been so tired lately, and why I've lost so much weight."

"Non-Hodgkin's," Rick repeated. He paused a beat in thought. "It can be treated, right? It can be cured?"

"Yes, it can be treated, and it's possible for it to be cured. I guess there are a lot of factors, but it's possible."

He drew a deep breath and stared into Sage's eyes, a flood of emotion affirming how much she meant to him. He didn't want to lose her. He *couldn't* lose her. Not now, not ever. The trail ahead was ominous to be sure, strewn with uncertainty and tendering no guarantees, but there would be no retreat. "We're getting married," he said with finality. "And we're going on a honeymoon to Mexico, just like you wanted." He looked down at her left hand. "Where's your ring?"

Sage held her fingers rigid, staring at the tan mark where the ring was missing. "I put it on the nightstand when I laid down to rest," she said. "It's been falling off my finger."

Rick smiled. "We'll, you'd better get it resized," he said, "'cause we're getting married."

He leaned forward and kissed her gently, feeling the warmth and softness of her lips. She pressed hard against him, her hand tracing down behind the belt of his uniform pants. He released an uneasy chuckle. "Just what exactly do you think yer doin'?" he asked out of the side of his mouth. Sage kissed him more passionately, causing his entire body to fever with desire. She wrapped her arms tightly around his neck as he lifted her onto a gray Formica countertop, both of them giggling when Sage's elbow knocked the metal lid off a glass jar of medical swabs. Rick tried to glance over his shoulder to check the narrow wired glass window of the exam room door. Extending his arm behind him, he managed to flip off a light switch, darkening the room. Sage clutched his neck with one hand and pulled him back, her breath warm and her skin soft and sweet. She reached for his belt buckle, tugging it loose and unbuttoning the top of his pants. His lips traced along her neck, now fragrant and honeyed with sweat.

The hushed passion inside the exam room was interrupted by a brisk knock on the wooden door followed immediately by the turning of the knob. The room filled with light. Rick's head swiveled to see Abby's nurse. She began to speak but stopped abruptly, her eyes opened wide and mouth agape as she stared at Rick and Sage. "I ... I'm sorry," she said, her face turning crimson. "I was just checking to see if either of you ... needed anything."

Rick turned to shield himself from her, fumbling for the top button of his trousers. He began to apologize, but before he could form any words, the nurse was gone.

"Oops," he said, biting the side of his lip. He and Sage looked at each other and giggled, much like two sophomores caught necking behind the high school gymnasium. Rick wrapped his hands around Sage's waist, helping her off the counter.

"You gotta admit," she said, "we have had a tough stretch of luck."

"I suppose," he replied. "Sometimes you get what you want, and sometimes you get what you need." He released a long sigh. "Then there's times you just get what you get."

Sage's eyes roamed over his face as she caressed his cheek. "You sure you want me?"

Rick kissed her again, lingering on her lips. "We're in this together," he said, his forehead pressed against hers as they tasted each other's breath. "And you can bet we're gettin' married."

• • •

Charlie walked slowly across the scorched landscape, his boots kicking up small clouds of white and gray ash. A dreary canopy of smoke hovered above him, shrouding the descending sun. Licking his dry lips, he scanned the sea of yellow shirts and helmets before eventually locating Mike Greer, who was speaking into a mic connected to the radio harnessed on his chest. Mike's face was covered with soot, his tired, sunken eyes shielded by a pair of clear wraparound safety glasses.

"Charlie," Mike said as he removed a glove and stepped toward the coroner. "It's been a while."

"Not seeing me for a while is a good thing," Charlie said with little expression, his eyes surveying the surrounding desolation. "So, what do we got so far? Where'd the fire start?"

Mike tugged his glove back onto his hand and pointed east toward an area a quarter mile into the black. "I figure it started over there, beneath those downed power lines. What caused that cable to snap is a mystery at this point."

Charlie's eyes traced from the power lines to the edge of the trees. The once-dense timber and verdant underbrush now resembled a graveyard of scarred, barren shafts that extended for miles. A sudden feeling of melancholy brushed over him as he contemplated the proud forest finding rebirth and rising again, strong and spirited as ever, long after Charlie had passed from existence.

"And the backpack?" Charlie asked. "Where was it found?"

"We're still figuring that out."

"Oh?"

Mike lifted his brow. "Rick didn't mention it had been moved?"

Charlie shook his head, biting the side of his lip. "No, he didn't."

Mike turned away, his head darting about in search of someone. He jabbed a pointed finger in the direction of a young woman resting on one knee as she stroked the head of a black and tan mid-sized dog. "Over here," Mike said as he walked toward the woman. Her thick dishwater-blond hair was pulled into a ponytail that flowed from beneath a weathered yellow ball cap, her head tilted forward and eyes downcast like a student in detention.

"Meredith, this is Charlie Duchesne, Dexter County coroner," Mike said, placing a hand on Charlie's shoulder and turning toward him. "Meredith has been working with Gallatin County SAR for about three years. This is the first time she and her dog have been over here."

She stood and began to extend her hand but reconsidered as Charlie folded his arms across his chest. "Three years?" Charlie grumbled. "I would think by now you would have learned not to move items found at a scene."

Meredith pursed her lips and looked down at her dog, who was brushing the side of his snout against her knee. "I apologize for that, Mr. Duchesne," she said. "It's just that Garrett is a friend of mine—"

"None of that matters," Charlie said with bite. "This isn't a game out here. It's not somebody's hobby. Someone's life—"

"You know," Mike interrupted, playing peacemaker, "if it wasn't for Meredith's dog, we probably wouldn't have located that backpack at all." The fire chief dropped to one knee, his gloved hand scratching beneath the dog's chin. "What's his name again—Tango? Yeah, that's it, Tango." He turned his head and looked up at Charlie. "Tango has been on the Gallatin team for about a year, Charlie. He's a damn good dog, and Meredith trained him herself."

Charlie dropped his arms to his side and looked away, bored and unimpressed. He flicked a thumb toward the charred forest. "How about we try to get a fix on where you found the pack," he said as gently as he could manage.

He started walking without waiting for a reply.

CHAPTER 21

Rick called Mike Greer early Saturday morning, hoping to persuade the fire chief to allow search teams back into the Crazies. With each passing hour, the clock was ticking on Garrett McRae's chances of survival.

Greer held firm. "We're still looking at Monday—at the earliest," he said. "We've had a bunch of snags reignite inside the burn area." Greer was using wildland lexicon for standing dead trees with fuel left to burn. Aside from the weakened state of the scorched timber, there also was the danger of stump holes, hidden pockets that formed when the root systems of larger trees secretly smoldered beneath the soil. The burn area had become a hazardous minefield.

Most of the state's limited assets were dedicated to fighting fires that dotted the Montana map from the Bitterroot to Miles City, but Rick managed to locate a helicopter crew in Bozeman that agreed to search the Crazies from the air on Saturday afternoon. After three hours of scanning endless miles of the Granite Peak Fire's simmering destruction, a pilot placed a solemn call to inform the sheriff their efforts had turned up nothing.

Rick spent the balance of the weekend doting on Sage and Abby, who were content to remain sequestered in the master bedroom, laughing and crying intermittently as the flat-screen television blared a romantic comedy marathon. Sage was scheduled to begin chemotherapy early Monday, and Rick expressed his desire to accompany her. She vetoed that plan, calmly explaining that her battle with NHL was going to be a marathon, not a sprint. "You need to work," she said. "Trust me—you need to work." Sage knew full well that Rick had sat through sessions of chemo with Christine, and she likely didn't want him to have to tread those coals again. Rick protested briefly but agreed to honor Sage's wishes. An odd rush of relief washed over him, coupled with a twinge of guilt.

They left the house only once all weekend, on Sunday morning to attend church, where the preacher quoted Matthew 6:27 to ask of the congregation, "Who of you by worrying can add a single hour to his life?" Rick sat stone-faced, staring at the pulpit as he worried like hell.

Sage was about to embark on her precarious duel with cancer. While she feigned outward hope, the journey she would navigate promised uncertainty and fear, her wooden ship in clear and present danger of foundering on the shoals.

Then there was Garrett McRae. The hunter had not been heard from for more than a week. They had found a backpack that contained no identification, although its uncommon blue-camo color made it sound like one that belonged to Garrett. Charlie Duchesne reported that the backpack had been charred in the fire, but he offered few additional details. The coroner planned to run tests for prints and possible DNA in the upcoming days.

Rick had promised to alert Amber McRae of any developments, and he should have contacted her immediately about the discovery. Her husband was missing, and she deserved to know. Why had he hesitated? To shield her from false hope? To spare her the anguish of thinking her husband had been incinerated in a wildland fire? The psychological torment he had experienced as the father of a missing daughter was something he would never wish on anybody. He now found himself playing God, a position well above his pay grade.

The preacher raised his volume toward the end of the scripture reading, shaking Rick from his trance. "Therefore do not worry about tomorrow, for tomorrow will worry about itself," the minister read. "Today has enough trouble of its own."

Rick swallowed, his forehead gathering beads of perspiration as he sat inside the suffocating warmth of the church, its sealed stained-glass windows sheltering the congregation from the smell of smoke. He felt Sage's hand wander onto his, the delicate skin on her fingertips squeezing the inside of his palm. He closed his hand on hers, his gaze remaining fixed on the preacher lest his eyes betray to Sage the turmoil he held within.

Indeed, he thought, today certainly has enough trouble of its own.

CHAPTER 22

Jack Kelly thought he had safely dodged a bullet when he told his wife that the initial search for Garrett McRae had been largely routine. Though he had reeked of smoke and his entire body was caked in dirt, Tamara generally appeared to embrace his account of events.

But that was before one of the local news outlets chose to report the harrowing tale of two law enforcement officers who had been caught well inside the Granite Peak Fire perimeter and nearly consumed by the flames. Tamara's reflexive response came in the form of an ultimatum that Jack resign from the sheriff's department or she would resign from their marriage. Over time, and with the assistance of a Bozeman spa day accompanied by a well-funded excursion to Macy's, she did manage to cool down, somewhat akin to the embers of the Granite Peak blaze.

Truth be told, Jack's flirtation with death in the Crazies had provided just enough adrenaline to reignite a fuse that had burned throughout his adult life. Much like a soldier who continued to request additional tours of duty rather than taming to civilian life, Jack couldn't seem to divorce himself from the lure of law enforcement, however benign the majority of incidents in Dexter County might be.

He'd wondered at times whether he possessed some sort of death wish, a tendency toward self-loathing, suppressed anger from his youth, or perhaps even some peculiar feeling of inferiority. He had more than one opportunity to discuss such topics with a variety of police psychologists—whom he was required to visit following incidents that required use of force—but he always managed to glide through those sessions with minimal dialogue, supplemented by a facial expression as immovable as stone.

Psychobabble be damned.

His initial plan had been to move West, enjoy his pension, and bask in a life of health and serenity. Montana was not Tamara's first choice, as she would have preferred a destination due south of Jersey, perhaps Florida or even the Carolinas. She acquiesced primarily because she'd hoped to quiet the prancing demons that had spent years battling for command of her husband's soul.

If there was any locale where Jack could find some measure of tranquility, it was Montana, which he fell in love with from the moment he was introduced to the state by Rick Morrand. With its gleaming mountain peaks, crystal streams, and carefree pace, Jack was instantly drawn in, and he allowed himself to dream that it was a place where perhaps his wandering, conflicted spirit might finally find remission. Yet, while he did enjoy fly fishing well enough, he likely would have found the experience more enriching had a sniper been planted somewhere among the pines.

Jack's assignment on Monday morning was to visit Kyle Ricketts, who had emerged from the Crazy Mountains in the company of Randall Boone, both men having only a casual regard for the absence of Garrett McRae. Despite losing contact with their hunting partner for more than three full days, they had set up shop in a saloon in Mariah, Garrett's well-being apparently the most distant thought from their minds.

According to the information he provided, Ricketts was employed at Len's Collision Center, a body shop located in an industrial section off I-90 in Bozeman. When Jack pulled into the parking lot, he spotted his man standing outside a garage door dressed in a striped denim jumpsuit and sucking nervously on a vape pipe as he leaned against the peeling paint of the gray stucco building.

"Morning, Kyle," Jack said as he lowered his window. "Got a minute to talk?"

Kyle stuffed the pipe inside his pocket and placed his palms beneath his armpits. He threw a nod toward the inside of the garage. "Sorry, but I need to get back to work."

"My mistake," Jack said, throwing his vehicle into Park. "I accidentally phrased my request as a question." He emerged from his truck and slammed the door behind him. Adjusting his aviator sunglasses, he took two steps forward. "What I meant to say was, 'Kyle, I need you to provide some answers.' That better?"

Kyle swallowed as he took full measure of Jack's six-foot-six-inch frame. His bloodshot eyes were covered with a watery film. He seemed about to cry. He blinked often, and his facial muscles delivered a symphony of random ticks. His chin was sprinkled with pinpoint sores. "I … I really don't know what else I can tell you besides what I already said."

"I'd like to talk to you a bit more about Randall Boone," Jack said. "You seemed … shall we say, a little ill at ease in his presence when we initially questioned you. I'm wondering if perhaps you could supply me with some additional details, now that we're alone."

Kyle nodded uneasily. "Sure," he mumbled.

"Good." Jack lifted a small notepad and pen out of his shirt pocket. "How long have you and Mr. Boone been friends?"

Kyle raised his head and squinted toward the sky. "Boone ain't my friend. He don't seem to be nobody's friend."

"So why were you hunting with him?"

"I was invited by Garrett," Kyle said with a shrug that was closer to a shiver. "We've known each other since we were kids. I've hunted with Garrett before, so I decided to go. I'd met Boone once or twice, but I don't necessarily know him." He lowered his eyes toward the ground. "I don't really like him, neither."

Jack folded his arms across his massive chest. "Have you had any contact with Mr. Boone since you got back?"

Kyle glanced at Jack, then returned his eyes toward the sky, scanning its expanse as though the arrival of aliens was imminent. Jack twisted his head toward the sky, following Kyle's line of sight, but he could see only a solitary plane headed east.

"Kyle!" Jack said sharply. "Have you been in contact with Mr. Boone?"

Kyle's eyes opened wide. "Boone called me a couple of times, saying he wanted to meet, but I blew him off." His gaze returned to the sky. "Damn," he said, wagging his head. "Another one."

Jack looked up at the sky once again. There was a second plane on the horizon. "Is there something going on up there that I should know about?"

"They're sprayin' again," Kyle said. "Two planes so far—more will be comin', I'm sure."

Jack stroked his hand over his close-cropped hair and scratched the back of his neck. "*Who* is spraying?" he said as he cocked his head. "And *what* exactly are they spraying?"

Kyle looked at Jack curiously. "You never heard of chemtrails?"

"Chem … trails?"

"That's right," Kyle said. "The chemicals come right out of the back of planes. I'm figuring it's the military. The chemicals spread out gradually. Before you know it, the whole sky is covered."

Jack raised his eyebrows, turning his head upward once again. "Most folks would refer to that as exhaust," he said, "or perhaps condensation."

Kyle reached into his pocket and pulled out his vape pipe, inhaling deeply before blowing out a stream of thick mist. "Condensation dissipates," he said. "If you look up there at those chemicals, they don't dissipate." He pursed his lips, shaking his head again. "You would think with all the smoke in the air, they'd give us a break."

Jack allowed himself one more glance toward the sky, all the while wondering who exactly "they" were, not to mention who Kyle Ricketts might be. The first plane had disappeared beyond the horizon, leaving a long trail of exhaust behind. At least, Jack *thought* it was exhaust. Perhaps he should have doubt, similar to the doubt he had regarding the veracity of anything that might trail out of Kyle's mouth. He tugged a handkerchief from his back pocket and cleaned his sunglasses, wondering all the while if coming out of retirement had been such a grand idea.

A compressor inside the garage rumbled to life, followed by the screaming sound of an air impact wrench loosening lug nuts. "Sir," Kyle said, his voice rising above the compressor, "I really need to get back to work."

Jack flipped through the pages of his notebook. "This won't take but a few more minutes. Tell me a little more about Boone and Garrett. How did Garrett know him? Are they good friends?"

Kyle rolled his eyes, sucking once more from his vape pipe. "They worked construction together," he said. "I don't know if they were good friends or not."

"Did they seem to get along?"

"How do I know?" he said with a shrug. "I wasn't around them that much." He glanced inside the garage. His face continued to twitch. "Can you please let me get back to work? I like my job."

"I like mine too," Jack said, staring at his notes. He placed the pad back in his pocket. "Mr. Ricketts, I've been doing this for quite a while, and there's this feeling I get when I think someone is not being entirely forthcoming with me." He stared at Kyle, hiking his eyebrows expectantly.

Kyle blew out a long sigh. "Look, Boone isn't all that great of a guy."

"So I've gathered."

"They had an argument."

"What kind of argument?"

"I really can't say."

"I won't be leaving until you do."

Kyle rolled his eyes as hit bit the side of his lip, eyes and cheekbones twitching. "There were rumors, okay?" he said. "Some bullshit about Boone having a thing for Garrett's wife."

"Bullshit?"

"I don't know if it's true or not."

Jack pursed his lips and took a step toward Kyle. "Is that what the argument was about?"

Kyle shrugged. "Could have been. I'd gone to gather some firewood, and when I come back, they were shouting at each other."

"What did you do?"

"I told them to knock it off, but I don't think they heard me."

Jack huffed a breath. "What happened next—you know, after they didn't *hear* you?"

"I don't know," he said with a shrug.

Jack glanced in both directions, then trained his eyes on Kyle. "What do you mean you don't know?"

Kyle slid along the concrete wall, trying to create more space between them. The compressor in the garage whirred once again. "I blacked out!" he shouted.

Jack squinted at him. "You what?"

Kyle nodded. "I tend to have seizures every now and then," he said through short breaths. "They come out of nowhere. When they do, I black out."

"Epilepsy?" Jack asked. "You have epilepsy?"

Kyle shook his head. "Doc told me they come on when I'm under stress." He cast his eyes toward the sky. "Or maybe it's those chemicals—I don't know."

Jack nodded toward the vape pipe in Kyle hand. "I'm sure sucking on that thing helps a lot."

Kyle drew on the pipe in defiance, blowing a narrow silver cloud from the side of his mouth. "Keeps me calm," he offered.

Jack rested his hands on his hips, closing his eyes a moment as his temples throbbed. "What was the next thing you remembered after you blacked out?"

"I woke up the next morning," Kyle said. "Boone was saddling up his horse, and Garrett was already gone."

"Did Boone say where he was going?"

Kyle blinked a few times. "He said he was going out to hunt."

"When did he return?"

"Late Monday morning." The air impact wrench squealed again. A car's ignition cranked, the tired engine hesitating before finally turning over. A cloud of exhaust spewed from the door of the garage. "Look," Kyle said nervously, "I gotta go."

Jack's eyes narrowed. "Monday morning, huh? So he was gone two nights without returning to camp?"

Kyle nodded. "He's got a couple of caches up in the Crazies. He could stay up there a while, if he wanted to."

Jack paused, considering Kyle's words. *What was Boone doing for two full days?* "Did he say if he'd seen Garrett?"

Kyle stuffed his vape pipe into his pocket and released a long sigh. "I'd rather not—"

"I don't care what you would or wouldn't like to say," Jack growled. "Did Boone say he'd seen Garrett or not?"

"He said he hadn't seen him," Kyle mumbled. "But he had Garrett's horse. He said he found it wandering along the trail, coming from the east side of the Crazies."

"Was any of Garrett's gear on the horse?"

Kyle shook his head. "There was a quartered cow elk on its back. It had Garrett's tag on it."

"Did Boone have blood on him?"

Kyle hesitated. "I don't remember."

"Another blackout?" Jack snarled. "It's a simple question."

"I *don't* remember," Kyle said more definitively, averting his eyes.

Jack felt his jaw tighten as he ground his teeth. It was a reflex left over from his Newark days, when his instincts told him someone was lying. His next impulse was to grab the man and throw him against a wall, urging him to reassess his powers of recollection. He drew a breath and reminded himself he wasn't in Jersey.

"Did you hear anything from Garrett after Friday night? You said he radioed on Saturday, telling you he was at Campfire Lake?"

"There was a lot of static," Kyle replied. "I might have heard him wrong."

Jack rubbed the back of his neck. "Why didn't you guys come out on Monday morning, when Boone returned with Garrett's horse? It was obvious he was out there somewhere—apparently on foot."

"I told Boone we should leave, but he didn't want to," Kyle said with a shrug. "He said he still had his bull tag, and he wanted to use it. We skinned the meat and boned it—you know, to keep it cool—then we put it in game bags that we hung in a tree. Boone told me to guard it while he went back out to hunt."

Jack cocked his head. "Guard it?" he said with a frown. "You have it up in a tree. It's safe from animals, and the cool air and shade will preserve it. No one needs to *guard* it."

"He insisted someone had to stay behind," Kyle said meekly. "We flipped a coin—sort of."

Jack chuckled. "Don't tell me—you lost."

Kyle lips curled downward, his eyes fixed on the ground. "It was like he didn't want me to go anywhere," he said. "Two separate grizzlies wandered through camp that night. I barely slept."

"And Boone ended up getting his bull?"

"On Tuesday, less than two miles from our camp," Kyle said. "He made me help him gut and quarter it. It was a six-by-six. He saved the head and rack for a mount."

Jack nodded as he studied Kyle's watery eyes and pockmarked face. He resembled a weak, frightened animal wary of larger beasts to whom he might fall prey. Boone was one such predator, perhaps. He seemed to have cast a spell of intimidation that had Kyle paralyzed with fear. Or was it an act? Was Kyle afraid or covering his tracks? Jack wasn't sure, but he doubted whether Kyle had told him everything he knew, mainly because there was so much more that wasn't known. Why didn't either of the men try to locate Garrett after Saturday morning? Why did they seem to have such little concern for Garrett's safety or whereabouts? Why didn't they leave camp and head east, following the tracks of Garrett's horse? Rick also had mentioned a bloody T-shirt, one that had mysteriously disappeared off Boone's back.

Jack reached through his window and pulled a small metal case off the dash. He handed Kyle a business card. "Let me know if you think of any-thing else."

Kyle stuffed the card into his back pocket. "I think I've already told you enough."

Jack opened the door of his truck, pausing as his hand gripped the window frame. "So Boone came out with two elk, one of them Garrett's?"

"Yes."

"And you bagged nothing?"

Kyle nodded sheepishly.

"How do you feel about that?"

"Can't say I'm happy."

"Why are you so terrified of this Boone guy?"

Kyle blinked rapidly. "I ain't terrified of him."

"No?"

Kyle turned toward the entrance of the garage, looking at Jack over his shoulder. "Like I said, sir. He ain't a good dude."

CHAPTER 23

Sage's forearm rested on a padded vinyl slab attached to a chair in Janice Tillotson's office, her fist opening and closing as her nervous young nurse searched for a vein. Sage had known Danielle Kingston since she was born, and she guessed her to be about twenty-two. Danielle was fresh out of Rimrock College in Billings, where she had received an associate's degree as a medical assistant. Having grown up on a ranch, Danielle had spent plenty of years assisting with animal vaccinations and helping her family chart the long, hard days of calving season. Sage was about to find out how well that experience translated into poking a needle into the blood vessel of a human being.

"Ouch!" Sage yelped, getting her answer. Danielle had gone after a bulging vein with the vigor of someone playing darts.

"I'm so sorry!" Danielle said, her voice sounding panicked as her eyes opened wide. "Do you want me to take it out?"

Sage looked at the pallid, puffy skin on her arm, where the needle dangled like a harpoon protruding from the back of a whale. "Looks like you hit the mark. No sense turning back now."

Danielle's hands tremored as she attached a plastic tube to the needle. Sage's eyes traced the tube up to a bag hanging from a metal stand. "How many times have you done this, Danielle?"

"This is my third," the young woman said.

Sage allowed herself a chuckle. "Glad I was able to help you practice."

Danielle's face was flushed. Her hands continued to shake as she placed a piece of tape over the needle casing, holding it in place. "This should be easier once they implant your port," she said, embarrassed.

"I can't wait."

"Dr. Tillotson will be in to check on you shortly." Danielle opened the door and quietly backed out, as if Sage were a child about to nap.

Sage shook her head and pursed her lips. She had no cause to complain. Janice Tillotson had told her the treatments could be done in something called a "cancer center" in Bozeman, but Sage didn't care for the sound of that. She tended to avoid Bozeman, considering the city was growing fast with what seemed like an endless stream of refugees from California. Janice was nice enough to arrange for her to have treatments in Riverton, although Sage would be traveling to Billings for an MRI to determine whether the cancer had spread.

The doctor wanted chemotherapy to start immediately, hence Danielle's insertion of an IV into Sage's arm. A port would be implanted sometime later that week, the routine outpatient procedure to be performed at Riverton's Memorial Hospital. Sage couldn't help but wonder why Janice was so eager for treatments to begin so quickly.

She released a lengthy exhale as she stared at the IV. She thought she felt a warm sensation as the chemicals entered her body. Dr. Tillotson had explained that the chemo drugs would function much like sedatives, making Sage feel numbed and tired. It was possible that she would even sleep through the hours of drug delivery, though Sage couldn't quite see that happening.

The warm feeling gradually felt more like a burn, and Sage welcomed it. She'd been sucker-punched by her diagnosis, not unlike one of the whiskey-soaked patrons who'd occasionally end up facedown on the faded wooden floor of her saloon. Now, she was fighting back. These chemicals, whatever they were, were coursing through her veins like a flaming river, destroying everything in their path.

"Fuck you, Cancer," she said as she stared at the tube in her arm, her teeth tightly clenched. "Do you hear me? Fuck you!"

The door opened. Dr. Tillotson entered and scanned the room to see if Sage was talking to someone. "You okay?"

"Never better," Sage said, forcing an artificial smile. She was starting to feel a little lightheaded.

"Where's Rick?" the doctor asked. "He didn't want to come?"

"No, actually he did."

"Why isn't he here?"

"I asked him not to."

"Because ..."

"He doesn't need to be here."

Janice tugged her four-wheeled stool out from under the counter and sat. Her frown suggested she was transitioning from physician to trusted friend. "Look," she said in a calm voice. "With what you're going through, you need all the support you can get. It's no time to put up walls."

Sage rolled her eyes. "It's not like that. Rick has that hunter lost in the Crazies, and I know that's weighing on him. This is the first … *missing* person on his watch. He seems to be taking it personally."

"Well, he *is* the sheriff," Janice said, hiking her eyebrows.

"I think there's more to it than that."

The doctor nodded knowingly. "It's been about a year since Chloe died?"

"A year ago this month. He's got a lot on his plate."

"So do you," Janice said. She released a sigh and folded her arms across her chest. "Let him support you if he wants to. It will be good for him—and for you."

Sage's eyes flitted around the exam room. "I really appreciate you allowing me to do this here," she said. "I wasn't too keen on the idea of schlepping up to Bozangeles."

Janice smiled. "Don't get too excited just yet. I'll need you to go over to Billings at some point."

Sage's brow tightened as she bit the side of her lower lip. "That's when I find out whether … *it* has spread?" She wasn't quite sure why she used the word *it* for her condition. Something about saying "cancer" in normal conversation suddenly intimidated her, somewhat akin to invoking the name of Satan.

Janice leaned forward, holding the tips of Sage's fingers. The doctor's skin was soft and warm, her eyes reassuring. "Let's think positive thoughts, shall we?"

Sage nodded, trying to ignore the cold sensation that raced up her spine. Dr. Tillotson patted her hand and gently released it. The doctor rose from the stool and slid it back underneath the counter. "Positive thoughts, right?" she said as she opened the door to exit the room.

"Positive thoughts," Sage repeated, watching the door close, leaving her in loneliness. She drew a breath, an eerie feeling convincing her she was the last human being on the planet.

Fuck you, Cancer.

• • •

When Rick called Charlie Duchesne on Monday morning, the coroner was still grousing about the fact that the backpack believed to belong to Garrett McRae had been moved from its original location. Charlie was punctilious about such matters, considering it his duty to provide a precise narrative regarding the facts surrounding the disappearance of a given individual, regardless of whether that person in question was alive or dead.

Charlie was most often referred to as a coroner, and rightly so, since he had been repeatedly elected to that position by the denizens of Dexter County. Yet, with a Montana physician's license in his possession, he also filled the role of medical examiner, and he believed that his exhaustive background as an investigator and forensic expert made him an asset when authorities were searching for a person who might yet be among the living.

"Were you able to lift prints off the backpack?" Rick asked as he drove his truck up Highway 191 along the eastern side of the Crazies. The wind had shifted again to the north, taking the smoke of the Granite Peak Fire along with it. The unyielding, nettlesome odor of burnt timber remained.

"There were definitely prints," Charlie said from his office. "I also found hair fibers, so there can be DNA as well."

"And you marked the place where you found it?"

Charlie blew out a breath. "I hope I did," he growled. "The woman who moved the pack took me to the location where she found it. She *swore* it was the exact spot. I don't know if that's true or if she was just covering her ass." Charlie paused a beat before adding, "Sorry—I'm probably not sup-posed to say stuff like that."

Rick watched himself lift his eyebrows and shake his head in his rear-view mirror. "So, that's about it?"

"That's it. Except for the shoes."

"What shoes?"

"Over the weekend, one of Mike Greer's guys found a pair of hiking boots wedged beneath the trunk of a fallen tree. They were about a mile south of the spot where the backpack was found—or, at least, where it *sup-posedly* was found."

"What size are the boots?"

"Ten and a half," Charlie said.

"What condition are they in? Old? New?"

"They look fairly new."

Rick thought of the photos he'd seen of Garrett McRae. A ten-and-a-half shoe would seem a good fit. "Let me know when you get some results on the forensics," he said, ending the call.

He continued north on uneven asphalt of the two-lane highway, its cracks and potholes having been repaired at random with tar and crushed gravel. The jagged, untamed crest of the Crazies dominated the landscape to the west. The regal peaks were both mystical and haunting, as though charged with the task of holding deep, cryptic truths that must forever remain hidden.

His phone vibrated on the console. "Jack," Rick said. "Did you get a chance to talk to Kyle Ricketts?"

"Interesting dude," the undersheriff replied.

"How so?"

"Let's just say he has issues."

"Such as?"

"You ever heard of something called chemtrails?"

"No," Rick answered as he shook his head. "What are chemtrails?"

Jack hesitated a beat. "I'll explain it to you later. Anyway, he said Garrett and this guy Boone got into an argument."

"What kind of argument?

"It was Friday night—before Garrett disappeared," Jack said. "I guess things got pretty heated."

"What were they arguing about?"

"Supposedly, Boone may have had an affair with Garrett's wife, and Garrett found out about it."

Rick's forehead tightened. "This is what Kyle told you?"

"Took a little effort, but, yeah, that's what Kyle told me. He claims he doesn't know exactly how it ended because he blacked out."

"Why would he black out?"

"From a seizure."

"Did you say *seizure*?"

"Like I told you, the guy's got issues," Jack said. "I'm thinking I should head up to Boone's place to see what else I can find out. Maybe we can learn more about that bloody shirt he was wearing."

Rick paused in thought. "Well, don't antagonize him."

"Can you define what you mean by *antagonize*?" Jack said in a defensive tone.

Rick regretted the comment. He was well aware of Jack's history in Jersey, but he meant no affront. "I know you're not a fan of Boone, and neither am I," he explained in a slow, controlled voice. "But as of right now, this is still a missing person case. We need this guy's help to find him."

"You think he's still alive?"

"Until I learn otherwise."

"Copy that, Sheriff," Jack said. "I'm off to Three Forks to see Boone." He added with a chuckle, "I'll do my best not to antagonize him."

• • •

Rick laid down his cell phone and turned left off the highway, gradually climbing the foothills leading toward the mountains. He quickly entered the black, where the Granite Peak Fire appeared to have begun in the tall grasses and sage before ascending into the trees. The initial blaze started on a Sunday, one day after the hunters may have last heard from Garrett McRae.

Rick considered the boots that had been found by a member of Mike Greer's wildland crew. It was not uncommon for a bow hunter stalking an elk to change from hiking boots to a soft-soled shoe, perhaps a moccasin, in the interest of silence and stealth. Could Garrett have shed his shoes, and later his pack, as he set off on foot in pursuit of an animal? Depending on how far he traveled, he surely would have been caught in the flames as he unwittingly tried to find his way back to his gear.

But how did Boone end up with Garrett's horse? Was the horse hobbled near the shoes or the pack? Did Garrett try to retrieve the horse after field-dressing his elk? Fresh off the argument between Boone and Garrett in camp, did matters escalate when they saw each other again?

Rick looked ahead through the soot covering his windshield to see Mike Greer waving at him with a gloved hand. The fire chief was leaning on a McLeod—a double-sided wildland tool that could be used as a rake or hoe. Mike's face was covered with sweat and soot, his yellow Nomex shirt soiled by deep-black charcoal that once had been healthy timber. He was hardly the kind of leader who would radio commands to subordinates from a secure distance. Whether the task was digging fire line, dropping snags, or handling mop-up, he enjoyed toiling alongside his troops.

Mike removed his white helmet and tucked it under his arm. Stepping forward, he tugged off his glove to grip Rick's hand. "We're still dealing with plenty of hotspots," he said as he looked over his shoulder at the carnage in the distance. He brushed his sleeve across his forehead, leaving a long black smudge. "This thing moved through so quickly the first time that there was plenty of fuel left to burn when the winds picked up late Friday. I think we may finally have it under control."

Rick surveyed the wisps of gray smoke and charred trees that extended as far as the eye could see. "I guess Charlie had a run-in with a member of your crew?" he asked Mike.

"He got a little upset about that backpack," Mike said. "Meredith is a good gal, and her dog is well trained. She just gets a little overzealous sometimes."

"But she was able to get Charlie to the spot where it was found?"

"Seems like it," Mike answered. "I have to give her credit for finding it in the first place. It was tucked beneath a juniper, and plenty of people walked right by. But she and her dog went right to it, almost like she knew where it was."

Rick nodded, pausing in thought. "What do you make of the hiking boots that were found?"

"He changed shoes," Mike said, echoing Rick's suspicion. "My lieutenant is a bow hunter, and he says that's what a lot of them do." He placed his helmet back on his head and folded his arms across his chest. "Makes no sense to me, of course. Tiptoeing around the forest seems like a great way to come upon a sow with cubs or maybe even a male eating a kill. There aren't supposed to be grizzlies in the Crazies, but I think there are plenty of them out there."

Rick cleared his throat. "So I've heard." He gazed again toward the horizon, scratching the stubble on his chin. "So we have this guy saying he's at Campfire Lake, then traveling due east, then heading north?"

"Not unusual, from what my lieutenant tells me," Mike said. "These bow hunters are a strange breed of cat. A lot of them scout during the summer, and they have their spots. If one place comes up empty, they move on. Once they find an animal, they'll follow it for miles to make sure they have a clean shot. There are no second chances."

"Especially with a bow," Rick said.

Mike nodded. "Exactly."

Rick exhaled. "Is there a search crew back out there?"

"Ben Westfall is with his guys now. The underbrush is all but gone, so it's hard to determine which way the hunter may have headed. They brought in a tracker, but he hasn't managed to find much."

"Looks like a good chance he could have been trapped in the fire," Rick said in a grave tone.

Mike nodded, the edges of his lips downward. "I'm afraid so."

Rick looked at the gravel road he'd used to drive up from Highway 191. "I went through a stretch of black on my way up here. Is that where the brush fire started?"

Mike wagged his head and motioned east beyond a distant ridge. "If you check out the towers back that way, you'll notice what looks like a downed power line. Not sure how it snapped—probably the wind, I would imagine, or maybe a falling tree. This thing started small, and we thought we had a handle on it. Then the wind changed."

Rick shook his head. "So Garrett probably wasn't even aware there was a fire over here."

"Probably not," Mike said. "At least, not until it was too late."

CHAPTER 24

Spencer Bible stared at the yellowed newspapers littering the front walkway of his father's house, the engine of his pre-owned Impala making a strange rhythmic clicking noise as it idled in the driveway. He recalled his father suggesting that timing chains tended to be an issue in Chevrolet vehicles, and he might be better off buying a Ford. He boldly purchased the Impala anyway, perhaps the solitary time in his life that he had defied his father's counsel. As with just about everything else, Cyrus Augustus Bible had been right.

Spencer's father had never judged him but instead offered a strong and patient guiding hand. Growing up, Spencer was never forced to do anything. He was introduced to fishing, which he enjoyed well enough, if for no other reason than it had allowed him to spend quality time with his dad. Hunting was another story, as evidenced by Spencer's retching behind a spruce tree when he was shown how to field dress an elk.

Although his father had natural athletic talent that enabled him to excel in both football and baseball at the University of Montana, that particular gene eluded Spencer, who eschewed sports in pursuit of interests such as mathematics, cinema, and chess. He had his father's full support when he attempted to establish a chess club at Great Falls High, but the endeavor fizzled after only a few weeks due to lack of interest. "The most successful people," Cyrus reassured him at the time, "are those who have failed the most."

Worthy wisdom aside, Spencer had resolved that he must never fail his father, whom he placed on a pedestal as if the man were chiseled from marble. To be certain, Cyrus was well worthy of the esteem. Considered a civic titan among the citizens of Great Falls, he took great care to lead by example as opposed to directive. It was that quality, perhaps, that Spencer admired most.

Spencer turned off the ignition and walked around the rear of his car. He studied the massive willow tree in the corner of the yard, recalling how he climbed it as a child, sitting by himself for hours at a time. He would wonder what his mother had been like, or how it would have been to have a brother or sister. Being alone with his thoughts felt safe to him, a respite from a world that demanded he succeed, even though no such requirement was ever formally made, least of all by his father.

A cool gust of wind kicked up, pushing a swirl of the great willow's fallen leaves across the yard and rattling the metal "For Sale" sign placed in the matted brown grass. With his father now in assisted living, the under-stated three-bedroom ranch house was no longer needed. After almost a year, there had been no takers. Perhaps local buyers had feared—much like Spencer—that they were incapable to doing justice to his father's legacy.

Spencer had not seen his father in more than a week, and his previous visit had been brief. Cyrus had been irritable, at one point pushing a lunch tray onto the floor and shouting at a nurse. His disease was overtaking him liking rising water over a drowning man. He was trapped within a shell of the icon he once was, the lack of a cure giving him no means of escape. It would only be a matter of time before he wouldn't recognize his only son, and that was something Spencer was not sure he could bear.

Spencer straightened the sign and pushed it deeper into the soil. He pulled his phone from the front pocket of his pants and dialed his office. After four rings, his secretary finally answered. "Rachel, did you contact the *Great Falls Tribune* and cancel the subscription? They're still delivering papers to my dad's house."

"They said not to worry about it," Rachel said with assurance. "We won't be charged for the paper because they have a special promotion going on."

"It's not a matter of *paying* for it," Spencer snapped. "Every time I come over here, there's a bunch of damn papers lying all over the place."

Rachel said nothing, perhaps stunned by Spencer's use of a cuss word, something Cyrus would never abide. Spencer's temples throbbed as he clasped his eyes tightly shut, absorbing the generalized pain of his predic-ament. The ache rooted in his heart radiated far beyond yellow newspapers that were about as significant as a broken shoelace.

"*Please*," he finally said, a strain in his voice. "We really need to sell this house."

He returned to his car and started his engine. Glancing at the cup holder in the front seat, he noticed the empty latte he'd purchased during his first visit to Starlight Coffee. He thought of the woman who worked there, the barista named Lizzie, who had come to visit him. She appeared to like him well enough, for reasons he wasn't quite sure of. He'd kept the first latte cup she had given him, as well as plenty of others that were now stacked in his office. He had visited Starlight nearly every day, exchanging small talk and fighting off hyperventilation as Lizzie prepared his drink. Dreaming of her deep-blue eyes and the way her curls tumbled over her delicate shoulders, he longed to ask her on a date, but sheer terror had kept that idea locked in fantasy.

Leaving the driveway, Spencer gazed once more at the giant willow in the front yard. He no longer enjoyed being alone.

● ● ●

Jack Kelly took the exit off I-90 toward Three Forks, looking for the trailer owned by Randall Boone. The address was located five miles south of town, off a barren stretch of Highway 287.

After making the turnoff and crossing an irrigation ditch, Jack spotted Boone's charcoal-gray truck outside a decaying double-wide about three hundred yards up the two-track. Exhaust spewed from the dual pipes at the rear of the vehicle. Boone burst out of the front door of the trailer, cigarette dangling from the side of his mouth, a large black hefty bag in each of his hands. He hurled both bags into the back of his truck.

Jack remembered Rick's admonition not to "antagonize" Boone, and he figured that playing chicken on a two-track would probably qualify. He swerved onto a dirt road that paralleled the irrigation ditch, rolling to a stop behind a collection of cottonwoods that shielded him from view. Peering through a patch of shrubs, he watched as Boone walked around the side of the trailer, where he reached into a rusted metal oil drum and pulled out another plastic bag. He threw it in back with the others, jumped into his cab, and put the truck in gear. His oversized tires kicked up gravel as he roared down the two-track, crossed the irrigation ditch, and accelerated north on Highway 287.

Jack turned his rig around and got out to the highway, falling in line behind a propane truck that provided an ideal buffer to tail Boone. Detective instincts took over. "Garbage day, Mr. Boone?" he told his empty cab. "One man's trash just might be another man's treasure." He followed Boone back toward Three Forks, figuring the hunter might stop off at the fenced-in green boxes on the south end of town. Instead, Boone continued north, taking a left onto the ramp for I-90 West. He drove for thirty miles, Jack following him at a distance, ducking behind semis while trying to maintain Boone's eighty-mile-per-hour rate of speed.

Boone veered off the interstate near the town of Whitehall, heading north on Route 399. About a mile in, he turned down a gravel road toward a small group of green boxes. Jack continued down 399, trying to avoid suspicion. He pulled over after about a quarter-mile, watching in his rearview mirror as Boone emerged from the disposal site and headed back toward I-90.

As he bounded through chuckholes leading inside the fence that surrounding the site, Jack studied the circle of containers, their green paint flecked with rust and displaying blanched white stenciled letters that read "NO METAL." He stopped his truck and reached into the storage compartment of the center console, then pulled on a pair of nitrile gloves. Walking alongside the containers, he searched for the three bags he'd watched Boone load into his truck. Most of the containers were filled with empty cardboard boxes or household trash in white plastic bags. He winced as he approached the fifth container, which had the hooves of a skinned elk dangling over the side, a collection of horse flies attacking the scant flesh that remained on its discarded fur. Placing his handkerchief over his nose and mouth to ward off the stench, he glanced briefly inside before continuing on. After scanning the smaller containers and finding nothing, he looked across the site to see two more. They were three times as large as the others, similar in size to those used to transport cargo. Jack spotted a discarded five-gallon paint bucket and used it to pull himself up the side of the container. Gasping for air from the effort, he looked down at the collection of trash and hit pay dirt. Three black Hefty bags were lying in the corner next to a dented baseboard heater and two torn window screens.

Using his stomach as a fulcrum, Jack reached for the closest bag. As he held his breath to ward off the foul odor of the container, his fingers feathered for the plastic. He could touch it but was unable to get a firm grip. He rose back up, drew a deep breath, and tried again. Gripping the metal side panel, he extended farther, his hips teetering on the edge. He grasped the bag and tugged it, but instead of pulling it toward him, he found himself losing his balance and plummeting into the container, landing flat on his back among the rubbish. Blinking rapidly as he stared at the sky, he wagged his head to regain his senses, his eyes drifting left to discover the unhappy remains of an Egg McMuffin. He raised himself up on his elbows, the sleeves of his uniform shirt now drenched in unidentifiable goo.

He rose to his feet, stared at his gloved hands, and wiped them on his pants. He tore into the first plastic bag. Empty beer bottles, two pizza cartons, nothing else. The second bag contained more of the same. "C'mon," he whispered softly as he gripped the third bag, spreading it wide as if opening a curtain. Among household trash he spotted a crumpled cotton T-shirt that was stiff from stains of dried blood. His lips curled into a broad smile as he held it in front of him, reading the faded words "Metallica, Frisco, 2008." Jack huffed a breath. "Figures," he muttered.

He heard a truck pull up outside the container. Two doors slammed, and a tailgate groaned open. Following an exchange of muffled voices, there was a loud grunt. As he slowly turned and squinted skyward, Jack saw a large object catapult over the side. He held up his forearm to shield himself, but he was too late. He felt backward into the trash, the remains of a bloody elk carcass landing on top of him.

"Goddamn it!" he yelled.

"Shit!" he heard a voice say. "There's someone in there."

Jack shivered as he feverishly wrestled the skin off of him. He struggled to his feet, clawing his way up the side of the container to see the truck speeding away, its tailgate still ajar.

His cell phone rang. He wiped the slime off the nitrile glove on his right hand and reached for his phone. "Yeah," he said as his chest heaved. "This is Kelly."

"You okay?" Rick asked. "You sound like you're out of breath."

Jack wheezed as he studied the interior of the container. "You might say I'm in the dumps," he said flatly.

Rick was silent for a moment, perhaps confused. "What happened with Boone? Everything go … *smoothly?*"

"Don't worry—I didn't antagonize him," Jack said. "In fact, I didn't even *talk* to him."

"Where are you now?"

"Whitehall."

"Whitehall?" Rick said, voice rising. "How did you—"

"I'm on my way back," Jack said, his breathing gradually returning to normal. "And I'm bringing the shirt."

"*The* shirt?"

"*The* shirt," Jack repeated. "I don't think he didn't want us to find it, but I did."

"Great work," Rick said.

Jack forced an uneasy chuckle and looked around the inside of the dumpster. "Yeah," he said. "Great work."

CHAPTER 25

Amber McRae kept looking at the gas gauge of her 2002 Tahoe, perhaps hoping her intense glare might somehow prevent it from sinking toward Empty faster than a setting sun. She'd checked her purse before she left the house, finding eleven dollars and scattered change. Her debit card was with her. Maybe that would work.

The physical therapy clinic, located just west of Bozeman in Belgrade, was willing to send a bill for her copay as opposed to requiring immediate payment for services rendered. She prayed they wouldn't realize that their previous three statements were sitting in a kitchen drawer, envelopes unopened.

The rearview mirror framed the sinless face of her child. Gabe was staring directly at her from his car seat, his bright-blue eyes twinkling with adoration. He seemed thoroughly convinced that his mother would take care of him, always doing what was best. On the days they visited the physical therapy clinic she felt like anything but a heroine.

As Amber exited the interstate at Jackrabbit Trail, Gabe's expression abruptly changed. "No doctor, Mommy!" he shrieked, his eyes flooding with tears. "No doctor!" Amber drew a deep breath when a solitary chime rang from her dashboard. She watched helplessly as an orange warning light indicated her tank was nearly dry. "No doctor!" Gabe shouted again.

"Don't cry, sweetheart," she said in the gentlest voice she could muster.

It was a common ritual. She would load Gabe into the SUV, changing the subject whenever he would ask where they were going. She hoped he would think they were bound for the market or perhaps a sitter. Once they exited Jackrabbit Trail, all hell would break loose.

The physical therapy provided by the clinic was purported to help increase mobility. Sessions were paid for with insurance from Garrett's place of work. Even with his employer paying half the premium, keeping the coverage in force presented the family with one of their larger monthly expenses. Amber had suggested that they explore a state-run program as opposed to private insurance, but Garrett wouldn't have it. He said the clinic was their best chance of helping her son. Amber reluctantly agreed, accommodating a husband pierced by overwhelming guilt.

She considered it sheer folly to think that her son would ever gain "mobility," as they had promised. The notion that he would frolic gaily in the tall Montana native grasses, the way he did in her dream, was pure fantasy. She was convinced the physical therapy served no other purpose than to stem the tide of Gabe's further deterioration, and it would be powerless to slow the steady, universal decay that was occurring within the McRae family home.

To make matters worse, Amber's husband was missing. That meant he wasn't working. No work, no insurance. With no insurance, there would be no clinic.

Amber pulled into a parking space. Her temples ached when Gabe wailed again from the backseat. "No, Mommy!" he yelled. "No doctor!"

She slammed the driver's side door and walked to the back of the Tahoe. The hinges of the rear door groaned as she tugged it open and reached inside to retrieve Gabe's tiny wheelchair.

It took everything she had to hold back tears of her own.

• • •

Meredith Hart paced the floor in the living room of her mother's house, cell phone pressed to her ear. She'd been trying to contact Brian Scott all morning, getting voice mail each time. She'd heard that the mission to locate Garrett McRae had officially resumed, but no one from the search dog team had notified her with a time to report for duty.

Monday was her regular day off from her job at the Forest Service. Her mother had fallen asleep. Thank God.

Brian finally picked up.

"Yes, Meredith?" he asked, his voice threaded with exasperation.

"Why haven't you called?" she snapped. "I heard the search for Garrett was back on, but—"

"The search is back on, but I can't let you be part of it."

Meredith's face twitched in disbelief. "You have to be shitting me. Why *wouldn't* I be part of it?"

"My call," Brian said. "I'm pissed you went rogue on Friday. People are lining up to rip me a new one."

Brian was normally an easygoing guy. Calm and collected. She'd liked him from the moment she joined Search and Rescue. They'd shared a beer or two. She considered him a friend. What wasn't he telling her?

"Is this about that friggin' backpack?" she shouted. "I made a mistake, okay? But I took that asshole coroner right to the spot where I found it!"

Brian paused before answering, calmly allowing Meredith's anger to dissipate like a ripple in a lake. "The backpack didn't help, either," he said in a measured tone. "But that's not the main reason."

"What then?"

She heard Brian exhale. "This one might be a little close to home for you."

A series of phlegm-soaked coughs rattled from her mother's bedroom. "Meredith?" the woman croaked. "Meredith! I need a glass of water!"

Meredith pressed the phone against her breast. "In a minute, Mother!" she shouted, her head about to detonate. She drew a breath and returned to the call. "Brian, what are you saying? What do you mean this is a little close to home?"

"I'd prefer not to get into it."

"No, Brian," she said, voice rising again. "You really *need* to get into it."

Another round of hacks echoed from the bedroom. "Meredith!" her mother shouted in a breathless bellow succeeded by a lengthy wheeze..

"You have to know there are rumors," Brian said.

"What kind of rumors?"

"About you and Garrett."

Meredith began to answer but hesitated. Yeah, boy, she knew of the rumors. She and Garrett were close. Everyone saw it. Once Garrett began experiencing problems at home, everyone assumed the obvious. Meredith could have denied them. She hadn't.

"I want to be on this mission," Meredith said in a desperate, shivering voice. "I *have* to be on this search."

"I'm sorry, Meredith. I've made my decision."

Meredith ended the call and walked into the kitchen. She laid her phone on the counter and began to fill a glass of water. Her entire body felt empty.

• • •

Amber McRae sat in the lobby of the clinic, her fingers tenderly stroking Gabe's blond hair as he sat in his wheelchair. He was quiet now but hardly calm, his fearful eyes void of trust.

She threw occasional glances toward the front desk, where a gray-haired woman with half-lens glasses busily tapped a keyboard while staring at a computer screen. Their eyes met a couple of times, but the woman offered only a tight smile. Amber wondered whether someone had discovered that the McRae account was seriously in arrears.

A toned thirty-something physical therapist appeared and squatted next to Gabe. She wore blue scrubs that matched her eyes, her brown hair tamed in a long ponytail that trailed down the back of her neck. "My name's Heather," she said, her lips curling open to expose rows of perfect white teeth. "This must be Gabe!" Amber flicked a cautious smile, having never seen Heather before. Gabe's eyes blinked with skepticism.

Heather caressed Gabe's face with the back of her fingers and stepped behind his chair. Amber began to stand, but Heather gently touched her arm. "Mrs. McRae, it's probably best that you stay out here."

Amber shook her head rapidly, glancing at Gabe and then back at Heather. "But I always go in with him," she protested. "He *needs* me in there with him."

"We want to make sure he is making progress. I'm told that with you nearby, he doesn't seem as focused."

I'm told? What is that supposed to mean? A flood of warmth flowed into her cheeks. Was this about their insurance, or perhaps the bills not being paid? She swallowed hard as she sat in her chair. Gabe's eyes filled with terror as Heather began to wheel him away. His torso twisted, both arms flailing over the side of his chair. "No!" he yelped. "Mommy!" Heather leaned down and said something in his ear, which did little to soothe him. "Mommy! Mommy!" he shouted again before disappearing down a hallway.

Amber slumped forward, her face buried in her hands. A sudden chill washed over her. "Can I get you something, Mrs. McRae?" she heard the woman at the front desk say. "A cup of water, perhaps?" Amber did not look up, instead wagging her head as her face remained glued to her palms. After several moments she slumped back into the chair and exhaled, her entire body weighted with exhaustion.

She stared straight ahead, her eyes zombied on a flat-screen television mounted in the corner of the waiting room. The sound was muted, streams of closed-captioned words trickling across the screen. A female reporter, hair blowing in a stiff wind, was interviewing a woman named Darla, all of four foot eleven, maybe eighty-five or so, her sun-weathered face splattered with liver spots. They were standing near the entrance of an Eastern Montana ranch that served as a haven for battered women. Turns out Darla had started the ranch after finishing a stretch at Deer Lodge for putting six slugs into the chest of her abusive husband. "When a woman's had enough, she's had enough," Darla pointed out.

A conglomerate named Newtrend was planning an oil pipeline that would run directly through Darla's land, forcing the ranch to close. The woman had carried her plight to the internet, creating a YouTube video that had already garnered more than a million views.

Amber turned her head toward the hallway that had swallowed her disabled son like the gaping mouth of a savage beast. Dense clouds of guilt descended upon her. She felt helpless, sitting idly by as Gabe had been spirited away to the torture chamber. *What kind of mother am I?* A silver-rimmed clock on the wall told her that only minutes had passed. Her eyes drifted back to the television, air leaving her lungs as the screen displayed a photo of her husband.

She rose from her chair and approached the TV, squinting to watch the words streaming across the bottom. "Authorities have discovered a backpack and hiking boots that are believed to belong to missing hunter Garrett McRae."

Missing backpack? Hiking boots? Amber's heart thumped. *Why wasn't I told?*

She stormed over to her purse and fumbled for her phone. Her hand was shaking as she scrolled through the list of recent calls, searching for the number of the Dexter County Sheriff's Office. Hitting Send and pressing the phone to her ear, her anger rose as she paced the blue-gray carpet of the waiting room.

"Dexter County Sheriff's Office, this is Helen. How may—"

"Where the hell is Morrand?" Amber said through gritted teeth.

"Excuse me?"

"Sheriff Morrand!" she repeated. "Where the hell is he?"

Helen sounded unfazed. "Sheriff Morrand isn't in the office at the moment. May I ask who is calling, please?"

"This is Amber McRae," she shouted. "I need to talk to Sheriff Morrand, and I need to talk to him now!"

"Yes, Mrs. McRae. We've met before. I'm sorry, but as I told you, he's not—"

"Then where is he?"

"I'm sorry, ma'am, but we don't disclose that information. Now, if I can take down your information, I can have him call you."

"He has my information!" Amber snarled, drawing a glare from the woman seated at the front desk. "He promised to call me if there were any developments involving my husband. Instead, I'm getting information from a goddamn news station!"

"I'm sorry that happened, ma'am, and I'm sure Sheriff Morrand will be happy to discuss it with you. If I could get your number again—"

"Ahhhh!" Amber cried as she ended the call, gripping her phone in an attempt to crush it. She doubled over, her face tightening into a grimace. When she stood, the room spun. The woman seated behind the front counter had dropped her jaw in astonishment.

Amber heard a sound from the hallway where Heather had taken Gabe. As she drew closer, she recognized repeated high-pitched screams that could only belong to a child. *My child.* "That's it! I'm done!" she shouted as she started down the hallway.

"Ma'am, you can't go down there," a voice called behind her.

Amber burst through a pair of double doors that opened up into a large mirrored therapy room filled with padded tables, walking ramps, and treadmills. Gabe lay on one of the tables, flat on his back, Heather raising his tiny left leg into the air and bending it into the shape of a wishbone. Her child appeared to be in unbridled agony.

"Stop!" Amber shouted as she stormed across the room. When Gabe heard his mother, he turned toward her, his face beet red and a torrent of tears gushing down his cheeks.

"Get away from him!" she screamed. "Get away from my son!"

Heather calmly laid Gabe's leg onto the table and stepped back. "It's not as bad as it sounds, Mrs. McRae. He's making progress; he really is. This is normal."

Amber's eyes widened. "Normal?" she shrieked. "You call this *normal?* I don't think so. You people should be arrested for child abuse." She gently lifted Gabe from the table and placed him in the wheelchair as Gabe continued to wail. "I'm so sorry, baby," she said, choking back emotion. "I should have never brought you here."

"Don't go, Mrs. McRae," Heather pleaded. "He's showing improvement."

Amber didn't answer as she wheeled Gabe out of the room, her chest aching as she listened to his muffled whimpers. She'd never felt so alone. Her mind and heart longed for her husband. Why had she forsaken him, getting tied up with a loser like Randall Boone?

She wondered what she had done.

• • •

Rick looked at his watch as he drove back toward Riverton. It was shortly after one o'clock, and he was less than ten minutes away from Janice Tillotson's office. He prayed Sage would still be there.

She explicitly instructed him to stay away from her first appointment, saying that she would be going through treatments for months, and his presence was not required. He'd finally agreed, but that did little to ease the hollow feeling he'd had in his stomach throughout the morning. If he'd learned anything in his fifty-three years on Earth, it was that women—most particularly Sage Fontenot—did not always say what they meant.

As he pulled into the small parking lot off Main Street, he spotted Sage's truck. When he approached the front desk, a nurse he didn't recognize rose from her chair as though expecting him. "Good morning, Sheriff," she said politely, brushing her hands across the flowered top of her scrubs. "My name's Bernadette. Ms. Fontenot should be done shortly, but I can take you down the hallway if you'd like to sit with her."

"I'd like that," Rick said, slightly above a whisper. He followed Bernadette down a lavender-carpeted corridor leading to a door that cautioned "Do Not Disturb." The nurse tapped the door with her knuckles before entering. Sage's chair didn't appear to be especially comfortable, but that didn't prevent her from leaning her head against the wall as she enjoyed a peaceful sleep. She wore ear buds that were connected to her phone, most likely listening to music she had downloaded.

As Bernadette quietly closed the door, Rick sat in a chair next to Sage, biting the side of his lower lip as he studied her features. He had known her since she was a little girl, maybe five years old. She had followed him around relentlessly, proclaiming her unabashed crush to anyone who would listen, ignoring the fact that Rick was nearly ten. Growing up in rural Montana, where schoolmates often lived miles apart, Rick took Sage under his wing, treating her as a kid sister, not knowing she would grow into a beautiful woman and trusted friend. She had loved him unconditionally through his years of relentless trials, never expecting or demanding that he love her in return.

But he did love her, much more deeply than he had ever imagined or had ventured to admit. This was her time of need, and her desire to shield him from her immeasurable fears was of little consequence. Tough as she was, she had to be scared to death. It was his turn and his time to share her burden.

He watched her eyes open as he gently touched the top of her arm. Her skin was warm, almost feverish. The corners of her lips rose into a smile as she reached for his hand and squeezed it. If she was upset that he was there, she didn't show it.

"Hello, Sheriff Morrand," she murmured. "I wasn't expecting you."

Rick eased closer to her, stroking the side of her face with the back of his hand. "How are you feeling?"

"I'm dying," she said, pausing a beat before adding, "of thirst."

Rick spotted a plastic pitcher of water on a nearby counter, a straw protruding from its pink lid. He eased the straw toward Sage's cracked, dry lips. She drank the water for several seconds before tilting her head back and drawing a deep breath through her nose. After removing her ear buds, she touched her phone. "Looks like it went dead," she said, her lips pushed sideways. "What time is it?"

Rick glanced at his watch. "One thirty."

"You're not supposed to be here," Sage said through a yawn. "I thought we agreed on that."

"*You* agreed on that."

"Whatever," she answered. "I didn't expect you to be here."

"I *want* to be here. Are you upset that I came?"

"Yes. I mean, no." Her eyes played coy as she squeezed his hand again. "I'm glad you're here."

Rick leaned forward and kissed her. He heard a quick knock before the door opened. Bernadette flashed a tight smile, a pink color spilling across her face. "Excuse me," she said. "Sheriff, if you can give me a moment, I can take some vitals and bring Ms. Fontenot out to the lobby. Will you be driving her home? It's probably a good idea."

Rick nodded. "Yes. Definitely."

"What about my truck?" Sage protested.

"Your truck can stay here," Rick said. "Last I heard, Riverton doesn't have a very high incidence of car theft."

A short time later, Bernadette brought Sage out to the lobby. She appeared fatigued and walked as if barefoot on hot asphalt. Rick lifted a jeans jacket off her arm and helped her put it on. She hooked her hand around his bicep, and they turned toward the door.

"Oh, Ms. Fontenot?" Bernadette said behind them. "May I take another look at your insurance card?"

"Is there a problem?" Sage asked, fishing it out of the top pocket of her jacket.

"Oh, I don't think so," Bernadette said with confidence. "Sometimes our photocopies come out a little blurry. I just wanted to make sure I had the correct number."

Bernadette smiled as she wrote down a string of digits on a sheet of paper that had black-and-white images of Sage's driver's license and insurance card. "Probably a computer glitch." She handed the card back to Sage. "Their phone lines get pretty tied up in the late afternoon, but I'll call them first thing in the morning."

Sage's forehead tightened. "Is there—?"

"Please don't worry, Ms. Fontenot," she said. "I'm sure everything is just fine."

CHAPTER 26

Charlie Duchesne gulped a mouthful of coffee as he stared at the computer monitor on his desk early Tuesday morning. Adjusting his peepers on the bridge of his nose, he lurched his chair forward, its ancient metal casters squealing on the tile floor.

He had discovered two sets of fingerprints on the backpack that he believed belonged to Garrett McRae. The prints had been sent to Helen Pritchard at the sheriff's office late Monday afternoon. Helen's duties, of course, extended far beyond simply handling dispatch, and it was Charlie's request that she forward the prints back east to the FBI's Integrated Automated Fingerprint Identification System or IAFIS. Charlie hadn't expected such a timely response, but Helen had a way of endearing herself to the personnel of various law enforcement agencies, possessing an authentic gift of gab that meshed seamlessly with her numerous years on the job. She was a far more accomplished people person than Charlie was, the coroner thought, smiling to himself.

Charlie was confident that one set of prints belonged to Garrett McRae. Though he didn't expect to confirm his assumption through the criminal justice system, he did in fact learn that Garrett had been arrested for driving under the influence. Charlie wondered whether the charge had resulted in a conviction, since it may well have jeopardized McRae's standing as an EMT, not to mention his role with Search and Rescue.

The report on the second set of prints was far more puzzling. Given what little he'd heard from folks at the sheriff's office, Charlie anticipated he would receive a generous rap sheet belonging to one Randall Boone. Yet, while he did receive a criminal record that included convictions for drug possession, domestic violence, and assault, as well as a warrant for a charge of attempted murder, there was no mention whatsoever of Randall Boone.

Charlie felt blood drain from his face as he looked at the screen. He began to type a new email before stopping abruptly, deciding his desire for a prompt answer would not be found in the digital age. He yanked the receiver off of his rotary phone and dialed the sheriff's office. Thankfully, Helen answered after one ring.

"Helen, it's Charlie."

"I know, Charlie," she answered. "We have Caller ID."

"Has the sheriff come in yet?"

"I'm expecting him shortly. Is there something—?"

"Did you happen to look at these fingerprint reports returned from IAFIS?" he asked, pronouncing the acronym *AY-fiss*.

"*Nooooo*," Helen answered skeptically, her tone suggesting she considered the question some kind of trap.

"I need you to contact the sheriff's office in Frisco, Texas. I think they're somewhere around Dallas. See what they can tell you about a James Edward Davis."

"Frisco is just north of Dallas," Helen said. "I had a cousin who lived there. Rose. Lived in Frisco all her life. Went to see her years ago and had to fly into Dallas. Do you realize they actually have trains going around inside their airport? And, oh, the traffic! Rose is gone now, of course—"

"Helen, I need this as fast as possible," Charlie said, his voice corded with urgency. "And I need a picture. It's very important that I get a picture."

"James Edward Davis," Helen said, her voice all business. "I'll get right on it, Charlie." She paused a beat. "Any chance you can tell me what's going on? Any info I should pass along to Sheriff Morrand?"

Charlie exhaled. "Well, I can't be sure until I see a picture. But it appears to me that Randall Boone is not Randall Boone."

● ● ●

Spencer Bible hesitated as he walked through the front door of his agency, his eyes fixed on the man who was already seated in his office. Rachel was at her desk, motionless with interlocked fingers, as though any movement might discharge an explosive device.

Taking a nervous sip from his paper Starlight Coffee cup, Spencer pointed toward the plate-glass window. "Is that …?" he asked in a whisper. Rachel nodded slowly, her face tensed with fright.

Walter Reynolds, Executive Vice President of Sales for Nexus Life and Casualty Insurance, was hard to miss. With his bodybuilder's physique and thick head of synthetic black hair, he looked much younger than his fifty-four years. A Rolex El Presidente perpetually gleamed from his wrist, and it was rumored that he would travel annually to Milan, Italy, for the singular intent of choosing a new batch of custom-tailored Brioni suits. Having once appeared on the cover of *Fortune Magazine*, he was considered the brains behind the largest insurance company in the nation—a company that underwrote nearly eighty-five percent of business on the books with Western Montana Insurance.

Though Nexus was based in Chicago, it wasn't uncommon for Walter to ride the company's Gulfstream G650 into some of the smaller burgs in the nation, bursting through the front door to check in on unsuspecting brokers as if he was auditioning for the next episode of *Undercover Boss*. With Montana's scenic beauty and opportunities for outdoor adventure, Great Falls had always been a favorite stop for Walter, who would often linger an extra day to hunt or fish. He had always been courteous and respectful to Cyrus Bible, likely due to the fact that Western Montana Insurance Company absolutely dominated the life, health, and casualty markets through the entire expanse of the Pacific Northwest. That is, until Cyrus Bible had the misfortune of falling ill.

Spencer stepped into his office, his senses assaulted by Walter's cologne. Drawing a deep breath, he placed his cup on the corner of his cluttered desk and extended his hand. "Good morning, Mr. Reynolds," he said. "I certainly wasn't expecting you."

Glancing at the papers strewn across the desk, Walter seemed to agree. He rose from his chair and shook Spencer's hand. "Hello, Spencer," he said flatly. "I'm glad you made it in. Do you always arrive after nine?"

Spencer absorbed Walter's greeting like a sharp slap across the face. "We open at nine" was the best he could offer.

"I see," Walter said, returning to his chair. He stared at his fingers, rubbing them together to shed unwanted dust, be it real or imaginary. He lifted a black leather folio off the chair next to him and spread it open on his lap. "Anyway, I had a few things I wanted to talk to you about."

Spencer sat down nervously, the back of his chair rolling into the credenza behind him. He jostled a few framed photos, knocking over one of his father. After straightening it, he turned back toward his visitor.

"Oh," Walter said, suddenly realizing he had forgotten something. "How is your dad?" The question appeared rooted in obligation as opposed to genuine concern.

"He's fine," Spencer said. "I mean, he's not *fine*, but … He's fine."

Walter nodded, apparently satisfied with the sliver of time he'd devoted to the subject. He began to flip through the pages of the notebook inside the folio. Spencer found himself staring at the toupee on Walter's head, wondering whether it might present some kind of fire hazard. In Spencer's experience, Montanans weren't all that big on artificial hair. When your hair fell out, it fell out. That was it. His father had told him that if a man was going to put something fake on top of his head, that probably was just the tip of the iceberg. Cyrus had never explicitly verbalized it, but Spencer assumed he was not a huge fan of Walter Reynolds.

"What can you tell me about Henry and Eleanor Gustafson?" Walter asked.

Spencer shrugged his shoulders. "They're clients," he said with measure. "Longtime clients. Great people."

"Great people and great clients," Walter said. "Owners of three life policies, as a matter of fact." He paused and stared at his watch, more in admiration than concern for the time. "So, we get a call at the main office from Mr. Gustafson the other day, and he wants to know how to cash out two of the policies and transfer the funds elsewhere. He claims you're the one who advised him to explore this option." Walter rolled his tongue on the inside of his cheek. "I'm sure that you are aware that whole life policies are profitable for the company?"

Spencer nodded.

"And that Nexus Life and Casualty is in business to make a profit?"

Spencer slid a finger along the inside of his collar, which suddenly felt snug. "Well, of course," he said, flashing a brief, uneasy smile. "Everybody—"

"Spencer, do you know what a persistency rate is?" Spencer began to answer, but Walter wouldn't allow it. "The persistency rate is the percentage of an insurance company's already written policies that remain in force, without lapsing or being replaced by policies of other insurers. Put simply, it's the amount of business you keep on the books."

Warmth flooded into Spencer's face. "I am aware what persistency is, Mr. Reynolds. I believe—"

Walter raised an open palm, commanding Spencer's silence. "Did you know that your father had the highest persistency rate in the country?"

Spencer nodded slowly, his brain drifting to the boxes of awards stacked inside a shed behind his father's house. The agency Cyrus Bible had built received countless sales honors over the decades, ones he declined to display in public lest he appear immodest. "I am well aware of my father's retention rate."

"*Persistency*," Walter said. "I prefer the word *persistency*."

"Persistency," Spencer mumbled. Walter's persistence made his head throb.

Walter straightened his watch. "I regret to say that the persistency rate of this agency under your leadership has, shall we say, *plummeted*. You are hardly in a position to be giving business away."

Spencer touched his forehead, which was clammy with sweat. "I wouldn't say I've been giving business away."

"What would you call it then?"

"Like I said, the Gustafsons are great people," he stammered. "I was trying to do what was best for them."

Walter sat up, resting his elbows on the arms of his chair and pressing his manicured fingers together to form a steeple. "Why isn't whole life insurance best for them?"

Spencer shrugged. "I just thought their money might be better invested somewhere else."

"With another company?"

"I was just trying to do the right thing."

"So now you're a financial planner?"

"Well, I did take a workshop."

"A workshop," Walter repeated, his tone colored with disdain. He straightened in his chair, adjusted his Brioni suit jacket, and cleared his throat. "Spencer," he said gently, perhaps shifting into good cop mode, "I would like you to consider something."

"Sir?" Spencer asked sheepishly.

"Perhaps the company can have someone come in to work with you."

"*Work* with me?"

"You know, provide some guidance," Walter said. "Let's face it, Spencer—with your father being ill, you are going through a tough time."

"I'm fine, sir," Spencer said rapidly. "My father built this agency, and I made a promise to him that I would run it. I really don't want any help."

"Think about it."

"Sir, I really don't need—"

Walter pointed his index finger toward Spencer. "*Think* about it," he repeated. Snapping his folio shut, he rose from his chair and extended his hand. "Please give your father my regards. I would have liked to have seen him, but—"

Spencer used the back of his trousers to quickly swipe the perspiration off his palm. "I'll give him your regards." He knew damn well his father likely wouldn't have a clue who in the hell Walter Reynolds was. He wondered whether patients with Alzheimer's had any control over the order in which people were forgotten. If that were the case, dispensing of the memory of Walter would have topped Cyrus Bible's list.

Rachel kept her head buried in paperwork as Walter breezed past her desk without heeding her existence. He glanced at his prized watch one last time before heading out the door and stepping into the backseat of a black Lincoln Town Car, the door held open by a uniformed man void of expression.

Spencer plopped into his chair and leaned backward, once again knocking over the photo of his father. Staring at the picture, he tried to swallow but found himself choked with emotion. He gently returned the frame to the credenza, folded his hands across his lap, and closed his eyes. Though the room was quiet, he felt a strange presence, as though he was being watched.

He slowly opened his eyes and jerked forward in his chair. Leaning against the door, her arms folded across her breasts, was Lizzie, the woman from Starlight Coffee. She wore a billowy white blouse tucked inside tight jeans that hugged her perfect hips. Tilting her head to one side, she blinked nonchalantly, exposing eyes that sparkled like iridescent opals. Her luscious lips formed a mischievous smile. "So, are you going to ask me out or what?"

CHAPTER 27

James Edward Davis was born in Portales, New Mexico, the son of a nameless father whom his mother swore was dead. Sadie Ann Davis described herself as a waitress, though she only traveled to the local diner for twenty hours a week at best. The majority of her income was derived from the parade of male suitors who would arrive each evening at her brown three-room adobe, usually staying no more than an hour at a time. James had strict orders to stay in his room, his moist eyes fixed on a snowy television screen as he tried to ignore the loud rhythmic thumping coming from down the hall. On more than one occasion, having heard the front screen door slam shut, he would peer into the living room, where he saw his mother dressed in a pink silk robe and perched on the edge of a stained and torn yellow couch, her eyes squinting through the smoke of her Virginia Slim as she counted the bills in her hand.

The closest thing he had to a male role model was a colored man named Virgil Skinner, who visited James's mother once or twice a week. As far as James could tell, Virgil and Sadie never had sex, even though Virgil would give her money on occasion. The two adults would sit in the kitchen and drink coffee most of the time, Virgil insisting to Sadie that the pathway to her salvation would require the immediate acquaintance of Jesus Christ. She would chuckle, then rise from her chair and pat Virgil on the shoulder on her way to the cupboard, where she would locate a bottle of caramel-colored liquid to sweeten her coffee. Sometimes she would drink too much, causing her to chase Virgil from the house with a flurry of expletives, but after a few days he would inevitably return.

Virgil took an interest in James, and he even convinced Sadie to let him take the boy hunting. It was Virgil who helped young James bag his first kill, a five-point buck.

When he was ten, James and Sadie moved north to Clovis, leaving Virgil Skinner behind. During his junior year in high school, his mother went missing, her body never found, and the cause of her disappearance undetermined. Virgil was the prime suspect, most likely due to the pigment of his skin. He wasn't charged, and no other suspects were questioned. A local family offered to take James in, but he declined, opting instead to move to Lubbock, Texas, where he landed a job working construction.

Given his upbringing, James was largely unschooled in exercising respect toward women, let alone courting them. He lied to himself, thinking that he didn't want to act like the men who had treated his mother like worthless chattel, somewhat akin to the child of an alcoholic swearing they would never drink. But his mother's loveless behavior had instructed him that women themselves were generally shallow and deceitful, void of self-dignity and destined to depart once they had milked you dry. James would be no Virgil Skinner, that was for sure.

If James possessed a low regard for women, they perhaps held an even lower opinion of him. Most of his early relationships were short-lived, often initiated during drunken stupors in run-down Lubbock roadhouses. The women he preyed upon possessed afflicted pasts born from poor decisions, and they would err once more when they accepted the company of James Edward Davis. He often would offer them a drink, followed by several shots of Cuervo Gold, which invariably led an invitation to a decrepit trailer located off a lightless gravel road on the outskirts of town. Rugged sex would ensue, often bordering on rape. More than one of his visitors had fled his trailer in terror, clothing clutched against her bare breasts, the cold blackness of the Texas prairie ringing with James's laughter as he slugged a longneck on his rotting front porch.

He was reported to law enforcement on two occasions, but prosecutors brought no charges.

After losing a third construction job, he was finally sent away on a burglary rap, serving his time at the Lubbock County Detention Center. Upon his release, he met Dana Avery, then a seventeen-year-old senior at Coronado High School. A church-going girl, Dana was convinced she could save James from eternal damnation. He would chuckle at the notion, reminded of his mother's friend, Virgil, who'd made countless attempts to expel Satan from her soul. James's relationship with Dana was fairly short-lived, but he was reluctant to let her go. She made the tragic error of going to a movie with a classmate, a basketball player named Daniel Rivera. Upon seeing them together, James attacked Daniel in the alley behind the theater, pummeling the boy's face into a bloody pulp while Dana screamed helplessly nearby.

As Daniel lay hospitalized in a coma, deputies sought to arrest James Davis, but he had disappeared. He was headed north to Montana, where he would obtain a fake drivers' license identifying him as Randall Boone. Bozeman was booming, and it was easy to land a job at Eagle Ridge Construction, where the owner possessed only a passing interest in background checks. Eight years into his tenure, Randall Boone befriended a new employee named Garrett McRae, whose wife was named Amber, perhaps the most perfect monument to womanhood Boone had ever seen.

• • •

After driving Sage to her house, Rick headed back to the sheriff's office, hoping to tie up a few loose ends before picking up Abby at school. When he breezed through the front door, Helen raised a palm to stop him, her eyes peeking over the rims of her glasses.

"You don't want to go in there just yet," she said.

Rick cocked his head. "Oh?"

"You ever been in a cage with a wet bobcat before?"

"Can't say that I have."

"Well, you're entering a cage with a wet bobcat."

Rick glanced at the frosted glass window of his office door, then back at Helen. "What exactly are you trying to say?"

"Amber McRae is in your office," Helen answered, pursing her lips. "She ain't happy, to say the least."

Rick blew out a breath and turned the knob to his office. Amber stood in front of his desk, her body rigid, her face blazing red and fire in her eyes. Her son sat in a wheelchair two paces behind her, his gaze fixed on Rick, seemingly curious how the sheriff might fare against the wet bobcat.

"Mrs. McRae, I owe you a sincere apology," Rick said, removing his hat and laying it on the corner of his desk. "I had intended to—"

"You had *intended* to what?" Amber shouted as she stepped toward him. "Did you *intend* to tell me that my missing husband's belongings had been found? When exactly, Sheriff, did you *intend* to tell me?"

Rick turned to close the door of his office and saw Helen standing there, her shoulder leaning against the jamb. She had no plans to move lest authorities be left without a witness to the execution of the local sheriff.

He looked beyond Amber at manila folders that were stacked on the lone chair in front of his desk. "Mrs. McRae, please sit down a moment." He gathered the folders and handed them to Helen, who promptly plopped them onto a file cabinet and stood sentry in the corner of the room.

"You promised to keep me updated on any developments," Amber hissed through her teeth. "You told me that as soon as you knew anything—*any-thing*—you would contact me. Instead, I find out things from watching the news. The goddamned news!"

Rick drew a deep breath and looked at Gabe, who watched him with sheepish eyes. "Mrs. McRae, I don't know if it's appropriate for us to have this discussion in front of your boy."

"No?" she yelled. "Where in the hell would you like me to stash him? This is Gabe's father we're talking about. Aren't we both entitled to know what is going on? That's what you promised." She motioned toward Helen. "Instead, I'm left talking to this bitch."

"Excuse me?" Helen asked, removing her glasses. She started forward as if poked in the back with a hot branding iron. Rick quickly stepped into her path.

"Helen, you need to return to your desk," he said sternly. "Close the door behind you, and give us some privacy."

Helen moved toward the door, eyes glued on Amber. "You need to choose your words more carefully, Sister." Glancing with disdain toward her boss, she slammed the door shut, rattling the frosted glass.

Rick moved his hat aside and sat on the corner of his desk. "Please accept my apology for not providing you with details about your husband," he said in a temperate tone. "I certainly didn't mean to keep you in the dark. I hesitated to call you because I didn't want you to have false hope."

Amber moved closer, her light-brown eyelashes squeezing into a squint. "And exactly who made you the judge of hope?"

Rick flicked his brow upward before averting his eyes. His reasoning had been sound. In the same manner that he had feared the worst when his daughter had gone missing, his hope that Garrett McRae would be found alive was fading by the day. Within his heavy heart, he believed that it was just a matter of time before Amber would walk through the gates of the hot, fiery corridor of horror that he had experienced himself. Offering Amber sporadic details of her husband's demise would only set up mileposts along the road to his inevitable doom.

Still, Amber McRae had a point. It was not his call to make. "Again, I apologize," he said, turning his eyes back toward her. "I promise to contact you the moment we have anything."

"I would certainly hope so." She took a step backward, placed her hands on her hips, and released a sigh. "So, Sheriff, what is it? Is my husband alive or dead?"

Rick looked past her toward Gabe, who blinked at him through weary blue eyes. "Mrs. McRae, we just don't have an answer at this point. I'm sorry."

Amber pursed her lips and shook her head. She released the brake on Gabe's wheelchair and began pushing him toward the door.

Rick cleared his throat and cast an index finger into the air. "Oh, Mrs. McRae—as long as you're here, I do have a couple of questions I'd like to ask."

She stopped, turned toward him, and rolled her eyes. "I really should go. It's been a difficult day, and my son needs some rest."

"This will only take a minute." He motioned toward the empty chair. "Please, have a seat."

"I'd rather stand."

"Suit yourself." He turned his eyes toward her. "I've been hearing some rumors, and I would really like some clarification. What was—or is—the exact relationship between you and Randall Boone?"

Amber's face flushed. "What do you mean?"

"It's not a trick question. It's my understanding that there may have been an extramarital affair."

"Your question is inappropriate, Sheriff. I can't believe you are saying something like that in front of my son."

Rick stood up from the corner of his desk. "A little while ago you wanted him to be all ears."

"Mommy, I want to go home," Gabe whined, now oblivious to the conversation. Amber stroked his silky blond hair. "We're leaving now, sweetheart," she whispered. Drawing a deep breath, she stared at Rick for several seconds. "Sheriff, my husband and I had our difficulties, okay? But that is between Garrett and me."

"That's not necessarily true." Wrath returned to her eyes. He wondered whether he had splashed fresh water on the bobcat.

"What does my personal life have to do with my husband going missing?"

"It may or may not."

"Mommy!" Gabe shrieked. "I want to go home! I'm hungry."

"We'd like to leave now," Amber said.

Rick walked toward his office door and held it open. Amber began to push Gabe forward but paused as she passed within six inches of Rick's face. He could smell her perfume, but she was about as alluring as a cobra. Her long glare made him uncertain whether she would spit or speak.

"Keep me informed, Sheriff," she said with venom. "You just concentrate on keeping me informed."

* * *

Abby walked slowly out of the front door of her school, a broad smile on her face as she admired the messages schoolmates had written on her cast. When she spotted Rick's truck, her lips flattened in disappointment.

"Where's Auntie Sage?" she asked as she climbed into his truck and clicked her seat belt. "I thought she was going to pick me up today."

"Good afternoon to you, too, young lady," Rick said with a chuckle. "Sage is home resting, so I guess you're stuck with me."

"Okay. I guess I'll see her at dinner."

Rick paused for a moment, rubbing his chin as his elbow rested on the console. "Actually, I figured we'd go out to the ranch tonight, let Sage get some sleep."

Abby twisted toward him. "Why? Wasn't today her first day of chemo? We need to take care of her!"

"The best thing we can do is leave her be. It was Sage's request. She doesn't want us fussing over her."

Abby wagged her head. "She's just saying that," she said, suddenly an interpreter of adult female dialogue. "We should be there with her."

"I'm thinking we can all be at the ranch tomorrow night. Maybe we can even move some more of her stuff over there."

Abby glanced at him. "You just don't want to sleep on her couch."

Rick took a short breath, a sharp jolt of pain reminding him that his ribs were only just beginning to heal. "That might be part of it," he offered.

Abby stared out the window. Two horses—a chestnut and an Appaloosa—frolicked across the toasted grass of an open pasture as though playing tag. "I don't see why you don't just sleep in the same bed."

Rick put his hand on Abby's shoulder and leaned toward the passenger seat. "I beg your pardon?"

Abby turned boldly toward him. "I mean, you're getting married. What difference does it make?"

"We're not married yet. That's the difference."

Abby shook her head and rolled her eyes. "Whatever."

The cab grew silent save for occasional bursts of static coming from the mobile radio. Rick studied his granddaughter, who had returned her gaze to the passing fields, this time zeroing in on two dozen Angus strung along a barbed-wire fence. As she edged toward the conclusion of her first decade of existence, Abby had begun to flirt with the outer boundaries of insolence. Rick didn't find this particularly alarming, since experience had taught him children of her age often viewed adults as dull and somewhat witless, unable to understand or keep pace with the complexities of the modern world. This behavior, or course, was a prelude to her becoming a teenager, when her elders likely would be cause for embarrassment, their only utility being their ability to supply food and shelter.

Rick shuddered as he considered Abby growing older, his mind drifting to the conflicts he'd had with Chloe. At times he felt like he had a younger version of his deceased daughter living in his presence. Hell, he would even slip at times and call her Chloe. She was exceedingly bright and insightful for her age, just like her mother had been. Would Abby inherit Chloe's mental illness? There supposedly was a genetic component, one that Rick loathed to consider. Would she fall prey to drug addiction as well?

"When am I going to see my dad?" Abby blurted out.

"I'm working on it."

"That's what you always say."

Bull's-eye. Rick wasn't *working* on anything. There was nothing really to work on. Abby was under the impression that her father was Chase Reddick, a man for whom the term "loser" was overly generous. Chase was incarcerated in Deer Lodge at present, but that was of little consequence. The fact of the matter was that Chase was not Abby's father, and Abby's real father wasn't even alive. The details were complex, to say the least, far beyond the limits of Abby's level of comprehension.

Or so he thought.

"You're probably just stressed," Abby said.

"I'm *stressed?*"

"Yep. That's what my counselor would say."

Rick squinted at her. "You have a counselor? When did you get a counselor?"

Abby shrugged. "A lady came into our classroom and told us that if any of us were feeling stressed, we could see her. I wasn't sure what *stressed* meant, so I asked her. She told me, and I decided I was feeling stressed."

"This is going on in fourth grade?"

"Sure. Why not?"

"What happened to the three R's?"

Abby turned toward him, her forehead crinkled. "What's that?"

"Reading, 'Riting and 'Rithmetic."

"That doesn't make any sense."

More silence. They drove another mile down Highway 89 before Abby lunged forward in her seat. "There's the turnoff to Auntie Sage's house," she proclaimed in a voice suggesting her grandfather had never been there before. They barreled down the road without losing speed.

"We're going to the ranch," Rick said. "You like spaghetti?"

Abby didn't answer.

CHAPTER 28

Abby shrieked when Rick walked into the kitchen on Wednesday morning. She stared at him for several seconds, eyes opened wide and mouth agape. "Do you like it?" Rick asked, stroking his palm across his smooth, hairless head, which he had shaved after Abby had gone to sleep.

"What? … How? … Why?" was all she was able to mutter.

"If Sage is going to be going without hair, so will I," he said with an innocent shrug.

Abby continued to glare at him as she took a bite of her buttered toast. She said nothing during the entire ride to school, opting to study Rick as if he were a museum exhibit. "You really did that for Sage?" she finally asked when they pulled up to the curb.

"Why not?"

She leaned toward him and allowed him to kiss the top of her forehead, their morning ritual. "Cool," she said as she exited his truck and vanished among a throng of chattering classmates.

Helen was on the phone when he walked into the sheriff's office. Her curious eyes watched him walk over to the nearby Mr. Coffee and pour a cup.

"Yes sir, I have placed the information on his desk," Helen said. "He just walked in, so I'm sure he will be calling you as soon as he's had a chance to review everything." She glanced at Rick again as her head bobbed up and down. "Yes sir, I realize that it's urgent. He'll be back in touch with you shortly."

Rick watched Helen hang up the phone. "So, what information is on my desk and why is it so urgent?" He took a sip of coffee, which tasted like burnt rubber. More than once he'd requested that Helen wait until he got in before putting coffee on. She never complied.

"Everything is organized on your desk," Helen said. "You probably want to see it to believe it."

Rick drank more coffee, strictly for purposes of loading up on caffeine. "Can you give me a hint?"

Helen picked up a pen off her desk and rolled it between her thumb and forefinger. "Let's just say it involves the alleged Randall Boone."

"The *alleged* Randall Boone?"

She flicked her head toward Rick's office. "It's all there sitting on your desk."

Rick started toward the coffee machine to refill his cup but thought better of it. He walked past Helen's desk, when she stopped him. "You okay, Sheriff?"

"Of course. Why do you ask?"

"Something about you looks different."

"I'm fine," he said, wagging his head. He entered his office, hanging his hat on a rickety wooden rack and placing his cup next to a closed manila file folder on his desk. Plopping into his chair, he used both hands to stroke the top and sides of his scalp. His skin was smooth and soft, aside from the scabs that remained from his grizzly encounter. Negotiating his razor around the remaining stitches had been a challenge.

There was a quick double tap on the glass portion of Rick's office door before it opened, Helen's normal mode of entry. She took two steps and froze. "Holy shit," she said.

"How's it look?"

"I never realized your ears were so big" was all Helen could offer. She stared at him a beat before looking at his desk. "Did you take a look at that file?"

"Not yet." Rick rolled his chair forward as his fingertips feathered the side of his temples. "Let's see what's so important and urgent involving Randall Boone." He opened the file and picked up a sheet of paper with the logo of the Denton County Sheriff's Office at the top. There was a large black-and-white photo in the middle of the page, showing a man with a goatee and a crescent-shaped scar above his brow.

"Damn! That's Randall Boone."

"Only it ain't Randall Boone."

"James Edward Davis," Rick said. "Wanted in Texas for attempted murder, among other things." He began turning the pages inside the folder, throwing occasional glances at Helen. "How did you come about this information?"

"Charlie. He was running prints through IAFIS and found this … discrepancy."

"Was that the sheriff from Texas on the phone when I came in?"

"Yes sir. Glenn Turley. Been sheriff down there for over twenty years. Quite a character, that one. Seems pretty eager to get his hands on Boone … or Davis, I guess I should say. He'll be faxing a warrant this morning. He wants you to hold the guy until they can get up here."

"Does Jack know about this?"

"Not all of the details," Helen said.

"Fill him in. Meanwhile, I'll give this sheriff a call."

Rick watched Helen nod and turn toward the door. "So you think my ears look big?" he shouted after her.

"Let's say that style might have to grow on me," she said over her shoulder.

Rick put his phone on speaker and dialed the Denton County Sheriff's Office. A few moments later a crawling baritone came on the line. "This is Glenn Turley," he said, his first name sounding like "Glynn." A loud bite of an apple followed. "How may I help you?"

"Sheriff, this is Rick Morrand in Montana."

"Well, hey, Rick," Turley drawled. "Thank you for calling me back."

"How're things down in Texas?"

"Hotter than a devil's dick. Must be that global warming they keep talking about."

Rick lunged forward and took his phone off speaker. "I understand you have some interest in a suspect we have up here?"

Turley took another chomp of his apple. "I'm told one of our shit stains managed to make his way to Montana."

Rick stared at his handset as he held it away from his ear. "If the *shit stain* you are referring to is named James Edward Davis, that would be correct, Sheriff. Up here, he's been going by the name of Randall Boone."

"He can call himself whatever he wants, but that's Davis," Turley continued. "I was involved in the original arrest of that butt-sucker. Now, there's one who shoulda been returned to the birth canal from the get-go. He beat up a young boy, Danny Rivera, who was pretty well liked in this town, even being Mexican. Amazing what the ability to shoot a three-pointer can do for ethnic relations." Rick heard a final bite of an apple followed by the clang of the core falling into an empty metal trash can. "Anyway, we just faxed a warrant over to you, and we'd be much obliged if you could pick him up. I'll be sending deputies up there A-SAP."

"I'd like to do that, Sheriff, but Mr. Davis doesn't live in our jurisdiction," Rick said. "He's in Gallatin County. The sheriff over there is a friend of mine. I'd be happy to—"

"What's his name?" Turley asked.

"*Her* name is Patricia Martin. We went to high school together."

"She's a girl, huh?"

Rick rolled his eyes. "I'd describe her more as a woman by now. A pretty tough one at that."

"Hmmm," Turley said. "Perhaps you could give her a holler on my behalf. For some reason, female officers don't always appreciate my style." He let out a chuckle. "At least, that was the case with the two I married."

"I'm stunned," Rick murmured as he rested his chin on the mouthpiece of his phone. He picked up the sheet of paper on his desk and stared at the photo of the man he had come to know as Randall Boone. *Shit stain.* The fact that his true name was James Edward Davis was just one of several unanswered questions surrounding him. From the moment Rick had laid eyes on him, he suspected foul play. The more he learned, the more his suspicions intensified. All he needed was more proof, and that would require time.

"You still there, Rick?"

"I'm here, Sheriff."

"Please call me Glynn."

"How quickly do you think you'll be sending people up here? As you might expect, the fires have strained all of our resources, and it might take Patty a day or so to round this guy up."

"We're anxious to get our hands on him," Turley said. "That sombitch is the worst piece of trailer trash ever to stumble out of a single-wide. As soon as y'all grab him, I'll put a couple of deputies on the road."

"Got it ... Glenn," Rick forced himself to say. "We'll be in touch."

• • •

Even though Rick and Sheriff Patty Martin had discussed official business over the phone on a few occasions, Rick hadn't seen her in years. He recalled her as Patty Barber at Jim Bridger High, her face sprinkled with freckles and her long auburn hair pulled tight into a long braid that reached the small of her back. Wearing patterned Western shirts tucked into her Levi's, she leaned a bit on the portly side, with broad shoulders, a muscular chest, and buttocks that could generously fill a saddle.

During their sophomore year, Patty found herself smitten with Rick Morrand and had followed him relentlessly through the Bridger hallways and all around campus. If the term "stalker" had been in fashion back then,

Patty most certainly would have fit the description. This didn't sit well with young Sage Fontenot, who was already several years into her own lifelong crush. The girls' crisscrossed yearnings produced inevitable strife, and even though Sage was smaller and two years younger, she and Patty engaged in a spirited hair-puller outside the girls' locker room before faculty managed to intervene. Fortunately for all concerned, Patty Barber was eventually swept off her feet by Wesley Martin, a two-hundred-sixty-pound lineman who transferred to Bridger from South Dakota. Last Rick had heard, they'd been married for decades.

As he picked up his handset and flipped through his Rolodex, Rick wondered whether Patty remembered their high school days. Her conversations with him were generally professional but tinged with a touch of flirtation. He hoped that Patty still thought of him with fondness, because he was in deep need of a favor—perhaps more than one.

"Gallatin County Sheriff's Office," a young female voice said.

"Sheriff Patty Martin, please. This is Sheriff Morrand from Dexter County."

The springs beneath his leather seat squealed as he leaned back in his chair and waited. After several seconds, Patty came on the line. "Rick Morrand," she said slowly, as though rolling his name off her tongue had triggered a trip down memory lane. "I was just thinking about you the other day."

Rick wondered why she was thinking about him but didn't venture to ask. "How are you, Patty?"

"I'm well," she said. "The sheriff business treating you okay?"

"So far, so good. How's Wesley doing?" he added, though he really didn't care how Wesley was doing.

"Wesley's Wesley," she said without enthusiasm.

"You're still married, aren't you?"

"Oh yeah. Why? You having second thoughts about you and me?" She let loose with a high-pitched, convulsive laugh that nearly split Rick's eardrums. Hearing that every day likely made Wesley want to swallow a pistol.

"Actually, I'm getting married … again."

"So I've heard. To Sage, right? Makes sense. She always had a thing for you."

"Yes, I suppose she has."

"Well, if you ever change your mind, you know where to find me," Patty said with more nettlesome laughter.

"What about Wesley?"

"What? A girl can't get a little on the side?" Rick braced for her laugh, but she turned serious. "Tell me—how's that search going? What was that fella's name again?"

"Garrett McRae," Rick said as he drew a deep breath. "No luck so far. In fact, I'm not so sure that hunter just disappeared on his own. I'm beginning to think he may have had some help."

"Oh?"

"That's one of the reasons I called, Patty. I'm going to be forwarding a warrant for a man wanted in Texas. He lives in your jurisdiction. He was on that same hunting trip when Garrett went missing. As far as I'm concerned, he's now a person of interest."

"What makes you interested?"

"For starters, he identified himself as Randall Boone, which is the name on his Montana driver's license. His real name is James Edward Davis. That's what you'll see on the warrant I send you. Same guy."

"I see."

"I was wondering whether you might be able to do me a favor," Rick said. "A couple of them, actually."

"Fire away."

"I'd like to be there when you arrest him. There are some more questions I need to ask him."

"Shouldn't be a problem, provided you respect the fact that you are in my jurisdiction and my deputies will be making the arrest."

"Understood."

"What else?"

Rick paused a beat, choosing his words cautiously. "I'd like you to hold him as long as you can. Maybe take your time letting the sheriff in Texas know we have the guy in custody."

There was a long silence. "Rick, I know you haven't been a sheriff all that long, but you're an attorney as well," Patty said. "You know I can't do that."

"Why not?"

"For one thing, that's up to the courts—I have no control over how long a prisoner is held. Second, we'd just as soon get the guy out of here as quickly as possible, for reasons of liability. Which brings me to number three, whereby this guy could find a slick lawyer who could petition for his release. Not likely, but it's possible. In that scenario, he might beat feet before the Texas deputies even get here. Next thing you know, he could be in Canada or Mexico. I would imagine the Texans wouldn't be too pleased with something like that."

Rick tapped his pen on his desk and stared once more at the photo of James Edward Davis. "I guess I just need more time. Something about him just doesn't seem right."

"What is he wanted for in Texas, anyway?"

"Attempted murder."

"And what is your suspicion?"

"Murder," Rick answered without hesitation.

"You don't even have a body, from what you told me," Patty huffed. "You have *any* evidence?"

"Like I said, I'm working on it. I need time."

Rick could hear Patty breathing into the receiver. "Tell you what, Rick. Let me review the warrant, and you are welcome to come along when we make the arrest. But keep in mind that I want you to respect my jurisdiction."

"I understand."

"Once we bring him in, you are free to ask questions and we'll take it from there. Fair enough?"

"Fair enough."

CHAPTER 29

Having reviewed the warrant from Texas, Patty Martin said she could make deputies available by early afternoon. The plan was for Gallatin County officers to apprehend James Edward Davis at his place of work, with Rick and Jack Kelly serving as backup.

Jack spent the morning at a fishing access far down the valley, where a twenty-nine-year-old alcohol-addled male had managed to shoot himself in the thigh while bait-fishing in the Yellowstone. He severed his femoral artery in the process, which necessitated a taut tourniquet and helicopter transport to Billings Clinic.

Rick had his truck running when Jack arrived in the sheriff's office. Sipping a thirty-two-ounce soft drink, the oversized undersheriff walked briskly across the gravel parking lot and hopped in the passenger seat. He immediately fixed his eyes on the side of his friend's shaved head.

"You get a haircut?"

Rick slowly removed his Stetson, exposing his gleaming skull. "What do you think?" he asked, a broad smile forming across his face. "I'm doing it to support Sage."

Jack rolled his tongue beneath his bottom lip, studying Rick's face. Suddenly, he burst into loud laughter. "Well, I guess that's a nice thing you're doing."

"What's so funny?" Rick protested.

"Honestly?"

"Honestly."

"I've yet to see a white guy who looks good with a shaved head," Jack said. "With brothers, it's a different story. Ladies *love* a brother with a shaved head. But white guys? Not so much."

Rick frowned. "What are you talkin' about?" He tilted his head back and forth as he looked into his rearview mirror. He lightly brushed his hand along the side of his scalp. "I think it looks pretty clean."

"Yeah, as in Mr. Clean," Jack said with a chuckle. He shook his head and broke into a toothy smile. "Like I said, it's a nice thing you're doing."

"You can join me anytime you like—especially since brothers look so good with shaved heads." He reached over and lifted off Jack's hat, exposing closely cropped salt-flecked hair that had receded far from the front of his forehead. "Looks like you don't have all that far to go."

Jack snagged his hat and put it back on his head. "Where we headed?"

Rick smiled as he wheeled his truck out of the lot and headed for the interstate. He was reminded again how Jack Kelly was irreplaceable, both as a personal friend and an undersheriff. Being a relative rookie in the daily rigors of law enforcement, Rick needed all the help he could get. While he would acknowledge that Jack sometimes viewed the letter of the law as scrawled in pencil, the former detective's experience and expertise had been instrumental in significantly shortening Rick's learning curve.

The two men were supposed to make radio contact with the Gallatin County deputies upon arriving at the construction site where Davis worked. They'd been strictly instructed that they were there to assist, and they should take no action until the deputies arrived.

When they pulled through the chain-linked fence bordering the site, Davis's truck was nowhere to be found. The foreman approached their vehicle, his face holding a pained grimace of a man trapped in a state of perennial constipation. Rick lowered his window.

"Hello again, sir," he said. "We're looking for James Davis."

The man squinted. "Who?"

"Randall Boone."

"He ain't here." The man grunted. "Left about an hour ago, saying he wasn't feeling well."

"Did he look sick?"

The foreman wagged his head. "Not really. If I didn't need him so badly, I would've fired his ass."

Rick looked at Jack. "You thinking what I'm thinking?"

Jack nodded.

Rick glanced toward the foreman. "You might want to put an ad on Craigslist," he said as he turned the wheel of his truck and hit the gas. The foreman filled the truck's rearview mirror, thumbs jammed in his front pockets as he stood in a cloud of dust, his face awash in confusion.

Jack radioed the Gallatin County deputies and received no response, so Rick called Patty Martin on his cell phone. "Change of plans, Patty. Our suspect isn't at his place of work, so we're headed to his residence. We tried to radio your deputies—"

"They're at an MVA out on I-90," Patty said, referring to a motor vehicle accident. "They shouldn't be too long. What's the address?"

"Forty-two Ressler Lane, Three Forks. We're headed there now."

"Got it," Patty said. "And just so we're clear, you two are to stand down until my deputies arrive. You copy?"

"I copy," Rick glanced toward Jack, who shrugged and rolled his eyes.

• • •

When they pulled along the irrigation ditch that bordered James Davis's residence, Rick had fully intended to acquiesce to Patty's wishes. That was before he and Jack spotted Davis's truck backed up to his trailer, the bed loaded with items that could well qualify as his personal belongings. The suspect was nowhere in sight.

"He's trying to skip," Jack said, peering through a pair of binoculars. "We need to move on him."

"Whoa," Rick said. "I promised Patty we would wait for her deputies."

"That could take a while." Jack continued to scan the property. "Meanwhile, this guy could skate right out of here. Would you like to wave at him as he drives by?"

"C'mon, Jack," he said as he heaved a sigh. "We're out of our jurisdiction."

"I understand all that." Jack laid the field glasses on the dash. "But as law enforcement officers, we can apprehend him if he's committing a felony."

Rick cocked his head. "And what felony would he be committing?"

"Not sure," Jack said with a shrug. "I'll come up with something."

Rick folded his arms and stared at the distant trailer. "I was afraid you'd say that."

"You want to lose him?"

Rick backed up his truck and pulled onto the two-track. "You figure he's inside?"

"Either inside or maybe out back. He probably has some kind of storage shed."

Rick eased his truck along the rugged two-track. He watched Jack unholster his firearm, check the ammo clip, and return it to his side. The ex-detective's jaw muscles quaked as if pulsing with adrenaline. "You planning on shooting someone?"

"Not unless they plan to shoot me," Jack said with a grin. "Don't worry—I'll try not to antagonize him."

Rick rolled his rig to a stop a few feet from where the Ford was parked, its engine running. His eyes roamed the front of the trailer. The white metal siding was dented and faded, rust stains bleeding from the aluminum frames of the windows. "I'm going to go to the front door," he said. "I want you to circle out back, in case he tries to take off." Turning toward his friend, he said, "Jack, you sure we shouldn't just set here a while and wait for those deputies from Gallatin County? Patty told us to stand down, and I promised your wife—"

"We need to move, Rick," Jack said, his eyes glazed with intensity. "His truck is running. He starts taking off, and all we can do then is rely on him committing that felony I told you about."

"What felony is that again?"

"Like I said," Jack answered, putting on his tactical glasses, "I'll think of something."

Rick watched Jack slide out of the passenger seat and ease toward the side of the house, his large frame in a crouch and both hands gripping his gun. Rick stepped out of his truck and walked toward the entrance of the trailer, the heel of his right palm resting on the Colt Python he'd used to replace his missing semi-auto. His handheld radio crackled on his belt before he twisted the volume control between his thumb and forefinger to reduce the sound. He pushed a breath of air out of his parted lips, feeling his heart pound as his brain rattled off the list of offenses on Davis's rap sheet. Among other things, the man who pretended to be Randall Boone had a history of violence, especially toward women. That didn't sit well with Rick Morrand, whose father had trained him to conduct himself as a consummate gentleman, regardless of circumstance. "Only cowards mistreat women and horses," his dad would say.

The entrance to the trailer was fronted by three wooden steps tilted to one side. The sole of Rick's boot had just creaked onto the second step, when he heard a loud crash of metal coming from the rear of the property, followed by a booming voice. "Son of a bitch!" Jack Kelly bellowed.

In seconds, Rick saw James Edward Davis running around the side of the trailer, losing his purchase and tumbling to the ground on the dirt-and-gravel driveway. He regained his feet almost instantly, his eyes focused on making a run toward his idling truck.

Rick jumped off the porch, ignoring the jolt to his injured ribs. He measured the distance Davis needed to go to reach the front of the truck and lasered toward it, breaking into a full sprint. During his football career as a kicker at San Diego State, not one single team had managed to score on a kickoff, primarily due to the efforts of Rick Morrand, who made more than his share of touchdown-saving tackles. Rick would relish the opportunity to lay out an opposing returner, often cutting off the speedster's path down the sideline. His teammates would roar their approval on the field and hold him in the highest regard in the locker room, which was all that mattered to a teen on the apron of manhood.

With Davis only a few yards short of the truck, Rick left his feet, soaring like a missile. Davis grunted loudly, air vacating his torso as Rick made contact. Both men landed with a thud on the ground, grinding across the loose rock. Placing his weight on the suspect's back, Rick fumbled for his handcuffs. As he reached for Davis's right wrist, he felt the thundering blow of an elbow crack against the side of his jaw.

Rick blinked rapidly, his vision blurred. He rolled off Davis in slow motion. Ears ringing, he shook his head vigorously, attempting to clear the fog. His eyes opened to see a mammoth fist falling like a meteorite toward him, connecting with his cheekbone. Another followed, pushing Rick further into a daze. Davis put his weight on a knee that pressed against Rick's injured ribs, shoving the sheriff's chest as he rose to his feet. Rick gasped for air, razors of pain in his rib cage sending spasms that rippled through his lower spine.

Davis stood over him. "I heard your dead daughter was a real fuckin' whore," the wanted man said.

He turned to move toward his truck, but Rick unleashed a thunderous growl and tugged him down by the bottom of his pant leg. Davis landed flat on his stomach. Teeth clenched in a grimace, Rick stood up and snared the suspect's ankles as though gripping a wheelbarrow, unleashing a merciless kick that connected just below the man's buttocks. Davis shrieked with the high-pitched howl of a wounded animal, but Rick wasn't finished. He clutched the back of the man's belt and grabbed a fistful of shirt behind the nape of his neck. Yanking him to his feet, Rick ran Davis headlong into the iron brush guard on the front of the Ford truck.

Davis whimpered as Rick pulled him back a foot and repeated the exercise. The man fell to the ground in a heap, blood streaming from twin gashes on his forehead. Heaving breaths, Rick rose to his feet and brushed off his pants, staring with disdain at his conquered foe. He prepared to move toward Davis again, when he felt a firm grasp on the back of his shoulders.

"Easy, Sheriff," he heard a voice say. He turned to see the two Gallatin County deputies standing nearby. "We'll take it from here."

Footsteps ground on the gravel behind him. Jack Kelly was wiping blood from a two-inch slice on his chin. His forehead glistening with sweat, he removed his tac glasses and stared at Davis lying facedown on the ground, apparently still unconscious. "What the hell happened?" he asked.

"Reckon he antagonized me," Rick said.

CHAPTER 30

pencer Bible squinted into the small mirror that hung on a wall inside his office Thursday morning, repeatedly checking the hair length on alternate sides of his head. He would most assuredly need a trim prior to his date with Lizzie on Friday night, when they would share dinner before attending a movie at the local cinema.

He'd made reservations at Papa Dante's, generally considered the premier Italian restaurant in Great Falls, with Pizza Village registering as a solid second. Spencer had made his reservation and then confirmed repeatedly, forcing the hostess at Pape Dante's to politely request that he cease and desist. He had no plans to visit Starlight Coffee the rest of the week, terrified that Lizzie might size him up and suddenly change her mind. Calling her at work to extend a formal invitation to her had been nerve-wracking enough, with Lizzie practically finishing his sentences for him before she excused herself to return to her duties.

A buzzing sound from the intercom on his desk startled him. "Are you available, Spencer?" Rachel asked. "There is a woman on the line who wouldn't say who she was or why she was calling. All she'll tell me is that she has a general question about insurance."

"Maybe she's interested in a new policy," Spencer said cautiously, praying Lizzie wasn't calling to cancel.

"I think I recognize her voice," Rachel said. "She called a couple of days ago. When I told her you weren't in and tried to help her, she hung up."

"Please put her through. Maybe I can answer her question."

"Hello, is this Mr. Bible?" a soft, quiet voice asked. His chest muscles relaxed. It wasn't Lizzie.

"You can call me Spencer if you'd like. How may I help?"

"I just had a question … regarding life insurance," she said.

"Sure," Spencer answered. "You need a policy?" He pulled a pen and notepad closer to him. "May I have your name?"

"That's not important."

The pen twisted between Spencer's fingers. His mind wandered to his conversation with Walter Reynolds, who had admonished him for lack of sales and threatened to insert a company representative into his agency to serve as babysitter. Unfortunately, a new policy for his current caller wasn't in the offing. "What is your question?" he managed to say.

"This is strictly hypothetical," the woman said. "If someone has a policy and goes missing, how long does it take before the benefit is paid?"

Spencer felt his forehead tighten. "Do you already have a policy with us, ma'am?"

"That's not important," came the refrain. "Like I said—this is hypothetical."

"Right." Spencer looked at the phone on his desk. His Caller ID read "Private Number." Perhaps the woman had been watching too many crime shows. Or maybe she was calling to settle a bet. It wasn't the first time an odd question had been posed. He decided to play along. "There are a lot of factors involved," he said. "But, simply put—and I hate to be indelicate— there has to be a dead body. We usually pay a benefit following the receipt of a death certificate."

"What if they don't find a body?"

"Well," Spencer said, drawing a deep breath, "it normally takes seven years before a missing person is declared dead."

"Seven years!" the caller shrieked. "Are you serious?"

"I'm serious," he answered, tapping his pen on the notepad. Given Montana's geographical size, sparse population, and rugged terrain, missing persons were hardly an anomaly. But with no death certificate, no benefit would be paid. In Spencer's limited career as an insurance man, folks never liked that answer.

"No exceptions?"

"No exceptions," Spencer said. "May I ask where you are from?" He waited patiently for several seconds, but received no response. "Ma'am? Are you there?"

The next sound he heard was a dial tone.

• • •

Rick figured that if he gave Patty Martin a day to cool off, she might be more receptive to his desire to interview James Edward Davis. But when he entered her office on Thursday morning, he found his one-time class-mate standing rigidly behind her desk, hands on hips, eyes piping with rage, veins pulsed on a forehead colored dark crimson.

"You got balls coming in here," she said.

"Good morning, Patty," he said calmly. "Mind if I sit down?"

"Hell, yeah, I mind if you sit down," she shouted.

He wiggled his lower jaw, which brought a sharp jolt of pain to the right side of his face. James Davis had raised quite a peach on Rick's upper cheekbone, and despite Sage's efforts to ice it down, a fair bit of swelling remained. "I believe I owe you an apology."

"Ya think?" Patty barked, apparently not in the mood for sympathy. She jutted her finger toward the west wall of her office, which was the general direction of her holding cells. "I got a prisoner in there with a concussion, facial lacerations, and just anything else that comes from an overall ass-kickin'. His one phone call was to a lawyer, which means I'm gonna probably get sued, you're gonna get sued—hell, the whole state of Montana'll proba-bly get sued. On top of that, what am I supposed to tell the boys who come in here from Texas?"

"Tell 'em Davis must have slipped," Rick said dryly, adjusting his weight and digging his thumbs behind his belt.

Patty's eyes widened. "You think this is a joke?" she sputtered. "You think this is *funny*?"

"He deserved everything he got."

"Oh?" Patty said, hiking her thick eyebrows. "How so?"

"He said something that crossed the line."

Patty turned away for a beat. She'd developed a slight paunch, which pro-truded over the belt of her uniform pants. She blew out a breath and looked back toward Rick. "Look, Sheriff, I realize you don't have a lot of miles as a peace officer, but I would think you would at least know that you can't go around beating the living crap out of a prisoner who smarts off to you."

"Like I said, he crossed the line."

"What did he say?"

"I'd rather not get into it."

"Well, you're going to have to get into it. And you also need to explain why you decided—against my strict orders—to make an arrest outside your jurisdiction."

Rick shrugged. "The man was in the process of committing a felony. The report said he was in possession of methamphetamine."

Patty's chin dropped, no doubt attempting to summon patience beyond her grasp. "Yes, he had meth on him," she said, her face reddening again, "but you and your deputy didn't know it at the time."

"Jack's my undersheriff."

Patty glared at him and pointed at a chair in front of her desk. "Rick, sit down."

"Actually, I'm fine, just—"

"Rick. Sit. Down."

Rick plopped into the chair, suppressing a grunt when a sharp pain stabbed his rib cage. He watched as Patty eased into her leather chair. She closed her eyes and folded her hands on top of her desk as if preparing to pray.

"Rick," she said softly, "my deputies told me that if they hadn't shown up, you may well have killed Davis. I realize that this guy is a dirt bag, but what in the hell could he have possibly said that would make you go off like that?"

Rick removed his hat and ran his hand along his shaved scalp. Patty flashed a quizzical look, which he ignored. He gazed out the window behind her chair. The sun was out, though veiled by what now seemed like an ever-present haze. Rain was nowhere in sight. He wondered whether the fires would burn forever. "The man said something about my daughter that I just couldn't abide."

"Care to tell me what it was?"

"He called my daughter a whore."

Patty nodded her head, biting the side of her lip. "Rick, your daughter has been gone less than a year," she said with a sigh. "There seems to be some anger—to say the least—which can be part of the grieving process. Have you considered any kind of … counseling?"

Rick forced an uneasy chuckle. "You a shrink now, Patty?"

Her blue eyes sparkled with compassion and sincerity. "I'd like to think I'm your friend."

Rick's face sagged in surrender. "You are my friend, and I appreciate what you're trying to do. I did try some of that grief counseling after Christine died, but I quit after only a couple of sessions. Seemed like I did better when I just rode my horse."

Patty leaned back in her chair and studied the bruising on Rick's face. "Looks like you took a couple of good ones yourself."

"I'm sorry about the trouble I've caused you."

"Aw, I'm a big girl," she said, leaning back and locking her fingers over her midsection. "We'll let them know he's here, and I'm sure it'll be a while before they come up here to get him."

"What do you plan to say?"

"I'll cross that bridge when I come to it," she said.

"Any chance of my questioning him?"

Patty blurted out one of her unpleasant laughs. "Oh, I don't think that's the best idea right now. You said you were trying to track down some evidence?"

"DNA," Rick said. "I need some time."

"Well, track down your evidence, and we'll talk after that."

Rick nodded and rose from his chair. The pain from his ribs robbed his breath. He used his hat to shield his grimace before placing it on his head.

Patty's eyes sharpened, her face tilting to one side. "You really don't like this guy, do you?"

His fingers smoothed across his downturned brim. "It's fair to say that I do not."

* * *

As his truck crested Bozeman Pass, Rick's phone lit up on his console. "Sage Fontenot Fan Club," he answered. His smile made his cheekbone ache, but he ignored it. "How may I help you?"

"Would you mind picking up Abby today?" she asked, her voice strained with emotion.

"Of course. You okay?"

"I have a problem."

Rick's brow furrowed. "What's wrong?"

"I'm so pissed right now."

"About what?"

"I don't see how they can do this."

"Who? Do what?"

"This is bullshit. That's what it is."

"Sage," Rick said in a measured tone. "Take a breath." He paused. "Tell me what is going on."

He heard his fiancée release a lengthy sigh. "You remember when we were at the doctor's office the other day, and they asked me about my insurance?"

"Yeah, I remember. She said it wasn't a problem."

"Well, it is a problem."

"How so?"

"It's a problem because I apparently don't have insurance."

"What do you mean? I saw your insurance card. You've had insurance forever."

"Apparently I don't *now*."

"Why not?"

"I guess it's my fault."

"Sage, start from the beginning. What's going on?"

Another deep sigh. "Okay, since we are getting married and we're eventually going to live at the ranch, I decided to have all of my mail forwarded to the Spur. I'm used to taking my mail there anyway and paying my bills in my office. Turns out, the quarterly insurance bill somehow got lost in the shuffle. When I called today to get it paid, they said I've been cancelled. I have no health insurance."

Rick slowed for a battered Ford Focus in front of him, its plates expired. He pulled into the passing lane and accelerated. "So, you pay the bill and they reinstate you. Isn't that the way it works?"

"Sure, that's the way it works—provided you don't have cancer. Problem is, I have cancer."

"They won't reinstate you?"

"Not a chance."

"That's bullshit!"

"Like I was sayin'."

Rick felt anger rising. Sage Fontenot was one of the most responsible people he'd ever met. In addition to being a talented musician, she was an accomplished businesswoman. Though the Spur did have its occasional skirmishes between patrons, it was a highly successful enterprise, a favorite destination in Riverton for locals and tourists alike. Sage paid her bills and filed her taxes on time.

"What's this I'm always hearing about no one can be denied insurance—even with preexisting conditions?" Rick asked. "Can we get a different policy?"

"Oh, sure," Sage said with a scornful snicker. "I've already checked into that. The deductible is sky high, and the premium is ridiculous."

"I can't believe this."

They both were silent for several seconds. "I'm thinking I'd better slow down the chemo until I sort this out," Sage said.

"You're not slowing down anything," Rick snapped.

"You realize how expensive that treatment is without insurance?"

"I don't care. I have money. We'll pay cash."

"I can't ask you to do that."

"You don't have to ask. I've already made a decision."

More silence. "But—"

"There's nothing else to talk about. You're going to be my wife." He paused. "Sage, stop being afraid of depending on me. You need to allow me to take care of you."

"I … I'm afraid," Sage said, her voice choked with emotion.

"You have to trust me."

"Looking at my past, trust isn't my strong suit."

"I don't care about the past," Rick said. "I care about now."

Sage wept softly into the phone. After nearly a minute, she gathered herself. "You know, I really can't wait to become Sage Morrand," she said between halting breaths. "I want that more than anything."

"Then trust me."

More tears, followed by a girlish giggle. "I promise to trust you, Rick Morrand," she said. "I *promise*."

CHAPTER 31

Rick used a gulp of coffee to wash down two Advil early Friday morning, trying to arrest ailments that ranged from a sore lower back to an aching cheekbone and throbbing ribs. At Abby's insistence, they had spent the night at Sage's house, which meant that Rick returned to the green velour sofa. Sleep had been fitful at best, his brain racing through a loop video of topics, everything from Garrett McRae's disappearance to Sage's cancer and the cancellation of her insurance. The flurry of images continued throughout the night, causing him to toss and turn until merciful slivers of daylight began to peek through the living room blinds.

Ben Westfall had called shortly after dawn to let him know that the Granite Peak Fire was fully under control, meaning it was possible for search teams to expand activity in the area. Rick planned to briefly stop by the sheriff's office before meeting up with Ben mid-morning on the Dexter County side of the Crazies.

He pulled into the parking lot to find Jack Kelly already there. The undersheriff was in his small office off the lobby, reading glasses propped on his nose as he pored over a stack of phone records. Rick filled a navy-blue Kiwanis mug with Helen's burnt coffee and stood next to Jack's desk. "Find anything interesting?" he asked.

"Well, it looks like our friend Boone—or James Edward Davis, I should say—had been in contact with Mrs. McRae. Davis initiated the calls, and it doesn't appear that they talked all that long."

"He also was there when I stopped out at her house," Rick said. He sipped his coffee, wincing at its painful taste. "Though she denies it, they seem to have ongoing familiarity with each other."

"He called her just a few days ago."

Rick nodded. "Anything else?"

Jack ran a pencil along the transcript of phone numbers in front of him. "Yeah, this is kind of strange. We know that Kyle Ricketts called Amber McRae from the Gold Bar in Mariah on the day they reported Garrett missing, right?"

"Correct."

"Well, for some reason, she called the Gold Bar again."

"The same day?"

"Nope," Jack said, wagging his head. "It was just a few days ago."

Rick frowned. "The bartender said he'd never met Garrett McRae. Why would Amber be calling him?"

"Good question."

"I'm going to meet Ben in the Crazies," Rick said. "I'll stop in Mariah on my way back."

• • •

Rick filled a Thermos with Helen's coffee, strictly for survival, and drove north out of Riverton, his hopes of finding Garrett McRae flickering like fading embers.

The deep-green conifers that had once blanketed the Crazies were now decimated, the barren landscape dotted with random puffs of smoke reminiscent of a war zone. Rick found himself experiencing a slow burn of his own, his mind drifting to Sage's insurance. After feeling humiliated at the doctor's office, she now was riddled with guilt, lashing herself with blame for a simple mistake that could happen to anyone.

During the years he'd spent as a trial lawyer in Southern California, he'd never been a huge fan of insurance companies. Though he did occasionally appear in courtrooms, his career was largely spent on the telephone, shuffling through a stack of files as he haggled with adjusters who would assert his cases bore no merit. He was routinely called an ambulance chaser, accused of loitering around accident scenes and emergency rooms, the butt of jokes that compared him to sharks, snakes, and other predators. He'd absorbed the barbs in good humor, accepting them as part of a profession that grew his bank account while supporting a lifestyle that featured Lakers tickets, shiny new Porsches, Maui vacations, and endless highways of cocaine.

He sometimes would shudder at the memories of those years, grateful he'd somehow made it safely back to his childhood home. Yet even when he was trapped in the haze of his alcoholism and addiction, he wondered why lawyers were pilloried while insurance companies were held up as pillars of virtue. They would blame trial lawyers for ever-increasing premiums, but insurance carriers were diversified financial juggernauts, paying hefty management bonuses while realizing unrestrained rivers of revenue. Though he now served as sheriff, Rick still possessed a Montana law license. He had offered to file a lawsuit to get Sage's policy reinstated, but she resisted the notion of suing anyone, regardless of the severity of their transgression. She preferred to rely on a dash of karma and a whole lot of faith, the latter being a quality of hers that Rick not only admired but longed to acquire himself.

Rick's back and ribs throbbed as he slowly navigated the rocky road that wound through blackened meadows to the Granite Peak Trailhead. He rolled to a stop and stepped out onto ground covered with ash. Ben Westfall was standing nearby, staring toward the gray naked hillsides, deep in thought as his fingers stroked his massive gray moustache. Four male volunteers wearing backpacks stood nearby. After a brief handshake and exchange of niceties, Ben offered his plan.

"Mike Greer has a small team that is going to continue to push west from the Lupine County side," he said. "My guys are going to head out to the hunters' base camp and move east from there, making sure we didn't miss anything."

Rick glanced at Ben's volunteers. "Looks like you're spread pretty thin."

"Mike has it worse than me. His guys have been fighting fire for a couple weeks straight, and now they're on a search mission. They're flat-out exhausted, but they're willing to help if they can."

Rick tugged the front brim of his hat, shielding his eyes from the rising morning sun. "I thought I may have heard a helicopter on my way in here."

"We managed to scare up another bird from Gallatin County, but they can only give us about four hours, same as last time," Ben said. "They have nothing to report just yet. We're also supposed to have a horse team, but they haven't arrived." He folded his burly arms across his chest. "You realize, Sheriff, that we're pretty much looking at a recovery mission at this point."

Rick nodded. He well understood the verity of the situation, but Ben's words drenched him like a bucket of freezing water. Garrett McRae was dead. At least, that was Ben's working assumption, and he was a man best suited to judge such matters. They would not be rescuing a husband and father but rather offering a family some closure. In his experiences with his daughter, Rick knew all about closure. There was no such thing.

"I assume Mike has a dog team on the other side?" he asked.

"No dogs."

Rick cocked his head. "No *dogs?*" In addition to such tools as GPS units and computer mapping software, the use of canines was a critical tool in the art of search and rescue. With a sense of smell that is one hundred times stronger than that of humans, they could efficiently track down a body submerged in water or buried deep in snow. A simple command could alert them to whether they were hunting for a live person or a cadaver. They were indispensable.

"The bloodhound team got called off to an Amber Alert east of Billings," Ben said. "Deputies tracked down the perp, but he was unwilling to tell him where the little girl is." He shook his head. "Four years old."

"How about that gal from Three Forks?" Rick asked. "She has that mixed breed that found the backpack."

"Meredith Hart? She's been told to stand down. It was Brian Scott's call—he runs their team." The handheld radio harnessed on Ben's chest crackled briefly with static. He twisted the dial to lower the volume. "It's a real shame too. When it comes to finding cadavers, Meredith's dog is one of the best."

Rick huffed a breath. "Did this Brian guy happen to give you a reason?"

"He thought she was too close to the situation," Ben said with a shrug. "Meredith and Garrett were on the same SAR crew in Gallatin County. The rumor was that they had a thing."

Rick lifted his brow. "A *thing*," he said. "Like, an affair?"

"I suppose."

Rick drew a deep breath and paused in thought for several seconds. "Well, she's got a damn good dog," he said. "We need to get her back out here."

Ben nodded calmly, his soft eyes blinking. As a long-time veteran of SAR teams, he likely was accustomed to that peculiar abstract time zone when a mission transitioned from search to recovery. The period that elapsed could vary widely with each incident. No words were spoken, but everyone knew.

Everyone knew.

•　•　•

Rick drove back through Mariah shortly after midday. When he pulled into the parking lot of the Gold Bar, Jesse Lone Wolf was outside, his torso buried beneath the hood of a twenty-year-old Dodge pickup, its silver paint faded and tires barren of tread. Jesse's gray shirtsleeves were rolled up to the elbows, his hairless grime-covered brown forearms corded with sinewy muscle. He brushed a shock of ink-black hair off his forehead, glanced at Rick briefly, and returned to his work.

The metal plate on the front side panel of the truck was missing, but Rick guessed it was a Ram 2500. "Those Cummins diesel engines can be tricky," he said. Rick didn't know whether Cummins engines were tricky or not, but it was the best icebreaker he could muster. Given that his previous encounter with Jesse had been less than amicable, he thought he should try a different tack. Jesse didn't speak, so Rick tried again. "The bar closed today?"

Jesse kept his eyes focused on the engine, methodically reaching for one of the tools scattered across a greasy blue towel draped over the top of the grille. "With the fire going on, I decided we shouldn't open until noon."

Rick chuckled. "Bet your morning clientele didn't like that decision."

"They can drink at home," Jesse grumbled.

Rick rested his hands on top of the truck's engine compartment and peered in at Jesse's handiwork. "I never was all that hot at working on engines," he said with lament, "but it looks like you're pretty good. You do it a lot?"

Jesse threw a brief glance toward Rick. "I do it enough. I like to buy used trucks, usually from someone who doesn't see the same value in 'em that I do. After I fix 'em up, I sell 'em." He stopped working and looked toward the front door of the Gold Bar. No customers had arrived. "Working as a bartender doesn't pay all that much."

"How'd you learn your skills?"

"My dad taught me. That is, before you guys killed him."

Rick removed his hands from the truck's side panel, adjusting his hat as he breathed a heavy sigh. Screw the Dale Carnegie routine. Time to cut to the chase.

"As I recall, Mr. Lone Wolf, one of the hunters used the phone at your bar when they came in on a Wednesday afternoon from the Crazies. Is that correct?"

"Yep," Jesse said, without looking up. "It was the small, skinny guy. Looked like a meth head, if you ask me."

"Kyle Ricketts?"

"If you say so."

"Mr. Ricketts was talking to the wife of the missing hunter, Garrett McRae?"

"I guess," Jesse answered. "I know he was talking to a woman, and she didn't sound happy."

"According to the bar's phone records, that call was to Amber McRae."

Jesse stopped working and glared at Rick. "So now you guys are looking at our phone records?"

"Perfectly legal."

"Legal don't make it right," Jesse said, ducking back beneath the hood.

"As it turns out, a call from the same phone number came into the bar last Saturday night, and we're assuming the caller was Mrs. McRae," Rick said. "When I showed you a picture of Garrett McRae last week, you said you'd never seen him before."

"That's right."

"Do you know Amber McRae?"

"Nope."

"Can you think of any reason she might be calling your bar on a Saturday night, considering you're about eighty miles from where she lives?"

Jesse grunted as he tightened a nut with his wrench. "No idea."

"So you didn't talk to her?"

"Nope."

"Anybody else working last Saturday night?"

"Crystal."

"Crystal," Rick said. "When is she scheduled to work next?"

"She ain't," Jesse answered, pausing his work again. "The fires pretty much shot hunting season around here, so the owner had me let her go."

"Does she live around here?"

"Don't think so. She was pissed when we fired her. I'm pretty sure she left town."

"Do you have a number for her?"

"I'd have to look for it."

Rick nodded slowly, turning his eyes toward the Gold Bar. Two bowl-legged ranchers emerged from a rickety yellow Ford truck nearly as old as them. Its windows were rolled down, and an ancient General Electric refrigerator was strapped to the back of the cab. The men hobbled toward the entrance, mumbling to each other when they found the door locked. One of them spotted Jesse working beneath the hood. He waved a crooked finger at him before heading across the gravel toward the truck.

"You still got that white Silverado?" the old man asked, his voice straining. "I was fixin' to buy it for my grandson."

"Got rid of it, Earl," Jesse said.

Earl continued toward the truck, tipping his straw hat at Rick. "Got rid of it? What the hell for?" he protested. "I told ya I was interested in it."

Jesse put down his wrench and wiped his hands on the towel draped over the front of the truck. "You didn't want that one, Earl," he said as he walked around Rick. "It was a 2004. That wasn't a good year for Silverados. That particular rig had a lot of electrical problems I couldn't seem to fix."

"Damn," Earl said, removing his hat and scratching the sparse strands of cream-colored hair on his pink scalp. "That truck looked pretty clean to me."

"It wasn't a good rig, Earl—trust me," Jesse said. "I'll find you something else. I promise."

Earl nodded and released a long exhale from a mouth that contained a random smattering of tobacco-stained teeth. He glanced toward the bar, where his friend was standing patiently, thumbs jammed behind red suspenders fastened to weary, faded jeans. "Well, I may as well get a cold one while I'm here. You open yet?"

"I'll be there in just a minute," Jesse said as he began to gather his tools.

"Looks like you got some customers," Rick said. "Before I go, can you tell me Crystal's last name?"

"Raintree."

"I need you to call me when you find her number."

"Sure."

"I assume you still have my card?"

Jesse stopped and turned toward him. He reached into the top pocket of his shirt, using two fingers to pull out Rick's business card. "Close to my heart, Sheriff," he said, his voice laced with sarcasm.

Rick said nothing as he watched Jesse walk away.

● ● ●

Spencer Bible got a late jump on heading to lunch, which meant that most of the specials at Lorraine's Diner were long gone. With her daughter Tilly having called in sick, Lorraine was forced to hold down the restaurant by herself, a circumstance that left her somewhat disconcerted. Spencer paid the price, Lorraine ordering him to sit at the counter so she needn't have to travel all the way to a booth in order to serve him. Of course he complied.

"You'll be having tuna salad," Lorraine informed him as he perused a laminated menu. "I can put that on a toast, maybe with a slice of tomato and mayo? It comes with coleslaw."

"Sure," Spencer said. "And a sweet tea, please."

"Sweet tea, coming right up," Lorraine said, snatching the obsolete menu from his hand.

Spencer interlocked his fingers and sat in silence for a moment, watching Lorraine pin the small green ticket to an order wheel. An unshaven cook, metal scoop in hand, adjusted his white paper chef's hat and reached through a rectangular opening to snatch the ticket and confirm what he already knew. Spencer loosened his tie and reached for the copy of the *Great Falls Tribune* he had brought along from his office. He separated the front section from the rest of the paper and began thumbing through the pages, careful not to place the paper directly on the counter lest Lorraine fuss about having to clean up the ink stains.

Thumbing through the pages, his eye caught a photo of a cement truck that had overturned near City Hall after failing to slow down when making a turn. The tow truck crew apparently had their hands full. Next, he read about an incident in Butte, where a man claimed self-defense upon firing a crossbow into the chest of an intruder who had appeared at the front door bearing an ax and demanding to retrieve some belongings. It appeared the victim would survive.

Lorraine arrived with the tea and set it on the counter, a lemon slice clipped to the edge of the glass. Spencer dropped the lemon into the tea and reached for the container of sugar, but Lorraine wrestled it away. "It's already sweetened," she said. "Too much sugar isn't good for you." She tended to mother him, perhaps assuming the fact he didn't have a mother required someone in town to take up the task. She'd even gone so far as to encourage him to date her daughter, a gawky and freckled redhead who might be considered somewhat pretty were it not for a smile that displayed too much of her gums. He was simply not attracted to her—at least not in the way he was attracted to Lizzie.

Spencer smiled at Lorraine, sipped his tea, and returned to his newspaper. A story at the bottom of page five caught his attention. "Hunter Still Missing in Crazy Mountains," the headline read. A thirty-eight-year-old man named Garrett McRae, resident of Three Forks, had become separated from his two companions while bow hunting in the Crazy Mountains. The reporter had interviewed his wife, a woman named Amber, who was caring for a four-year-old disabled child. Despite the relatively short time frame her husband had been reported missing—and the fact that no body had been discovered—Amber seemed convinced that the severe fires that had stampeded through the Crazies had eliminated any hope of her husband's survival.

Lorraine placed Spencer's tuna salad sandwich on the counter, but Spencer ignored it. He looked again at the story. The name McRae sounded vaguely familiar, though he wasn't quite sure why. Perhaps Garrett had grown up in Great Falls before settling in Gallatin County? Suddenly, a shiver crawled up Spencer's spine. He recalled the curious phone call he'd received the previous day, when an anonymous female caller had inquired about some of the specifics concerning life insurance. Could that have been Amber McRae? He wagged his head and shrugged, placing the paper on the stool next to him and sliding over the plate that held his tuna salad sandwich.

The toast on Spencer's sandwich crunched as he bit into it. He removed two napkins from a dispenser and wiped the mayonnaise from the side of his mouth. Lorraine had often touted her tuna salad as the best on the planet. He respectfully disagreed, though he would never dare tell her.

Spencer took another bite of his sandwich, dabbing his lips. His eyebrows furrowed as he stared again at the newspaper lying on the chair.

"How's the sandwich?" Lorraine asked.

"Um-hum!" Spencer as he chewed.

"You shouldn't talk with your mouth full," she said.

* * *

Amber had just put Gabe down for his nap when she heard her cell phone ring in the kitchen. Frantically waving her open palms over her son, she prayed the sleeping child would not awaken.

She plucked her phone off the laminate counter, answering without checking the number. "Hello?" she asked in a hushed tone.

"Are you crazy?" the caller asked.

"Who is this?"

"You know who this is," Jesse snapped. "Did you call the bar Saturday night?"

Amber didn't answer.

"That sheriff has been out here twice now. He said he had phone records showing that you called the bar on Saturday night."

"So?"

"So," Jesse said, his voice rising, "they are wondering why you would be calling me."

"Who says I was calling you?"

"The sheriff, that's who! I can't believe you would do something so stupid."

"There's no need to raise your voice to me," Amber said in a loud whisper. "Just let me handle the sheriff." She glanced at the number on the screen of her phone. "What number is this? Where are you calling from?"

"It's a burner phone. What do you plan to tell the sheriff? You know he's going to ask why you called here."

"I'll figure it out," Amber said. "You need to relax."

"Relax?" Jesse snarled, his voice rising again. "That guy Boone was wearing a shirt loaded with blood. Is he involved?"

Amber released a sigh as her eyes roamed the kitchen. She stared at a framed photo beside the window, one showing her and Garrett during happier times. "Don't worry about Boone."

"Have they found anything?"

"Guess you must not watch the news. They found his backpack and his shoes."

"No remains?"

"Not yet."

Jesse grew silent. "Please don't call the bar again."

Amber didn't answer as she ended the call.

CHAPTER 32

Spencer arrived at Papa Dante's at five-forty sharp, twenty minutes early, his fist tightly wrapped around a large bouquet of roses and lilies cradled in fresh wildflowers. He'd paced the tan carpeted floors of his apartment for nearly an hour, returning to the bathroom mirror numerous times to straighten his collar or check for lint on his black felt sport coat.

He was greeted at Papa Dante's by a young man with slicked red hair who introduced himself as Alfredo even though Spencer had known him in high school simply as Fred. He was led toward the back of the restaurant to a private canopied booth, where silverware and water glasses were neatly placed on opposite sides of a candle that flickered in the center of a red-checked tablecloth.

A waitress appeared and introduced herself as Fran, making Spencer briefly wonder why the restaurant didn't force her to be called Francesca. "Would you like something besides water?" Fran asked. She tugged at the tails of her black blouse, which briefly relieved the strain on the buttons. Spencer guessed she was in her fifties, judging by the gray strands sprinkled through her short brown hair.

"Water is fine, for now," Spencer said.

"Special occasion?" Fran asked, looking at the bouquet lying on the table.

"Uh, sort of," Spencer muttered, feeling warmth flow into his face.

"Anniversary?"

Spencer wagged his head. "No, just a date. Kind of a special one, I guess."

Fran nodded and disappeared for a moment, then returned with a glass pitcher dripping with condensation. She filled the water glasses, her warm smile suggesting Spencer had triggered some pleasant faraway memory. "I leave you to wait for the lucky lady," she said. "In the meantime, let me know if you need anything."

Spencer flicked a half smile at Fran and stared toward the front door of the restaurant. He'd washed and vacuumed the Impala on three different occasions during the week in anticipation of picking up Lizzie at her residence. However, she said it would be easier to just meet him at the restaurant since she lived only a short distance away.

Shortly after six o'clock, she appeared, walking briskly past an awestruck Alfredo when she spotted Spencer in the booth. She wore a tight blue dress that hugged her hips as it descended to an abrupt end at mid-thigh. Black-strapped dress sandals paid homage to her perfect legs. Her eyes sparkled, red lips breaking into a warm and eager smile.

Spencer struggled to get out of the booth, nearly tugging the tablecloth along with him. He nervously snared the flowers off the table and presented them to her. She admired them briefly, drawing in their fragrance, then wrapped her arms around him in a warm embrace, leaving him intoxicated by her perfume as her full flowing hair briefly pressed against the side of his face.

Fran approached the table as they took their seats, flashing a raised eyebrow toward Spencer to signal her approval. "May I get you something to drink, miss?" she asked.

"We'd both like a glass of red wine," Lizzie said with assurance. "Are there any specials?"

"Our entrees are special every night," Fran said as she handed leather-bound menus to each of them. "I would recommend the lasagna. It's the best around."

Spencer pursed his lips and nodded, figuring "best around" extended the reputation of Papa Dante's lasagna clear to the Canadian border. "Lasagna it is, then!" Lizzie said brightly, handing the menu back to Fran without opening it.

Fran turned toward Spencer. "Lasagna sounds great," he said with a smile. She nodded and returned moments later with two glasses of wine. Lizzie raised her glass toward him, her eyes filling him with as much warmth as the red.

"So what movie are we going to see tonight?" she asked.

Spencer winced slightly. "I hope you don't mind, but the Roxy puts on a 'Classic Night' once a month, and it just so happens that's what is going on tonight. We don't have to go if you don't want."

"What's the movie?" she asked.

"*Double Indemnity.*"

"What's it about?"

"Unfortunately, it's about insurance. At least, I guess that's the best way to describe it."

"I'm sure it's fine."

"It's black and white," Spencer said, clenching his teeth. "Like I said, we don't have to go if you don't want."

He felt Lizzie's palm cover his, sending a bolt of passion that rocketed through his loins. "No, let's go," she said. "I'm sure it will be fun."

The lasagna didn't disappoint. Two more glasses of wine quickly followed during the meal, making Spencer feel more at ease. He found talking to Lizzie to be relaxed and effortless, unlike any interaction he'd ever had with a woman before.

The Roxy was a refurbished, two-screen theater with a lobby piped in neon and filled with bright art deco features that made it drip with nostalgia. They ordered soft drinks and smiled broadly at each other when they both chose Milk Duds, as though their selection of the candy represented some sort of mystic, predetermined fate.

Spencer had watched *Double Indemnity* twice before, since it happened to be one of his father's favorite movies. He smiled wistfully each time Fred McMurray referred to Barbara Stanwyck as "Baby." Lizzie slipped her arm inside his and pressed against him, her eyes fixed on the screen as they shared the bucket of popcorn on Spencer's lap. He wondered whether he would someday call her "Baby."

Lizzie remained close to him as they strolled out into the cool evening air, her hand curled beneath his arm. He stared at her perfect profile, which glistened beneath the bright marquee of the movie theater.

"So, when they talk about double indemnity, the insurance policy pays twice as much if the person dies in an accident?"

Spencer nodded. "That's correct. When Fred McMurray agreed to murder Barbara Stanwyck's husband, they wanted to make it look like an accident. Unfortunately for Fred McMurray's character, he didn't get away with it."

Lizzie chuckled. "So the girl ended up getting all the money."

"You got it!" Spencer said lightheartedly.

Lizzie tugged his bicep. "Tell me more about insurance."

Spencer frowned. "You can't be serious."

"No, I am. Is there always only one beneficiary?"

He shook his head. "Not always. There's what's called a contingent beneficiary. If something happens to the primary beneficiary, the second person would move up in line."

Lizzie nodded. "I see."

Lizzie leaned her head against his shoulder, making him wish the night would never end. "Enough talk about insurance," he said. "What would you like to do now? Maybe get a cup of coffee?"

Lizzie laughed again. "Uh, I'm kind of around coffee more than I would like."

Spencer tapped his fingers on his forehead. "I'm sorry. That was stupid."

"You're not stupid," Lizzie said, her breast pressing against his arm. "Do you live around here?"

Spencer swallowed. "It's not far."

"Why don't we go to your place? We can relax and talk. After all, it's Friday night."

Spencer hesitated for a beat. "Sure," he said, running a checklist through his mind. Was his apartment clean? Bed made, clothes picked up, no dishes in the sink? He hadn't anticipated that his first date with Lizzie would bring such unexpected fortune.

They rode in his car the short distance to his apartment. He hoped Lizzie wouldn't notice his hand shaking as he struggled to get his key into the front door. Cracking it open slightly, he turned toward her, feeling somewhat abashed. "Could you give me a brief moment?" he asked sheepishly. Lizzie didn't answer, instead offering a nod and coy smile. She swayed slightly as she placed her hands behind her back.

Spencer slipped inside and darted to the kitchen, where he took a stack of dishes out of the sink and stashed them in the dishwasher. Next he went to the bedroom, kicking underwear and socks beneath the bed and unfurling the comforter like an open parachute over the ruffled sheets. Out in the living room, sofa pillows were quickly straightened before he stuffed three insurance magazines and the control to his Xbox into a drawer.

When he returned to the front door, Lizzie was standing as he had left her. She raised her eyebrows slightly, prompting Spencer to say, "Please, come in."

"This is nice," Lizzie said as she glanced around the living room. She gracefully nestled onto the couch and smiled at him. "I'd love a glass of wine."

"Wine? Right!" Spencer said nervously, his index finger pointed upward. He sometimes received bottles of wine from friends and associates as Christmas gifts. He opened the cupboard above the sink. Pushing aside two bottles of chardonnay, he found a dusty bottle of red. The wine at dinner had made his mouth feel dry, but he decided red suited him.

He was relieved the bottle had a twist-off cap. The only two wine glasses he owned had a strange film on them, so he ran them under water and quickly dried them. He filled both glasses three-quarters full.

The wine and conversation flowed easily, the red giving way to one of the bottles of chardonnay. The more he drank, the greater at ease he felt. He found himself moving closer to Lizzie, lured by some hypnotic spell. Her lustrous eyes entranced him, extending an irresistible temptation to relinquish full possession of his very soul.

• • •

When Spencer awoke, Lizzie was gone. His head throbbed, his throat feeling like a dry creek bed. The morning light invading his bedroom caused his eyes to burn. He could still smell her perfume, if not the fresh irresistible aroma of her skin. He propped himself on one elbow, covered by a thin bedsheet. An uneasy sensation washed over him as he realized he was without a stitch of clothing.

He assembled the events of the previous evening. He recalled being on the couch, fully content to be kissing Lizzie's soft and generous lips. Before long, she had gently taken his hand and led him to his bedroom, where she had transported him to places of lust and pleasure he had never known to exist. He wasn't a virgin, but he wasn't all that far off. The extent of his sexual exploits had come during his college years, when he dated Debbie Swenson, an earthy farmer's daughter from Wisconsin who found it unnecessary to shave her legs. Their sexual encounters had been brief and uneventful. Debbie didn't seem to like sex all that much, and Spencer had too brief a track record to form an opinion. As the son of devout Christians, he liked the sexual sensation well enough, but he didn't care much for the subsequent feelings of extreme guilt.

With Lizzie, things were different. Having engaged in relations with a woman of her beauty had made him feel he was standing at the summit of a towering mountain peak, master of the universe, captain of his destiny. The world that had so intimidated him now appeared broad and limitless, his for the taking, fit to be conquered. He propped a pillow against the headboard, interlocked his fingers behind his head, and lay back on his pillow. If he had a cigarette, he would have smoked it. He was nothing short of indestructible.

A cool sensation crossed over him. Where was Lizzie? Why had she left? Was the night as magical for her as it was for him? Would he see her again?

His eyes caught sight of a piece of paper lying on the edge of the bed. He reached for it. The cursive was gentle and flowing. "Had to go to work and wanted to let you sleep. Absolutely loved last night. See you tonight, maybe?" Below the writing was a 406 phone number, which Spencer assumed was Lizzie's cell phone. He read the note two more times before laying it gently on the bedspread.

Indestructible indeed.

CHAPTER 33

Charlie Duchesne asked Rick to come to his office at nine o'clock sharp Monday morning, saying he expected to have DNA results from the shirt belonging to James Edward Davis, also known as Randall Boone.

When Rick walked in, the coroner's eyes were glued to a computer screen on the right side of his desk. "Interesting," Charlie muttered, keeping his eyes fixed on the monitor. He acknowledged Rick's presence by pushing a pink cardboard box of donuts in his direction. Rick selected an old-fashioned with no icing, judging that it posed the least harmful threat to his coronary arteries. The legs of a heavy wooden chair groaned on the linoleum floor as he took a seat.

"Three types of blood on the shirt," Charlie said. "There's a fair amount of animal blood, belonging to either a deer or an elk. There are some drops belonging to your person of interest. That would make sense, I guess, since he said he cut himself while field-dressing an elk."

"Field-dressing Garrett McRae's elk," Rick said with an edge.

"I suppose," Charlie answered. "Either way, it's not all that unusual for a hunter to have some of his blood on his own clothing. Your hands can get nicked and scratched out there."

Rick nodded politely. "What other blood did you find?"

Charlie turned away from his computer screen and sat squarely at his desk. He spun the box of donuts toward himself, plucked out a maple bar, studied it for a moment, then tossed it back. "There was blood belonging to Garrett McRae, and there was plenty of it," he said solemnly. "Not only drops of blood but plenty of spatter."

"That seems to indicate there was a struggle," Rick said, cocking his head sideways as he leaned back in his chair. "I knew that shit stain had—"

"Shit stain?" Charlie asked, looking up from his computer. "That's a new one."

"Whatever," Rick snapped. "That guy had something to do with Garrett's disappearance."

"I'm not going there," Charlie said. "At least, not yet."

"What then?"

"I don't know for sure. I need more evidence."

"Like what?"

"A body is always nice."

Rick pursed his lips, deferring to Charlie's experience and wisdom, at least for the time being. He picked up his donut, which lay on a napkin at the corner of the desk. It was far from fresh. He took a bite, sending a cascade of crumbs onto his uniform pants. Without hesitating, he swept them onto Charlie's floor, causing the coroner to hike his bushy gray eyebrows.

"I need to ask you something," Rick said. "You ever hear of a guy named Justin Spotted Bear?"

"Spotted Bear?" Charlie repeated. "Sure. Guy got a raw deal, as I recall. Why do you ask?"

"His son works up in Mariah at the Gold Bar, where those two hunters came out of the Crazies—without Garrett McRae. He seems to absolutely despise law enforcement. Claims that officers 'murdered' his father, Justin Spotted Bear."

Charlie reclaimed the maple bar and took a quick bite, then placed it on his desk. He held up his hand as he chewed, shoving his chair backward and rising to access a gray file cabinet in the corner of his office. He pulled a manila folder from the second drawer, and his eyes quickly scanned its contents. He nodded slowly as he sat back down. "This one was surrounded by a lot of controversy."

"How so?"

Charlie laid the open file in front of him. "You must have been living in California at the time," he said. "Justin Spotted Bear was pretty outspoken—to say the least—when it came to the rights of Native Americans. He was especially sensitive about Indian burial grounds."

"What happened to him?"

"The guy really liked the firewater, which didn't help matters any," Charlie said. "His drinking got worse and worse."

Rick chuckled. "I know how that goes."

"The more he drank, the more he tended to mouth off. At first he'd just rail against the government, kind of the Indian version of Ruby Ridge. Over time he started talking about stockpiling weapons, killing judges, murdering cops."

"Law enforcement tends to dislike that sort of thing."

"Correct," Charlie said. "So, he apparently drew the attention of the Feds, particularly the Bureau. One night, Spotted Bear is out drinking at a roadhouse off the res. Deputies usually went easy on him, especially since he wasn't that far from home. They would just follow him through the darkness, make sure he didn't go off the road."

Charlie took another bite of his maple bar and washed it down with a gulp of coffee. Mouth half-full, he continued. "Anyway, this is the night the federal agents decide to serve him a summons for threatening a government official. They slap a berry on the roof of their unmarked vehicle and blow right past the deputy. Even though Spotted Bear is shit-faced, he knows it's not a regular stop. He parks in the middle of the road, jumps out of his vehicle, and starts walking toward them. His hand is supposedly behind his back, as if he's carrying. The agents are behind their doors, telling him to drop his weapon. They say he just kept walking."

"Suicide by cop?"

"Maybe—except he didn't have a weapon," Charlie said. "For all anyone knew, he was tucking in his shirt."

Rick heaved a sigh and shook his head. "But they shot him."

"Eighteen times."

"*How many?*"

"Eighteen," Charlie repeated. "Says it all right here."

"Sounds a little excessive."

Charlie's eyes widened. "Oh, I'd say so. All hell broke loose on the reservation. There were protests for months, especially after the two agents got off with a slap on the wrist." He took another sip of coffee. "Surprised you didn't hear about it," he said as he swallowed. "Now that I think about it, the national news covered the story."

Rick briefly considered the blur of alcohol and drugs that made up his life in California. "I believe I was preoccupied."

"I'll bet," Charlie said, knowing his friend's history well.

"I'll bet you'd bet," Rick said, causing them both to burst into laughter.

The phone jangled on Charlie's desk. He picked it up after the second ring. "Duchesne," he said. Charlie listened intently to the caller, at one point raising his eyebrows toward Rick. "Actually, the sheriff is right here. I would imagine we can get up there before noon." Charlie hung up the phone and rose from his chair.

"What's up?" Rick asked.

"That was Mike Greer. He said the team on the east side of the Crazies might have found some remains."

• • •

Meredith Hart knelt behind a green side-by-side, trying to bury her emotions in the thick fur of her search dog, Tango. No matter how hard she tried, audible sobs kept coming, rivers of tears pouring from her eyes. A search team member stood with his hand on her shoulder, trying to comfort her. Tango's tongue wagged excitedly, saliva dripping from the corners of his mouth. He lurched forward, wanting to return to the site of his discovery, bursting with pride that he had done his job.

When she had been summoned to rejoin the search, Meredith knew full well that she was on a recovery mission. The Dexter County sheriff who had insisted on her participation was not so much interested in her abilities as those of her canine. When it came to locating cadavers, Tango was without peer. If there was any chance of a body being found, he would find it.

Unfortunately, Tango did not discover a body but rather only part of one. Meredith had briefly caught sight of what appeared to be a bone protruding from a shredded, blood-soaked pant leg. The clothing had burned considerably, but enough remained that she noticed blue camouflaged fabric, similar to that worn by Garrett McRae. The scene was gruesome enough that the volunteer searcher who had accompanied her emptied his breakfast in the scrub nearby.

To say that Meredith worshipped the soil Garrett tread upon would hardly be an exaggeration. She had been infatuated with him from the moment they first met, during a joint training between search crews and dog teams. She desired him instantly, ignoring the wedding band on his finger as if it was a high school ring. There were occasional interludes of guilt when she would confess to herself that the difficulties Garrett had with his wife were closely tied to the tragedy that had befallen their child. She knew that extreme misfortune had left Garrett weak and vulnerable, at times as flightless as a wounded sparrow. Meredith reasoned that it was her calling to rescue his soul, to restore his self-worth, and return him to the life he deserved, a life that most certainly would include her.

Guilt had no place in her fantasy. She would be Garrett McRae's savior. She wanted to have him. She *had* to have him.

"Meredith, I'm going to have someone drive you home," a gentle voice said. It was Brian Scott, who had ordered her to stand down shortly after her run-in with Charlie Duchesne. Maybe Brian had been right. Perhaps the search for Garrett was "too close to home." Given their history, would she be prepared to absorb the finality of his death? She told herself she had been compelled by duty. She knew that she and Tango were ideal for the task at hand. They had located plenty of corpses before. Grisly business, to be sure, but they would know where to look.

Meredith nodded as Brian helped her to her feet. Tango was more tranquil now, nuzzling his head against her thigh, perhaps sensing his owner's anguish. Meredith gingerly opened the hatchback of her Subaru, ordering Tango into a crate and placing her backpack beside it.

"I can drive, Brian," she said as she opened her car door.

Brian rested his hand on the top of the window frame. "That doesn't sound like such a good idea."

"It's not up for negotiation," she said, flashing a tight counterfeit smile. "I really need to be alone." She started the engine, closed the door, and put the car in gear. Tango barked twice before emitting a mournful wail and lying on the floor of his carrier.

The inside of the car grew deathly quiet.

● ● ●

Charlie was less than pleased to learn that Meredith Hart was no longer at the scene, but, given their history, her exit was probably best for all concerned.

"I'm sure I can catch up with her tomorrow," Rick offered. Charlie responded by grumbling something incoherent.

Mike Greer looked like he hadn't slept in days, his dual roles as fire chief and search team member having taken their toll. He said nothing as he quickly shook their hands and motioned toward a four-seat side-by-side. "It's a little ways in, but not too bad," Mike said. "We got the area taped off."

"That's the least they can do," Charlie murmured beneath his breath. Rick flashed him a stern look as they boarded the vehicle. They drove for two miles down a dozer trail that wound through a graveyard of timber and ash. The once-lush forest of the Crazies was ravaged and desolate. Restoration would take decades. Rebirth would begin the following spring, when rich underbrush splashed with alpine flowers would surround the naked blackened timbers. Huckleberry shrubs and conifer seedlings would come next, the trees growing perhaps a foot per year as they reached for the bright sunshine. Nature's redemption was pure and bountiful, but it was painfully slow.

A pair of search crew members stood outside the crime scene tape, nodding toward the men as they approached. The evidence was sparse, but the tale it started to tell appeared distressing, if not grotesque. There was a small part of a shredded pant leg, blue camo in color and soaked in dark-brown blood. The fabric was half-twisted around a human bone, a significant one at that.

"Looks like a fibula," Charlie said flatly, hovering over the discovery, hands gripped above his kneecaps. "DNA will tell us more from here."

Rick swallowed as he removed his hat. He brushed a hand across his head, his fingers finding the wound left by a bear attack only a couple weeks earlier. "Grizzly?" he asked.

"I don't like to jump to conclusions, but it looks like something with powerful jaws took a chomp right out of his calf. There looks to be a lot of blood loss." He dropped to one knee to get a closer look. "Do you know if the missing hunter ever had a broken leg?" he asked Rick. "It appears this victim suffered a fractured fibula at some point."

"I'll ask his wife," Rick said glumly, dreading the conversation that lay ahead.

Charlie turned toward Ben. "Is this it?"

Ben nodded. "For now. The dog may have lost the scent."

"Either that or that woman lost her nerve," Charlie snapped.

"Go easy on her, Charlie," Rick said. "Without that woman and her dog, we'd be lookin' at a whole lot of nothin'."

"If it was a bear, we're figuring he was dragged off," Mike said. "We'll have a tracker in here tomorrow, and we're hoping another dog team might be available." His eyes roamed the decimated Crazies. "Of course, the fire has complicated everything."

Charlie walked around to the small bed on the back of the side-by-side, then yanked out a canvas bag filled with equipment. He laid the bag on the ground and unzipped it, then pulled out a digital camera. "Let me start by getting some photos."

• • •

Sage's shoulders fell against the wall of her master bathroom, her head throbbing as her nostrils begged for fresh air. Wiping the spittle trailing from the side of her mouth, she clawed at the lever on the toilet, flushing its contents. After retching over the white porcelain bowl for nearly a half hour, she finally had been granted a reprieve.

Her chin fell to her chest as she pinched teardrops from her watery eyes. Another brief wave of nausea passed over her, followed by chilled sweat gathering on her forehead. She felt like she was going to die—no, she *knew* she was going to die—a haunting sensation that was becoming all too common.

Sage had just finished her second round of chemo at Dr. Janice Tillotson's office. She was following a treatment called R-CHOP, so named to honor the drugs that comprised the regimen: Rituximab, Cyclophosphamide, Hydroxydaunorubicin, Oncovin, and Prednisone. Shortly after her physician had boldly announced that they were going to "kick cancer's ass," Sage decided to fully embrace the medications that would assist her in winning the battle against Non-Hodgkin's lymphoma. They would become loyal allies, her most trusted girlfriends, almost like bridesmaids, tending to her needs as she marched toward victory over cancer.

If the drugs were her bridesmaids, they might as well have been taking turns screwing her groom.

First, there was Rituximab, a monoclonal antibody designed to target B-cell lymphocytes in the body by destroying a specific protein on the surface of the cell. A noble endeavor indeed, except for the fact that the drug had a wide range of side effects. There was the drop in blood pressure, which made Sage feel like she was going to faint whenever she wanted to stand up. Allergic reactions ranged from rashes to coughing and wheezing, followed by flu-like symptoms.

Cyclophosphamide was designed to prevent the division of cells. While achieving that mission, it also caused mouth sores, joint soreness, and easy bruising. Hydroxydaunorubicin was supposed to prevent the replication of cancerous DNA and RNA, provided Sage didn't mind the flushing, eye itching and redness, joint and lower back soreness, and painful urination. She didn't even want to think about the realistic possibility of heart issues. Oncovin, more recently called Vincristine, was another drug that prevented cell division, but it could cause constipation and tingling in the hands and feet. Then there was Prednisone, a steroid to help with anti-inflammation. Mood swings in the recipient were common, as her fiancé might attest. In many cases, the drug also resulted in loss of appetite, heartburn, sweating, nausea, and vomiting.

All of which left Sage sitting on a cold slate bathroom floor, puking her guts out when there was nothing left to puke. If side effects were pool balls, she had run the table. Yep, she felt like she was going to die, and the feeling was more than just a physical symptom.

She had told Rick about luck, more specifically *bad* luck. Sage had come from a long line of it. Her grandfather briefly survived a lightning strike, only to be killed by a second one as he stumbled across a flooded parking lot toward the ER. Her daddy had perished as a direct result of being a luckless gambler. When she was just a little girl, young Uncle Frank survived Vietnam, returned home, and promptly choked to death on a long slice of his celebratory rib eye.

Yes sir, hitching your wagon to a Fontenot was risky business indeed. Rick had ignored her warnings, of course, even though you needn't be prescient to connect the dots. The curse was continuing right before their eyes, and it apparently was contagious. How else could you explain one man falling in love with two women who had cancer?

Damn, Sage thought, she sure could use a drink. Janice Tillotson had said alcohol was okay in moderation, but Sage considered that a waste of time. She had abstained in the year since Chloe died, and she saw no reason to take it up again now. After all, she wouldn't want any unnecessary side effects, now, would she?

Her phone rang. She looked at the screen, took a deep breath, and wiped the wetness off her high cheekbones. "Hi," she said softly.

"You okay?" Rick asked, no doubt sensing the teardrop in her voice.

"I'm fine," she answered. Oh yeah, she thought, just F.I.N.E. *Fucked up, Insecure, Neurotic, and Emotional.* "I'm totally *fine.*"

"Did the chemo go okay?"

"It went … fine," Sage mumbled.

"You don't sound very convincing."

"No, it was okay—honest. Where are you?"

"I'm with Charlie up in the Crazies," he said. "I saw I had a signal, so I thought I'd call."

"That's sweet of you."

"You need anything?"

"Can you pick up Abby?"

"Of course. What do you want for dinner? I'll stop somewhere and get whatever you want."

Sage's stomach gurgled, her cheeks puffing with air. The thought of food—any food—made her want to gag. "You go ahead and get something for you and Abby. I think I'm going to lie down for a while."

"Anything I can do?"

She bit her lower lip, choking back tears. Here was a man who had lost a wife and then a daughter, but he somehow had managed to proffer a deep love for her. Sage could feel it, as certain as warm afternoon sunshine on her face. How could she be so selfish as to make him carry this burden? *Her* burden. She felt guilty she had pushed their wedding plans. Maybe he wasn't ready. Should they postpone? Should she leave somehow? That would kill him. Then again, so would her dying.

"Sage, are you there?" Rick asked.

"I'm right here."

"You okay?"

"I'm fine," she said.

* * *

Rick started the engine of his rig while Charlie threw his gear into the rear bed. The aging coroner grunted as he wrapped his hand on the grab handle and eased himself into the passenger seat.

"You doin' okay, old-timer?" Rick asked with a chuckle.

"Watch yourself, son," Charlie answered. "You're gonna be here soon enough."

Their levity was short-lived, given the grim scene they had witnessed. Rick released a long sigh and shifted into gear. The men wobbled in their seats as the truck bounced down the rugged dirt road leading to the state highway. They didn't speak for nearly a mile, each of them perhaps lost in a private requiem for Garrett McRae. The odious discovery of a leg bone among what appeared to be Garrett's clothing drenched in blood seemed to slam the door shut on his chances of survival.

"I'll get more DNA tests run on the evidence," Charlie finally offered.

"You have a theory?" Rick asked.

Charlie bit the side of his lip. "He could have been working on that elk and a grizzly came along. Poor guy probably never knew what hit him. Wouldn't be the first time that's happened."

Rick's chest grew tight as his mind flashed to the attack he had endured in the blackness of the Crazies. The bear's snarls had been laced with an unrelenting fury, producing a bone-chilling sound Rick would carry to his grave. The beast's strength was nothing short of astonishing, the sow tossing Rick about like a rag doll, its hot, acrid breath feeling like a blowtorch. The skin on Rick's skull tightened, an ice-cold sweat gathering on his neck.

"You figure it was a bear?" he managed to say.

Charlie pursed his lips and nodded. "That's what they tend to do. They feed for a bit, then drag their kill off to somewhere where they can protect it."

"So that's your theory?"

"That's my theory, but it's only a theory," Charlie said. "I'd like to see more evidence. For one thing, it would be nice to know where the elk was before that guy Boone took off with it. What's his real name again?"

"Davis," Rick said. "James Edward Davis."

"Right."

Silence filled the cab once again. Rick pulled onto the ash-colored pavement of Highway 191 and headed south toward Big Timber. The rig's mobile radio crackled with static a couple of times before Rick reduced the volume. "I guess we need to keep searching."

"Yep."

"If they plan to stick with search dogs, they ought to keep using that gal from Three Forks," Rick said. "I know you're not a fan, but she seems to know what she's doing."

Charlie huffed. "Yeah, she really knows what she's doing alright. Kind of interesting, isn't it?"

"What?" Rick asked. "What's *interesting*?"

Charlie turned toward Rick. "The stuff we've found so far wasn't exactly on the beaten path, but she and her dog managed to find it."

"Dog must be good."

"Right. The *dog* must be good," Charlie said with a laugh.

Rick's eyebrows furrowed. "What are you getting at, Charlie?"

"Just sayin' is all," Charlie mumbled. "Just sayin'."

CHAPTER 34

Rick had slipped a quarter-inch sheet of plywood beneath the seat cushions of Sage's sofa, but it didn't seem to help all that much. He had resigned himself that he likely would have a sore spine all the way to their wedding day, the vial of Advil in his pocket now his new best friend. His encounter with James Edward Davis had done little to mend his ribs, but he had written that off as a cost of doing business.

Sage had been asleep when he and Abby got home, leaving them to watch cable news as they ate Chinese from paper cartons. Rick chuckled when Abby opened a cookie to a fortune that read "You will be hungry again in ten minutes," although his granddaughter appeared less than amused.

Sage stirred when he went to say good-bye early Tuesday morning. Beneath her head, clumps of hair lay on her pillow, leaving blank patches on her scalp. His chest felt thick as his heart filled with compassion. She rested peacefully, her breathing slow and measured. He gently kissed her cheek.

After dropping Abby off at school, he drove toward Three Forks, intending to give Amber McRae an update on the status of the search. He realized he would be facing a woman whose husband, the father of a young son, most likely was deceased.

When she answered the door, Amber had her hair pulled back and was wearing no makeup. Her eyes were red and watery, dark circles betraying a lack of sleep. She wore a denim shirt that trailed down to a pair of tight white shorts that hugged her upper thighs. Without saying a word, she stepped outside the screen door into the cool morning air, arms folded across her chest.

Rick considered removing his hat but thought against it. He guessed he wouldn't be staying long. "Mrs. McRae, I have some news."

"You mean about my husband being dead?"

Rick's eyes narrowed. "Ma'am?"

"He's dead, isn't he?"

"We don't know that for certain."

Amber rolled her eyes. "They found his remains, didn't they?"

Rick cocked his head. "Now, where did you hear that, Mrs. McRae?"

"It was on the local news this morning, Sheriff," she said. "You ain't exactly quick to the draw."

Rick bit his lip as his eyes roamed the front porch. A weathered swing hanging from the white wooden ceiling creaked as it swung in the breeze. "I apologize for that. There must have been some kind of leak."

His words sounded foolish, and Amber reaction was understandable. "A leak?" she said, her eyes widening.

"We don't have conclusive evidence that your husband is deceased," he said softly.

"So what I've heard is fake news?"

"What I'm saying is that there is nothing conclusive." He paused a beat, drawing a deep breath. "Can you tell me if your husband ever suffered a broken leg?"

Amber shifted her weight, clamping her hands on her hips. "Football. Junior year in high school. He came back the next season to be named league MVP." She peered at him through her full natural eyelashes. "Why did you ask, Sheriff? Did they find a bone that had been fractured?"

Rick didn't immediately answer.

Amber rolled her eyes and huffed a breath. "Things sound pretty conclusive to me, Sheriff," she said as she wrapped her fingers inside the tarnished brass handle of the screen door, preparing to go back inside. "Tell you what: as soon as you find something you consider *conclusive*, you let me know."

Rick pursed his lips and rubbed his chin. It was an ideal time to exit the porch and be on his way. A voice inside his head told him exactly that, just as it had told him to allow Amber to leave his office without him bringing up her affair with Randall Boone, aka James Edward Davis. Considering Rick's face-to-face interactions with Amber had been infrequent, he wanted to make the most out of them as far as gathering information was concerned.

"Mrs. McRae, would you mind if I asked you a couple of questions?"

She released the door handle and blinked rapidly, harnessing her emotions. "Please be quick, Sheriff," she said, her voice revealing a slight quiver. "My son will be waking up soon."

"What can you tell me about Meredith Hart?"

Amber's forehead flushed with color, her jaw muscles starting to twitch. She scratched her eyebrow with the broken nail of her forefinger, folding her arms again as she shed any hint of frailty. "You mean the woman who was fucking my husband?"

Her words stunned him for a moment. "Are you sure that was actually occurring? I mean, do you know that for a fact?"

She moved closer to him, filling his nose with an odd but pleasant scent of shampoo and talcum powder. "If you're asking me whether I was actually there, I would say no, Sheriff. But, yeah, they were screwin', all right."

From the first time he'd met her, Rick figured Amber McRae had a temper fiery enough to match the reddish tint of her hair. When he visited her home, she struck him as a sensitive, doting mother. Now she'd developed a hard edge again, using language more common to a shit-faced sailor six hours into leave. Perhaps it was frustration or anger. Add to that a dose of desperate fear, since she now faced the real prospect of raising a disabled child alone.

"Can you tell me the reason for your suspicions, Mrs. McRae?"

Amber's eyes opened wide. "My suspicions? Let's see, first there were their *training* hikes for Search and Rescue," she said, making air quotes around the word *training* for emphasis. "Then it was important for them to *study* together, since she wanted to be an EMT."

"It was Garrett's goal to become a paramedic, is that true?"

"Oh yeah," Amber said, her tone laced with sarcasm. "He would have gotten a two-dollar-an-hour raise."

"So they hiked together and studied a few times—"

"Don't forget the emails," Amber interrupted, "and the texts."

"They corresponded a lot with each other?"

"They were regular old pen pals," she said with bite. She glanced over her shoulder toward the inside of the front door, perhaps anticipating Gabe waking from his nap. "Can you tell me why this is important, Sheriff?"

"I'm just trying to get an accurate depiction of the relationship between Ms. Hart and your husband."

Amber's eyes sharpened. "Let me paint you a picture, Sheriff. My husband can't be excused for his behavior, but it was that bitch moving things along. She was after him from the first time they met. She knew that Garrett and I were having difficulties, especially after Gabe's accident."

Rick nodded and blew out a breath. "I thank you for your time, Mrs. McRae," he said, tugging the brim of his hat. "We'll be running some tests on the … things … we found. I will be sure to let you know of anything that comes up."

"Oh, I'm sure you will, Sheriff," she said with a smirk as she opened the screen door. "I'm sure you will."

• • •

Spencer strolled into his office at mid-morning, his late arrival causing Rachel to draw a deep breath and glance at her watch. He ignored her as he grabbed three phone messages off her desk, rifled through them, and stuffed them into his shirt pocket. "Back in a bit," he said as he headed out the door.

He whistled his way down the street to the newspaper box in front of Lorraine's Diner, dropping in four quarters to secure the final copy of the *Great Falls Tribune*. Taking a seat at the counter, he allowed himself a lengthy yawn as he unfurled his newspaper onto the counter. Lorraine approached with a pot of coffee, holding a steady glare on the newspaper making unobstructed contact with her freshly wiped Formica. Spencer disregarded her as well, stroking his Adam's apple through the top of his unbuttoned shirt while he slowly turned a page. He heard Lorraine sniff, perhaps reacting to the new cologne Spencer had liberally splashed onto his face before he left his apartment.

"No work today?" Lorraine asked. "I see you're not wearing a tie."

"Oh, I'm working," Spencer said flatly. "May I have a menu?"

"It's pretty late for breakfast. I might be able to do oatmeal, but that's about it."

Spencer lowered his newspaper and fixed his eyes on Lorraine. "I'd like to see a menu," he repeated. "Your establishment *does* offer a menu, does it not?"

Lorraine's eyes opened wide as though she'd just taken a whiff of smelling salts. Her lips quivered before she reached beneath the counter and produced a plastic-covered breakfast menu, then laid it on the counter next to Spencer. He took a long sip from his cup as he watched her walk away, his mouth curling into a grin. Returning to his newspaper, his mind gracefully glided to Lizzie. Following their initial date on Friday, they had been together three more nights, sharing his bed with lovemaking and laughter. She had filled his senses with the softness of her luscious lips, the sweetness of her breath, the scent of her skin. He would lean his chin on her bountiful curls as she rested her head on his bare chest, the tips of her fingers gently stroking the lines of his physique. Her touch was magical, that was for sure.

She had left early each morning, insisting she needed to get to work. He would watch her from his front window as she used two long manicured fingernails to blow him a soft kiss while stepping into her blue Toyota Corolla. He thought he was awakening from a dream.

He knew so little about Lizzie—not even her last name. He wanted to send flowers but didn't know where she lived. She said she grew up in Butte but would quickly deflect questions about family. Spencer didn't know if she had siblings or whether her parents were alive or dead.

Despite this dearth of information, he felt like he had known Lizzie all his life. She would giggle while she wondered about what their children might look like, where they might travel, or what kind of house they would build together. The conversations were silly, of course, their love affair just having taken wing. He was ruled by infatuation, which hurled him into an intoxicating bliss that defied all reason. It was as if he had sipped some sort of enchanted potion that infused him with the power of a paladin, self-confidence oozing from every pore. With Lizzie by his side, no longer would anyone kick sand in the face of Spencer Bible, no sirree.

He would cling to this sensation at all costs. The world from which he'd transcended would cease to exist. He was crazy about Lizzie. He would do anything for her. *Anything.* He vowed he must never lose her.

"Have you decided?" Lorraine asked, peering over the top of her reading glasses.

"Eggs Benedict," Spencer said, turning another page of his newspaper. He heard Lorraine heave a lengthy sigh as his eyes caught a wire story at the top of Page Five. "Possible Remains of Hunter Found," the headline said. The article was brief and did not specify what was meant by "remains." Nor did it specify whether the hunter had died of natural causes or possible foul play.

A cool shudder crawled up his spine. He fumbled into the top pocket of his shirt and pulled out the three pink phone messages he'd glanced at only briefly when leaving his office. The first two were leads for individual health insurance policies. Pretty straightforward. The third was more peculiar. *Amber McRae* was written in Rachel's cursive above a 406 phone number. Below the number was the sentence: "Same person as last week?"

He glanced back at the newspaper article about a missing hunter named Garrett McRae. A line at the bottom of the story said that Dexter County

Sheriff Rick Morrand was heading up the investigation, but he was not available to comment. Spencer folded his newspaper and looked at Lorraine.

"I decided I'm not hungry," he said. Dropping a five-dollar bill on the counter, he headed out the door. He needed to contact this sheriff named Morrand.

• • •

The home where Meredith Hart lived in Three Forks was modest and orderly, its exterior adorned with the kind of white faux-wood siding they peddled on late-night cable TV. The fence around the yard was reinforced with wire netting, likely to discourage deer, rabbits, and other critters from accessing the flower bed that extended from the front stoop to the edge of the house. The grass had begun to brown, reluctantly bidding farewell to another fleeting summer. All was quiet, aside from the rustling of fading leaves clinging to a poplar tree shading a section of the green asphalt roof. No vehicles were parked in the gravel driveway, which trailed to a separate single-car garage.

Rick knew little about Meredith aside from the fact that she was responsible for discovering any and all evidence pertaining to the case of missing bow hunter Garrett McRae, thanks primarily to the efforts of her diligent search dog named Tango. Charlie found Meredith's timely discoveries to be somewhat odd, but, then again, the coroner considered it his professional duty to determine everything somewhat odd. Charlie was renowned for frolicking on the fringes of conspiracy, engaging Rick in spirited presentations ranging from the shot fired from the grassy knoll to the dubious explanations for the collapse of the Twin Towers.

What captured Rick's interest was Meredith's alleged affair with Garrett. Like many rumors in rural Montana, that one had caught on like wildfire but had yet to be sufficiently vetted. It did appear that Meredith and Garrett did have a friendship of some nature, perhaps less strenuous than the one he had with Amber McRae, who seemed hot and cold toward her husband in turns. Meredith might be able to shed some light on Garrett's home life, though Rick would certainly have to filter her personal bias. Did Meredith know the man who called himself Randall Boone? Did Amber and Boone actually have an affair? What was the nature of Garrett's friendship with Boone? Did Meredith know Kyle Ricketts? Was there any conceivable reason these men would lose contact with Garrett and not report him missing for more than three full days?

With these thoughts ruminating beneath the surface of his skull, Rick entered through a creaky wooden gate and stepped onto the front porch. The storm door was closed, but he could see through the glass that the wooden entry door was open. He pressed the cracked flickering doorbell, but he couldn't be sure if he heard it ring. Two of his knuckles rapped on the storm door. "Hello?" he said. He thought he heard a faint voice. He knocked again, harder. "Law enforcement. Anybody home?"

This time a voice inside sounded louder. "You break that glass and you're gonna pay for it," a woman barked. Her pronouncement was followed by a series of hacks, a torrent of phlegm thundering through her throat.

"I'm Sheriff Morrand from Dexter County," Rick said. "May I come in?"

More coughing. "Come in, come in," she said. "You're wasting my oxygen."

Rick stepped inside to find a woman in a cotton nightgown sitting on a faded brown sofa, nasal cannula plugged into her nose. A walker leaned against a wooden coffee table. Next to a dimly lit lamp were a pack of L&Ms, a yellow Bic lighter, and an ashtray filled with extinguished butts. Years of sun had leathered the woman's face. She studied her visitor, her mouth shifting from side to side. If she owned teeth, they were elsewhere. Her unwashed silver hair was combed straight back. She pushed a loose strand behind her ear, making a vain attempt to look fetching.

Staring at Rick seemed to soften her mood. "Where'd you say ya was from?"

"Dexter County, ma'am," he said. "My name is Sheriff Rick Morrand."

Her eyes squinted. "You're a bit off your reservation, ain't ya, Sheriff Morrand?"

Rick removed his hat and stroked the stubble that had begun to grow on his scalp. "We've been searching for a lost hunter over in Dexter County. I'm sure Meredith must have mentioned it, seeing she's been part of the mission."

"I knew Meredith and that dog of hers were up to something, but I wasn't sure where," the woman said. "I did know they were looking for that McRae boy." She reached for her pack of cigarettes, then pried one out with her finger and put it in her mouth. "Have they found him yet? Meredith hasn't said much, and I don't watch the news. Makes me too depressed, if you know what I mean."

"We haven't found him yet," Rick said in a somber tone. "Is Meredith not home?"

"No sir. She's at work."

"You're her mother, I would guess?"

A hint of sparkle flashed from her blue eyes. "I was hoping you'd ask if I was her sister," the woman said, her chuckle cut short by another thick hack. "Yes, I'm her mother. Name's Patricia."

Rick stroked the crown of his hat. "Would you mind if I asked you a few questions, Patricia?"

"Please sit down." A shaky, wrinkled index finger pointed to a billowy tan Barcalounger. "Want a beer? I got some ice cold Keystones in the fridge."

"No, thank you." His ribs stabbed him as he gingerly perched on the front of the unsteady chair, fearing that sitting back in it might take him to a point of no return. "Can you tell me how well your daughter knew Mr. McRae?"

Patricia picked up her lighter and lit the cigarette dangling from her mouth. She drew a long drag, delivering another blast of torture down her trachea. "I know they were both involved with that search outfit," she said as she exhaled. "And I guess Garrett had convinced her she needs to become one of those EMTs. Seems like a waste of time to me—no money and all—but she's pretty set on it."

"Did you ever see them together?"

Patricia tapped her cigarette on the edge of the ashtray and took another drag. "Maybe only once or twice, but she sure talked about him a lot," she said, smoke sputtering from her mouth as she spoke. "There were starting to be some rumors floating around about the two of them. In Three Forks, it don't take much to spark a rumor. It was no secret that McRae couple had their difficulties, given what happen to their son and all. I told Meredith she needed to keep her distance. Give them folks some space, as the young people like to say."

Rick drew a breath, pursing his lips in thought. "Would you know if they were more than just friends? That is, maybe they were in a relationship?"

A giggle rattled up Patricia's throat. She blew a cloud of smoke toward the ceiling. "Now, Sheriff, that kind of talk makes me blush. Like I was saying, all I know about are the rumors."

Rick nodded and slowly rose from his chair, his knees aching and his wind cut short by his ribs. "Well, Mrs. Hart ... Patricia ... I thank you for your time." He reached in his top pocket and handed her a business card. "Would you be so kind as to have your daughter call me? I see no sense in bothering her at her place of work."

Patricia puffed her cigarette as she studied the card. "Sheriff Richard Morrand. You are quite a looker, Sheriff. Tell you what … If I were twenty years younger—"

"I guess that would be my misfortune you're not, ma'am," Rick said with a brief smile as he placed his hat on his head. He started toward the door, then stop abruptly. "One other thing, Patricia. Do you happen to know where your daughter was the weekend after Labor Day?"

"Probably out camping somewhere in the mountains with that dog of hers. She takes a backpack and heads out every weekend, sometimes even when it snows. Hell of a place to be shopping for a husband, if you ask me."

"Does she go with someone?"

Patricia gagged, then stamped out her cigarette in the ashtray. "Just her and the dog, usually."

Rick cocked his head. "Does she let you know where she is headed?"

"Oh yes," Patricia answered. "She writes it down so I know where she is in case they get lost. She should be more worried about her coming home and finding me croaked." She twisted her neck toward the kitchen. "See that top drawer under the counter? There's a black notebook in there. Would you mind fetching it for me?"

Rick walked toward the kitchen. He pulled open the drawer, which contained a stack of bills wrapped in a rubber band. Next to the stack were two Montana road maps and a page of stamps that said *LOVE* on them. Always good to tell your creditors you're fond of them, he guessed. No sign of a black notebook.

"Are you sure this is the drawer, ma'am?" he asked.

Patricia turned her head and squinted at him. "You don't see it?" She eased forward on the couch and began to paw at her walker. "Here, let me take a look."

"No, please don't get up," he pleaded, fearful one of her next breaths might conclude her life. "It's not critical at the moment. If you could just have your daughter call me, I would appreciate it."

"Got your card right here next to the ashtray. You sure don't want to stay awhile, maybe sit down and have a Keystone? They're ice cold."

"Perhaps some other time, Patricia," he said, tipping his hat toward her. "I appreciate your assistance."

CHAPTER 35

Rick pulled his truck into the parking lot of the Gallatin County Sheriff's Office slightly after noon. Nearly a week had passed since his thrashing of James Edward Davis, and he'd hoped that Patty Martin's mood had tempered to a degree that would allow him to question her prisoner.

Assuming, of course, Davis hadn't already been spirited away by Texas deputies.

Patty was between bites of a deli sandwich when he walked into her office. She stared at him with curiosity, her lips suspended open to display an unsightly half-chewed blend of ciabatta, ham, lettuce, tomato, and mayonnaise. She laid her sandwich in a wrapper on her desk, thumbed a dollop of mayo from the corner of her mouth, took a loud sip through the straw of her large soft drink, and sat back in her chair. "Back so soon?" she asked.

Okay, so maybe her mood hadn't tempered all that much.

"Good afternoon, Patty," Rick said. "You told me I could question my suspect once I have some evidence, and I definitely have some evidence."

Patty hiked her eyebrows. "Oh?"

"Yes."

"And what is your evidence?"

"A shirt belonging to the suspect was covered in blood. There was animal blood, which isn't surprising. There was the suspect's blood, which also isn't overly surprising."

Rick paused as Patty pulled her chair forward, drained a final sip of her soft drink, and dropped it into a wastebasket under her desk. "I'm listening."

"The shirt had a lot of blood containing the DNA of the missing hunter, Garrett McRae." Rick said. "According to another hunter who was present, Davis and McRae had argued the night before Garrett disappeared. Next thing anyone knows, Davis is trotting back into camp with Garrett's tagged cow elk, which happened to be sitting on the back of Garrett's horse." Rick lifted his eyebrows and cocked his head to the side. "That sound like evidence to you?"

Patty picked up a pen off her desk and studied the inscription on its side as though considering the services of whoever provided it to her. "A lot of interesting *circumstances*, I'll give you that."

"Circumstances backed by hard evidence," Rick said. "Blood evidence."

Patty dropped the pen on her desk. "Did you seek professional help, like I told you to?"

Rick hesitated, rubbing his chin. The question pricked him. *Told me to?* As a fellow sheriff, she didn't have the authority to tell him to do anything. Then again, if he did not comply, she had threatened to call for a full investigation into his confrontation with James Davis. "I'm working on it," he finally said.

"*Working* on it?"

"A shrink isn't someone I'm just going to Google."

"Not a shrink—a therapist," Patty said. "I'm sure your daughter used a therapist?"

Rick felt warmth flow into his face. "Let's leave my daughter out of this."

Patty raised an open palm. "My apologies. But I'm serious about you getting help—or else."

"I understand."

She stared at him, her eyes saying she didn't believe a word he was saying. She was correct.

"I need to speak to your prisoner," he said.

"I'll give you ten minutes."

• • •

The recently rechristened James Edward Davis was slumped over a gray metal table, hands folded in front of him, wrists married by shiny metal handcuffs. Color drained from his face when he saw Rick walk through the door of the interrogation room. His eyes widened. Sitting erect, he inched his chair backward in fear.

Patty Martin stood in the doorway. "Mr. Davis, Sheriff Morrand would like to ask you a few questions. You are under absolutely no obligation to answer them since they do not pertain to your previous arrest in Texas, which is the sole reason that you are currently being held."

Her words appeared to embolden him as his eyes drifted back toward Rick. A pair of two-inch gashes, held together by sutures, decorated his forehead, Rick recalling man meeting brush guard. Rick allowed himself a tight smile, staring at the wounds more with admiration than regret.

"May we have the room?" he asked over his shoulder.

"Over my fat, dead ass," Patty said, clearing the doorway to allow a burly deputy to enter. The man was not introduced as he moved to the corner of the room. His copper-colored hair was slicked straight back, sideburns trimmed level with his earlobes. He held his hands over his belt, freckled biceps wrapped tightly in the fabric of his uniform shirt. Rick looked at Patty, who cast a thumb at a one-way mirror along the wall beside the door. She formed her index and middle fingers into a V-shape, pointing them toward her cautioning eyes and then at Rick before quietly leaving the room.

Davis's eyes were black holes, a pair of dead-end streets. His glare said he had nothing to lose, and in fact all had been lost. He would be returning to Texas and likely would be headed for a long prison sentence, probably some garden spot like Huntsville. Chances of his answering Rick's questions were slim, and Rick knew it.

The door burst open. A man in an ill-fitting blue suit, standing all of five foot five, quickly entered the room. "What the hell is going on here?" he demanded, gawking at Rick through oval glass frames. His light-brown hair was thick on the sides, sprinkling flecks of dandruff onto his shoulders. What appeared to be narrow rows of wheat adorned the top of his head, where he'd apparently embarked on a hair transplant with a woefully insufficient budget.

"Who are you?" Rick asked.

"Errol Nash, Attorney at Law," the man said, forcefully sliding a card across the table. He blinked his eyes and twitched his nose, the latter a hooked assemblage of bone and cartilage resembling the beak of a peregrine. "I assume you are here to further harass my client?"

"I didn't harass him to begin with."

The lawyer's eyes widened. "Is that right?" He pulled a sheet of paper out of his briefcase and pointed at it. "Concussion, facial lacerations, testicular contusions—"

"Testicular contusions?" Rick asked. "Is that what they call getting kicked in the nuts these days?"

Nash squinted. "Sheriff, does the suffering my client has endured somehow amuse you?"

"Not in the least, Mr. … Nash," Rick answered, staring at the man's business card. "All I would like to do is ask Mr. Boone—Davis—a few simple questions."

"Not going to happen," Nash said. "This gentleman is a plaintiff in a civil lawsuit against Gallatin County, not to mention you personally. I'm astonished the attorney general hasn't brought criminal charges."

"You mean when this gentleman resisted arrest during the commission of a felony?"

"You and I both know that is patently untrue, Sheriff. It is men like you that give law enforcement a bad name. By all rights, you probably should be behind bars."

Rick's forehead tightened. "I would suggest you temper your remarks, Counselor."

Nash hiked his eyebrows. "What are you going to do, Sheriff? Beat me senseless as well?"

"Awfully tempting," Rick answered. He fixed his glare on Nash, who averted his eyes.

The door opened once again. "All right, that's it," Patty Martin barked. "Deputy, take the prisoner back to his cell."

"Wait!" Davis said. "I want to answer his questions."

Nash placed his hand on Davis's shoulder. "Mr. Davis, please do not utter another word!"

"Get your hand off me, Dipshit," Davis said. "I want to answer his questions. I ain't done nothin' wrong."

Patty blew out a breath. "You realize, Mr. Davis, that anything you say can be used against you in a court of law?"

"I know what Miranda is, trust me," Davis said. "I ain't done nothin' wrong."

Patty folded her arms across her chest and pursed her lips. After a beat, she said, "Okay, Mr. Davis, it's your decision." She cast her eyes toward Rick and wagged her index finger. "Don't push it, Sheriff. I'll be right on the other side of the glass."

Rick didn't respond, instead taking a seat directly across the table from Davis. He drew a deep breath and stared for several seconds, causing the suspect to fidget in his chair. "I guess we should just cut to the chase, Mr. Davis. It's my understanding that you didn't like Garrett McRae all that much, is that correct?"

Davis shrugged. "We were friends at one point."

"You were friends before you began sleeping with his wife?"

Davis huffed a breath. "Garrett's marriage to Amber was over—it had been over for a long time. I knew it, Amber knew it … The only one who didn't seem to know it was Garrett."

"Mrs. McRae told me that she and her husband had experienced difficulties," Rick said. "That's understandable considering the tragedy they had to endure with the injury to their son."

"From what Amber told me, Garrett wasn't exactly a saint," Davis said. "I heard he got a little on the side as well."

Rick ignored the comment and forged ahead. "According to Kyle Ricketts, Mr. McRae was already gone on Saturday morning when you left camp as well, is that accurate?"

"If that's what Kyle says."

"Next thing anybody knows, you're riding back into camp with Garrett's horse, complete with a dressed cow elk on its back. Seems awfully convenient, to say the least. Sure was nice of Garrett to pack that meat for you."

"Garrett didn't dress that elk—I did."

"Oh?"

Davis drew a deep breath. "I found his horse wandering on the trail. I continued on about a quarter mile and found the elk. It hadn't been dead long. It was still warm."

"Was it tagged?"

Davis nodded.

"How fortunate," Rick said. "You roll up on a freshly killed cow elk that's already tagged, and, lo and behold, you happen to have a horse to transport the meat." Rick's forehead tightened into a frown. "You sure Garrett didn't dress it for you?"

Nash placed his hand on his client's wrist. "I want to remind you, Mr. Davis, that you don't have to answer any more questions."

"Do. Not. Touch. Me," Davis said, grinding his teeth. "That's the last time I'm going to tell you that."

"Careful, Nash," Rick said. "This one likes to prey on people who are smaller and weaker than him. I'd say you qualify." As he spoke, Rick's eyes were trained on the inside of Davis's forearm. Below the scripted blue ink of the name "Boone" in the area where Davis's radial artery and veins pulsed blood to and from his wrist, he had another tattoo. It was an upside-down pentagram surrounded by a thick round border. The head of a horned goat was emblazoned in the center of the pentagram, and a pair of eerie claws clutched the lower part of the outer circle. Pinkish razor-thin scars ran perpendicular to the base of Davis's wrist, indicating his wounds had been inflicted intentionally. Rick watched Nash slowly remove his hand, clear his throat, crack his neck, and interlock his fingers as he rested his arms on the table.

Davis turned toward Rick. "As I've said already, McRae wasn't there. He may have started to gut the elk—there was a hole in its belly—and then got run off. Maybe a bear got to it, I don't know. All I can tell you is that when I got there, McRae was gone."

"You're saying a grizzly was in the area?"

"I *know* there was a grizzly in the area," Davis said. "I saw one right before I came up on the kill. Fired a couple of shots over his head and off he went."

"So you fired two shots. I would imagine Kyle probably heard them?"

"Mr. Davis," Nash said, bowing his head and wagging it in despair. "Please don't—"

"You'd have to ask Kyle," Davis said. His eyes narrowed. "What are you gettin' at?"

"I plan to ask Kyle about the shots," Rick said. "To be clear, you claim a bear got at Garrett's elk?"

Nash released a sigh, his face anguished. Davis glanced at the lawyer, then looked at Rick and shrugged. "Don't know for sure, but it coulda been a bear. Either that or McRae was pretty sloppy. There was a hole in the animal's gut. Almost looked like it was ripped open. Blood was streaming out, and she hadn't been dead long. When I reached inside, the organs were still warm."

Rick paused for several seconds. Could Garrett have killed the cow elk and then encountered a predatory grizzly? It was not beyond the realm of possibility—Rick could attest to that. "If you saw a bear in the area, weren't you concerned it might come back?"

"Nope," Davis said. "Unlike McRae, I'm smart enough to carry a gun."

"Were you concerned that something might have happened to Garrett?"

"Not necessarily," Davis said with a shrug. "It wasn't like we were best of friends at that point. Like I said—he should have had a gun."

By eschewing firearms, Garrett indeed had severely compromised his safety. Had he been attacked, he would have been forced to defend himself with his bow and perhaps a hunting knife, two weapons glaringly inadequate when facing a grizzly fighting over a kill.

"Did you happen to find any of Mr. McRae's belongings in the area?" Rick asked. "For example, did you see his backpack?"

Davis wagged his head. "No backpack," he muttered.

"Is there a reason we would find your fingerprints on his pack?"

Davis paused to consider the question. "I probably touched it at camp. I might have moved it because it was in the way."

"*Several* of your prints were on the pack," Rick said. "It seems like you handled it extensively."

Davis shrugged nonchalantly, his snide expression suggesting he thought he had gained some sort of upper hand.

Rick persisted. "How do you explain Garrett's blood being on your shirt?"

"Mr. Davis …" Nash said. He almost placed his hand on Davis's forearm, but his client's cold glare made him retreat.

"McRae and I had a fistfight," Davis said. "I hit him pretty hard in the nose, might've even broken it." He flexed the fingers of his right hand, snickering as he stared at his knuckles with satisfaction. "He had blood gushing out of his nostrils, dripping all over the place. I'm sure that's how it got on my shirt. You can ask Kyle—he saw the whole thing."

Rick's forehead tightened. "Kyle said you guys were arguing, and he blacked out."

"Yeah, *right*," Davis huffed. "Nope. Kyle saw the whole thing. I looked right at him when I was on top of McRae, pounding his face. Kyle stared back at me, and he didn't look all that interested in stopping us."

Rick pursed his lips. "So, let me get this straight. You and Garrett get into an argument, likely because you had an affair with his wife. He leaves camp, and you head out afterward, only to return with his horse, which is carrying an elk he killed and tagged. Your fingerprints are on his backpack, and his blood is on your shirt. Then, you wait until the following Wednesday before you report him missing." He leaned forward, placing his interlocked fingers on the table. "Do you see why we might find all of this a bit suspicious, Mr. Davis?"

Rick cast his eyes toward Nash. The lawyer had his eyelids closed, thumb and forefinger massaging his temple and forehead.

"I didn't do nothin' to Garrett," Davis said. "I ain't got nothin' to hide."

"If you're so innocent," Rick said, "then why were you so intent on getting rid of your shirt? You drove thirty miles out of your way to dump it."

Davis's eyes widened. "Because of all this!" he said, raising his voice. "I managed to stay out of trouble for over ten years. Then this shit happened. I knew if I told you the truth, you would never believe me."

Rick nodded. "You're right about that."

Davis clenched his teeth. "I didn't kill Garrett."

"So you say, Mr. Davis." Rick nodded toward the deputy, who stood as rigid and still as a statue. "I'm done here—at least for now."

* * *

Rick steered his truck through the twisting turns of Bozeman Pass, unwrapping a deep-fried drive-thru sandwich that purportedly contained fish, though there was strong doubt its contents had ever been out to sea. His stomach rumbling from hunger, he took two quick bites and stuffed half of the sandwich back into the bag, burying the sleeve of French fries he'd received in place of his requested order of onion rings.

His cell phone rang. Helen.

"Sorry to bother you, Sheriff, but there's an insurance man on the line who wants to talk to you. This is the third time he's called."

"I don't find myself much in the mood to be talking to insurance people these days."

"He's not a salesman," Helen said. "He said he has information that might have some bearing on the Garrett McRae case. At least, that's what *he* seems to think."

"Did he give you any details?"

"He insisted on talking to you personally. Should I patch the call through to you?"

"Sure," Rick said. He brushed crumbs off his fingers and waited. A soft, measured voice came onto the line.

"Sheriff?" the man asked. "Is this Sheriff Morrand?"

"Yes sir," Rick answered. "Whom do I have the pleasure of speaking to?"

"My name is Spencer Bible."

Spencer Bible. Now there's a peculiar name. Had he heard it before? He couldn't quite place it. "How may I help you?"

"Well, Sheriff, I'm calling about the missing bow hunter, Garrett McRae?" Spencer said. "I assume he hasn't been found?"

"No, he has not," Rick said solemnly. His mind flashed to the grim discovery of a fibula surrounded by what was assumed to be Garrett's bloody clothing. "Would you have information regarding his whereabouts?"

"Not regarding his whereabouts, no," Spencer said. "It's my understanding some of his remains may have been found?"

"Nothing is official," Rick said tersely, still piqued that information had leaked to the press. He found himself growing impatient. "Can you tell me your interest in this case, Mr. Bible?"

"I manage Western Montana Insurance Company, located in Great Falls. We sell home, auto, and group health policies, as well as life insurance. In any case, my office received a couple of peculiar calls during the last week, both from the same woman. She wouldn't identify herself during the first call, but the second time she did."

Rick's brow tightened. He picked up an untouched fountain drink purchased from the drive-thru, a Diet Coke that was actually Dr. Pepper. He rolled his eyes and shook his head. "What did the woman say?"

"I only talked to her once myself, and she wouldn't give me her name," the insurance man said. "She was asking me hypothetical questions about life insurance."

"What kind of hypothetical questions?"

"She asked how long it took to receive a payoff on a policy if someone goes missing. I explained that we would need a death certificate to pay on a policy. If we had no death certificate, there would be a delay of up to seven years. She got really upset by that."

Rick nodded slowly as he bit the side of his lip. "What else did she say?"

"That was it. She hung up on me."

"But she called again?"

"Yes, she did—just this morning," Spencer said. "I wasn't in the office, but she left her information with my secretary. Amber McRae—same last name as the missing hunter. When we checked our files, it turns out that we sold a life insurance policy for $500,000 to Garrett McRae not too long ago. My secretary did the original application and submitted it—that's probably why it didn't immediately ring any bells." He paused a beat. "Things have been a bit hectic around our office. My father actually owns the agency, and he has fallen ill."

"I'm sorry to hear about your father."

"Thank you," Spencer said quietly. "My secretary told me she remembers the application—I guess she found Mr. McRae to be fairly good-looking. He told her that his wife had insisted he get the policy because they have a disabled son, and she was concerned about his care if something happened to him. From what my secretary says, it sounded like his wife was really adamant about it. Rachel said Mr. McRae seemed amused by the whole thing."

Rick straightened in his seat and took another draw of Dr. Pepper. "I assume the beneficiary on the policy is Amber McRae?"

"That's correct," Spencer said.

"Did your secretary tell you the reason Amber called?"

"Absolutely. Mrs. McRae wanted to file a benefit claim on the life insurance policy. Rachel told her the same thing I did—we can't pay a benefit claim until we receive a death certificate. Am I correct in assuming there has been no death certificate issued?"

Rick hesitated. "No, there hasn't," he finally said.

He knew that the chances of finding Garrett alive were virtually nonexistent. Convincing evidence pointed to a fatal grizzly attack, a rare but credible occurrence in the Montana Rockies. In most cases, hikers and hunters had survived intense bear encounters to recite their tales of peril. Such had been Rick's good fortune. Perhaps Garrett McRae had not been so lucky.

Still, Rick continued to maintain his strong suspicion of James Edward Davis as though gnawing on the grizzle of a flatiron steak. There was both tangible and circumstantial evidence to suggest that Davis brought harm to Garrett McRae. Why was Amber McRae, who had been involved in a romantic affair with Davis, so eager to collect on her husband's life insurance policy?

"Sheriff Morrand?" Spencer Bible said, jarring Rick from his thoughts. "I'm wondering if maybe I'm making too big a deal out of all this. I just thought—"

"No, I appreciate you calling, Mr. Bible," Rick said. "You done good, son. You done really good."

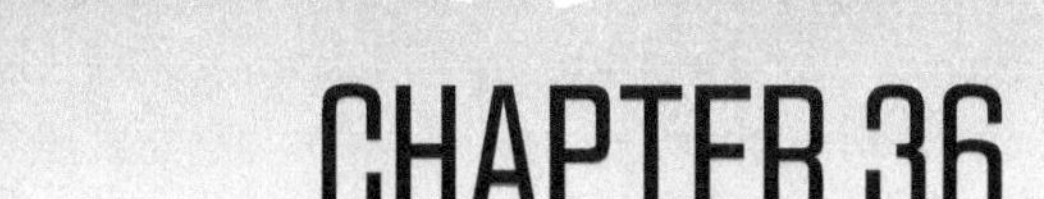

CHAPTER 36

Rick awoke Wednesday morning to find a shapely blonde standing in his kitchen, her red plaid cowgirl shirt tucked inside the tight jeans wrapped around her faultless hips. The pleasant aroma of thick-cut bacon filled the air as it crackled and popped in an iron skillet on the stove. A fresh pot of coffee gurgled as it finished brewing on the counter nearby.

"Well, what do you think?" Sage asked as she whirled around to face her fiancé. She tilted her head and raised her eyebrows, her lips curling into a mischievous, alluring grin.

She had requested that they all stay at the ranch for the time being, given its ample size and overall tranquility. Rick had slept in the master bedroom, with Sage taking the guest room, although she had tiptoed down the hall shortly after midnight and crawled in bed with him, retreating before Abby awoke. Had she known, Abby likely would think they were being silly to be so secretive. Sage certainly did.

"I like it," Rick said, blinking the sleep from his eyes so he could study Sage's new look.

"Not too Dolly Parton, is it?" Sage asked, flicking golden curls off her shoulder.

"You can never have too much Dolly Parton," Rick said with a smile. He eased closer to her. "You sure you want to be making breakfast?"

"I got a family to feed," Sage said. "It's time for me to get back to livin'. I find that more appealing than focusing on dyin'."

Rick cocked his head and nodded with approval. "Does that mean we should keep working on our wedding and honeymoon?"

Sage placed her cup on the counter and stepped toward him, her arms wrapping around his waist. Her breath was warm, her skin sweet, eyes deep and inviting. "As long as your offer still stands."

Rick shrugged. "I was kind of on the fence, but this new look put me over the top."

Sage rolled her eyes and started to turn away, but Rick pulled her back toward him. He pressed his lips against hers, and they became lost in a long, deep kiss. He felt her midsection knead with his, arousing his senses. Her fingers dug deep into the thick muscle of his spine, her soft breasts tight against his chest.

"Gross!"

They started to giggle at the sound of Abby's voice, their foreheads pressing together in resignation. "Now why do you go saying something like that?" Sage said, turning toward her.

"'Cause it's gross!" Abby said.

"What's gross about it?"

Abby paused in thought. "Well, no offense, but you guys are kind of old."

Sage's eyes widened. "Old? Abby Morrand, we're not old!"

Rick burst into laughter. "Tell you what, Abby, you just go ahead and think kissing is gross until you're … say … twenty-five. Sound alright?"

"Don't worry, I don't like boys," Abby answered. "They're boring."

Sage cast a glance toward Rick. "Yeah, you might have a point there."

"C'mon," Rick protested. "That's two against one."

They laughed in unison, perhaps relishing their rare moment of mirth. The death of Chloe Morrand, daughter and mother, had cast a gloomy pall over their family, one that only recently had begun to lift. Then came Sage's illness, the outcome of which remained treacherously uncertain. Any interlude of joy was welcomed, regardless of how fleeting it might be.

Abby stood on her toes to reach into a cupboard, tugging a box adorned with a tropical bird and the word "Choco-Puffs" across the front. She then reached into the fridge for a carton of milk.

"Talk about gross," Rick said. "You're having chocolate for breakfast?"

"I like them," Abby answered. "And they're better than eggs."

"I thought you liked eggs," Sage said, handing Abby a bowl and spoon.

Abby's face crinkled with distaste. "They're gross. You're eating a baby chick!"

"Not necessarily," Rick said. "Chicks only come from eggs that have been fertilized."

Abby cocked her head. "How do they become fertilized?"

"From a rooster," Rick said. "It happens when a hen and rooster mate."

Abby thought a moment, seemingly constructing a visual picture in her mind. "Gross!" she shouted.

They burst into laughter once more.

• • •

Rick drove directly to Charlie's office, the coroner having received results of DNA tests on the fibula found in the Crazies. Surprising to no one, the sequence matched that of Garrett McRae, generating a ghastly scenario in which a large creature—presumably a grizzly—had sunk its teeth deep into the calf of its prey, removing the entire rear bone of the lower leg while tearing loose a sizeable chunk of flesh. The thought of such occurrence sent a frigid chill racing the length of Rick's spine, his stomach churning as he considered his recent harrowing brush with death.

Charlie had more news. "We need to get back up to the Crazies," he said as he pulled a brown Carhartt jacket off his wooden coatrack. "Looks like they found more remains."

"A body?"

"Nope. I'd say it was more like … remains. The searchers are saying they found what appears to be rib bones, and maybe some more clothing."

Rick swallowed deep into his throat. "Where did they find this stuff?"

"Northeast of where the leg bone was found," Charlie said. "A dog picked up a scent and led them to the second scene."

"Was it the same dog as before? That dog belonging to Meredith Hart?"

"Negative," Charlie said. "I used a bloodhound owned by Corky Rollins."

"Don't know him."

"Out of Billings. He's got a good dog—true bloodhound."

"What happened to Meredith?"

Charlie shrugged. "No one was able to get in touch with her." He began to walk out the door. "She seems to have vanished."

Rick snagged Charlie's bicep. "Wait a minute. What do you mean *vanished*?"

"I mean, she is nowhere to be found," Charlie answered. "I tried to tell you that there was something about her that didn't seem quite right." He flicked the light switch in his office. "Are we going to get going or what?"

• • •

The scene where the latest evidence was found was as gruesome as the previous one had been. The fire had seared what was left of a blood-soaked flannel shirt. A pair of rib bones, stained with dried blood, lay on a pile of what looked like bone crushed to the fine texture of sawdust.

Charlie's eyes traced back down the pathway that had led to the evidence. He walked slowly across the burnt underbrush, scanning the scorched earth along what had once been a narrow game trail. He stopped on occasion, bending down to have a closer look at the ground. Rick, Ben Westfall, and one of two search team members watched him attentively, as if he were conducting a seminar.

Seventy-five yards into his search, Charlie reached into his back pocket for a pair of nitrile gloves. "Sheriff!" he shouted at he dropped to one knee. Rick walked purposefully through the charred thicket, his boots kicking up clouds of ash. As he approached, he realized Charlie was staring at a blackened billfold lying in the brush. The coroner took a knife from his belt and used the tip to open the flap of the wallet and reveal a driver's license holder. Rick knelt next to Charlie, staring at the wallet. The plastic covering the license was shriveled and brown, partially obscuring the photo, but Rick could easily make out the word *McRae*.

Air left his chest. He glanced at Charlie and back at the license, eyes widening in an odd disbelief. He was well aware that Garrett's chances of survival had severely diminished over the previous two weeks, but he found himself unprepared to accept the finality of the man's death—the first death on Rick's watch not attributed to natural causes. His mind flashed to the photo of Amber and Garrett that adorned their refrigerator, their beaming smiles illuminating a future of happiness and promise. His face tightened into a wince as he considered Gabe, the disabled child who now was likely fatherless.

"I hate to say it, but I think he was alive at this juncture—at least, *temporarily*," Charlie said solemnly. "It's possible the first bite didn't kill him, and he may well have dropped his wallet before he bled out."

"Hoping we could follow his trail?" Rick asked.

Charlie nodded.

Rick felt a shiver, once again reliving his own grizzly attack. His nostrils flared as his eyes darted about his surroundings, his senses filling with the phantom smell of the bear's fetid stench.

"You okay?" Charlie asked.

"Yeah, sure, fine," Rick said, snapping alert. "So, you figure he's … dead?"

Charlie pulled a plastic bag from his jacket and used his knife to edge the wallet inside. "I wouldn't say that just yet, although I honestly don't see how anyone could possibly survive the blood loss I've seen so far." He nodded up the trail. "There seems to be a couple of rib bones among those remains. I'm going to run tests on those, just to confirm the DNA matches up."

Rick nodded. "You figure there are more remains?"

"Being a coroner, I prefer to have a body—even if I have to piece it together," he said. "I'm thinking this animal—I'm assuming a grizzly—dragged its prey along this trail, likely trying to take it somewhere to stash it. Apparently, the bear decided to have a snack or two along the way."

Rick's stomach churned. "You mean he was headed to a den or something? Where do you figure that might be?"

Charlie flicked his chin to the north. "Up in that mess somewhere," he said, pointing toward what looked like dense snarls of burnt brush tangled with an endless labyrinth of crisscrossed fallen timbers.

"You think this grizzly could have made it through all that?"

Charlie chuckled. "A grizzly can make it through anything."

• • •

As he and Charlie rode in Ben's side-by-side back toward their vehicles, Rick noticed a young uniformed man leaning against a US Forest Service truck, arms folded across his chest. He walked hastily toward them.

"Sheriff, I'm Special Agent Rob Deering," he said, extending his hand. "I've been working with Chief Greer on the investigation into the origin of the Granite Peak Fire."

"Nice to meet you, Officer Deering," Rick said, gripping his hand. "What have you determined?"

Deering had a slight build, his close-cropped hair leading to patches of fuzz posing as sideburns. A maiden attempt at a moustache was penciled across his upper lip. Rick had heard about him. Though Deering looked like he was only months out of Bridger High, he had quickly developed a reputation as being a bright investigator with a meticulous attention to detail. Rick was eager to hear what he had to say.

"We're confident the fire was caused by an electrical wire," Deering began. "In most cases those wires are snapped by a fallen tree. This time around there were no trees in the area where the break occurred. As you know, this whole thing started with a brush fire."

"How do you figure that wire broke?"

Deering shook his head and pursed his lips. "We don't know for certain at this point, Sheriff. But the way the wire was frayed, it almost looks like it might have been severed by a bullet."

Rick's head cocked backward. "What kind of bullet? A rifle?"

Deering's face crinkled in frustration. "Had to be, but it's hard to tell. Finding a casing in that area is like looking for a needle in a haystack." He paused a beat. "A burnt haystack, I guess."

Rick scanned the blackened descending foothills to the east, which gave way to endless acres of grasslands. The distant fields were dotted with rolled-up bales of hay, each resembling a toasted cinnamon roll propped up on its side, the yield from the second cut of the season. Most of the cows were gone, having been hauled away in long trailers swiftly carrying them to an abrupt fate they never saw coming. Perhaps humans and cattle were similar that way.

"There are some cattle ranchers in this area," Rick said. "Have you talked to them, asked them if they saw anything?"

"I'm working on that," Deering answered. "I saw some four-wheeler tracks down closer to Highway 191. They were in tight circles, maybe kids doing donuts or something. That would be my guess, anyway. I'm going to find out who exactly lives around here."

"Keep me posted," Rick said. "I'm especially interested in finding that shell casing. If someone set that fire intentionally, there might be a tie-in to my investigation."

Deering nodded. "You got it, Sheriff."

• • •

When they arrived back in Riverton, Charlie vowed to overnight the latest evidence to the lab in Missoula, claiming he would make sure the findings were processed at warp speed. Rick was amused by the promise, given that "warp speed" was not the phrase he would normally associate with the everyday progression of events in Montana. He also knew that Charlie had called in some favors to receive quick results, and his capital with the lab might soon be running low.

As he pulled onto Main Street, he heard his phone vibrate on the console and checked caller ID. Patty Martin.

"Got some bad news," she said in a tone that was both abrupt and businesslike. "Looks like two marshals will be up from Texas next Wednesday to pick up your boy."

Rick winced. "Davis?"

"That's the only boy of yours I'm holding here, unless there's somebody else."

"You can't let him go," Rick said.

"Excuse me?"

"I'm not done with him yet."

"Not *done* with him?" Patty coughed up a half-laugh as if discharging a hairball. "Oh, I think you're done with him. By the middle of next week, he'll be gone."

"Can't you stall them?" Rick pleaded.

"Negative. I'm not in the business of *stalling* anybody. Besides, this dirt bag has been here so long that he's gone way beyond stink. One of my deputies put a drunk driver in with him, and Davis ended up beating the crap out of the guy."

"Sorry to hear that," Rick murmured.

"I'm sure you are," she snapped. Patty blew out a sigh, filling Rick's ear with the forceful sound of her breath. "Rick, I'm not sure why you have such a hard-on for Davis, but maybe it's time to let it go. Trust me—he'll get what's coming to him in Texas." She paused a beat. "Besides, didn't I hear there were more remains found in the Crazies?"

"How'd you hear that?"

"I'm sheriff of Gallatin County, in case you might have forgot," Patty said. "What did they find this time around?"

"More bones," Rick answered. "Charlie Duchesne is thinking they might be … ribs."

"Ribs," Patty repeated. "Sounds like this bow hunter just might have been dragged off by a grizzly, as disheartening as that may be. Why is it so hard for you to wrap your head around that?"

"Something just doesn't add up."

"Well, I would suggest that you figure out what doesn't add up within the next few days," Patty said. "By next Wednesday, Davis will be gone."

CHAPTER 37

Jack Kelly always hated liars, which essentially meant he harbored contempt for just about every crime suspect, person of interest, domestic abuser, meth head, drug dealer, or garden-variety gangbanger he had encountered during his lengthy career as a detective in Newark. As he pulled up to the workplace of Kyle Ricketts on Thursday to follow up on his initial interview, he realized how little things had changed.

Ricketts was at his customary post outside the garage, sucking on a vape pipe as though it were delivering mother's milk. When he spotted Jack's rig, he darted around the corner of the building down an alleyway right into a sixteen-foot barbed-wire fence that proved impossible to scale. Jack tugged on the back of Kyle's belt, easing him back down to earth.

"You lied to me," Jack said, his tone suggesting the concept astonished him.

"I don't know what you are talking about," Kyle said, making a feeble attempt to break around Jack to freedom.

"See now, you just lied again," he said, grabbing Kyle with one hand and pinning him against the chain-link fence.

Kyle's face twitched, his head wagging back and forth, pupils dilated and vacant, face tightened in terror.

"What are you trying to hide?"

"I … I'm not hiding anything," Kyle said, his voice trembling.

"Why did you lie to me?"

Kyle's lips quivered, exposing the spaced teeth of a jack-o-lantern. "I … I guess I didn't want to get involved."

"Well, you *are* involved," Jack said. "A hunter goes missing in the backcountry, and you don't bother to tell anyone for almost four days? I need to know why you lied to me." He clenched his teeth and shook his head. "Damn, I just *hate* it when people lie to me."

"Hey, what's going on here?" a voice behind Jack barked. Holding Kyle in place, Jack looked to see a short, round man standing at the end of the alley. "That's one of my employees you have there."

Jack squinted, adjusting the aviators resting on the broad bridge of his nose. "You the owner of this place?"

"That's right," the man answered, temporarily emboldened.

"You might want to consider implementing a drug-testing program."

"He's a good worker."

"I'm sure he is," Jack said, "provided he's all jacked up on whatever he's jacked up on." He ran his tongue across his upper lip and flicked his head toward the building. "Now you go ahead and go back to work."

"I'd like to know what's going on," the man protested.

"Duly noted," Jack answered. "Now get the hell out of here!"

The owner mumbled something and waddled back toward the front of the building. Jack turned toward Kyle, who had beads of sweat forming on his ashen forehead.

"I'm going to release my grip, but I want you to stand still," he said. "At least, I want you to stand as still as you can."

Kyle blinked and nodded. Jack calmly took a step back from him. He folded his aviators and hooked them inside the top of his open collar. "Now, as I recall, you told me that you blacked out when Garrett threw down with this Davis character."

"Who?" Kyle asked, appearing confused.

"Davis. Boone. Whatever his name is," Jack snapped. "You told me that when the two of them started arguing, you blacked out. We've come to find out that's not necessarily true, now, is it?"

Kyle cast his eyes toward the ground and shook his head.

Jack lifted Kyle's jaw with his thumb and forefinger. "Keeping in mind that we're now telling the truth, you want to tell me what actually happened?"

Kyle averted his eyes, wiping his brow with a filthy shirtsleeve. "We were settin' around the fire, passin' a bottle of Jack Daniels, and somehow Amber's name came up," he said. "Boone didn't seem to want to talk about her, but Garrett kept pressing him, egging him on. I stepped away for a minute to piss, and when I came back, they were trading blows."

"According to Davis—*Boone*—Garrett's nose might have been broken," Jack said.

Kyle's fearful eyes glanced at Jack before darting away. "He was bleeding, yeah," Kyle answered. "And that was pretty weird. Garrett was—*is*—one tough dude. He was always sticking up for people, including me. I was surprised to see Boone getting the better of him."

"What happened next?"

Kyle shrugged. "Eventually, they quit. We all went to sleep, and when I woke up, Garrett was already gone. Not long after that, Boone took off himself."

"That was Saturday?"

"Yeah."

"And on Saturday you thought you heard Garrett on your radio."

Kyle wagged his head and pursed his lips. "I think so."

"Did Boone come back to camp that night?"

"No."

"Did you find that unusual?"

"Not really. These guys have caches of supplies in different places."

"When did Boone come back?"

"Early morning on Monday."

Jack paused a moment, stroking his square jaw. "Did anything unusual happen while you were sitting around camp for two days?"

Kyle squinted. "What do you mean?"

Jack shrugged. "Oh, I don't know. Did you see anything, hear anything?" He leaned forward, dipping his head to make eye contact. "Don't forget— we're being honest."

Kyle thought a moment. "Uh, yeah, I guess there was something," he said. "Early in the morning on Sunday, I heard a couple of gunshots."

"What kind of gunshots?"

"They were pretty loud. I'd guess it was a long rifle. I thought it was strange, being bow hunting season and all."

"Did you ask Boone about the shots when he got back to camp?"

"No."

"Why not?"

"I …. I guess I didn't want to upset him."

"Did Boone have a rifle?"

Kyle nodded. "Sure," he said. "Most bow hunters have one in a scabbard on their horse. If you're smart, you also carry a sidearm."

"How many shots did you hear?"

"Two."

"You sure?"

"Positive. At least, there were two that day."

"What do you mean?" Jack said, tilting his head. He placed a firm grip on Kyle's clavicle. "Just the truth."

Kyle nodded, the bridge of his nose growing taut, mouth compressed as if he'd tasted something sour. "I … I may have heard other shots—maybe a day later," he murmured. "Like I was saying, it was weird to hear that during bow season."

Jack placed his hands on his hips and heaved a sigh. "You sure you're telling me everything?"

"Yes sir."

"*Everything?*"

"Yes sir. I'm positive."

Jack hiked his brow, eyes opening wide. "You realize, Mr. Ricketts, that if for some reason Garrett McRae is in fact deceased, and if he didn't perish due to natural causes, you might well be an accessory?"

Kyle swallowed hard, color leaving his face. "I didn't do nothin' wrong, and I don't want no trouble, sir," he said. "I'd like to keep this job. It's hard for me to get a job with my record."

"You have a record? What for?"

"Possession, mostly."

"I'm stunned," Jack said. He looked at his watch and cast a thumb over his shoulder. "Guess you best get back to work, then." Kyle shuffled away briskly, likely in urgent search of a restroom.

Jack walked slowly toward the end of the building, where he was met by Kyle's boss. The man's face was as round as his torso, his nose flat and lips thin and pink. The top of his head was bald, wrapped in a hula skirt of short black hair. An oval patch reading "Mel" was sewed to the breast of his white open-collared shirt. "You really should go easy on him, Deputy," he said. "He's not a bad kid."

"Think so, huh? First of all, he lied to me. Second, it looks to me like he uses drugs."

"He told me he's clean."

"Case closed, then," Jack huffed. "You actually believe that?"

Mel released a breath. "He's got other issues."

"Such as?"

"Mental illness. He's been diagnosed."

"With what?"

"He told me once," the boss said, lifting his phone out of the top pocket of his shirt. "It's called dissociative something." He scrolled a pudgy thumb on the screen. "Here it is … dissociative identity disorder. It used to be called multiple personality disorder."

Jack folded his arms across his massive chest. "Tell me more."

"DID, as it is called, is characterized by a person having two distinct personality types," Mel read. "The illness can feature memory gaps that are more severe than ordinary forgetfulness."

Jack's brow furrowed. He tapped his index finger in Mel's direction. "Can you read me that last part again?"

Mel shrugged. "He forgets things, I guess. There can be long periods of time when he has no recollection of what he might have said or done. He assured me that it rarely happens. As far as I can tell, it hasn't affected his work." He slipped his phone back into his shirt. "Like I said—you should go easy on him."

"Sorry for causing an interruption at your place of business," Jack replied, quickly entering the cab of his truck. "I thank you for your time."

* * *

Despite her protests, Rick insisted on driving Sage to her MRI exam in Billings. If he knew anything about his fiancée, it was that she didn't like being startled and she had a powerful aversion to being in small places. He wanted to be there for her, figuring that his presence—combined with the benzodiazepine of her choice—would help pull her through the diagnostic procedure.

Neither of them had slept well, anticipating the imaging test that would give an early indication whether the grueling treatments Sage had endured at Dr. Tillotson's office were having any positive effect. Sage certainly wasn't saying much during the ride, except for touching on trivial topics such as the weather getting cooler, the uninspiring scenery of Eastern Montana, and her mouth being dry.

"Do you still keep bottled water in your truck?" she asked.

"Can't give you water until after the exam," Rick said. "You know that."

"Right," Sage murmured while fixing her eyes on a flock of sheep strewn across the landscape. "Guess I forgot."

They roared past the exit to Columbus, forty miles west of Billings. "Tell me," Rick said, his tone becoming solemn, "how is it that you became afraid of being confined? I don't seem to recall that being an issue for you when we were kids."

"You really want to know? The more you learn about me, the worse things get."

"Don't worry. It's not like you're marrying an Eagle Scout."

"Well, when I was a little girl, my mother's version of a timeout was to lock me in the pantry. It wasn't so much that I was confined, I guess, but more the darkness. I couldn't see a thing, and sometimes I'd be in there for three hours or more."

"Had she been drinking when she did that?"

"Ya think?"

Rick shook his head. "I saw your mother around plenty of times. I didn't even know she drank."

"People aren't always what they seem," Sage answered. She paused a beat. "There's something else I want to tell you."

"Wait, let me guess," Rick said, shooting a glance toward her. "I'm not the first man you've had relations with."

Sage slapped his bicep with the back of her hand. "Very funny. No, it's something else."

"What then?"

"She wasn't my real mother."

Rick whipped his head toward her. "Your mother wasn't your mother?"

"Nope," she answered. "My dad had an affair, and my biological mother got pregnant. I think Mom might have resented me for that."

Rick's jaw fell as he squinted toward Sage. "You look just like your mom."

"The woman who raised me and the woman who gave birth to me are both Crow. At least my father had to decency to stick with the same tribe."

"Damn," Rick said, shaking his head as he stared through the windshield at the pavement in front of him. "Why didn't you tell me this before?"

"You were never going to be my husband before."

Rick chuckled. "Anything else I need to know?"

"Nope. That about does it."

They rode in silence until Rick exited the interstate and pulled into the parking lot of the Billings Clinic. As they walked to the entrance, he held Sage's hand, which was clammy and cold. She offered a half smile, a vain attempt to mask what seemed like intense fear.

After filling out several pages of paperwork, Sage was led through a pair of cream-colored double doors, a pair of black plastic placards reading

"Radiology" beneath each of the narrow wire-mesh windows. Another half smile, no more reassuring than the first. Rick sat for a moment, then walked to the counter where Sage had delivered her paperwork. An ivory-haired woman was working on a computer screen, peering over a pair of clear-framed glasses connected to a silver chain that trailed behind her neck. She finished her task and turned toward Rick.

"May I help you, sir?"

Rick tugged a checkbook from the back pocket of his uniform pants. "I'd like to settle up with you on Ms. Fontenot's bill. Can you give me a total?"

The woman returned to her screen, typing in Sage's last name from the paperwork lying on her desk. "It looks like you are paying cash, is that correct?"

Rick felt a flash of rage run through his blood, his anger at Sage's insurance carrier suddenly rising well beyond a simmer. "That is correct," he managed to say through gritted teeth.

"After the ten-percent discount for cash, today's procedure is a total of $1,884.70."

Rick stared at his checkbook, which he was tapping against the palm of his other hand. "That's after the cash discount, huh?"

The woman smiled. "Yes sir, it is. Are you also interested in paying for the services our technicians have performed at Dr. Tillotson's office? I'm assuming that will be cash as well?"

Rick let out a shallow cough. "Sure," he said, prying the word from his throat.

"The balance for the treatments thus far is $12,797.43."

Rick felt air race from his lungs, blood leaving his face. "I assume that's also with the discount?" he muttered.

"You bet, sir," she said, her tone strong and confident. "That includes the discount."

Rick placed his checkbook on the counter. He spotted a faded plastic mug holding a pair of pens, each with a cheap plastic flower taped to it. "Can I get a grand total?" he asked, glancing toward her.

"Sure. That will be $14,682.13."

"Would it be possible to see the bills?"

"I'm so sorry, sir, but I can't do that. There is detailed information about her treatments on those bills. That would be a violation of HIIPA laws."

"She's my fiancée," he protested.

"I'm sorry, sir. That's different than being married."

Rick shook his head and began to write the check. He had known Sage's bills would be exorbitant, and savings from his one-time law career in California had given him the money to pay them. That wasn't the issue. What troubled him was the fact that Sage had paid premiums for years, only to be turned away by her insurer at her greatest time of need—all because of a single missed payment. Making matters worse, the insurance carrier had told her they could underwrite a new policy, accepting her now *preexisting* condition, provided she agree to a sky-high deductible and a hefty monthly premium, which they would be happy to deduct directly from her checking account. Even with a new policy, it would take days, weeks, maybe even months for her to see a new doctor and begin treatment. For Rick, the last part was a deal killer.

"Damn, I hate insurance companies," he mumbled as he wrote his signature.

"Sir?" the administrator asked.

"Nothing," Rick said as he handed her the check. "Would it be possible to send all of Ms. Fontenot's future bills to my office? I'm the sheriff of Dexter County. I can provide the address."

"Sorry, Sheriff, no can do," she said. "That would be—"

"Right. It would violate HIIPA laws."

"That's correct, sir. I really do apologize."

Rick nodded and walked away from the counter. He plopped into one of the several blue-cushioned chairs in the waiting area, sliding his checkbook into his back pocket. His phone vibrated inside his shirt pocket.

"Morrand," he whispered as he met the glare of an elderly patient across the room.

"There you are!" a voice loudly cackled, followed by a series of phlegm-filled hacks. "Your office said you weren't in, so I thought I would try your cell phone!"

Though Rick had spoken to Patricia Hart on only one occasion, he would recognize her voice anywhere. "Hello, Mrs. Hart," he said softly. "I'm at the doctor's office. May I call—"

"Doctor's office!" she croaked. "Sheriff, are you okay?"

"I'm fine, Mrs. Hart. I'm just—"

"What's with this Mrs. Hart business, Sheriff? You need to call me Patricia."

"Sure, Mrs. Hart—Patricia," Rick said. She sounded like she'd tossed back a few Keystones. "I'm sorry, but I'll have to call you back."

"This won't take but a minute," she said, brushing him aside. "Do you remember when you asked me where Meredith went camping the weekend after Labor Day? As you may recall, I couldn't find my address book. Well, guess what? I found it!"

The elderly woman continued to watch him, her eyes blinking as she peered above the top of a quilting magazine. He sent a tight smile her way, raising an index finger in a plea for patience. She thrust her head toward a sign that read "Please Silence Your Cell Phones" before shaking her head in disgust and returning to her reading.

"I'm happy to hear you found the address book, ma'am," Rick said. "If you can—"

"Well, I already gave the information to your secretary—the woman named Helen. She is your secretary, right?"

"Actually, she's our dispatcher, but—"

"Your dispatcher," Patricia said. "Well, I gave your dispatcher the information."

"If you can tell me where Meredith went camping, Mrs. Hart, that would be great," Rick said, seared by the stare from across the room.

"The weekend after Labor Day would be September eighth and ninth, correct?"

"Yes."

"Says here that she was going to Campfire Lake, wherever that is." Her throat sounded cluttered with gravel.

A cold sensation rippled through Rick's skin. "Campfire Lake?" he said loudly, ignoring the woman across the room. "Are you sure?"

"Yes, I'm sure. It says it right here." Her tone grew somber. "Sheriff, Meredith isn't in any kind of trouble, is she?"

"You're sure it's Campfire Lake?"

"Yes, Sheriff," Patricia repeated. "Please tell me if—"

"Have you told Meredith that I would like to speak to her?"

"I would, Sheriff, except I haven't seen her. She left a message saying she would be down in Yellowstone, attending some trainings for the Forest Service. She didn't tell me when she'd be back. Sheriff, is she—"

"Thank you for following up with me, Mrs. Hart," Rick said, ending the call. He sat slumped in his chair, numbed by the news he'd just received. He opened the internet browser on his phone, searching for the US Forest Service office in Bozeman. The woman across the room rolled her eyes as he put the phone to his ear. A receptionist answered with a buoyant, youthful voice.

"This is Sheriff Morrand from Dexter County," Rick said. "I'm trying to reach Meredith Hart."

"One moment, sir," the receptionist said, placing him on hold. The elderly woman looked at him, but his glare chased her away. The Forest Service receptionist returned. "I'm sorry, sir, but Ranger Hart is not in today."

"It's my understanding that she may be at a field training, perhaps down in Yellowstone?"

"One moment, sir," the receptionist answered, again placing him on hold. One minute later, she returned. "I'm not seeing anything scheduled, Sheriff. I also checked with my supervisor, and she confirmed there are no ongoing trainings." She paused. "Is there any other information I can provide?"

"No," Rick said, releasing a long sigh. "Thank you."

● ● ●

Sage slept for most of the entire drive back to Riverton, waking only briefly when Rick pulled into the parking lot of the sheriff's office. "I need to check my mail and see if I have any messages," he said as he gently stroked her forearm. Her damp, cool skin loosely draped over her radial bone. Sage nodded briefly without opening her eyes, adjusted herself in the passenger seat, and returned to sleep.

When Rick walked into the office, Helen was stationed at her post. He rarely saw his mail, let alone checked it, mainly because Helen usually beat him to it. She wasn't all that adept at taking messages either, since she viewed herself as a highly capable gatekeeper who could answer any question and arbitrate any citizen issue, many of which she considered trivial. Rick was there to seek her assistance on a specific matter, this one pertaining to James Edward Davis, who continued to live rent-free within the confines of the sheriff's head.

"Helen, I need to speak with you about something," he said in a hushed, somber tone as he opened the door to his office. "Can you come in a minute?"

Helen followed him in, closing the door behind her. Rick sat in his chair and pulled a white pad of paper from his desk drawer. He glanced at Helen, whose face was a ghostly white.

"Am I fired?" she asked, her voice trembling.

"Hell no, you're not fired," Rick said quickly. "Most of us will probably be dead before that ever happens." He motioned toward the chair in front of his desk. "Please, sit down."

"You sound awfully serious, Sheriff."

"My apologies—I guess I got a lot on my mind" He tapped a ballpoint pen on the blank pad. "Remember about six months ago, when you took time off to help out your family up near Kalispell?"

"Sheriff, if I am taking too much personal time—"

"Helen, please," Rick said, using his thumb and forefinger to massage his temples. "This has nothing to do with personal time, vacation time, or anything else." He drew a breath. "As I recall, you had a niece who was having some problems, correct?"

"My sister's daughter," Helen said, pushing her lips to one side. "She's a drug addict."

"How's she been doing?"

"She just jumped the fence on her fourth rehab. So I guess the answer would be 'not so good.'"

"Sorry to hear that," Rick said. "Didn't you tell me that at one point she ran off with some kind of cult?"

"She sure did," Helen answered. "That's when I went up to Kalispell. My sister was at the end of her rope."

"Do you recall which cult your niece was in?"

Helen wagged her head. "I don't remember the exact name, but the word Satan was in there somewhere, that's for sure. Why do you ask, Sheriff?"

Rick leaned on his desk and began sketching the tattoo he saw on James Davis's wrist. First, he drew the upside-down pentagram, surrounded by a round border. Next came the head of the horned goat, followed by the claws gripping the outer circle. He cocked his head to one side, studying his handiwork. The artwork looked like something Abby might have drawn—perhaps when she was three. He turned the pad toward Helen.

She paused as she studied it. "That a moose?" Helen cracked. "Or maybe a reindeer?"

"No, it's a—"

"A horned goat. Sorry, Sheriff. I don't take these folks too seriously, mainly because I have a solid faith in the Lord."

"Personally, they give me the creeps," Rick murmured. He thumped his index finger on the drawing. "You have a pentagram in a circle, a horned goat and some claws. I'm wondering if you recognize this symbol. I noticed it tattooed on the wrist of James Davis."

"The former Randall Boone?"

"The same."

Helen's eyes darted between Rick and the drawing. She rolled her tongue inside her cheek. "When my niece went missing, I did some research on cults, probably more than I would have liked."

"That's what I figured."

"You'd be amazed how many there are—right here in Montana."

"I probably don't want to know."

Helen lifted the pad off the desk. "I'll do some more research to get you a solid answer. You're thinking this somehow ties in to the case of Garrett McCrae?"

Rick leaned back in his chair, interlocking his fingers across his stomach. "It might," he said. "Let's just say I have this hunch."

CHAPTER 38

Spencer was seated at his desk late Friday, flicking periodic glances at the clock on his office wall. Lizzie would be arriving soon, meeting him for their evening date at Papa Dante's. His heart began to race when he saw her walk through the front entrance, a blue V-cut dress hugging hips that swayed as though she were striding down a Paris runway. Lizzie threw a half-smile toward Rachel when she whisked past the secretary's desk.

Clutching a bouquet of roses he'd purchased an hour earlier, Spencer rose and kissed Lizzie's cheek. The dress ignited her eyes. Her glossed lips were flawless and full, the sweet scent of her perfume seizing his senses. "Please sit down," he said, extending his upturned palm toward the chair in front of his desk. "I'm just finishing some paperwork." Lizzie sat and crossed her legs, straightening her dress before resting a gold clutch purse on her lap.

Rachel appeared at the door. "Excuse me," she said. Spencer looked up from his work, watching her place a manila folder into a metal basket on his desk. "That's the file you wanted to review. The McRae policy?"

Spencer nodded. "Good. Great. Thank you."

"I know it's not five yet, but do you mind if I take off?" Rachel asked. "I still need to go to the post office."

"Totally fine," Spencer said with a nod. "See you on Monday."

"Yes, Monday." Rachel delivered a skeptical stare toward Lizzie and turned away from the door.

"I don't think she likes me," Lizzie whispered.

"Oh, Rachel just takes a little while to get to know people." He shrugged. "I know *I* like you."

Lizzie giggled, her plush eyebrows raising. "I guess I like you too."

Spencer reviewed the form on his desk, then picked up a pen and signed it. "I just need to make a couple copies of these, and we'll be on our way." He cast a brief smile, rose from his desk, and left his office.

With his eyes glued to the document he needed to copy, Spencer puckered his lips and whistled an uneven tune, blissfully anticipating his date with Lizzie and the carnal events that were sure to follow. He loaded the document and pressed the copy button before releasing an exasperated breath. *Out of paper.*

"This might take a minute," he said as he walked back toward his office. "I need to go into the storage closet and find—" Lizzie was perusing the file that Rachel had placed on his desk. She quickly closed the folder and returned it to the metal basket. Spencer's eyebrows furrowed as he tilted his head.

"Oh, I'm sorry," Lizzie said nervously. "I … guess I was being nosy." She paused a beat. "It's just that I've never seen an actual insurance policy before, and I was … curious."

"I see," Spencer murmured, nodding. He pointed down the hallway. "Anyway, I, uh, need to get some copy paper from the storage closet."

Lizzie rose and exhaled, a brow lifted. "What kind of storage closet is it?" she asked, eyes tinged with mischief. "I mean, is it large enough to—"

"We really need to go," Spencer said with a laugh, his face growing warm. "We have a reservation."

"Oh, all right." She pressed her soft, full lips tightly against his, evaporating the world around him.

• • •

Spencer tucked Lizzie's arm under his as they entered Pape Dante's. Frequent visits to the venue of their first date had become somewhat of a tradition, to the extent that their nascent love affair could have such a thing. Lizzie had lightheartedly explained to him that Italian food contained aphrodisiacs, secret love potions that would assist in launching them into an evening of passionate lovemaking. The thought aroused him, although Lizzie's eager and explorative manner in the bedroom already fed him with a desire that had little to do with his diet, be it basil manicotti or macaroni and cheese.

A hostess escorted them past the buzzing voices and clinking glasses of the happy-hour crowd, leading them through an archway to a table in the back of the restaurant. The din of the bar area faded, giving way to the voice of Andrea Bocelli flowing gracefully from speakers in the ceiling.

"I like this song," Spencer said.

The hostess glanced over her shoulder. "I never get tired of it—it's so *romantic*," she said. "It's called 'Time To Say Goodbye.'"

Spencer turned toward Lizzie. "Do you like this song?" She was staring straight ahead and didn't answer. "Lizzie?"

Her eyes blinked rapidly. "I'm sorry. Did you say something?"

"I was asking … never mind," he said, helping with her chair.

After they had ordered, Lizzie offered only occasional glances toward him. Her smile seemed forced and distant as it flickered in the dim light of the glass-encased candle resting at the center of their table. She responded with one-word answers while her fork poked at the sliced olives and feta cheese sprinkled across the top of her dinner salad.

"Are you sure nothing's wrong?" Spencer asked as he watched her sip red wine. An innocent wag of her head was followed by a long period of silence.

"I wanted to ask you something," she finally said.

Spencer wiped his mouth with his cloth napkin. "Please do."

"Your secretary gave you a file for someone named McRae. Is that the missing hunter?" She took a quick drink from her glass. "I mean, if it's none of my business, just say the word."

"No, it's fine," Spencer said, laying his fork on his salad plate. "Yes, a man named Garrett McRae has been missing. I'm surprised you knew about it."

"It's kind of hard to miss," Lizzie said. "I mean, it's been on the news as well as social media."

Lizzie paused, holding her glass aloft and swirling her wine. "Did they find him?"

"Not yet," Spencer said. "They don't know if he's alive or dead, although I have to say it's not looking good." His eyes roamed the restaurant before he turned back toward Lizzie. "He has a policy with us—a life insurance policy. It's been kind of a strange situation."

Lizzie stared expectantly at him. "How so?"

"His wife has called our office a couple of times. The first time she called, he hadn't been missing all that long. She didn't give her name, and she was asking vague questions about life insurance. This week, she demanded payment on the policy."

Lizzie nodded. "If I remember correctly, she has a disabled child, doesn't she?"

Spencer shrugged. "I'm not aware of—"

"I'm sure of it," Lizzie said. "She has a young child in a wheelchair. I saw a picture. I think someone was trying to start a GoFundMe account. She's really strapped for cash."

"I don't know if—"

"So, what do you think?" Lizzie asked. "Are you going to pay?"

"Pay what?"

She flipped her hand as she took another sip of wine. "The policy, the benefit, whatever it's called."

"It's called a benefit," Spencer said as he exhaled, "and, no, we don't plan to pay it. We require a death certificate to do that."

"How long has the hunter been missing?"

"I guess now it's closer to three weeks."

"Have they found any trace of him?"

"Oh yeah," Spencer said, eyes opened wide. "They found some of his belongings … and more than that."

Lizzie's eyebrows furrowed. "Like what?"

"Remains."

"I think they mentioned that on the news. Did they find his body?"

"Some bones," Spencer said. "They think he may have been attacked by a grizzly."

"Bones? A grizzly?" she asked, wincing. "How sad. I feel so sorry for that woman—especially with a disabled child. Why don't you just pay the … What is it called again?"

"Benefit."

"Benefit," Lizzie repeated. "Why don't you pay the benefit? It sounds like her husband is dead."

"It doesn't work that way," Spencer insisted. "We need a death certificate. The coroner needs to determine that the man is deceased."

"What if the coroner doesn't issue a death certificate?"

Spencer shrugged. "Then they have to wait seven years."

"Seven *what*? That's so wrong!" Lizzie huffed, emptying her glass. She searched for their waiter, the guy named Fred who masqueraded evenings as Alfredo. He quickly shuffled toward them with a bottle of Chianti, refilling Lizzie's glass and offering more wine to Spencer, who waved him off.

"Your entrees will be ready shortly," Alfredo offered, perhaps reading Spencer's concern about Lizzie drinking on an empty stomach.

"Thank you," Spencer said abruptly. He watched the waiter walk away and turned toward Lizzie. "What do you mean, it's so *wrong*?"

"It just is," Lizzie said, taking a drink from her replenished glass. "It's obvious the man is dead, and his wife is left to care for a disabled child. Insurance companies have tons of money. Why not just pay it?"

"Tons of money?"

"Absolutely," Lizzie said. "Insurance companies are loaded. Everyone knows that."

Spencer rolled his eyes. "Insurance companies invest their money wisely, if that's what you mean."

"Whatever," she said, drinking more wine.

Spencer stared at her glass. "Do you think maybe you should slow down a bit?"

"Excuse me?"

"You seem to be hitting the wine pretty good. We haven't eaten yet."

Lizzie sneered at him, defiantly lifted her wine, and downed it. She motioned to Alfredo, glass extended. Alfredo filled it. Spencer stared at her, rendered impotent as she took another gulp and placed her glass on the table. She stood unsteadily, picking up her purse and holding it against her chest. "I'll be leaving now," she said as she plucked a light sweater off the back of her chair.

Spencer stood. "But we haven't had our food," he protested.

"I don't plan to eat with you."

"Why not? What have I done?"

"You obviously are not the man I thought you were."

Spencer was speechless. He squinted at Lizzie, mouth agape. "What do you mean?"

"I mean I'm out of here."

"At least, let me go with you."

"No thanks," Lizzie said dismissively. "I'll walk. It's not far."

"You can't walk alone."

"Oh, really?" she smirked. "It's Great Falls, for Christ's sake. Good-bye!"

Spencer watched helplessly as Lizzie stormed toward the front door, her perfect bare legs rising from the ankle straps of her suede high-heeled shoes. She grasped the back of a chair from a nearby table, steadying herself against the alcohol. Spencer sat back down, slumping in his chair. He lifted his eyes to find Alfredo, who was standing in front of him, an entrée in either hand.

"I guess you'd better pack those to go, Fred," Spencer mumbled. "I seem to have lost my appetite."

There would be no need for aphrodisiacs on this night.

CHAPTER 39

Rick sat at his desk late Monday morning, a cup of Helen's coffee cradled in his hands. He took a sip, wincing as though he'd just had a shot of cheap whiskey. He lifted the window behind his chair and tossed the coffee out, figuring it was better to destroy the evidence than hurt Helen's feelings.

His office door opened as he shut the window, making him wonder whether he'd been caught in the act. Jack Kelly appeared, holding a cup of Helen's coffee in one hand. His massive frame settled into a heavy wooden chair in front of Rick's desk. He wore a half smile tinged with concern.

"How's Sage?" the undersheriff asked. "She doing okay?"

"We should know soon enough," Rick answered. "She had an MRI last Thursday to find out how the chemo is working."

Jack cocked his head. "Last Thursday? Shouldn't they have something by now? I thought all that stuff is computerized."

"It is, but they say they need *comprehensive* results," Rick huffed. "Probably covering their asses so they don't get sued."

"Damned lawyers."

They both laughed before Rick turned serious. "Meanwhile, Sage had to spend the weekend on pins and needles waiting for the results." The room fell silent as they mourned the thought. "Anyway, tell me about your interview with Kyle Ricketts. How'd that go?"

"The guy is a real piece of work."

"So you said."

Jack lifted a spiral notebook from the top pocket of his uniform shirt. He licked his thumb and rustled through the pages. "Ricketts did confirm that he heard two shots—most likely a long rifle—sometime Sunday morning. So Davis saying he fired a couple of shots to run off a bear apparently checks out."

Rick shook his head. "It does and it doesn't."

"How so?"

"You confirmed that Davis fired a rifle, but we *can't* confirm exactly *what* he was shooting at."

Jack eyes narrowed. "What's your theory?"

Rick shrugged. "Not sure if I have one—at least not fully developed. Thing is, I don't have a whole lot of faith in anything Davis says."

Jack's eyes drifted back down to his notebook. "Here's something else. Ricketts claims he may have heard more shots, possibly on Monday. He said they sounded like they were far away, but he thinks they had the echo of a rifle."

"Monday?" Rick asked. "Morning or afternoon?"

"Not sure. Why?"

"That's the day the Granite Peak Fire kicked up," Rick said. "It was a brush fire on Monday, and they thought they had it contained. It started to get away from them later that day."

"Tell me about it," Jack said, recalling the near-death experience he would have two days later. "What do gunshots have to do with the Granite Peak Fire?"

"The guy investigating it for the Forest Service finds the fire suspicious, to say the least. He claims it was started when a downed power line fell into the scrub, and the power line snapped because it was severed by a bullet."

Jack lifted his eyebrows, pressing his lips together into a flat line. "That sounds like a reach."

"Rob Deering, the agent for the Forest Service, is pretty confident it happened," Rick said. "I trust his judgment."

"So, back to my original question: What's your theory? Why would Davis decide to start a wildland fire?"

"I'm still working on it," Rick said. "I'm not quite there yet, but I think I'm getting closer." He laid his palms flat on his desk. "You have anything else?"

Jack nodded. "As a matter of fact, I do," he said, returning to his notes. "You ever hear of something called dissociated identity disorder?"

"I'm afraid I do," Rick said, pinching his lips to one side. "That was Chloe's diagnosis at one point. As I recall, the person can go for periods of time and not remember their actions. In Chloe's case, they concluded that behavior resulted from drugs, not her mental illness."

Jack shrugged. "Ricketts supposedly has that diagnosis. He did claim at one point that he blacked out. Maybe he had some kind of episode and forgot exactly what he did. Maybe—"

"I thought he and Garrett were close."

"Gotta tell ya, dude struck me as bat-shit crazy," Jack said. He winced, holding his eyes tightly closed. "Sorry, Sheriff—poor choice of words."

Rick wagged his head. "No worries—you're good." He released a long sigh. "Let's take a look at how close Ricketts and McRae actually were. After all, neither of those hunters seemed overly concerned they left Garrett behind."

The office door opened, and Helen poked her head in. "Sorry to interrupt, but I have a complaint down in the valley and no one else is available."

"What's the complaint?" Rick asked.

Helen drew a breath. "Stitch Hogan was moving his cattle down East River Road, bringing them back from summer pasture. Apparently, he and his crew didn't do a good job of cleaning up."

Rick frowned. "How bad can it be?"

"Probably nothing a good rain couldn't cure," Helen said. "That is, if we had a good rain."

"Who called in the complaint?"

"A woman named Abigail Alton. She's called a few times. New to the area—thick New York accent. She said Hogan's cows made her get dung all over the tires of her Porsche Cayenne."

"Shit," Jack said.

"Exactly," Helen said, throwing him a glance.

Rick looked at Jack. "You have anything on your schedule at present?"

"Nope," Jack said as he rose from his chair. "It's situations like these that attracted me to Montana law enforcement."

Helen began to follow Jack out of the office. "Helen, just a second," Rick said.

"Sheriff?"

"Did you have any luck finding out anything about that tattoo we discussed?"

Helen nodded. "Matter of fact I did. Let me get my notes." She returned moments later and closed the office door behind her. "I have this friend up in Kalispell—I made her acquaintance when my niece ran off. Her name is Sally. She's somewhat of a cult guru."

Rick lifted his chin. "Interesting specialty."

Helen shot a scolding glare before continuing. "She said that symbol might belong to a group out of Idaho. She thought the name might be Worshippers of Darkness, but she wasn't quite sure. Pretty loose bunch that didn't last long. To quote my friend, they were a pack of country boys trying to get laid."

"Helen!" Rick said with a burst of laughter.

"Excuse the sentiment, Sheriff. My friend isn't quite as refined as I am."

"I'll bet the women they attracted were real keepers," Rick said, continuing to chuckle.

"No comment."

"Do they have any rituals?" Rick asked. "Maybe drinking animal blood, anything like that?"

"They were devil-worshippers, all right," Helen answered, shaking her head to grieve their forfeited souls. "When a couple of young women went missing up there, it was rumored that the cult was into human sacrifice. I guess they enjoyed the notoriety, but nothing ever came of it."

Rick leaned forward in his chair and squinted at Helen. "Human sacrifice? Did your friend happen to say what that entailed?'

"Seems to be self-explanatory, doesn't it? They take a knife, cut someone open, disembowel—"

Rick held up his palm. "I get it, Helen—let's not spoil my lunch. You think this group actually did stuff like that?"

"Doubt it," Helen answered. "I'm told that when it came to the cult business, they were pretty much amateurs. But you never know."

The office grew silent, both of them contemplating the macabre nature of their discourse.

"Sheriff, if you don't mind me asking, where are you going with all this?"

Rick picked up a pen and began tapping it on his desk pad. "I don't mind you asking," he said, "but I'm not ready just yet to share my thoughts on this one. You just might think I was crazy."

CHAPTER 40

Rick walked into the Forty-Niner to find Charlie seated in the corner booth, drinking coffee and thumbing through the obituary section of the *Riverton Herald.*

"Any names ring a bell?" Rick cracked.

"All of 'em," Charlie said, barely above a whisper.

"What then? Looking for typos?"

Charlie folded the paper and laid it on the table. "You're quite the comedian," he said without smiling. He took another sip of coffee and cast his eyes toward the newspaper. "You know, plenty of folks these days die alone. Only way you get information about them is a neighbor or friend. Other times, you enter a home and encounter a spouse, a sibling, or perhaps an adult child. They're almost always sitting on some faded couch, cold and numb, glaring intently into nowhere. Most are filled with grief, others perhaps relief. Either way, they're sad—despondent, if you will. I utter words of comfort by rote, almost like I'm following a script. The family member will nod their head, thanking me for my *thoughtful* words. I may know the family personally, but with all the people moving up here, that has become less frequent. I study the scene, ask some questions, maybe get a list of medications. I close the zipper on that black body bag, nod toward a deputy to help me lift the body onto the gurney, then head out the door. It's the same tired routine. I may act solemn, but as many times as I've done this, I may as well be taking out a Hefty bag full of trash." He took a deep breath and released a long sigh, tapping a finger on the newspaper. "So, yeah, I read the obituaries. Maybe it comes from guilt; I don't know. I feel like I have an obligation to discover exactly who is in that bag."

"I apologize, Charlie," Rick said. "I didn't mean to make light—"

Charlie shook his head. "No need to apologize. You've done nothing wrong. I'm getting a little melancholy, I guess. Must be my age." He took a long sip of coffee. "Anyway, I was thinking about your missing hunter. What was he like? Was he a good husband? A good father? A good son? A good friend?" He paused in thought. "Was he a good *man*?"

"From what I gather, Garrett McRae was all of the above," Rick said.

"How about his wife? Did she love him?"

"Well, they had their problems, especially after the accident with their son."

"But did she *love* him?"

"No one can be sure of that," Rick answered. He studied the deep creases in Charlie's leathery skin. The strands of gray hair on the side of his head were uncombed, his clothes wrinkled, tired eyes conflicted. "Charlie, you doing okay? Everything get worked out with Dora?"

The coroner shook his head. "I would say no, things aren't worked out with Dora," he mumbled. "In fact, she's gone to stay with her sister for a while."

"She say when she'd be back?"

"Nope," Charlie answered. "She still swears I've been gamblin'."

"Well?"

"Hell, no!" Charlie snarled. "Are *you* going to start with me now?"

Dodge, the usual waitress, appeared at their table, her faded T-shirt tugged over a paunch that pressed against the buckle of her torn jeans. A row of silver metal studs lined the rim of her outer earlobe. The side of her head was shaved, giving way to hair colored lavender. Her tattooed arm topped off Charlie's cup before filling one for Rick.

"That a new shade, Dodge?" Rick asked, studying her hair.

"Indeed it is," she replied. "Do you like it?"

"Looks good on you."

Dodge smiled. "Y'all need menus?"

"I'll have the special," Rick answered.

"Same here," Charlie echoed.

"Care to know what it is?"

"I'm sure it's fine," Rick said. "Usually is."

Both men watched Dodge head toward the kitchen. "Why do you figure her parents called her Dodge?" Charlie asked.

"Not sure." Rick chuckled. "Some folks call their daughters Mercedes, so why not Dodge?"

"I imagine someone will eventually give birth to a Tesla, if it ain't happened already," Charlie mused. He picked up a sugar dispenser and held it above his coffee cup, watching it pour like sand from an hourglass. "How's Sage? She coming along okay?"

"So far, so good," Rick answered. "One day at a time."

Charlie nodded, his lips curling into a knowing smile. He drank his coffee and licked his lips, seemingly pleased with the sugar content. "Now, where was I?"

"We were talking about Dora."

"Before that."

"You were asking me about Amber McRae," Rick said. "You were wondering whether she loved her husband."

"Right, Amber McRae," Charlie said with a nod. "You know, she called me yesterday. Second time she called me this week."

"She called twice? Why?"

"Said I needed to issue a death certificate."

Rick cocked his head. "That seems a little aggressive."

"Ya think?" Charlie said, eyes widening. He scanned the restaurant then looked back toward Rick. "I've had people request a copy of a death certificate that was already issued, but I don't recall anyone *demanding* that I issue one."

"Almost sounds like she might be in some kind of hurry?"

"You said it, not me," Charlie answered. "Anyway, that's why I was wondering about their marriage."

"She's a hard one to figure, to be honest. At times she sounds like she's speaking the God's honest truth, straight from her heart. Other times I feel like she's sellin' me a timeshare." Rick took a sip of coffee. "What did you tell her?"

"I politely said I couldn't issue a death certificate until I—*we*—completed our investigation," Charlie said. "I'm just not there yet."

"Have you heard anything back on those remains discovered the other day?"

"The rib bones?" Charlie asked. He took a sip of his coffee, then dumped another truckload of sugar into the cup. "The DNA is a match for Garrett McRae. No real surprise there."

Dodge appeared at the table, sliding a steaming dish in front of each man. Rick stared at his plate.

"What we got here, Dodge?"

"The special," she answered. "Liver and onions."

Rick pushed himself back in the booth as though a scorpion was strolling across his plate. "Liver and onions?" he said in shock. "I don't care much for liver and onions, Dodge. Why didn't you tell me?"

"You didn't want to know. Y'all care for anything else?"

"No," Rick said as he watched her whirl and walk away. He shoved his plate to the side and looked at Charlie. "You have any thoughts?"

"I like liver and onions," Charlie said, tucking a napkin into the top of his shirt. "You gonna eat your Texas toast?"

Rick pursed his lips. "I mean, do you have any thoughts about Garrett McRae?" he said, tossing the two thick slices of yellow bread onto Charlie's plate. "Do you have a theory about what might have happened?"

Charlie took a bite of toast. "At this point, I'm still thinking bear attack," he said as he chewed. "From what I've seen so far, he lost a ton of blood. In my experience, a guy who lost that much blood would have absolutely no chance of survival."

Rick watched Charlie dump a load of catsup onto his liver and onions. He considered his own plate, pondering whether burying the entrée beneath condiments might make it palatable. He decided he wasn't hungry enough to test the theory.

Charlie eyed him curiously. "What are you thinking, Rick?"

Rick drew a deep breath. "Call me foolish, but I believe more and more that James Davis—aka Randall Boone—is somehow involved. I know he and Garrett got into a fistfight at their camp, more than likely over Davis's involvement with Amber McRae. Garrett leaves camp, no one hears from him, and then Davis trots back into camp with Garrett's horse and a cow elk with Garrett's tag. Davis's fingerprints are on Garrett's backpack, and Garrett's blood is on Davis's clothes."

Charlie leaned back in the booth. "Maybe Davis was messing with the backpack in camp," he said, "and we already know Garrett bled during their fight—"

"I know, I know," Rick said, holding up his hand. "But there's more to it than that."

"Go ahead," Charlie said, scooping a fork-load off his plate. "I'm all ears."

Rick stared at the coffee cup cradled in his hands. "I had Helen doing some research. Davis has this tattoo on his arm—a pentagram and horned goat. For some reason, it struck me as kind of strange. Helen looked into it, and she told me that Davis must have belonged to some kind of cult."

Charlie frowned. Rick continued. "I forget the name—and I don't even know if they still exist—but apparently these guys liked to drink blood, devil-worship, the whole bit. They sacrificed animals … and maybe even humans."

Dodge appeared at their table, topping off their coffee cups. "Can I get you gentlemen anything else?" she asked. Rick glanced at his plate, looked at Dodge, and shook his head.

As Dodge walked away, Charlie rested his elbows on the table, his fingers forming a steeple beneath his chin. "I assume you are going somewhere with this?"

"Kyle Ricketts told Jack that he heard two gunshots on Sunday morning. Let's say there was another confrontation between Davis and McRae, and Davis shot him. Could have even been an accident, who knows? Davis panics, knowing that nobody is going to believe his side of things. He decides to make it *look* like a bear attack."

"You're not suggesting—"

"Look, Davis is a sociopath," Rick continued. "He may have belonged to a cult that was into human sacrifice."

Charlie's eyes sharpened. "*Allegedly* into human sacrifice."

Rick leaned forward, dropping his voice to a whisper. "He starts chopping up McRae's corpse likes he's gutting an animal. He leaves an evidence trail that makes it look like a grizzly killed him. It wouldn't surprise me if Davis set that fire as well, maybe figuring he could cover his tracks and make our job all the more difficult."

Charlie shook his head as he poured more sugar into his coffee and stirred it. "I think I'll stick with bear attack as my working theory for now."

Rick slapped the table top with his open palm, casting his eyes toward the ceiling. "So, are you going to issue a death certificate? You said he couldn't have survived the loss of blood."

"That is what I said, but I'm still not ready to close my end of the investigation."

"Why?"

"I need more evidence," Charlie answered.

Dodge approached the table. She tried to refill Charlie's cup, but he covered it with his hand. "No more for me, Dodge. My socks are going up and down as it is."

Rick handed the uneaten plate of liver and onions to Dodge.

"You didn't care for it?" she asked.

"Didn't bother tasting it."

"You should expand your horizons, Sheriff."

"Duly noted."

She filled his coffee cup and departed. "Charlie, how do you plan to find more evidence?" Rick asked. "You have about a quarter-mile of dense, burnt thicket before coming to the edge of a canyon. It drops probably six hundred feet down to the drainage. Steep, vicious, unforgiving terrain. The weather has been warm this fall, but snow is coming soon. It would take—"

"It's going to take as long as I need," Charlie said. "My investigation may carry over until spring."

"What about Amber McRae?"

"Mrs. McRae is going to need to be patient."

"Good luck with that," Rick huffed. He took a sip of his coffee, which was lukewarm. "I believe James Edward Davis murdered Garrett McRae. There's plenty of evidence."

"A lot of it is circumstantial."

Rick tapped his index finger on the table, pausing in thought. "There were clothes with the remains you found, right?"

Charlie nodded.

"Did they extract any DNA from the clothes?"

The bridge of Charlie's nose wrinkled, his eyes squinting as he paused in thought. "I figured you mainly wanted to confirm the bones belonged to McRae," he murmured. "I'm calling in favors for the lab to turn these results so quickly. I thought I should narrow the focus."

Rick nodded. "I don't have a problem with that, Charlie. But you didn't test the clothing for DNA belonging to Davis?"

"Not as of yet, no. You have to figure that if the two men got into a fist-fight, Davis's touch DNA would be on McRae's clothes."

"Not necessarily," Rick said without hesitation. "Garrett was hunting with a bow. He's going to want to get as close as possible to his target. To make sure he has no scent, he probably changed into bagged hunting clothes before heading out. He won't go into the field smelling like sweat and whiskey and God knows what else. I'd be willing to bet on it."

The word *bet* caused Charlie to hike his bushy eyebrows. "No offense, of course," Rick said.

"None taken," the coroner said with a chuckle. "I guess if Davis's DNA was on the clothing we found, that could place him at the place where the death seems to have occurred. I'll be happy to get additional test results." He leaned backward again, folding his arms across his chest. "You sure you're not engaging in a bit of tunnel vision?"

"How so?"

"You seem to have a real bugaboo about this Davis fella, going all the way back to the days we knew him as Randall Boone."

"It's not just him."

"Oh?"

Dodge stopped by and laid the lunch ticket on the table. Rick picked it up and reached for his wallet. "Let's say I'm not overly comfortable with Amber McRae being so eager to get her hands on that insurance money."

Charlie nodded. "Especially after her having had an affair with your suspect?"

"Exactly," Rick said. "Which makes me realize why you asked your original question. Did she love her husband? I'm sure at some point she did. But, as I said, she's a tough one to figure."

Dodge whisked past the table and picked up the lunch ticket, along with Rick's credit card. "Can I chip in, Sheriff?" Charlie asked. "After all, you didn't even eat anything."

"I got it, Charlie," Rick said. "I'll gladly pay for not having to eat liver."

Charlie flicked his index finger toward Rick. "Almost forgot. Were you able to track down that other woman?"

"What other woman?"

"The one with the dog."

"Meredith Hart?"

"That's the one. I hear she was camping in the Crazies the same weekend Garrett McRae went missing."

Rick frowned. "How'd you hear that?"

"Jack."

"How did Jack know?"

"Helen must have told him."

Rick rolled his eyes. "Good to see everyone keeps a tight lid on things around here," he said. "To answer your question, I haven't talked to her. At the moment, I'm having trouble locating her."

Charlie's flattened lips jutted to one side. "Struck me as kind of strange, her being in the Crazies that same weekend."

"You and me both."

Rick tapped the table, preparing to leave. A wave of gloom rippled across Charlie's weary face. He appeared saddened the lunch was over, leaving him to return to the solitude of his thoughts, a prisoner being led back to his cell. "Charlie," Rick said softly, "this thing with Dora … it's all gonna work out. I know it will."

Charlie nodded his head slowly. "I hope it will," he said, releasing a deep sigh. "I'd sure hate to die alone."

CHAPTER 41

"**W**ho the hell is Amber McRae?"

Spencer Bible felt blood drain from his face, hair rising on the nape of his neck. He had barely sat down at this desk on Tuesday morning when he was greeted by a voice of doom. *His* doom.

"Good morning, Mr. Reynolds," he told the executive vice president of sales for Nexus Life and Casualty Insurance. He wanted to say something else, but his throat felt clutched in a stranglehold. He looked through the plate-glass window of his office at his secretary, Rachel, who was dabbing her nails with polish as if putting the finishing touches on the Sistine Chapel. *Why hadn't she warned me?*

"You there, Spencer?" Walter demanded. "Who the *hell* is Amber McRae?"

Spencer's mouth felt as dry as an autumn creek bed. "She's … her husband … was … is … a … client," he managed to mumble.

"Was or is?"

"Technically, he is, sir," Spencer said. "He has a life insurance policy with us. Thing is, he went missing a few weeks ago."

Spencer could hear Walter pushing air from his nostrils, like a bull pawing the dirt. "So I've heard. Her husband has a life insurance policy, and Mrs. McRae is the beneficiary?"

"That's correct, sir."

"Well, Mrs. McRae also happens to be a social media sensation!" he barked.

"I … I'm not sure I follow you, sir."

"Damn, you really do dwell beneath a mushroom, don't you? This woman is posting videos all over the internet how her husband died in the mountains and she's getting jobbed by his insurance company. The shots of her handicapped kid really put the whole thing right over the top. I'm getting calls from brokers all over the country, telling me clients are switching carriers like rats jumping off a sinking ship."

The line was silent for several seconds. "It sounds like they're overreacting, sir."

"Overreacting? *Overreacting?*" Walter growled. "Yeah, Spencer, I'd say they're overreacting, all right. Who wrote the goddamn policy?"

Spencer felt his jaw tighten. "Rachel, sir. My secretary."

"So, she interviewed the husband?"

"Yes she did, sir," Spencer said. "She said he seemed like a nice enough fella."

"A nice enough fella," Walter repeated with bite. "Well, I did some research, and he certainly is an *interesting* fella. He's an EMT who wants to be a paramedic, which means he likes to spend time in speeding ambulances. He rides a Harley without a helmet when he's not off-roading on dirt bikes. Being a bow hunter, he tiptoes through the woods right before grizzlies head into hibernation. What's wrong, Spencer? No bull riders or base jumpers available that day?"

"I'm sorry, sir."

"Sorry doesn't cut it, son. This policy wasn't rated to take into consideration this gentleman's lifestyle. No premium rate. No exclusions, no limitations. You'd think the most dangerous thing this guy ever did was watch Netflix." He paused a beat. "Your secretary may have written it, but it's *you* who's responsible for it."

Spencer swallowed deep into his throat. "I explained to his wife that we can't pay the benefit without a death certificate."

"Well, you sure pissed her off."

"I didn't mean to piss … I didn't mean to upset her, sir. I simply explained that until we receive a death certificate, the benefit couldn't be paid for seven years."

"Well, she's not exactly embracing that concept. She's posting videos saying that her kid in a wheelchair is going to starve to death, courtesy of Nexus Life and Casualty Insurance. Do you realize how much this policy is worth?"

"As I recall, it was five hundred thousand dollars," Spencer mumbled sheepishly.

"Negative!" Walter shouted. "The talk is that this guy got killed by a bear. You ever hear of ADB?"

"Double Indemnity," Spencer mumbled, his voice a shade above a whisper.

"Beg your pardon?"

"Uh … ADB means Accidental Death Benefit," Spencer said. "If a person dies an unnatural death, a rider in the policy allows for an additional benefit, usually equal to the amount of the original policy."

"Bingo! That is precisely the benefit that is called for in this policy. Were you at all curious why an ADB rider was requested for this policy?"

Spencer stared out the window of his office. Rachel was still seated at her desk, lips puckered as she blew air on her freshly painted nails. "He told my secretary that his wife wanted him to get the most comprehensive coverage possible. It kind of sounded like the whole thing was her idea."

Walter cleared his throat. "I assume you have E and O insurance?"

"Sir?"

"Errors and omissions, Spencer," Walter said. "It appears to me that your agency left out some critical information."

"To answer your question, sir, we do carry E and O coverage."

"Do you happen to know the limit? One million? Two million? There's a chance you might need it."

Spencer shuddered as if someone had yanked back his shirt collar and dumped crushed ice down his spine. "There is suspicion that he was killed by a bear, but there also is the possibility of foul play," he stammered. "The sheriff—"

"Foul play?" Walter growled. "As in *murder*? Sorry, Spencer, murder is still considered accidental death."

"What if his wife was involved?"

"Whoa!" Walter said. "Better be careful there, son. That's a pretty strong accusation. What makes you say that?"

"Well, it's just kind of suspicious how aggressively she has been trying to collect on this policy. She's called this office more than once. It also seems strange that she encouraged him to get the policy."

"That's it? A woman with a disabled child wants to make sure her family is taken care of in case something happens to her husband. Fearing he is deceased, she wants to collect on his insurance policy to take care of her child. That's not exactly a conspiracy theory."

"The sheriff in Dexter County is skeptical," Spencer said. "Having talked to her myself, I just have this gut feeling that something isn't right."

"A *gut* feeling," Walter huffed. "You're not serious, are you?" His breath filled the phone line with a forceful exhale. "Look, Spencer, I've known your family for a while, and I always admired your father. Thing is, this isn't just a financial issue, it's a *severe* public relations nightmare. To mend the company's reputation—not to mention our stock price—someone is going to have to take a bullet for this."

Spencer's eyes blinked rapidly. "I'm not sure what you mean, sir."

"You may want to talk to that sheriff you mentioned, learn some more details," Walter said. "Sorry, but I need to go."

Before Spencer could say anything more, the line went dead.

• • •

Rick was reviewing paperwork in a file on his desk when Sage burst through the door of his office. The shiny waves of golden hair flowing from beneath her hat cascaded over her shoulders, appearing as full and natural as a spirited alpine waterfall. Her cotton dress, splashed with the purple and yellow hues of Texas bluebells, followed the lines of her body as it descended from beneath her denim jacket down to the pull straps of her Rocketbuster boots.

She took the sheet of paper he held in his hand and gently placed it on his desk pad. Slipping her left leg over his thighs, she straddled her future and final husband, knees pressing firmly against his hips. Rick cast a cautionary glance to his office door, but she directed his attention back toward her, cradling his face in her hands while exciting him with soft teases of her strawberry-glossed lips. He slid his hands beneath her jacket, feeling her ribs beneath her dress as he caressed the sides of her body. They engaged in a long kiss, allowing him to bask in the fragrance of her skin, the balm igniting the far reaches of his senses.

"I'm not sure what the protocol is for this type of situation in the Dexter County Sheriff Department Manual," Rick said.

"Shhh ...," his fiancée whispered, her hands clinging to the base of his neck as she pressed her lips against his.

"Something tells me you have some good news."

"Indeed I do," Sage said. "But it can wait." She adjusted her dress as she pulled closer to him. He felt the heat of her midsection press against his arousal.

"Wait a minute," he said. "Are you—"

"That is correct, Sheriff. I'm ridin' bareback." Her hands reached down to his waist, where she eagerly began to loosen the buckle of his uniform pants.

There was a slight tap on the glass of his office door before it quickly opened. "Oh! Oh my!" he heard Helen's voice say. "I'm so sorry. Oh! Oh my!"

The door clicked shut. Rick felt warmth flood into his face as he stared frozen at Sage, who curled her lips into a mischievous smile, eyes sparkling with delight. "Between here and the hospital, we're going to get a reputation as the horniest couple in town."

"Guilty as charged," Sage said with a giggle. She cupped her hands around his cheeks, planting a firm kiss on his mouth before climbing off his lap. Sage's fingers tugged at her dress to straighten it as he pushed the intercom button on his desk phone.

"What is it, Helen?" he asked.

"I … uh … sorry to interrupt you, Sheriff Morrand," she said nervously. "I wanted to let you know that Rob from the Forest Service is here."

"Rob Deering is in town?"

"That's correct, sir. He said he was on his way to Bozeman, but he has some information for you, and he figured he'd stop by and give it to you in person."

"I'll be right out," he said, eyes fixed on Sage. He stood and held her close to him. "You didn't get a chance to tell me your good news."

Sage's eyes brightened, the tip of her tongue arcing across her upper lip. "Well, I'm a long way from being out of the woods, but let's just say I have some hope."

"What were the test results?"

"The PET scan indicated the SUV was going down," Sage said.

"SUV?"

"Standardized Uptake Value. It's complicated, I know. But it basically means the tumors are shrinking." Her eyes brightened. "Like I said—I have hope."

Rick's throat suddenly tightened. A fleeting moment of relief—even joy, perhaps—was blindsided by an odd cascade of fear and gloom. He had been here before. His wife, Christine, had gone into remission for a period of time before her breast cancer returned with a vengeance. He forced a smile, masking his thoughts. "That's great news," he said softly. "How do you feel?"

Sage laughed as she drew closer to him. "To be honest, I've pretty much gotten used to feeling like crap. But I guess I would say that today is a good day." She looked up at him, her eyes searching his face. "Can you maybe meet me for lunch?" she asked, her voice threaded with longing. "Maybe finish what we started?"

Rick smiled. "Wish I could. After I visit with Rob, I need to follow up with Charlie."

"Tonight, then? Maybe bring some carryout from that Mexican place? We can celebrate."

"Can you eat Mexican food? Isn't it too spicy?"

"Why not? I asked Janice, and she told me one night won't kill me. She also said I can have a margarita."

"Careful," Rick said with a grin. "You're a little out of practice."

● ● ●

As he watched Sage leave from the door of his office, Rick cast a quick glance toward Helen, who was as red as a rose. "Any messages?" he asked. She wagged her head without looking at him, causing him to smile.

Rob followed him into the office and took a seat. His green slacks and khaki shirt were freshly pressed. Thick, shiny hair was neatly parted and slicked to one side as though he were auditioning for a Brylcreem commercial. A clean-shaven jaw and even high-cut sideburns suggested a man of extreme precision. "I hope I'm not barging in on you, Sheriff."

"Not in the least," Rick answered. He sat back in his chair, propping his right ankle on his left knee. "You have some news?"

"I do, sir," Rob said. "I interviewed several ranchers on the east side of the Crazies, and it turns out there were some kids in that area on the Monday following Labor Day."

"Kids? How old?"

"Teenagers. I had noticed some four-wheeler tracks down near Highway 191, so that's what I focused on. Turns out one of the ranchers has a son who was in the area with some of his buddies. The father said the kids like to go hunt gophers."

"So they had a rifle with them? Maybe a .22?"

Rob grimaced and shook his head. "The kid claimed they didn't. He wasn't overly forthcoming at first. Seemed a bit nervous."

"Did they hear or see anything unusual?"

"After I'd talked to him a while, he said they saw someone on a horse. The kid claimed the guy looked pretty creepy."

"What color was the horse?"

"He said it was hard to tell," Rob answered. "He thought maybe it was brown."

"A Red Dun maybe?"

Rob cracked a half smile. "Those horses do look brown for sure, but the kid wasn't all that specific."

"How close did they get to the guy on the horse?"

Rob shrugged. "Maybe two hundred yards. They were pretty wary of him, since he had a rifle in his scabbard."

Rick uncrossed his legs and leaned forward. He picked up a pen and began tapping it on his desk pad. He pictured the eastern foothills of the Crazies, where the Granite Peak Fire had begun. It was a long way from the hunters' base camp but not all that far from where Garrett McRae's remains were found. "Did you talk to any of the other kids?"

"I managed to track another one of them down. He lives with his grandparents, and they're blocking me from talking to him at the moment."

"*Blocking* you? Why?"

Rob threw open palms in the air. "Your guess is as good as mine. I'm going to make another run at them in the next day or so."

"Keep me posted?"

"You bet."

CHAPTER 42

Once he had acknowledged that his fate was sealed, Cyrus Bible had the foresight to negotiate the terms of his own long-term care, not unlike a condemned prisoner choosing his manner of execution. He selected Serenity Pines, generally regarded as Riverton's finest assisted living facility even though its name and tenor were more suggestive of a funeral home.

Spencer Bible had returned to Great Falls from his abbreviated studies at Montana State to learn that his father had plunked down ninety thousand dollars for a tidy one-bedroom apartment at the tree-shaded red-brick facility, its front entrance adorned with a long welcoming white canopy. The check Cyrus wrote represented no equity but rather was considered a "down payment" as he descended through the various stages of care that would ultimately lead to his grave.

Stricken with an extremely aggressive form of Alzheimer's, Cyrus's decline was much more rapid than he would have anticipated or preferred. He would last less than a year in his small apartment, eventually landing in a small room one might expect in a hospital ward. Spencer would visit his father twice weekly, an unbearable exercise that involved sitting idly in a padded blue chair staring at a frail, incontinent man whom he had previously known only as an unconquerable giant.

A short fifty-something Latina woman stood at the door of his father's room on Tuesday afternoon, the rectangular blue name tag that read "Camila" pinned to her pink-flowered scrubs. Her braided hair was pulled back to reveal warm, rounded eyes peeking out from coffee-colored skin. "He had a rough night," she said. "He took a fall while trying to get to the bathroom on his own. He's been pretty stubborn that way."

Spencer threw a glance toward his father, who was lying on a pillow with eyes closed. "Is he okay?"

"He should be fine," Camila said. "He had a shot of morphine not long ago, so he might talk a bit and then nod off."

Spencer trudged toward the bed. His father slowly opened his eyelids to greet him as "Jimmy," the name of a cousin with whom Cyrus had spent several summers during his youth. From a few black-and-white photos Spencer had seen, there was indeed some resemblance. He had corrected his father on previous occasions until he realized his efforts proved futile. "Hello, Dad," Spencer said softly as he pulled the blue chair closer to the bed.

"I like the staff here, Jimmy, but I may have to make some changes," Cyrus said, his empty eyes reaching out the room's only window toward a stand of tall Ponderosa pines. "The good news is that they tell me we're just about full, so it's good to know we're in the black."

His father had begun speaking about staff changes at the facility for about three weeks before Spencer realized that Cyrus was under the impression that he *owned* Serenity Pines. The fact that his faltering brain would entertain such a notion was understandable considering Cyrus had captained his own ship for the vast majority of his life.

"I'm sure you'll figure it out, Dad," Spencer said. Cyrus nodded as he struggled to keep his lids from lowering over his eyes. Spencer turned his face away, drenched by a surge of emotion as his mind recounted his morning conversation with Walter Reynolds. Spencer swore to himself he would never cry in front of the man who taught him to be a man, but that vow was now perilously close to fracturing.

He buried his face in his hands, elbows propped on his thighs. "I'm sorry, Dad," he said, his voice trembling. "I'm so sorry."

Cyrus turned toward him, squinting into a ray of sunlight that briefly peeked through the window. "Jimmy," he said, his dry, raspy voice threaded with compassion. "What is it?"

Spencer sat up in his chair, drawing a deep breath to recapture his composure. "I made a terrible mistake—a *terrible* mistake. I'm not sure what can be done to make it right." He looked at his father, who now wore a blank stare directed toward the ceiling.

"It's okay, Jimmy," his father muttered, having no comprehension of Spencer's offense. "Everyone makes mistakes." Cyrus Bible then drifted off to sleep.

Spencer sat for several seconds before placing his palm on his father's hand, the man's skin bruised and discolored from endless pricks of intravenous needles. He rose quietly from his chair and started to leave the room.

Camila's motherly, mournful eyes greeted him from the doorway. "Are you going to be okay?" she asked, gently touching his forearm.

"I don't know," he said.

• • •

Spencer walked down the hallway and out the front door of the facility, emerging from underneath the canopy to random drops of rain falling through the trees from a single dark cloud overhead. The smell of wet bark filled the air as he stepped gingerly through broken twigs and scattered pinecones.

His stomach churned, his chest crushed beneath an anvil of sudden gloom. He blinked back the wetness in his eyes, trying in vain to rein in his emotions as he considered the vacant, rudderless vessel his father had become. If the God his family professed did in fact exist, Cyrus Augustus Bible would soon be relieved of his present piteous existence and welcomed into a much better place.

At that point, of course, Spencer would be alone. All alone.

He had naively believed Lizzie could prevent such a circumstance. He had dreamed they would marry, purchase a home, have children and build a life together in Great Falls. That's what they discussed, wasn't it? He drew a deep breath, casting his eyes toward the ground, conceding he had been blindly intoxicated by a tonic of pure fantasy.

The raindrops increased. He opened the Impala's door, its hinges groaning, and slid behind the steering wheel. Staring out the windshield, his mind drifted to the sight of Lizzie's flawless figure storming out of Papa Dante's. He had assumed it was a simple spat, influenced by alcohol and empty stomachs, easy to resolve.

His repeated texts and numerous phone calls had gone unanswered. The bouquet of roses he sent to Starlight Coffee had been rejected, the manager explaining that Lizzie no longer worked there. Spencer would have checked her apartment had he known where she lived.

He was alone. Lizzie was gone. Long gone.

But where?

CHAPTER 43

Amber McRae rarely had visitors, and she preferred it that way. Chances were good they would disturb her son—who desperately needed his rest—and possibly carry germs that could cause infection. She especially relished the late afternoons, when Gabe would nap and she could lie on the living room sofa, the entire house tranquil save for the ambient whirr of the air purifier and the periodic buzz of her balky Frigidaire.

The ring of the front bell late Tuesday afternoon both startled and angered her, especially when it was followed by three solid raps on the aluminum frame of her screen door. Amber rose from the couch, tossing a glance in the direction of Gabe's room as her stockinged feet carried her purposefully across the wood floor. Tugging back the curtain, she peered through the glass at an overweight, disheveled man wearing a stained gray hoody, his head swiveling as he glanced nervously in opposite directions. Amber cracked the wooden entry door open only slightly, keeping the security chain latched. "My son is sleeping!" she whispered with attitude through the screen. "What is it?"

"I'm sorry to bother you, ma'am," he said through lips surrounded by a black untamed beard. "I ran out of gas about a quarter mile from here, and yours was the first place I saw."

Amber wagged her head. "I'm sorry, but I can't leave the house. You'll have to go somewhere else."

"Please, ma'am," he pleaded. "I just need a little gas to get back to town. Would you happen to have a can around? I can walk to my truck."

Amber glanced above the door where a wooden gun rack cradled a Henry .22 rifle, usually reserved for the execution of gophers. "I don't have any gas in the house. I'm sorry I can't help you." She began to close the door.

"Wait!" he said. "I'm begging you. I need to make a delivery before five o'clock or I'll lose my job. I have a wife and kids. *Please.*"

She studied him through the screen, his face full of grime and hands covered in grease. She wondered what kind of woman might marry him, let alone collaborate in the production of children. He had a desperation in his eyes that begged for pity as he interlocked his fingers in petition. "Please?" he repeated.

Amber looked toward the hallway leading to Gabe's room. She heard no sound. "I might have a can in the shed," she whispered. "I don't know if it has gas in it or not." The man flicked a half smile in gratitude.

She pulled on her boots, which were stationed next to the door. After unhooking the latch, she stepped out onto the porch. The wind had begun to pick up, rattling the surrendering leaves of the aspens and poplars that circled the house. Amber measured the face of the stranger in the afternoon light. His left eye was fixed on her, while the other wandered far to his right. "My name is Willard," he said from a mouth of stained and scattered teeth. "I greatly appreciate your kindness."

A gust caused the rusted chain of a porch swing to creak. "Willard," Amber repeated, offering neither her name nor her hand. She flung a nod over her shoulder. "The shed is over here."

The McRaes' cedar-sided storage shed contained an unreliable power mower, snow shovels, and assorted garden tools, many of them in need of repair. Anything of value or utility was kept in the barn. Amber lifted the thin slice of weathered pine that served as a makeshift latch, waving her hand in front of her face as she inhaled the smell of decay. "Sometimes our barn cats leave dead mice in here," she said apologetically. "Garrett usually ..."

Her voice trailed off, and the man didn't seem to notice. His head glanced in both directions, much like it had on the porch, making her uneasy. She reached inside the shed to the right of the door, her hand fumbling along a dusty shelf. She grasped a flashlight and pointed it toward her eyes, clicking the switch on and off twice. It was dead.

Amber pinned back the door, using the fading daylight to peer inside. Her eyes trailed along the dirt floor littered with strands of hay mixed with dead grass. Beyond the tired mower, at the far end of the shed, she spotted a two-gallon gas tin. "If you can hold this door a second, I can grab the can," she said. "There might be something in it."

Willard allowed Amber to step inside, then followed her. As she reached the back of the shed, she heard the door slam shut, ink-black darkness surrounding her. She picked up the gas can and stood frozen, panic enveloping her as she waited and listened. There was a flicking sound, followed by a flash of light. She looked toward the entrance, where the hulking stranger stared at her from behind the generous flame of his lighter. Her senses stung with the smell of butane mixed with his foul body odor. "She didn't tell me how beautiful you were," he said through dry, cracked lips, his left eye carrying a diabolical glare.

"What are you talking about?" Amber asked, her quaking voice failing to mask her fear.

"You needn't worry about it. It's not important." His chin lowered behind the flame. "This really doesn't have to be unpleasant." He fumbled beneath the bottom of his sweatshirt, unbuckling his weathered leather belt as he scanned the curves of her petite body. "In your case, I would prefer to take my time."

Amber took a step back. "My husband will be home soon. I'm expecting him any minute."

"Now, Amber, you and I both know that isn't true," he said in a deep bellow. "Your husband is *never* coming home."

"Who are you? Who sent you? How do you know my name?"

"Enough!" he snarled. He drew a deep breath. "Look—I can make this as painless as possible. I suggest that you do as I say. It will make things much less difficult for your child."

Amber's jaw muscles clenched. "Do you even *think* of harming my child."

The man lifted his left brow. "Surely you wouldn't want your handicapped boy to grow up without a father *or* mother, would you?"

Amber drew a short breath, tightened her grip on the gas can, and swung it wildly, clanking it against the side of Willard's head. He staggered backward, the lighter soaring from his hand onto a bed of dry grass.

Smoke began to fill the shed. In the flickering flame, Amber pawed along the wooded slats behind her, urgently grasping for a discarded tool that might prove useful to her desperate defense. A sharp object stung the palm of her hand. She recognized it as the broken wooden handle of a garden implement, perhaps a hoe or rake.

Raising the handle in front of her, she could see she was tightly grasping the shaft of a pitchfork. Her lips curled into a smile—not one of joy but rather functional madness. Adrenaline gushing through her veins, she charged at her distracted foe, plunging the pitchfork through his sweatshirt and deep into the flesh beneath his rib cage.

Willard backpedaled, crashing through the door of the shed and into the sunlight. Arms and legs flailing like a tortoise stranded on its shell, his left eye glared at the garden tool submerged in his torso. He spoke no words, emitting only terrified moans followed by shrill whimpers.

She glared at the predator who had become her prey. "You really want to mess with a mama bear?" she snarled through gritted teeth. Her entire body shook as she stormed back into the shed, where the gas tank of the mower had caused the walls of the structure to ignite. Using the crook of her elbow to shield her from billows of black smoke, she emerged from the doorway yanking the pull cord on an eighteen-inch chainsaw. With Willard watching in horror, Amber got the saw to fire up on her fifth try. She heaved rapid breaths, eyes wide as she stared at the whirring blade. Her index finger squeezed the throttle trigger, playfully toying with the chain speed. "Nobody threatens my family!" she shouted over the whine of the saw.

Willard's fingertips were clenching the dry dirt beside his body, his heels desperately searching for purchase as he tried to slide away from her. "Please," he cried. "I didn't mean to—"

Amber stomped her left boot onto his breastbone. She squeezed the trigger of the chainsaw, holding it directly above his neck. "Who sent you?" she screamed as she allowed the saw a momentary idle. She revved the saw again. "Damn it, who sent you?"

Willard's eyes watered with fright. His lips moved, but he seemed unable to form words. Amber put weight on her boot, lowering the chain closer to his throat as though she planned to sever a log for firewood. "This is the last time I'm going to ask you!"

The smell of smoke filled her nostrils, the salty taste of sweat crossing her lips. She could feel the heat of the fire, hear the wood cracking and popping as the shed neared collapse. Amid the depths of her frenzy, she thought she heard shouting. To her right, she saw movement. Her eyes trailed over her shoulder.

A Gallatin County deputy was crouched nearby, eyes widened, his hands nervously wrapped around a sidearm aimed directly at her.

CHAPTER 44

Rick awoke Wednesday morning to the sound of his vibrating cell phone. "Hey, Charlie," he whispered, not wanting to awaken Sage, who was lying beside him. "What is it?"

"Hope I'm not calling too early," the coroner said. "I got what you needed."

"What time is it?"

"Eight o'clock."

"Shit," Rick said. "I must have overslept." He heard the sound of the bathroom door opening down the hall. Abby was awake. He slipped on a pair of gym shorts that had found their way to the hickory floor, then tugged his faded San Diego State T-shirt over his head.

"Would you like to meet me in town?"

"No," Rick whispered. "Tell me what you got."

"So we looked for your suspect's DNA on clothing that was found near both sets of remains," Charlie began. "There was DNA from two people—Garrett McRae being one of them—at both scenes."

"The other person has to be James Edward Davis."

"You might think so," Charlie answered, "but they are calling their findings *inconclusive*."

"Inconclusive? Why?"

"Uh, because the samples are *inconclusive?*"

"There's must be a mistake," Rick said as he shook his head. "It has to be Davis. *Has* to be."

"Don't shoot the messenger," Charlie said. "They're saying inconclusive." He drew a breath. "But there's more."

Rick glanced over his shoulder at Sage. She lay peacefully on her back, her chest rising and falling rhythmically. "What else?"

"We were able to lift DNA from the wallet. There was a match."

"Davis?"

"Yes, Davis," Charlie said. "Keep in mind he easily could have touched the wallet back at their base camp. He could have been rummaging through Garrett's backpack for all we know."

"Or, he could have placed the wallet on the game trail to make it look like Garrett somehow left it behind."

"That's just one theory," Charlie murmured. "One of a few."

Rick looked at Sage once again, watching her nose and eyelids twitch as she rolled onto her side, the smooth skin of her cheek sinking into a feather pillow. Her clean-shaved head did not diminish her attractiveness but rather enhanced it. When they had made love hours before, he noticed the stark beauty of her features, from the richness of her eyes to the perfection of her lips.

He gently sat on the corner of the bed. "What do *you* think, Charlie?"

"It doesn't happen often, but I'm not sure what to think," the coroner said. "About all I know is that I have some bones torn from his gut, as well as a foot-long bone from his leg. Those two factors, as well as what I perceive as extreme blood loss, makes me fairly certain that this man is no longer living. Now, just exactly how he got to that point remains open to conjecture."

Rick locked his teeth. "I'm telling you, Charlie, this guy Davis had something to do with it."

"Yeah, yeah, I know," Charlie said with a chuckle. "You're in love with Davis." The coroner paused a beat. "You sure this isn't personal?"

"I gotta go," Rick said, ending the call. He rose to his feet and walked lightly around the bed. Turning the brass knob on the door and slowly pulling it open, he winced as its hinges made a yawning creak. As he stepped into the hallway, he locked eyes with Abby, who was standing in front of the sink inside the bathroom, toothbrush dangling from a mouth surrounded by a halo of baby-blue foam. She stared at Rick for a moment before pointing her eyes toward the room where Sage was sleeping. Abby's glare returned to her grandfather before she repeated the entire exercise, implying some form of explanation was required. Neither of them spoke for several seconds. Abby shrugged her shoulders with nonchalance, spitting a mouthful of toothpaste into the sink as she resumed brushing.

Rick walked briskly down the hall, searching his phone for the number of the Gallatin County Sheriff's Office. "Sheriff Martin, please," he said. "This is Rick Morrand." He pushed the Start button on a coffeemaker resting on the granite kitchen counter and opened a cupboard door to grab a mug.

"Sheriff Morrand," Patty said, her tone threaded with suspicion. "How might I help you today?"

"Patty, I need a favor."

"Go figure."

"I want you to hold your prisoner," Rick said, his words filling with urgency. "I have more evidence that can tie him to the murder of Garrett McRae. Strong evidence. There were kids who may have seen him in the area where Garrett's first remains were found. Now, we have a wallet—"

"Pump the brakes, Cowboy," Patty said. "My prisoner, as you prefer to call him, is no longer here."

"Where is he?"

"I would imagine by now he's back in Texas."

"He's not in Montana?" Rick stammered. "You said they wouldn't transport him until Wednesday. That's today."

"I know what day it is, Rick," Patty snapped. "Two deputies flew in on a fixed wing yesterday afternoon, picked him up, and headed back." She paused to take a sip through what sounded like a straw. "I'm kind of glad he's out of here, to be perfectly honest with you."

Rick slammed his palm on the counter. "I can't believe you did this."

"Get ahold of yourself, Sheriff," she shot back. "*I* didn't do anything. James Edward Davis was never my prisoner. I was simply holding him for another jurisdiction. They didn't teach you that in Sheriff 101?"

Rick massaged the front of his skull. "I know he wasn't your prisoner, Patty. I apologize."

"You're sure doin' a lot of apologizing these days."

"I apologize for that as well."

She let out an uneasy laugh. The line grew quiet. "I do have something you might be interested in," Patty finally said, her voice more subdued. "When is the last time you spoke to Amber McRae?"

"Amber?" Rick asked himself. "I don't know, maybe a few days. Why?"

"Well …," Patty said slowly, "one of my deputies ended up going to her house yesterday afternoon."

"What for?"

"We don't have all the facts nailed down just yet, but it appears someone tried to kill her."

Abby entered the kitchen, likely having heard her grandfather's earlier outburst. Rick walked past her, stepping out onto the deck of the ranch house. The gray wooden boards were covered in frost, untouched by sun trying to crawl over the mountains. He ignored the chill on his bare feet as he leaned one of his forearms on the railing. "Did you say someone tried to *kill* her?"

"I didn't stutter," Patty said. "According to her story, this guy showed up saying he ran out of gas. Next thing she knew, he had her trapped in a toolshed, fixin' to assault her."

"Is she okay?"

"She seems to be fine, but this fella didn't fare as well," Patty said. "My deputy happened to see smoke rising from Amber's property and went to investigate. When he rolled up, he saw a guy lying on the ground, a pitchfork sticking out of his gut. Amber was standing over him holding an eighteen-inch chainsaw right above his face. All she was missing was a goalie mask."

"Is the suspect alive?"

Patty took a slurp of her drink. "Fortunately, my deputy got Amber to stand down before she turned the guy into firewood. The pitchfork has been removed, and he is resting comfortably—cuffed to his bed with an officer guarding his room."

"What hospital?" Rick asked as he began to walk along the deck. "I need to—"

"Question him? I don't think so, Sheriff. Based on your recent record, I've decided your interrogation privileges in Gallatin County are permanently suspended."

"At least tell me his name. I have an ongoing investigation."

"Not a problem," Patty replied. He heard her rummage through papers on her desk. "His name is Earle Thomas Babcock. Goes by the name of Horsemeat."

"*Horsemeat?*"

"That's what the detective in Great Falls told me."

"The guy is from Great Falls?"

"Affirmative. His sheet is filled with burglaries, selling stolen goods, DUI, possession—petty stuff, mostly."

"Any arrests for assault?"

"None. Seems like he might have ventured beyond his normal pay grade."

"I'll say," Rick said, blowing out a breath of cold air. He heard a door open behind him. Sage's head was cocked sideways, forehead crinkled into a frown. She stared at his bare feet, which were surrounded by sparkles of melting frost. Rick held an index finger in the air, causing Sage to roll her eyes and retreat back inside. "If he's from Great Falls, what was he doing in Three Forks?" Rick asked Patty. "And why—"

"He was a little defiant at first, until we informed him he was looking at attempted murder," she said. "He'd served all of his time in county jails. Once we fully explained the intricacies of everyday life at Deer Lodge, he became more cooperative."

"What was his motive?"

"He claims someone hired him. A woman, actually."

"Did you get a name?"

Patty took a final draw from her drink and clanked it into a trash can. "No name," she said, her words suffocated by a belch.

"Physical description?"

"He only saw her once in person. He says she was attractive."

Rick paused in thought, rubbing his arms to stave off a shiver. A rooster crowed from a honeycombed-fenced pen beside the barn, followed immediately by cackles from hens. "Did she give him any money?"

"She *promised* to give him money," Patty said. "He claims she promised him a lot of things."

"I trust Horsemeat ain't much of a looker?"

Patty let out a burst of laughter. "No, he's not. Ain't much of a thinker either."

"Do you believe him?"

Patty paused. "That's a tough one. He doesn't know the woman's name, he can't contact her, and has no clue where to find her. Then again, why would a guy from Great Falls try to kill someone in Three Forks if no one had hired him?"

Sage reappeared at the door, holding Rick's hat, a cowhide jacket, and a pair of fur-lined moccasins. He recognized the moccasins from the previous Christmas—they had far less than a mile on them. He took his Stetson, offering Sage a half smile as he declined the other items. She shook her head and closed the door.

"Great Falls, huh?"

"That's correct," Patty said. "Is there any tie-in to your case?"

Rick exhaled. "The company holding a life insurance policy on Garrett McRae happens to be in Great Falls, but it could just be a coincidence. There also is a woman in our area whom I can't seem to locate. She supposedly had a relationship with Garrett."

"Care to share any additional details?"

"Not at the moment, Patty. But thank you for your help."

He ended the call and stepped back inside the ranch house, wiping his bare feet on a carpeted mat. Sage was standing at the stove, the back of her hand propped against her hip. Her other hand gripped a spatula and waited to flip pancakes cooking on a griddle. "Dang, it's cold out there," Rick said, vigorously rubbing his biceps. Sage swung her head back and forth, not turning around. Abby was leaning against the kitchen counter with her arms folded, her secretive, knowing smile and fluttering eyelids still celebrating the sheriff being busted as he exited Sage's bedroom earlier that morning. "You about ready for school, young lady?" he asked without expression.

"Do I have to go?" Abby whined. "I'm already late."

"It's a Wednesday in late September. Of course you have to go."

Abby groaned as she headed down the hallway to retrieve her backpack. Rick walked up behind Sage, wrapped his arms around her waist, and began to trace gentle kisses across the side of her neck. "Careful, fella," she said. "You don't want to be startin' something you can't finish."

Rick chuckled. "You're probably right. Abby and I need to grab a quick bite and get on our road."

"What's the hurry?" Sage asked as she swiveled toward him.

He offered a half smile. "Something tells me it's going to be a long day."

• • •

Rick walked into the sheriff's office and found his exasperated dispatcher intermittently nodding her head and rolling her eyes as she spoke into the phone.

"Yes ma'am," she said. "I understand, ma'am. Yes ma'am. I will take care of it, ma'am. Yes ma'am. I will let him know, ma'am. You bet. You have a nice day, now, will you?" She hung up and blew out a series of breaths as if she'd just climbed three flights of stairs.

"Mrs. Ulberg?" Rick asked.

"How'd you know?"

Rick smiled. "Just a wild guess. What is it that she would like me to know?"

"She says the Murdochs' dogs are still barking at night, and she's concerned they are unsettling her chickens."

Rick bit the side of his lip and hooked his thumbs beneath the front of his duty belt, tapping his fingers in cadence. "She has a six-hundred-acre ranch. The Murdoch place is a mile away."

Helen shrugged. "The sound carries, I guess."

"What makes her think the chickens are *unsettled?*"

"She claims their egg production is down."

"Has she considered psychotherapy?" Rick asked.

"For her or the chickens?"

"Both."

Rick shook his head and approached the door of his office. "Give a call to Jess Murdoch and ask him to try to calm his dogs down," he said as he began to turn the brass knob. "That's about all we can do."

"Oh, Sheriff?" Helen said. "You have a visitor."

"A visitor? Where?"

Helen flung her head over her shoulder. "She's in your office. Been here a while, actually—already asked to use the restroom. Seems a little skittish, if you ask me."

Rick raised his eyebrows and rubbed the side of his neck. "Does my visitor have a name?" he asked in a loud whisper.

Helen glanced at a notepad on her desk. "Meredith Hart. Says she's from Gallatin County Search and Rescue? Seems I've heard her name before. She said she planned to call but thought it better to meet you in person. As I mentioned, she appears to be on edge. I offered her coffee, but she declined." Her face brightened. "Would you like a cup of coffee, Sheriff?"

"No thanks, Helen," Rick said, placing his hand back on the doorknob. "Not right now."

"You don't like my coffee much, do you?"

"Your coffee is just fine, Helen."

"You don't have to fib, Sheriff," she said. "My girlfriend got a job at the new hair salon across the parking lot. She's able to see your window from her work station. She was curious as to why you like to water plants with caffeine."

Rick felt a rush of warmth flood into his face. He pressed his chin against the top of his chest and raised his eyebrows. "Do we have to do this now, Helen?"

"No, Sheriff," she said, turning her chair away and beginning to flip through a stack of papers on her desk. "Not at all."

CHAPTER 45

Meredith Hart sat erect in her chair, brown leather hiking boots firmly planted on the pine floor, fingers securely gripping her kneecaps. She wore the customary gray shirt and green trousers of the US Forest Service, her blond hair pulled back in a tight ponytail that intensified her sharp cheekbones and catlike blue eyes. Her fixed stare followed Rick's every step as he closed the office door and walked toward his desk.

"I understand you've been looking for me," she said flatly.

Rick hung up his nylon uniform jacket on a wooden coatrack, then placed his Stetson on the hook beside it. "Yes, I have, Ms. Hart," he said, his eyes tracing across the parking lot toward the salon employing Helen's trusted informant. "I wanted to contact you to discuss the nature of your relationship with Garrett McRae."

Meredith shrugged. "We were friends, if that is what you're asking."

"How close of friends were you?" Rick asked. "It's my understanding you spent a lot of time together." He leaned back in his chair, offering Meredith a polite smile.

Meredith's eyes slid away, her gaze focused on nothing in particular. "We trained together as members of Search and Rescue, and sometimes afterward we'd hang out." She turned back toward him. "I'm also working on becoming an EMT, and Garrett was helping me with that."

Rick leaned forward, interlocking his fingers on his desk. "I don't mean to be indelicate, but I'm sure you are aware that there were rumors."

Meredith cast her eyes toward the ceiling, pursing her lips as she wagged her head. "That's exactly what they were—rumors. To be honest, I almost wish they had been true, but Garrett just wasn't that kind of guy."

Rick nodded. "What kind of guy was he?"

"Kind, gentle, caring, unselfish," she said without hesitation. Her voice was kneaded with emotion, her eyes glazed with sadness. "He was crushed by what happened to his son, and he was deeply hurt by the troubles with his marriage."

Rick lifted a box of tissues from the corner of his desk and offered them to Meredith. She pulled two sheets from the box and dabbed her eyes. She didn't appear to be wearing makeup, and he deemed her smooth skin and distinct features made it unnecessary. "Can you tell me why you went back-packing in the Crazies the same weekend Garrett went missing?"

"I needed a break, and I wanted to get away," she answered. "I love the Crazies."

"Did you know that Garrett was going to be up there?"

"Yes, I did."

"Did you see him up there?"

"No."

"You're sure?"

"Positive," she said, her words strangled by another surge of anguish. "I wish I had." She blinked rapidly as she dried her eyes again.

Rick picked up a pen and rolled it between his fingers, his eyes remaining fixed on Meredith. "You told your mother you had some field trainings to attend in Yellowstone. But when I called the Forest Service office, I was told there were no such trainings."

"I had some vacation days," Meredith replied without hesitation. "I drove to Portland to visit some friends."

"Any particular reason you lied to your mother?"

Meredith's eyes scanned the ceiling before returning to him. "I prefer not to let my mother know my every move. Her insistence on telling you I went camping in the Crazies seems to have caused some suspicion."

Rick nodded. "Indeed it has. To be honest, some members of our team are also questioning how you were able to find evidence others missed."

Meredith flung her hands in the air and cocked her head. "Seriously?" she said, raising her cinnamon eyebrows. "Am I supposed to apologize for having a well-trained dog?"

Rick studied her face, weighing truth versus deception. Her tears had left her eyes road-mapped with red. Her closed lips quivered as she attempted to bridle her heartache.

"Have you ever met Amber McRae?"

Meredith nodded rapidly. "On a couple of occasions," she said, regaining composure.

"What did you think of her?"

"I didn't especially like her." She emitted an uneasy snicker. "Maybe I was biased, since I didn't think she treated Garrett very well."

"Were you aware that someone tried to take her life yesterday afternoon?"

"What?" Meredith blurted out, her voice rising. She leaned forward, eyes widened. "Is she okay? Is Gabe all right?"

"They're both fine, to my knowledge. We have a suspect in custody, and he claims that he was hired to kill Amber. Says he was hired by a woman."

"Well, I'm not that woman," Meredith said dismissively. "I would never want harm to come to Garrett or his family. Especially his son. Why would I?"

"Strong affection can cause folks to do some drastic things."

She blew out a breath. "I've already told you, Sheriff—we were *friends*."

Rick noted that Meredith freely spoke about Garrett in the past tense. Of course, why wouldn't she? He hadn't been seen for weeks. The odds of finding him alive appeared to be slim and none.

"Did he ever talk about his family—that is, aside from his wife and child?" Rick asked.

Meredith shook her head. "He didn't really have any other family that I knew of. He told me that his parents died in a car accident when he was really young, so he mostly was raised in foster homes. He was separated early from an older sister, who ended up dying from an overdose. The only family member he ever mentioned was his niece."

"He has a niece?"

"His sister's daughter," Meredith said. "He told me he wanted to try to help her, given she'd had a rough shake."

"Did you know her name?"

"He may have told me, but I can't recall it now," Meredith said. "I believe he was trying to help her get through school." She averted her eyes as grief crept back into her voice. "That's the kind of man he was—always putting the needs of others ahead of his own."

"Would you happen to recall where the niece was going to school?"

Meredith's eyebrows narrowed as she paused in thought. "If I remember correctly, it might have been Great Falls."

●　●　●

Rick arrived in Great Falls in the early afternoon. He drove down the town's busy Central Avenue, rolling to a stop in front of a storefront window with the words "Western Montana Insurance Company" arching across its surface. Two elderly women, shoulders hunched beneath outdated wool coats, glanced at the side of his truck and squinted skeptically through his windshield before continuing on their way.

Rick found a receptionist seated at her desk and typing on a keyboard as she stared at a computer screen. "May I help you, sir?"

"I'm here to visit with Mr. Bible. I'm Sheriff Morrand from Dexter County."

"I'm sorry, he's been out of the office since early this morning, and I'm not completely sure when I expect him back. Did you have an appointment?"

"I typically don't need appointments," he answered. "Is it possible for you to contact him?"

"I tried to do that a few minutes ago, but it went right to voice mail." She cast her eyes toward two chairs separated by an oak table with a ceramic lamp and fan-shaped stack of magazines. "You're welcome to wait, Sheriff. My name is Rachel. I'll be happy to make you some coffee, if you would like."

"No thank you, Rachel. I've had enough coffee for now." He walked to one of the chairs and sat. The wall above Rachel's desk was decorated with large framed paintings of a bison and a wolf. Toward the back of the room, outside what he assumed was Spencer's office, Rick saw a mount of a pronghorn sheep. He turned his head behind him to see trophies of a bighorn sheep and five-point elk on the wall above him. "Is Mr. Bible a hunter?"

Rachel shook her head. "No, his daddy is … *was*," she said. "Spencer not so much."

"His dad no longer hunts?"

"Unfortunately, Cyrus has fallen ill."

Rick nodded. "Mr. Bible mentioned that."

"Alzheimer's," Rachel said.

"Alzheimer's. I imagine that's difficult … for him and his son."

"Spencer has taken it pretty hard."

They sat in silence for several minutes. Rick started to reach for a hunting magazine but stopped when he heard the front door open. A young man walked in with familiarity, then stiffened when he took notice of a law enforcement uniform.

"Spencer, this is Sheriff Morrand from Dexter County," Rachel said.

"Oh, yes—we've talked on the phone," Spencer murmured skeptically as he approached Rick and extended his hand. His palm felt soft and clammy.

He had the joyless face of a man who had just attended a funeral, perhaps his own. "How many I help you, sir?"

"Would you mind if we had a word?"

"No problem at all," Spencer said, lips innocently downturned as he wagged his head.

Spencer was tall, slight of build, his blond hair freshly cut high and tight. He wore navy slacks and brown dress shoes. A narrow striped tie with a small knot descended from the button-down collar of his powder-blue dress shirt. Like most millennials, his clothes appeared two sizes too small.

Rick followed Spencer into a small, tidy office. The young insurance man settled behind a dust-free desk adorned with only a computer screen, phone, paperweight, stapler, and unblemished desk pad, all of which were neatly arranged in a manner that signaled an acute lack of business activity.

"It's nice to put a name with a face, Sheriff," Spencer said, his tone failing sincerity. "What is it that brings you to Great Falls?"

Rick crossed his legs and propped his Stetson on his kneecap. "Well, I suppose I'll just cut to the chase, Mr. Bible," he said. "I'm here concerning Amber McRae."

Spencer cast a half smile. "I am quite familiar with Mrs. McRae," he said uneasily. "I have spoken to her on several occasions."

"It appears someone tried to kill her yesterday afternoon."

Spencer swallowed as color drained from his face. "Excuse me, sir?"

"We have a man in custody who likely will be charged with attempted murder. Our suspect is a career criminal from Great Falls. He claims he was hired by a woman from up here."

Spencer wet his lips and coughed faintly into his closed fist. "I'm not sure how this involves us."

"I don't know that it does involve you, Mr. Bible," Rick said. His index finger stroked the crown of his Stetson. "I'd like to discuss the insurance policy issued to Garrett McRae."

Spencer hesitated for a beat. "Sure—absolutely," he said, reaching toward the metal basket on his desk. "I believe I have it right here." He placed the file in front of him and opened it.

"Can you tell me if there are other beneficiaries besides Amber McRae?" Rick asked.

Spencer issued another artificial cough as he turned over the first page of the policy. "What you would be referring to is a contingent beneficiary," he said, sliding his finger down the page. "Here it is—there is one contingent beneficiary by the name of Elizabeth Anne Cooper."

"So, if something were to happen to Amber, this woman named Elizabeth Anne Cooper would become the primary beneficiary, correct?" Rick asked.

Spencer nodded.

"Do you know who she is? Does it list her relationship to the insured?"

Spencer's chin flicked to one side, and he adjusted the knot on his tie. "It says here that she is Mr. McRae's niece," he croaked.

"Would you know if Ms. Cooper—

"Let me call my secretary in, Sheriff," he said. "She is the one who actually wrote the policy."

Spencer bit the side of his lip and pressed his intercom. "Rachel do you have a moment?" Rick looked over his shoulder through the plate glass at the front of Spencer's office. Rachel was seated at her desk, rhythmically licking her thumb as she paged through a magazine. She checked her wristwatch and rose from her chair. "Yes sir?" she said as she appeared at the office door.

"Would you have any information on the contingent beneficiary on this policy? Her name is Elizabeth Anne Cooper. The policy says she's Mr. McRae's niece."

"That's correct."

"And she's his only niece?" Rick asked.

"Yes, she is, Sheriff." Rachel said. "She was added to the policy later on, perhaps a couple weeks after Mr. McRae originally came to our office. He mentioned that, besides his wife, his niece was the only other family he had."

"And she lives here in Great Falls?"

Rachel shook her head. "I can't be sure of that. He didn't say."

Spencer remained silent, staring at the insurance policy on his desk. His face was the color of ash. He appeared seasick, perhaps seated on the deck of the *Titanic*. "Is something wrong, Mr. Bible?"

"No, I'm fine," Spencer said.

"Did you ever happen to meet Ms. Cooper? Given Garrett McRae's age, I would guess she's somewhere in her early to mid-twenties."

Spencer hesitated. "Thank you, Rachel," he mumbled as he glanced toward his secretary. "That's all for now."

Rachel stared at him, studying his appearance. "Are you okay, Spencer? Can I get you something? Water, perhaps?"

Spencer shook his head as he stared at the insurance policy. "No, thank you, Rachel. Please give us some privacy." Rachel held her eyes on Spencer as she backed through the doorway, casting a quick nod and tight smile toward Rick as the door clicked shut.

Rick rested his elbow on the arm of his chair, massaging the stubble on his chin. He leaned forward. "So, Mr. Bible, did you ever meet Ms. Cooper?"

"I … *may* have," he said. He fidgeted in his chair, nervously rubbing his fingers together. "I believe I know who she is."

"I'm listening."

Spencer licked his lips. "There's this woman I've been … dating. She goes by the name of Lizzie."

"You mean, like, short for Elizabeth?" Rick asked, helping him along. "Did you happen to catch her last name?"

A sunset of pink descended over Spencer's face. "No sir, actually I didn't."

"Sounds like a deep relationship."

"Actually, it was," Spencer said defensively. "At least, I *thought* it was."

"How well did you know her?"

Spencer drew a deep breath. "We started dating a couple of weeks ago—"

"Not to interrupt, but can you define dating?" Rick asked. "That seems to encompass all kinds of things these days—everything from riding bicycles to ride 'em cowboy."

Spencer stole another glance toward Rick before turning his eyes away. "We were intimate, if that's what you're wondering. I thought we had developed a nice … bond."

"Even though you never caught her name," Rick said. His eyes briefly roamed the ceiling. "You wouldn't happen to have a photo, would you?"

Spencer picked up the smartphone on his desk and unlocked the screen. He turned the display toward Rick, showing him a selfie. Spencer and Lizzie were cheek to cheek, all smiles with eyes glistening. Rick studied Lizzie's face. She was pretty—gorgeous, even. Her hair was full, eyes magical. Spencer appeared oblivious that he was far out of his depth.

"We had a disagreement a few days ago, and we broke up," Spencer said. He looked at Rick with eyes laced with sadness and defeat. "Is she in some kind of trouble?"

Rick pursed his lips. "As I mentioned, someone assaulted Amber McRae yesterday. The guy claims the person who hired him is an attractive woman from Great Falls, and Ms. Cooper looks like she could qualify." He cast his chin toward the policy. "Since she also is the contingent beneficiary, I'd be less than truthful if I didn't consider her a person of interest."

Spencer's neck bulged as though he was trying vainly to swallow. "I see," he said. He straightened the pages of the policy and stared at the open folder.

"Tell me, Mr. Bible, did Ms. Cooper know she was a beneficiary on the policy?"

Spencer paused, eyes still fixed on the folder. "I suppose she would if Mr. McRae had told her."

"Would she have any other way of knowing?"

Spencer shrugged. "I suppose if she saw the … *file*," Spencer said, the word *file* momentarily trapped in his throat. His mind flashed to seeing Lizzie sitting in his office, her eyes blinking innocently as she held the McRae folder in her hand.

Rick cocked his head to the side. "Why is it that I think there is something you're not telling me, Mr. Bible?"

Spencer closed the file, opened it, then closed it again. His eyes blinked, nose twitching. "Look, Sheriff," he said. "I didn't know that Lizzie was … Elizabeth. I swear I didn't. I'm sure you can appreciate that some might view my dating Mr. McRae's niece as some kind of ethical issue …"

"I'm not overly concerned with ethical issues at the moment," Rick said. He drew a deep breath, stood from his chair, and placed his Stetson on his head. "What I might recommend is that the next time you bed a woman, you might want to catch her last name."

The office turned deathly quiet before the hum of an inkjet printer outside Spencer's office pierced the silence. A moment later, Spencer's secretary knocked on the door. "Yes?" he said.

Rachel poked her head in. "Sorry to bother you, sir. I thought you would want to know that we just received an email pertaining to the McRae policy." She handed a piece of paper to Spencer. "It's a copy of a death certificate. They'll be sending the original overnight."

"A death certificate?" Rick asked, lifting his brow. "Charlie Duchesne sent you a death certificate for Garrett McRae?"

Rachel squinted at Rick. "It's for Mr. McRae," she said, "but I'm not familiar with anyone named Charlie Duchesne. The death certificate came from Lupine County."

CHAPTER 46

Charlie considered Lupine County Coroner Pernell Crawford to be incompetent, unethical, or senile—quite possibly a combination of all three. For that reason, the men certainly had their share of disagreements over the years, on two occasions nearly coming to blows.

The first run-in occurred on Charlie's forty-second wedding anniversary, when he and Dora were celebrating at the Grand, a white-tablecloth establishment in Big Timber. Pernell spotted Charlie and wandered over from the bar, claiming he wanted to introduce himself to Charlie's wife. Dora looked especially fetching that evening, having gussied herself up for the occasion. After kissing her hand not once but twice, Pernell proceeded to make a few suggestive comments to Charlie's bride, his alcohol-addled words serving as the flint to ignite sparks of jealousy that soon hurled Charlie into a blaze of rage. By the time a waiter and two bystanders intervened, the two men had pressed their foreheads together like a pair of bighorn sheep during the rut, Charlie's hand tightly clutching a steak knife still dripping with the juice from his lamb chop.

On another occasion, the Lupine County Sheriff's Office had asked Charlie to help investigate the mysterious death of a fifteen-year-old Native American girl found in a shallow grave less than a mile from Highway 191. The sheriff was primarily interested in Charlie's skills as a medical examiner, given Pernell did not hold a medical degree. Rather than welcoming outside expertise, Pernell was downright red-assed. By the time Charlie arrived on scene, potential evidence was either nonexistent or compromised. Charlie interviewed the parents of the girl—a straight-A student—and determined she would have had little reason to leave home. He suspected she'd been kidnapped, raped, and left to die, a sad, all-too-common occurrence for young Native women.

Pernell ruled that the girl was a runaway whose death was simply accidental, a sudden snowstorm trapping her on the wind-lashed high plains of Lupine County. The girl's parents, he claimed, had shamed her after having learned that she'd had sex with her boyfriend and possibly others. Charlie believed Pernell had scant regard for the Native peoples, and he felt compelled to let him know it. Despite his protests, Pernell's determination stood.

Charlie now was waist-deep in the investigation of Garrett McRae, reluctant to issue a final ruling until he'd navigated every tributary of inquiry. Pernell Crawford had usurped his efforts, claiming Garrett McRae's pursuit of a precious cow elk had caused him to drift into Lupine County, and that was where his remains were found.

Slamming the door of his SUV, Charlie stormed across the potholed driveway in front of Pernell's farmhouse, a decaying gray clapboard structure surrounded by a fence that was a patchwork of rusted tin and warped plywood. Charlie often wondered how voters had reelected Pernell for decades. Granted, there was the fact he'd almost always ran unopposed. Second, given the paucity of crime in sparsely populated Lupine County, residents weren't afforded the opportunity to appreciate the full measure of his ineptitude.

"Get on out here, you old bastard!" Charlie growled toward the front entrance of the house, its screen door hanging askew as it clung to rusted hinges. "Get your sorry ass out here—now!"

Charlie clutched the gate. It wouldn't budge. He shook it violently, rattling the entire fence. Suddenly, he froze. Out of the corner of his eye he saw two brown pit bulls, their bared teeth dripping with saliva as they sprinted around the side of the house. Charlie lurched backward in terror, arms flailing as he fought to keep his balance. The dogs propped their paws on the top of the gate, their sinewy muscles quivering as they barked menacingly.

Pernell emerged from the front door of the house, stumbling down the decrepit wooden porch, shotgun cradled in the crook of his arm. He wore faded denim overalls, half the bib unstrapped to reveal a thermal shirt stained with remnants of his most recent TV dinner. His thin gray hair looked like a trampled hayfield, his chin flecked with stubble, a wad of chew ballooning the right side of his jaw. Charlie guessed the coroner had spent the afternoon in the company of Jim Beam.

"Get these dogs outta here and face me like a man!" Charlie screamed over the incessant cacophony of barks, yelps, and howls.

"You're trespassing!" Pernell shouted back, drawing down the shotgun on his intruder. "I gotta good mind to cut these dogs loose and change your name to Alpo. Better yet, I could just pepper you with buckshot right there in your tracks."

"I'm sure you'd consider it self-defense, you incompetent old fool!" Charlie yelled. "Tell me—how much did they pay you?"

"How much did *who* pay me?"

"Whoever paid you to issue that death certificate, that's who!" Charlie snarled. He took a step forward, only to make the dogs more agitated.

"Nobody paid me nothin'," Pernell said, spitting a stream of tobacco juice on the ground for emphasis.

"I haven't finished my investigation, you bastard!"

"It ain't *your* investigation," Pernell said. "That boy died in my jurisdiction. Anybody can see that he was attacked by a bear while field-dressing an elk. Why don't you let him rest in peace?"

"I'm not convinced of that." Charlie answered. The barking of the dogs subsided, the beasts content to glare at Charlie while their clenched jaws slobbered amid a hum of steady growls. "If you didn't get paid off, what was your hurry?"

"Have you no sense of decency?" Pernell shouted. "The man's widow not only lost her husband, she's got a handicapped kid. I think it's fair to say she's suffered enough! How'd you like it if it was your wife?"

"Don't you dare mention my wife."

Pernell spewed another stream of tobacco juice. "Well, she seems like a mighty good woman. And she's one hell of a looker, that's for sure. How'd she ever end up with a broken-down gelding like you?"

Charlie rattled the gate again, sending clanging ripples along the fence line. The entrance remained stuck. One of the pit bulls lunged at his hand, puncturing the flesh. Charlie clutched the wound, grimacing as he stared at the dog through squinted eyes.

"Serves ya right," Pernell snapped.

"Damn mongrel probably has rabies!" Charlie replied. Behind him, he heard the sound of rubber grinding gravel. He spun to see an SUV from the Lupine County Sheriff's Department. A young deputy struggled to get out of the vehicle, his body better suited for devouring chili fries and watching the Broncos than handling the rigors of law enforcement.

"Everything okay here, gentlemen?" the deputy asked, sizing up Charlie before turning toward Pernell.

Pernell grabbed a fistful of fur and skin on each of the dog's necks, tugging them into a sitting position and quieting their barks. "He was just leavin'," he said, nodding toward Charlie.

Swiping his hand across the thigh of his jeans, Charlie examined the severity of his wound. "Sure, I'm leavin'," he said, glaring at Pernell. "But this ain't over. Before I'm done, this county will have a new coroner—you can bet on it."

Pernell turned his head to the side, sending a final stream of tobacco juice out of his mouth. "Aw, go on and git."

CHAPTER 47

Following several miles of ardent internal debate, Rick took the Three Forks exit off I-90 shortly before five o'clock, succumbing to the unenviable yet requisite task of visiting Amber McRae. He found Garrett's widow sitting in the swing on her front porch, wearing an oversized weathered sweatshirt with the faded image of a wolf on the front. Her legs were crossed, ankles tucked beneath her thighs, sleeves pulled over her hands for warmth as she cradled a glass of what appeared to be white wine. She briefly glanced at Rick's approaching vehicle before returning her vacant gaze toward a horizon full of nothingness.

Rick turned off his engine as his truck rolled to a stop. After studying the charred ruins of what had once been the McRaes' toolshed, he stepped out and walked toward the porch. A cool wind swirled, sending bright-yellow aspen leaves dancing across the walkway. Rick ascended the creaky wooden steps, removing his hat. Amber continued to stare into the distance as if he wasn't there.

"It's good to see you are okay," he said, offering the best icebreaker he could muster. "I understand you had quite a fright."

Amber threw her head back and stared at the porch ceiling. "Yeah, Sheriff, I had quite a *fright*," she said, her piercing tone a blend of contempt and mockery. She whipped her face toward him. "I guess maybe now you might believe I didn't kill my husband." She took a long sip of her wine. Her glazed eyes suggested the glass wasn't her first.

"I never said you killed your husband, ma'am," Rick said, his voice slightly above a whisper.

"You didn't have to," Amber snapped.

The porch grew silent for several seconds. The chains of the hanging swing squeaked. More leaves rustled. A wind chime tingled somewhere. The air was turning cold. "I realize this is a trying time for you, Mrs. McRae, but I would like to ask you a couple of questions."

Amber tipped her glass, finishing her wine. "Fire away, Sheriff," she said, setting the glass on the gray-colored floor of the porch.

Rick scratched his eyebrow and briefly studied his Stetson. "Would you have any idea who might want to harm you?"

"Your guess is as good as mine, Sheriff. But, then again, you're not a very good guesser, are you?"

Rick stepped closer, leaning against a post supporting the roof of the porch. "Do you have any acquaintances in Great Falls?"

"No."

Rick tugged his notebook out of his top pocket and flipped it open in one hand. "How about someone named Elizabeth Anne Cooper?"

"Oh, her," Amber huffed dismissively. "Great Falls, huh?" She began to reach for her wine glass but remembered it was empty. "I didn't know where she was. Either way, I wouldn't call her an *acquaintance*."

Rick closed the notebook and returned it to his pocket. "It's my under-standing she is Garrett's niece?"

"Yes, she is," Amber said, flicking a quick glance at him. "Garrett's sister raised her back east, I think in Pennsylvania. After Wendy died, Garrett figured it would be a good idea for her daughter to come out here. We knew her as Beth. She moved in with us, but that didn't last long. She had a bad habit of helping herself to my purse. We also had a few cowboys show up from the local bars looking for the contents of their wallets."

"So it's fair to say that you and Elizabeth didn't get along?"

Amber laughed. "I'm not a big fan of anyone who steals from me. It wasn't like we could afford it."

"Do you know if Garrett stayed in touch with her?"

Amber shrugged. "I demanded he not speak to her again, but with Garrett you never know. He was always trying to help other people—fix them, you might say." She blew out short breaths through parted lips, chok-ing back emotion. "Maybe he should have taken better care of himself."

Rick returned his hat to his head and folded his arms across his chest, his eyes drifting beyond the porch. A wild turkey waddled nonchalantly through a gap in a split-rail fence desperate for repair. Two horses frolicked playfully in the distance, kicking up clumps of soil in a field of tawny grass. "Did you know that Elizabeth Cooper is a secondary beneficiary on his life insurance policy?" he asked as he turned toward Amber.

"What?" she shouted, eyes opened wide. Heaving a sigh, she shook her head. "I don't believe it." She paused a beat. "So, if she is on that life insurance policy, she's the one who sent that guy to kill me."

"It's a possibility," Rick said. "Do you know why Garrett would have made her a beneficiary?"

"I have no idea, and it really doesn't matter, does it? It was Beth who was trying to have me killed. Has she been arrested?"

"Gallatin County is handling that investigation," Rick answered. "I'm sure they will try to locate her."

Amber snared her glass off the porch and quickly rose from the swing. "I need to check on Gabe, and I really could use a little more wine." She walked toward the front door of the house. "Would you care for a drink, Sheriff? Beer? Wine? Whiskey, maybe?"

"No ma'am," Rick answered. "I don't drink."

"That would figure," she said with a derisive chuckle. "You strike me as a bit stiff."

She began to swing open the screen door but suddenly stopped, staring beyond Rick at a red Toyota Sienna grinding gravel as it came up the driveway and rolled to a stop. A man wearing a green satin jacket stepped out of the driver's side and adjusted the faded ball cap covering his silver hair. His eyes were somber. He waited in front of the van until he was joined by a short, portly woman clinging to the handle of a brown shopping bag. "I'm sorry we're showing up unannounced, Amber," he said, placing his arm around the woman's shoulders. "We'd been traveling in our RV and just learned the news yesterday. We thought we'd stop by to see how you are getting on."

"That's very thoughtful of you, Coach Benson," Amber said. She glanced at her wine glass and quickly placed it on a windowsill between a pair of potted plants. There was a lengthy, awkward silence before the elderly couple climbed the stairs of the porch. They both hugged Amber, the woman offering her the bag she was carrying.

"We brought you a ham from Town & Country," she said. "Have you ever had one of their hams?"

"No, I haven't," Amber said, peering into the grocery bag. "I'll bet it's delicious."

"We figured you couldn't possibly have time for any cooking," the woman said. "Not with … well, you know."

Amber nodded her head rapidly, her eyes glassy and jaw muscles twitching as she tried in vain to offer a smile. "That's very thoughtful of you," she repeated.

Rick stood quietly nearby, as quiet and rigid as a sculpture. Amber finally glanced toward him. "Sheriff, this is Coach Bob Benson and his wife, Anita. Garrett played football for Coach Benson at Three Forks High."

Rick extended his hand. "I thought I recognized you. You're the winningest coach in Montana high school football history. You're a legend."

Benson chuckled. "I wouldn't go that far. I suppose I won a few games."

"More than a few," Rick said with laughter. "A couple of them came against my old school, Bridger High."

Amber took a step forward. "If you'll excuse me, I need to check on Gabe. I also want to get this ham in the refrigerator."

"I'll help you," Anita said as the women entered the house.

The coach briefly removed his ball cap, scratching a head of gray crew-cut hair. He had a solid build for a man of his age. His jaw was square and as firm as a wooden block, eyes filled with purpose. All he was missing was a silver whistle between his lips. "It's a shame what happened to Garrett," he said, returning his cap to his head "Never seems right when someone dies so young."

"No, it doesn't," Rick agreed. He swallowed, images of his deceased daughter clicking through his brain. After a beat, he asked, "Tell me, Coach, what was Garrett like when you coached him? What kind of athlete was he?"

"One of the best I ever coached. He had plenty of God-given talent, and he made the most out of it. He also was tough as nails."

Rick frowned. "Tough? How so?"

His lips curled into a warm smile, his eyes softening as if recalling the birth of his first child. "We had a playoff game up in Townsend against Broadwater High," he said. "They were a tough group to begin with, but they had a coach who had played semipro ball, and he taught his kids a few things that weren't all that sportsmanlike." He adjusted the bill of his ball cap and released a breath. "Garrett had gone for well over one hundred yards in the first half alone. Early in the third quarter, one of their linebackers speared him in the lower ribs, beneath his shoulder pads. Another guy hit him at the same time, right above the kidney." The coach cupped his hand and ran his fingers along the bottom of his rib cage and around his side. "Our left tackle swore he heard bones crack. I told Garrett he needed to sit out, but he wouldn't have it. He went back in and ran for another hundred yards and the winning touchdown. Later on, we took him to the hospital and had some X-rays done. Turns out the kid had three cracked ribs and two others that had broken clear off."

Benson's blue eyes looked like moist crystals, his lips starting to tremble. "Like I said, one tough kid."

Rick bit the side of his lip, his chest feeling weighted and thick. He almost clutched his aching torso, wondering how anyone could carry a football with injured ribs. Glancing toward the entrance to the house, he said, "Sounds like you stayed in touch."

"Yes, definitely," the coach answered, blinking back emotion. "Garrett was like another son to Anita and me. He even lived with us for a while."

"Oh?"

"After his mom and dad passed," Benson said. "We were foster parents, and we occasionally took in a lot of kids over the years. Garrett lived with us for about a year and a half. Him and Jesse."

Rick's chin jerked backward. "Did you say Jesse?"

The coach nodded. "Jesse Lone Wolf," he said. "He came to us from the res after his daddy died. His mother couldn't stay sober and lost custody. Jesse was a pretty troubled kid when we first got him, but he and Garrett hit it off. They were inseparable."

Inseparable? Jesse Lone Wolf had denied any knowledge of Garrett McRae, as well as any association with Amber. Rick paused, trying to process the information he'd received. "Have you kept in touch with Jesse?" The words caught in his throat.

Benson shook his head. "Unfortunately, no. I believe he still lives in Montana, but we haven't seen him for years." His eyelids opened wide. "Do you know him? Have you—"

The murmur of voices interrupted them, Anita and Amber emerging from behind the screen door. "Are you sure you can't stay for dinner?" she asked Anita. "Gabe and I would love to have you." She looked at Rick. "I'm sure the sheriff will be leaving soon."

"That's kind of you, Amber, but we really can't," Anita answered. "Perhaps another time?"

An uneasy silence followed before Coach Benson looked at his wife. "I was just telling the sheriff here about Garrett and Jesse living with us."

Amber glanced toward Rick, whose glare made her blanch. She quickly averted her eyes.

Anita flashed a smile. "Those boys could be a handful," she said, her lips pressing together as she shook her head. "And don't forget about Clay."

"Clay?" Rick asked. He looked at Amber. Her eyes blinked rapidly as she listened to the Bensons.

The coach snapped his fingers and pointed toward his wife. "How can I forget Clay Bonner?" he exclaimed as he turned toward Rick. "He was our quarterback. The three of those kids went everywhere together."

"Does Mr. Bonner still live in Montana?" Rick asked.

Coach Benson looked at Anita, his brow furrowed. "As I remember, he went to college at A&M, same place as Garrett. I guess he took a liking to Texas—I haven't seen him since."

Amber bit the side of her lip. "Well, I'm sure you folks need to get going. You probably want to get caught up after being away so long."

Anita gave Amber a long, lingering embrace. Placing her hands on Amber's shoulders, she squared the incipient widow toward her. "Now, as I've already told you, if you need anything—anything at all—I want you to call us *immediately*."

Amber nodded, her eyes growing moist. Bob said nothing, stepping forward to hug her gingerly, the gesture appearing foreign to him. The couple both nodded at Rick and eased their way off the porch. They waved once more as they drove away in their van.

"You never mentioned that you knew Jesse Lone Wolf," Rick said, hands on hips.

Amber averted her eyes. "I didn't think it was important."

Rick drew a deep breath through his nose. "You know, people are really getting into the habit of determining for me what is or isn't important. I'd really prefer they wouldn't do that." He watched Amber shrug, then asked, "So, can you tell me why you called the Gold Bar on the Saturday night after your husband was reported missing?"

"I thought they might be able to give me more information, especially since you weren't able to do so," she shot back, hiking her thick eyebrows.

"Did Garrett stay in contact with Jesse Lone Wolf?"

"I'm not sure," she said. "I know I haven't seen Jesse in years."

Rick stared at the western horizon. The bright-orange sun was gently sinking into a bed of cottony clouds. The temperature had dropped. Darkness would arrive soon. "What can you tell me about Clay Bonner?"

Amber rolled her eyes and flicked her hair over her shoulder. "Look, Sheriff, Gabe is going to be hungry, and I need to prepare something for him. Is all of this really necessary?"

"If you can just answer my question, I'll be on my way."

Amber's face now appeared flushed, likely from the wine. Alcohol didn't seem to favor her. "Garrett would get together with Clay and some of his other college buddies once a year," she said. "They would pick out an Aggies home game each fall and spend the weekend together. I wasn't crazy about it because they would end up getting pretty drunk. Once Gabe got hurt, Garrett didn't even want to go. I insisted, even though we really couldn't afford it. I figured it would do him good. Finally, he agreed to go this year. I forget who the Aggies were playing. He got back the week before his bow hunting trip. He seemed to be in good spirits." She squinted at Rick, tipping her head to one side. "Why are you interested in one of his college friends?"

"I guess I'm really not sure," Rick answered. He looked down at his watch, realizing he hadn't spoken to Sage the entire day. "I guess I best be going."

"When will Beth be arrested?"

Rick drew a breath. "As I mentioned, the attempt on your life is a Gallatin County investigation."

"You sure have an interesting concept of what's important," Amber said.

Rick adjusted his hat and tipped it toward Amber. "I suppose you're right," he said, ambling down the wooden steps and walking toward his truck.

CHAPTER 48

Abby sat silently in the passenger seat as she and Rick rode toward Riverton on Highway 89, her eyes staring intently at the side of the road.

"You counting fence posts again?" Rick asked.

His granddaughter shook her head and said nothing.

"You okay, Abby?"

She shrugged.

Rick leaned in her direction, trying to make eye contact. Her eyes were moist.

"Can you promise me you won't die?" she said.

Rick turned back toward the road in front of him. Resting his elbow on the console, he used his forefinger to scratch the side of his cheek. "Well, you understand that everyone has to die someday."

Abby rolled her eyes. "I *know* that, Pa-Pa," she said. "I just don't want you to die right away."

Rick shrugged. "Well, I certainly don't plan on dying anytime soon. What is making you so worried about this?"

Abby glared at him, eyes opened wide. "*Really?*"

"Yes, really."

"Well, my mommy died," she said, her voice cracking. She paused a moment, blinking back tears. "How about Auntie Sage having cancer? Or how about you almost getting eaten by a bear?"

The inside of Rick's chest felt like hardened clay. He reached for Abby's hand. Her skin was cold. "Well, the doctor is saying Sage is going to be fine, and I didn't get eaten," he murmured. "So far, so good." He slowed his truck as they came into town. The morning was brisk, but the sun was out and the sky was clear, nighttime rain having washed away the smoke. "You miss your mommy, don't you?"

Abby nodded but didn't speak.

Rick squeezed her hand as they rolled to a stop in front of her school. "You go out and have a good day, okay, sweetheart?" he said. "I love you."

Abby grabbed her backpack, opened the door, and slid off the seat onto the sidewalk. "I love you, too," she said. "Just don't die."

Rick watched his granddaughter run toward two of her classmates, the three girls sharing carefree laughter as they entered the school. Children were so pliable, he thought, able to experience injury and emotion and then quickly forget.

He found his head suddenly clouded by the memory of Chloe's murder. Gloom seized him at random as though he were being trailed by a haunting ghoul perpetually poised to strike. If time heals all, how long would it take for an eternity to pass?

• • •

Rick drove six blocks and parked in front of the Spur, Sage's establishment on Main Street. It wouldn't open until noon, but the lights were on and the front door unlocked. He walked along a dim hallway illuminated by neon before entering a high-ceilinged room filled with round tabletops and rimmed by large flat-screen TVs.

Birdie Hallin sat at the far end of the bar, a ringed check binder and pile of envelopes sprawled out in front of her. "Hey, Sheriff," the young woman said, glancing up from her work. "You here to pick up Sage's mail?" She released a sigh. "There isn't all that much left after I sorted out all the bills."

Dr. Tillotson had ordered Sage not to work, which was akin to asking a cowboy to cease riding horses. The patient reluctantly agreed to cut back, asking Birdie to prepare payments to various vendors so all Sage needed to do was sign the checks.

Birdie had green eyes and a contagious smile to go with her athletic figure, honed from her career as a barrel racer. As a high school junior, she had served a stint as queen of the Riverton Roundup Rodeo. For reasons not quite clear, she shared the same nickname as her mother and grandmother, which likely caused a measure of confusion at family gatherings.

At twenty-eight, Birdie now was one year away from an online accounting degree from Montana State, which would distinguish her as the first Hallin to graduate college. She had worked at the Spur for ten years, and Sage trusted her implicitly.

"I think I have everything in order," Birdie said, using a paper clip to attach a check to an invoice. "The only thing I'm not sure about is what to do with these medical bills."

"I'll take those," Rick said.

Her forehead crinkled. "Are you sure, Sheriff? Sage didn't mention—"

"It's okay, Birdie," he said, extending his hand. "It'll be fine."

Birdie slowly handed him several envelopes. "I'll just let Sage know that—"

"No, Birdie," Rick interrupted. "Sage doesn't need to know." He drew a long breath. "Look. I don't want Sage to worry about this stuff. When these bills come in, I'd like you to set them aside for me. Can you do that?"

Birdie nodded. "I understand, Sheriff." After a pause, she smiled and said, "I hope someday I find a guy who cares for me like that."

"I'm sure you will," Rick said as he winked and headed for the door. Sitting in his truck, Rick slipped his thumb beneath each of the envelopes. One of the invoices, from Billings Clinic, already had been paid. The others were not. There were bills for hospital services, treatments, labs, and even a pair of specialists whose names he didn't recognize. He would be writing another five-figure check.

He tossed the envelopes on the passenger seat. Warmth flowed into his face. Shifting into gear, he felt himself immersed in a slow boil.

● ● ●

Rick found Helen grinning broadly as she stirred cream into her coffee and cast a nod toward the coffeepot on the table nearby. "Coffee is ready, Sheriff. Hazelnut-flavored. You really should give it a try."

"I'm fine for now, Helen."

"Seriously," she said brightly, taking a sip from her cup and licking her pink lips. "I got it at Costco. I think you'd like it."

"Maybe later," Rick said, marshalling patience. "Any messages?"

Helen placed her coffee mug to the side and pulled her message pad toward her. "Rob Deering called from the National Forest Service. He interviewed the teenagers again in Lupine County. One of the boys says he's positive that the truck they saw was white, and it was a Chevrolet."

"Call Rob back and ask him if the kid had any idea what year it was. Also, ask whether it had Montana plates." He paused a beat, watching Helen write down his instructions. "Dodge trucks are big around here, followed maybe by Ford. See how many white Chevrolet trucks are registered in Dexter and Lupine counties."

"I'll get on it, Sheriff," Helen said, tapping her pen on her notepad. "Is there something in particular you are looking for? I mean, hasn't Garrett McRae been declared dead?"

"I'm not quite positive what I'm looking for. All I know is something is telling me I need to keep looking."

The coffeemaker made a hissing sound, spewing a puff of steam from beneath its lid. The hazelnut flavor created a pleasant aroma. "Maybe I'll give that new coffee a shot," he said.

• • •

Rick sat at his desk, leaned forward, and took a sip of coffee. It tasted like scorched peanuts. He clamped his eyes shut and shook his head vigorously. Within minutes, Helen gave a quick knock and entered his office holding a sheet of paper. She was a far better researcher than barista. "How's the coffee?" she asked as she placed the paper in front of him.

"Delicious. What's this?"

"You were right," Helen answered. "There aren't a lot of Chevy trucks around here. Rob wasn't available, so for now I just ran registrations going back twenty years. Here is the most recent list of what's out there on the road."

Rick scanned the paper, holding it away from his face so he could read it. The fourth entry on this list was for a white 2004 Chevrolet Silverado registered under the name Jesse Lone Wolf. He shuddered as he put on a pair of readers and drew the paper closer. After placing a checkmark next to Jesse's name, Rick handed the list back to Helen. "Run a vehicle report for that VIN number," he said. Helen nodded and walked briskly from the room.

CHAPTER 49

Highway 89 north was notorious for deer darting across the pavement out of nowhere, but Rick didn't care. Adrenaline pumping, he pressed the sole of his boot firmly on the accelerator of his rig, watching the speedometer tickle ninety miles per hour before he eased off, recalling Abby's admonition that morning to "not die."

Helen had learned that the white 2004 Silverado was reported stolen by Jesse Lone Wolf on the exact same afternoon Rick visited the Gold Bar, when the elderly patron name Earl inquired about the vehicle for his grandson. Rick figured Jesse was covering his ass after the sheriff had overheard him tell Earl that the truck had been sold.

But why?

When Rick pulled into the gravel parking lot, Jesse was under the hood of another vehicle, this one a red Ford Mustang. As the sheriff's truck approached, Jesse picked up a rag off the grille and began wiping down a sizeable socket wrench. He slammed the hood with attitude.

Rick stepped out and walked within a few paces, resting the heel of his hand lightly on his sidearm. "Need to ask you a few questions, Jesse."

"I really don't have much time, Sheriff," he answered. "I'm supposed to open the bar soon." He continued wiping down the wrench. "If we're going to talk, it will have to be inside."

"Sounds fine to me. That'll give me a chance to see whether that illegal shotgun has turned up behind your bar. I'd say I have reasonable cause."

"So you're here to harass me then?"

"I don't see it like that."

Jesse shook his head, running his fingers through hair as dark and slick as fresh tar. He tossed the wrench into a metal toolbox, clicked it shut, and started walking to the entrance of the bar, his ink-colored eyes casting a glance of disgust toward the sheriff.

The inside of the Gold Bar was cool and dark, the stale air inside carrying its customary mix of spilled beer, perspiration, burnt popcorn, and cow dung. Jesse placed his toolbox on the floor and clicked on a few light switches, the dim flickering bulbs doing little to brighten the establishment's aura of hopelessness. There was a time when this would have been Rick's kind of place.

Jesse wrung a gray weathered towel in the sink and began wiping down the bar, which was littered with dried rings left by beer mugs, pitchers, shots, and highball glasses. Though he attempted to portray otherwise, he appeared ill at ease. "What is it that you need to know, Sheriff?"

"Let's start by you telling me why you never mentioned you knew Garrett McRae."

Jesse shrugged. "Garrett and I knew each other as kids."

"I understand you lived together for a while. Your high school football coach said you were like brothers."

Jesse stopped wiping the bar for several seconds, then resumed with a slow, caressing stroke as if waxing the hood of a classic coupe. "I suppose we were close—back then."

"When was the last time you saw him?"

Jesse pressed his lips together, the corners of his mouth downturned. "Been years. If he came in here before those guys went hunting, I wasn't around. Crystal opened that day."

"What about those two guys who were with Garrett? Did you know them?"

"Why would I know them?" Jesse answered. "As I remember, they were from Three Forks."

"So was Garrett, and you knew him well. I'm sure you also knew Amber."

Jesse flicked a glance. "Where are you going with this, Sheriff?"

"You seem to have more acquaintances than you prefer to let on," Rick answered. "That troubles me." He studied Jesse's face. The bartender was Garrett's age, but his smooth brown skin made him appear younger. His lips were pressed firmly together, his piercing eyes perpetually filled with the promise of payback.

A sudden ringtone drew Rick's eyes toward a phone vibrating next to the cash register. Jesse cast a look toward it before continuing to wipe the bar. "You can answer that if you want to. I got plenty of time."

"Nope," Jesse answered. "Whoever it is, I can call 'em back."

"Fair enough," Rick said. He stared at the phone. It was cheap, likely a burner. He waited for it to stop ringing. "Tell me about Clay Bonner. I heard you and Garrett were friends with him. You keep in touch?"

Jesse wagged his head as he dipped his rag into the sink and wrung it out. "Haven't seen Clay since high school."

Rick tapped his fingers on the wet, tacky surface of the bar, his brain feeling as twisted as the filthy rag Jesse squeezed in his hands. He had been showered with a jumble of puzzle pieces, none of which seemed to fit.

"You need anything else, Sheriff?" Jesse asked. "I'll likely have some customers coming in soon. No offense, but seeing a sheriff's rig out front might make them feel uneasy, especially if they're already drunk." He stared at Rick, his eyes becoming as dull as black charcoals.

"What can you tell me about your Silverado?"

The question appeared to catch Jesse off guard. "What Silverado?" he said, averting his eyes.

Rick's face turned to stone. "Your white 2004 Silverado," Rick said flatly. "Last time I was here, you told a fella named Earl that you had sold it. Now I come to find out that you reported it stolen. Which is it? Did you sell it, or was it stolen?"

Jesse tossed the rag in the sink. "It was stolen. I wouldn't report it stolen unless it was."

"Why'd you tell Earl it was sold?"

"Didn't think he'd believe me."

"Can't say I blame him." The sheriff shrugged. "I can't remember the last time a truck has been stolen around here. You may as well be stealing someone's horse—and I would imagine the consequences would be the same."

The burner phone next to the register rang again. Jesse tried to pay it no mind. "You should go and answer that," Rick said. "It seems like someone is really trying to get in touch with you."

Jesse's nostrils flared as he drew in a deep breath. He picked up the phone and tossed it in a drawer beneath the register. "Like I said, Sheriff, I'll have some customers coming in soon. So unless there is something in particular you need to know—"

"No, I'm done here—at least, for now," Rick said, waving an open palm. He rapped his knuckles twice on the surface of the bar and straightened his hat. "And I'll tell you what—I'm not even going to ask you about your shotgun."

● ● ●

Rick jumped back into his truck and speed-dialed the sheriff's office on his cell phone. "Helen, has Jack come in yet?"

"He's come and gone," the dispatcher answered. "There's a nude man causing a ruckus at the Antler Motel."

"Why is the man causing a ruckus?" Rick asked. "And why the hell is he naked?"

Helen cleared her throat. "I believe he's causing a ruckus because his wife or girlfriend locked him out of his motel room. I would imagine he's naked for the same reason. Perhaps they were having relations and—"

"I get the picture, Helen," Rick interrupted. "When he clears, ask Jack to give me a try on my cell phone. In the meantime, I'd like you to see if you can track down a person by the name of Clay Bonner. He may go by Clayton. He went to school in College Station, Texas, and it's likely he's settled in the area somewhere."

"Middle name?" Helen asked. "Date of birth?"

"No on the middle name, but he should be around the same age as Garrett McRae."

"I'll see what I can find."

• • •

Rick's phone rang within twenty minutes, just as he was approaching Riverton. "You rang, Sheriff?" Jack Kelly asked in his low, baritone voice.

"Did you need to make an arrest at the Antler?"

"Negative."

"Why not?"

"I didn't want some naked guy in the back of my truck," Jack said. "Especially since I didn't know exactly what he'd been up to before I arrived."

"Where is the man now?"

"I managed to persuade his paramour to open the door and give him his suitcase. Seems she's a local gal, and he was visiting from Duluth. They met last night at the Mint and headed back to her place. I guess they were regular soul mates until she found out he was married."

"Ouch."

"She owns a pistol, but fortunately she didn't use it," Jack said. "I pointed him toward Minnesota, and off he went."

Rick allowed himself a laugh as he drove across the Yellowstone River, its low tumbling waters wandering through stands of aspens, their milky bark rising through chestnut-colored thistle and reaching toward honey-colored leaves that quaked in the soft autumn wind. A fly fisherman stood calf-deep in the current, smiling broadly as he repetitively cast toward the same shallow riffle, his drowsy effort indicating that the notion of landing a fish was of minimal consequence.

"I need you to do me a favor," Rick told Jack.

"You name it."

"We'll need a warrant for a burner phone owned by Jesse Lone Wolf."

"The reason for the warrant?"

"I suspect that he may be engaging in criminal activity," Rick said.

"Can you be more specific?"

"Not at the moment."

Jack chuckled.

"Look," Rick said. "We already know that Amber McRae called the bar on the Saturday after her husband was reported missing. Lone Wolf claims he wasn't there that night, but I'm not buying it. I'm also interested in whomever else he's been talking to."

"Anything in particular I should be looking for?"

"Let's start with any calls outside the 406," Rick said, referring to Montana's area code. "Their landline had mostly local calls, and the same probably would hold true for Jesse's personal phone. But the burner, who knows?"

"I'm on it," Jack said.

. . .

When Rick rolled up to the ranch house in the late afternoon, he spotted Abby standing outside the corral, her florescent-green cast dangling to one side as she used her other hand to stuff fistfuls of hay into the face of Big Sky. The horse attacked the fodder with vigor, acting as if he hadn't eaten in weeks.

"Watch your fingers," Rick said as he approached his granddaughter. "I've heard horses love to eat the fingers of little girls."

"Very funny, Pa-Pa," she said, glancing at him.

Rick placed an arm around Abby's shoulder and tugged her against his hip. He used the outside of his fingers to gently brush the golden hair on the side of Big Sky's face, which seemed to bring both horse and human a measure of peace. "He is one beautiful animal."

"Does that mean we're going to keep him?" Abby asked, gazing up at him.

"Of course we're going to keep him," Rick said. "If fact, I'm thinking he could use a friend. A lot of people get ornery when they don't have someone else around. I would suppose horses aren't much different."

"What kind of friend will Big Sky get? Can we get a mare, so we can have ponies?"

"Uh, excuse me!" a voice behind them said. It was Sage. "You mind filling me in on your plan for horses? After all, I seem to be hanging around this ranch quite a bit these days."

She wore a tender smile. Rick studied her face, which was framed beneath the yellow silk scarf she used to cover her scalp. Her skin had regained some color, her eyes showing a hint of sparkle. Rick gently kissed her lips, which were glazed with a balm carrying the taste and scent of strawberries. She had completed her first round of chemotherapy, and the results were promising. More chemo was to come. Depending on continued test results, it was possible that her future treatments could require only an oral tablet. Time would tell.

"This property always used to have horses on it," Rick said, his eyes roaming the expansive amber range that surrounded them. "I was just telling Abby that Big Sky could use a companion."

"Is that right?" Sage asked, her eyes glancing back and forth at each of them. "How about we not do anything rash right this second?"

"I have a birthday coming up," Abby suggested.

"Like I said," Sage replied. "Not right this second." She looped her arm beneath Rick's bicep and turned him toward the house. "Abby, supper will be ready soon. Don't forget to leave time to wash your hands." Abby didn't respond, her focus returning to feeding Big Sky.

The inside of the ranch house looked and felt like home, the aroma of elk chili wafting into the living room from the large stockpot simmering on the stove. Rick sat on the leather couch, moving aside one of the many pillows Sage had used to adorn the place and provide it with more of a feminine touch. She was a companion indeed and far more. After Christine died, Rick had entered a long period of grief and loneliness that he had accepted as some sort of necessary penance, a painful rite of passage from which there would be no reprieve. Sage had filled a void, once he had allowed her to do so, and perhaps he had done the same for her. The thought of losing each other had become unthinkable.

Sage plopped on the couch and leaned her head on his shoulder. "The local paper had a story today about the missing hunter," she said.

"I didn't notice any quotes from you. Did they try to get in touch for comment?"

"They may have called, but I probably missed them. Which is good since I have no comment."

"Really?" Sage asked, gazing up at him. "I thought the case was closed."

"Some people might think so, but I'm not necessarily among them."

Sage returned her head to his shoulder and nestled closer to him. "It's a shame what happened to their little boy."

"I think about that every time I look at Abby," Rick said. "When she fell off Big Sky, I was determined to never let her ride again. But how do you tell a kid growing up in Montana she can't ride a horse?"

"You can't," Sage said with a chuckle. She released a long sigh. "It's too bad they can't do anything for their son."

"I'm sure they would have if they could."

They sat in silence for several moments. "Strange case," Rick finally said. "Something just doesn't seem to add up."

"Anything in particular?"

"I just got a feeling in my gut."

Sage sat upright and gazed intently into his eyes. "Then I guess you have to go with your gut."

CHAPTER 50

Spencer Bible had never seen a check for one million dollars before.

He came to a stop on the gravel driveway outside the home of Amber McRae, turning off his ignition to silence the spiteful clicking noise from his Impala's timing belt. It was shortly before nine o'clock on Friday morning, the sun rising just enough to coax a silver glimmer from the morning dew. Spencer slid the check halfway out of its pristine envelope, counting the impressive number of zeroes printed on the certified funds that he would be handing to the widow of Garrett McRae. Amber had strongly suggested that he simply overnight a check, but he politely refused, his father having trained him that the personal presentation of life insurance benefits doubled as an opportunity for proper condolence.

He would have preferred having bamboo shoots wedged beneath his fingernails or being bitten by a snake. While he realized that the company protocol had merit, he lacked his father's interpersonal skills. On the few occasions when Spencer was tasked with presenting a check to a client, he found himself standing dumbfounded in front of the bereaved, unable to muster a single word that might provide comfort. The heartbreak of losing a loved one wasn't simply washed away by the purchase of a new fishing boat or summer cabin.

Spencer cast his eyes toward the front porch of the McRae home before looking again at the check. This endeavor promised to be far more difficult than most. His mind drifted to thoughts of his father, whom he planned to visit the minute he returned to Great Falls. Cyrus's health had declined rapidly in recent days, almost to the point of freefall. Spencer wondered what his father would do if he was faced with the same situation, seated in his car in front of the home belonging to Amber McRae. He quickly realized his father would not have been in the same situation. Cyrus always paid strict attention to detail, careful to write and rate life insurance policies by the book, his dedication to the client far outweighing any thirst for a commission. He loved the insurance business, almost as much as Spencer despised it.

Spencer closed the door of the Impala and trudged up the creaky wooden steps onto the porch. Amber had placed a piece of black electrical tape over the doorbell, presumably to prevent visitors from waking her son. Spencer stood stoically, hands crossed over his midsection in a funereal pose, hoping that Amber had heard him drive up. After nearly a minute, she appeared at the door and stared at him through the glass. Her lips were flat, her eyebrows pinched with the self-righteousness of someone collecting a delinquent debt.

"Good afternoon, Mrs. McRae."

"Please keep your voice down," she scolded. "My child is sleeping."

"First of all, ma'am, I wanted to express my deepest sympathies," Spencer whispered. "I can't imagine how—"

"I'm not in the market for sympathy, Mr. Bible," Amber interrupted. "I've received plenty of sympathy over the past few years, and it hasn't bought me all that much."

Spencer tried again. "I realize that this has been a difficult process for all of us. I can only hope—"

"*All* of us? Is that what you said?" she asked, jerking her head backward. "I lost a husband while caring for a disabled child. Between you and that sheriff in Dexter County, I was accused of being a liar, an unfaithful whore, even a murderer." Her nose flared, her breathing audible. "What is that you guys have on your website? You're always there—"

"We're always there when you need us," Spencer muttered.

Amber snapped her fingers and pointed at Spencer. "That's it!" she said mockingly. "We're always there when you need us. Was that the case with the McRae family, Mr. Bible? Were you there when we needed you?"

Spencer stood frozen. He may as well have been a facing a huffing, jaw-popping sow grizzly protecting her cub. Submission was the best course. Don't fight back. Play dead.

Amber stared at the check in Spencer's hand, awakening him from his trance. "I'm sorry, ma'am," he said uneasily. "Here is your check."

Amber opened the screen door slightly and snared the check, rapidly looking inside the envelope like a shylock ensuring he hadn't been shorted. She leaned against the door frame, her eyes seeming to soften as she studied

Spencer's face. "Mr. Bible, have you ever loved someone? I mean *really* loved someone, more than your next breath?"

Spencer felt warmth flow into his face. He thought of Lizzie and their impassioned yet turbulent affair, a fleeting sojourn up the crumbling steps of his dark cellar of loneliness into the brilliant daylight of love. "I … I thought I was in love once," Spencer said, "but maybe I was wrong."

"Garrett and I met when we were young kids," Amber said. "I adored him. Did we have difficulties? Yes. But we still loved each other. My husband deserved a lot better than the fate he suffered."

Spencer drew a deep breath. "Yes ma'am. It certainly was a tragic way to die."

"I'm not talking about the way he died," she said, flicking her head to one side. "I'm talking about that little boy sleeping in the bedroom. The accident that occurred could have happened to anyone. Garrett was never the same after that. That is when my husband died."

"Yes ma'am," Spencer said quietly.

Amber pursed her lips, her forehead wrinkling as she paused in thought. "I'm sorry I was so hard on you, Mr. Bible. I imagine you were just doing your job. I just thought your insurance company was being a bit … difficult."

"You are probably right, ma'am. In fact, you and I might have more in common than you think." He stared at the envelope in her hand, his mission complete. "Again, my deepest sympathies."

Amber closed the front door without speaking. Spencer turned and slowly stepped off the porch, pausing briefly to look back toward the door. Amber was watching him through one of the window panes, her hand pushing aside the curtain. When he caught her eye, she quickly vanished.

He sat in his car in the driveway for several moments before placing the keys in the ignition. He picked up his phone, which lay on the console in front of an ashtray he never used. The screen had a string of messages saying only "Missed call."

As he laid the phone down, it rang. "Spencer?" a voice asked.

It was Rachel. "Yes?" he murmured softly.

"Spencer, you need to call the rest home," she said, her voice threaded with emotion.

"I'm headed back. I'll be there in about an hour."

"No, Spencer, you need to call them *now*," she said with urgency.

"Why?"

"Just call them. They've been trying to reach you."

"Rachel, what is going on?"

The secretary was crying, gasping for breaths as she released her tears. "It's your daddy, Spencer. He passed early this morning."

CHAPTER 51

Rick arrived at the sheriff's office to find Jack seated at his metal desk in a small room off the lobby and squinting through turtle-shell reading glasses as he pored over a stack of telephone records. He was nodding his head rhythmically between sips of Helen's coffee, which he seemed to tolerate rather well.

"Find anything interesting?" Rick asked as he peered through the door to Jack's office.

"Possibly," the undersheriff replied. "Got a minute?"

Helen stood from her desk and walked a pot of coffee into Jack's office, then refilled his cup. "Care for some?" she asked Rick.

"Not just yet," he replied, causing Helen to roll her eyes.

Rick took a seat in an armless chair in front of Jack's desk. "What ya got?"

"Well, Helen did manage to track down someone named Clayton Bonner," Jack began. "He lives in San Antonio, where he's a partner in a medical group called Lone Star Orthopedics. Looking at their website, it appears they specialize in sports medicine."

"Did Amber McRae happen to reach out to him?"

"There were no calls from Amber's cell phone, but there were plenty from Garrett. I checked the records before his phone went dead. He had placed several calls to Bonner in August and again when he came back from Texas in September."

Rick shrugged. "Doesn't seem all that unusual. They were longtime friends, and Garrett was headed down there for the A&M football game."

Jack removed his reading glasses and leaned back in his chair. "You wouldn't think it was unusual. But I got Bonner on the phone this morning. All I wanted to ask were some routine questions—Garrett's state of mind, whether he appeared troubled by anything, the usual stuff. He asks me if something has happened, and I explained that Garrett had gone missing and was presumed dead. Suddenly, he clams up. He starts telling me any conversations he had with Garrett are privileged."

Rick stroked his thumb on the stubble beneath his chin. "Wonder what they were discussing. You'd think that since Dr. Bonner is an orthopedist, they'd be talking about Garrett's son."

Jack lifted his eyebrows. "Could be. Thing is, I've done this stuff for quite a while, probably a lot longer than I should. I get this odd feeling when something isn't adding up. This guy sounded really skittish, to say the least."

Rick paused in thought. "Any luck on that burner phone belonging to Jesse Lone Wolf?"

Jack flashed a contented smile. "I managed to track down Judge Enright sighting in his rifle at the shooting range yesterday, just before dark. I plan to have that phone in my possession this afternoon, and I expect us to get the call records tomorrow."

Rick stood from his chair. "You work quickly."

Jack grinned again. "Like I said, I've been at it awhile."

• • •

Rick invited Charlie to have a late breakfast at the Forty-Niner. His friend had been sulking ever since Pernell Crawford had outmaneuvered him and issued a death certificate for Garrett McRae, concluding an investigation Charlie did not consider complete.

Charlie ordered fried chicken and waffles as opposed to his usual omelet, perhaps mindful of the egg on his face. Rick shook his head, believing fried chicken had absolutely no place at a breakfast table let alone desecrating a waffle.

"I think it might be time for me to hang it up," Charlie murmured.

Rick pinched together his thumb and forefinger and rubbed them together, mimicking playing the world's tiniest violin. "Do you know what this is?"

"Knock it off," Charlie growled.

"C'mon, Charlie. You're excellent at what you do. We're lucky to have you in our county, as opposed to someone like Pernell."

Charlie poured an avalanche of sugar into his coffee. "I'm telling you— someone got to that guy. He's shameless."

"So, say Pernell's conclusion is wrong. Do *you* have a theory?"

"I pretty much have concluded that Mr. McRae is dead," he said. "I mean, besides the bones we discovered, there's just too much blood for him to have survived. But rather than a grizzly killing him, I think he was murdered. I think Davis placed Garrett's clothing to make it *look* like a bear attack. You said yourself Davis was a freak, didn't you? You told me he was into human sacrifice?" Charlie slurped his coffee, wiping his lips with the back of his sleeve. "Have you changed your mind?"

Rick released a sigh. "Well, if it was Davis, I'm not all that sure we'd be able to prove it," he said in a somber tone. "What about Kyle? His boss told Jack he has something called dissociative identity disorder. He could have done something to Garrett and not even realized it."

"Doubtful," Charlie said. "There's no physical evidence that places him at the scene where Garrett died." His eyes sharpened. "What's gotten into you? The other day you were positive it was Davis."

"I thought Davis was doing it for Amber, but that was before Horsemeat tried to kill her."

"Who?"

"Horsemeat," Rick said. "The guy they arrested was called Horsemeat."

Charlie huffed a breath. "Well, I still think James Davis is the guy. If I'd been given the opportunity to finish my investigation, I believe I could have proven it."

Dodge appeared at the table, sliding plates in front of them. "Care for more coffee?" she asked. Charlie pushed his cup toward her.

Rick sat in silence, staring at his eggs and bacon, uncertain what to think. He heard a sudden crunching sound. Charlie, apparently hungry, was attacking his fried chicken like a pit bull.

Rick's cell phone rang. It was Rob Deering. "Hey, Rob. Helen passed along your information. It was definitely helpful."

"There's more," the investigator said.

"Oh?"

"I finally managed to speak to that one boy being shielded by his grandparents. The family name is Steele."

"Seems I've heard of them."

"Big ranch, old money. Guess they prefer to keep to themselves. Anyway, the boy's name is Shane. Turns out he not only saw a white Silverado, but he also saw someone *driving* it."

Rick looked at Charlie, who was oblivious to the conversation as he devoured a leg bone. "Did he get a good look at who was driving?"

"The kid claims the guy nearly ran him over," Rob said. "Shane was riding his four-wheeler near 191, and the guy comes out of the brush like a bat out of hell."

Rick continued to stare at Charlie. After assaulting the leg bone, the coroner tore off a wing and began gnawing his way across it, apparently planning to pick it clean. In his zeal, he broke off a narrow bone in the center of the wing. He pulled it from his grease-covered lips, stared at it a moment, and tossed it on his plate. He returned to the wing, which otherwise remained intact.

"So you have a description?"

"Maybe something better," Rob answered. "I pulled up a shot of Garrett McRae off social media. I showed the picture to Shane, and he swears that's the guy."

"Is he sure?"

"Says he is."

Rick fixed his eyes on the bone lying on Charlie's plate, a frigid sensation rumbling up his spine. His chest pounded, his mouth feeling dry. "Great work, Rob," he murmured, ending the call.

"You gonna eat or what?" Charlie asked, his mouth full of food.

"I gotta go," Rick said rapidly. He tugged a twenty out of his pocket, his hands shaking slightly as he tossed the bill on the table. "Breakfast is on me."

"Where are you going?"

"Texas," Rick said as he slid out of the booth.

"Wait!" Charlie protested. "Are you going to track down James Edward Davis? Can I go with you?"

"No," Rick said flatly. "And no."

CHAPTER 52

Helen managed to find a flight that would leave Bozeman in the late afternoon, routing through Salt Lake City and landing in San Antonio at 10:35 that night. Carrying a leather travel bag Sage had packed for him, Rick rented a Ford Taurus and managed to walk into his room at the Alamo Inn and Suites shortly before midnight. Following a quick call home, he descended into a deep, dreamless sleep.

Lone Star Orthopedics opened at nine o'clock Friday morning. The clinic, founded by Clayton Bonner and his two partners, was located on top of a hill, its facade featuring large glass windows framed with thick cedar timbers, the pitch of the roof resembling a mountain chalet. Rick walked across a black-tar parking lot beneath dark low-slung clouds. The air was sultry, thick with the smell of rain. Three reserved parking spaces were located at the front of the lot, one occupied by a spotless silver Range Rover, its license plate proudly proclaiming its owner as "BONE DOC." A bronze Texas star was mounted above the main entrance of the building, and automatic sliding doors opened up into a spacious, pristine lobby that displayed several framed action photos of players from the San Antonio Spurs, the clinic's most prized client.

"I'm here to speak with Dr. Bonner," Rick told a petite blond receptionist at the front desk. The name "Jenna" was scripted with blue thread into her pink-and-white-flowered scrubs.

"Do you have an appointment, sir?" she said with a bright smile, her accent suggesting Texas was her birthplace.

"Actually, I do not," Rick said. His hand slipped beneath the lapel of his suede sport coat and produced a wallet badge. "My name is Sheriff Rick Morrand from Dexter County, Montana, and I need to visit with Dr. Bonner."

Jenna scanned an appointment book sprawled out in front of her, tapping her pen repeatedly as she pressed her thin lips together and shook her head. "Dr. Bonner's schedule is packed clear to mid-afternoon. Is there a chance you could come back then?"

"I'm afraid that won't work," Rick said. "I have a flight headed back to Bozeman at four o'clock."

"Well, let me call our office manager and let her know you're here," Jenna said, reaching for the multiline phone on her desk. "It will be up to her if—"

Rick leaned forward, his downturned palm hovering above the phone. "Please tell her this is an informal visit, lest we alarm your staff," he said. "The sooner I can have a word with Dr. Bonner, the sooner I'll be on my way." He smiled briefly and walked away from the reception desk, taking a seat next to an overweight man with his arm in a sling, the thumb of his free hand scrolling through his smartphone. The sheriff removed his Stetson and placed the crown on his lap. His fingers swept across the top of his head, his hair now the length of an average buzz cut.

After about fifteen minutes, a nurse opened a door adjacent to the reception desk and said, "Mr. Morrand?"

Rick rose quickly and walked toward her. Without smiling, she turned and led him down a long hallway, where they entered through a mahogany door with a brass plate that read "Clayton Bonner, MD." The nurse motioned toward two crimson leather chairs stationed in front of a large spotless cherrywood desk, its glass top furnished only with a phone and a lamp. "I'll let Dr. Bonner know you are here, Sheriff."

Rick smiled and tipped his hat toward the nurse as she turned to leave, her face still void of expression. He interlocked his fingers on his lap and perused the office. The lower part of the walls had a dark hardwood wainscot that gave way to forest-green wallpaper the texture of velvet. Matted frames boasted Bonner's undergraduate diploma from A&M, alongside his doctor of medicine degree from Vanderbilt. A massive credenza and bookcase stretched along the rear wall, matching the width of his desk. Rows of medical books were neatly aligned on the shelves, along with an autographed football and an array of framed photos. One had a man competing in a race, perhaps a triathlon, his face contorted in a painful grimace as he crossed the finish line. Other pictures appeared to show Bonner's family. His wife was attractive, her sparkling smile revealing strength and loyalty. Two young children, a boy and a girl, seemed healthy and carefree.

The door opened. Clayton Bonner entered. At first glance, he appeared more bookish than athletic. His dark hair was meticulously parted to the side, his black oversized glasses perched above the sharp features of a clean-shaven face—a regular Clark Kent. He walked toward his visitor, rubbing his hands together as though he'd just finished washing them.

"I appreciate you taking the time to see me on short notice, Doctor," Rick said as he rose from his chair. "I don't plan to take up much of your time."

Bonner didn't answer. His lips began to curl into a tight smile before he nervously flattened them. He walked behind his desk and sat, sliding his high-back leather chair forward and interlocking his fingers on the spotless glass. He drew a deep breath. "I'm really not sure why you came all the way down here, Sheriff. I've already spoken to your deputy and—"

"Actually, Jack's my undersheriff. He has a lot of experience in law enforcement, far more than me. There was something about your demeanor that made him uncomfortable."

Bonner tilted his head to the side. "I'm not sure what you mean."

"Well, when Jack got you on the phone, you didn't ask a lot of questions about what happened, how Garrett McRae might have died, that sort of thing. Before Jack knows it, you're talking about HIPPA. Are you saying that Garrett was a patient of yours?"

The doctor briefly averted his eyes. "He was my friend, and he was a patient. We discussed medical issues. I wanted to protect his privacy."

"What kind of medical issues?"

"As I told your … undersheriff, is it? I am unable to discuss these things due to—"

"Right. HIPPA," Rick said. The sheriff bit the side of his lip as he studied Bonner's face. "Tell you what—would you mind if I asked you some hypothetical questions?"

Bonner offered an uneasy shrug. "Sure," he said without conviction.

"Your old football coach—Bob Benson—told me that Garrett played an entire half of a football game with cracked ribs, two of the bottom ones having broken clear off."

"The ones that broke off were floating ribs," Bonner said. "They are attached to the spine, but not the sternum." He glanced at his silver watch, likely a Tag Heuer. "Look, Sheriff—"

Rick removed his Stetson and waved it toward Bonner. "Now, stick with me on this. Again, we're talking hypothetically. Wouldn't a football player with loose ribs in his gut want to have them removed? I mean, once they're broke, they're useless. And, from what I understand, the bottom ribs don't have much of a function to begin with."

Bonner pursed his lips impatiently. "I wouldn't say that they have no function. They are part of the rib cage, which protects internal organs."

"Yeah, I get that," Rick said. "Thing is, I Googled floating ribs—I just *love* Google—and I learned that floating ribs are sometimes called *false ribs* because they aren't nearly as essential as the ribs connected to the sternum. Would you say that's true? Are false ribs nonessential?" He paused. "I mean, could a patient remain healthy even if false ribs were removed?"

Bonner shrugged. "I suppose that an argument could be made—"

"Good!" Rick said. He placed his Stetson on his head, interlocked his fingers, and sat back in his chair. "Now tell me, Doctor, out of the two hundred and six bones in the human body, are there any *others* that are nonessential? For example, how about a fibula? Is a fibula essential?"

Color fled from Bonner's face as his jaw muscles flexed. His Adam's apple bulged before disappearing beneath his necktie, making him appear as though he were trying to swallow an oversized chunk of prime rib. "What are you getting at, Sheriff?"

Rick shrugged. "I'm just gathering more information on the musculoskeletal system." He cast a thumb toward the degrees framed on the wall. "Says right there you're an orthopedist."

"The fibula is often a preferred option in bone grafts," Bonner said. "It can be used in long bone reconstruction, where bone has been lost due to injury or other causes such as cancer. Or perhaps bone from the fibula can be used in mandible reconstruction—that is, the jaw."

Rick felt his phone vibrate in his pocket. He fished for it and saw that Jack Kelly was calling him. He declined to answer, training his eyes on Bonner.

"If you are removing the fibula for a graft, how much of it is used? Can it be removed completely?"

Bonner's eyes blinked rapidly. He tried to clear his throat. "I'm not sure why you are asking this."

"Hypothetically, Doctor," Rick calmly said. "Hypothetically."

Bonner's bowed his head and used one hand to massage his temples. "The upper part of the fibula has a nerve wrapped around it and is not taken, due to risk of nerve damage. The lowest part of the bone is part of the ankle joint and gives stability to the ankle."

"That seems to leave a lot of bone to work with."

"The removal of a large section does not affect leg function, if that's what you're asking," Bonner said. He propped his elbows on his desk and interlocked his fingers. "Sheriff, should I be contacting my lawyer?"

Rick frowned. "Well, in addition to being a sheriff, I happen to be a lawyer, and I guess now I'm wondering why you would need one. That is, unless you've done something out of line."

A knock on the door caught Rick's attention. He turned to see a young nurse with a blond pixie cut and blue scrubs poke her head inside the office. "I'm sorry to interrupt, Dr. Bonner—"

"Not now, Janet," Bonner snapped.

"You have four patients waiting," Janet persisted. "All of the exam rooms are full."

Bonner glared at her. "I said, not now!"

Janet's eyes opened wide as she retreated, quickly pulling the door shut. Rick turned toward Bonner, whose lips were quivering. "Let me cut to the chase," Rick said. "I'm thinking Garrett came to you and asked you to remove those floating ribs. That would make perfect sense, since those ribs were useless to him." He lasered a glare on Bonner. "But I believe Garrett went a little further. I think he wanted you to remove his fibula, and you complied. That would qualify as a completely unnecessary surgery, almost like playing around with a living, breathing cadaver. I'm no expert, but that doesn't seem to be in sync with the Hippocratic Oath."

Bonner averted his eyes for a beat and huffed a breath. "And why would Garrett want me to do that, Sheriff?"

Rick stiffened his spine and pointed toward Bonner. "I was hoping you would tell me."

Bonner sat back in his chair, his slumped shoulders signaling a surrender of sorts. "Look, Sheriff, it is true that I removed Garrett's fibula. As far as I know, that doesn't qualify as a crime."

"I suppose you're right," Rick answered. "It only qualifies as malpractice."

Bonner shrugged. His jaw shimmied. "Garrett asked me to do it."

Rick's head listed to one side. "And why would he make such a request, Doctor?"

"He didn't tell me, okay?" Bonner said. "He said it was better that I didn't know."

"So we're clear: you removed two ribs from his torso and also his fibula?"

Bonner swallowed hard. "Yes sir, I did," he answered. He flicked his eyes toward the wall with his degrees. "You have to understand something, Sheriff. I had to do this for Garrett. I *owed* him."

Rick's jaw grew slack. "How did you *owe* him?"

Bonner stroked his lips with his forefinger. He appeared conflicted whether to speak. "If it wasn't for Garrett, I wouldn't be sitting here today."

Rick's forehead tightened. "Oh? How so?"

"I'd rather not talk about it."

"I'd rather you did," Rick shot back. "It would be a shame for your medical board down here to learn that you are removing a perfectly viable body part from a patient when the procedure isn't necessary. In a sense, you mutilated your patient for no good reason."

Bonner released a lengthy sigh. He placed his glasses on his desk and rubbed his eyelids. "After I graduated from A&M, I first went to Baylor College of Medicine. As a student, I was allowed to write prescriptions, provided I had a resident or doctor cosign them." He stared down at his desk for a beat before turning his eyes back toward Rick. "I had dislocated my shoulder in a pickup basketball game, and I was in a lot of pain. I got a prescription for Percocet from a doctor and fell in love with them. Next thing you know, I'm writing my own prescriptions and forging signatures of doctors and residents. People around me could tell something was wrong. Wasn't long before I got caught."

"What happened?"

"I got expelled—that's what happened," Bonner said with rancor, perhaps still loathing himself for his misdeed. "The first thing I tried to do was kill myself. I tried to overdose—a coward's way out—but I obviously wasn't successful. I called Garrett—he had been my best friend in college. He drove through the night from Montana, an old Samsonite suitcase tossed in his backseat. This was before he got married. He moved in with me and slept on the couch while I kicked." He shook his head at the memory. "I was puking my guts out; I had chills, hallucinations, the whole deal. Garrett was there for it all. He got a job in construction down here, even attended NA meetings with me. If it wasn't for Garrett—"

"Sounds like a true friend."

Bonner trained his eyes intently on Rick. "There's no better friend than Garrett McRae. When he went back to Montana, he called me every day. After I had been clean for a year, he encouraged me to start applying to med schools again. He told me not to give up—to *never* give up. Finally, Vanderbilt cut me a break."

Rick's phone chimed with a text from Jack. "Call me" was all it said. Rick put the phone back in his pocket. He scanned the wood-paned windows lining one side of the office. The wind outside had picked up, causing a row of maple trees to sway. Drops of rain began to patter on the glass.

"When you removed the ribs and fibula," Rick said slowly, "did Garrett ask you to preserve them?"

Bonner hesitated. "An unusual request, I would agree. But it's not unheard of."

"And he took the bones with him?"

Bonner nodded.

"But he gave you no indication of why he would want you to remove the fibula?"

"None at all," he answered. "Like I said before, he told me it was better that I didn't know. He claimed he was protecting me."

"Perhaps he was. I'm thinking that Garrett figured that if he left some bloody clothes and a couple of ribs to make it look like he was attacked by a grizzly, we might be convinced. But if he left a sizeable bone from his leg … well, that would be far more persuasive." Rick huffed an abrupt laugh. "I mean, talk about commitment!"

Bonner wagged his head rapidly as he held his open palms in front of him. "Wait a minute," he said, his voice tremoring. "You mean to tell me that Garrett had me remove those bones so he could fake his own death?"

"Not only that," Rick said, "he also defrauded an insurance company."

Bonner blinked in disbelief. "But why? I mean, why would Garrett ever do that?"

"Doctor, you have kids," Rick said, nodding at the framed photos on the bookcase behind Bonner's desk. "People do desperate things for their children." The words stuck in his throat as if they were creeping through sludge. The visage of Chloe flashed into his brain like an oxygen-injected roar of flame. His desperation hadn't been able to save her, hard as he tried. That failure had relentlessly persisted, a piercing blade repeatedly plunged deep inside his chest. He drew two short breaths and gathered himself. "Tell me something. Did Garrett ever speak to you of Gabe, his son?"

"All the time," Bonner said without hesitation. "I assume you're asking me about whether his child could be helped?"

"Correct," Rick said with a nod.

"I'd say he was obsessed with finding a cure."

"What did you tell him?"

"I told him the truth. The *only* possibility that little Gabe might have was to receive infusions of embryonic stem cells. There are some experimental procedures out there that might work depending on the particular injury and the damage it caused. But they are definite longshots."

"Where are these procedures being done?"

Bonner blinked as his adjusted his glasses. "Stem cell infusions? Not in this country, that's for sure."

Rick froze. "Then where?"

Bonner's eyes briefly roamed the ceiling. "Places where regulation might be a little more lenient, yet they still practice medicine with a certain degree of sophistication. Maybe countries like Argentina or Brazil."

"How about a place that can be reached by car? Is Mexico a possibility?"

"It's possible. Sure."

"Would you happen to know where in Mexico?"

"There are plenty of places doing some aggressive procedures," Bonner said. "I'd have to do some research." He exhaled, his face drawn and eyes glazed. He looked at his shiny watch again. "Look, Sheriff, I really have to—"

Rick waved an open hand toward him. "Please go right ahead. I'll be happy to show myself out."

Bonner began to leave, then suddenly stopped. "Sheriff, I have a family," he said, flicking his eyes toward the photos behind his desk. "I hope—"

"You said Garrett kept you in the dark, and I'll take you at your word—at least, for now," he answered. "At the moment, it's him I'm interested in."

Bonner nodded and walked from the office, leaving the door ajar. Rick winced as he rose from his chair, his wounded ribs still sore. He needed to push forward. Garrett McRae was alive and likely in Mexico.

Rick just needed to know where.

CHAPTER 53

A storm had blown in, sending torrents of rain across the parking lot. Rick walked briskly toward his rental car, fumbling for his keys as his clothes quickly became drenched. He jumped inside, laying his hat on the passenger seat as he struggled to remove his sport coat. Rain blurred the windshield. The hot, muggy interior carried the stale scent of soaked suede.

He started the ignition, relieved to feel the cool air coming from the vents. After several minutes, the storm subsided. Rick dug into his pocket and retrieved his phone. Jack had been trying to reach him.

"How's Texas?" Jack's cavernous voice asked.

"Hotter than a goat's ass in a pepper patch."

Silence followed before Jack chuckled. "I needed a moment to process that one," he said. "Any luck with the doctor?"

"Some. It kind of depends on how you did with that burner phone."

"Well, Mr. Jesse Lone Wolf made it easy on us. There's only one call to a 406 area code. Everything else is out of state—out of the country, in fact. The majority of calls he made or received are to a single number that we traced to Mexico. Do you think this guy is running drugs or something?"

"This one isn't about drugs," Rick said, his heart starting to pound. "Can you tell me what city in Mexico?"

"A place called Alamos. It's in the northwest part of the country, in the state of Sonora. It's a small town. You can barely find it on a map."

"What is the closest big city?"

"Looks to me like it would be Ciudad Obregon," Jack said. "They have a population of about a half million."

"That means they have an airport."

"I would imagine." Jack paused briefly. "Wait a minute … You're not—"

"Have Helen book me a flight from San Antonio to Cuidad Obregon," Rick said. "I'm going to find Garrett McRae."

• • •

The best flight Helen could find was scheduled to leave the following morning, with a layover of more than eleven hours in Mexico City. That wouldn't work.

There were other mitigating circumstances. While Rick was carrying a passport card—which he had acquired in preparation for his honeymoon trip to Mexico—he would not be able to carry his gun on an international flight. His prized Colt revolver, gifted from his father, would need to be left north of the border while Rick traveled through sparsely populated areas of Mexico with no means of self-defense. He'd heard far too many stories of law enforcement officers beheaded or flayed by Mexican cartels for him to travel unarmed.

His solution would be to take a domestic flight to Tucson, declaring the weapon in his luggage. He'd rent a car and make the four-hundred-mile trek south across the desert through the cities of Hermosillo and Ciudad Obregon before finally reaching Alamos. When he crossed the border through the town of Nogales, he would make no mention that he had a weapon on hand.

"Are you sure you don't want to think this through a little bit?" Jack suggested as Rick entered San Antonio International Airport. "The Federales find out you're packin', and we might not see you for a while."

"Sage insisted I carry," Rick said. "To say the least, she's not thrilled I'm heading down there."

"I'm just thinking we should regroup. You know—do it by the book, maybe get the Feds involved?"

"We don't have time to regroup," Rick answered, "and the last thing I want to do is wait around for the Feds to screw this thing up." He paused for several seconds. "Besides, I still consider this a Dexter County matter."

Even if his suspect was nearly seventeen hundred miles away.

CHAPTER 54

After passing through the desperate and mournful poverty of Nogales, Rick drove his rented black Durango into the wide expanse of the Sonoran desert. The setting sun cast a red-orange flame over unlimited rolling hills of saguaros, which stood like infantry among the gold poppies and brittlebush scattered across the rock-strewn pink and brown floor. The blistering heat of the late afternoon had surrendered to the cool stillness of evening, the air now windless and innocent.

As he traveled along a black-tarred highway across occasional stretches of unblemished white sand, it was hard to believe that such a peaceful setting could serve as the backdrop for godless barbarism, shame, and piteous sorrow. Human smugglers used this immaculate stage to prey on the young and helpless, suffocating hope and destroying lives before they could begin. Drug-traffickers gushed their poison northward, creating a seemingly limitless supply of cruel shattered dreams and heartbreaking statistics.

Rick wondered whether he was making a mistake. He was following his instincts, believing that Jesse Lone Wolf's stolen Silverado had not been stolen at all but rather it had been left on the east side of the Crazies to be used by Garrett McRae to escape across the Mexican border, leaving all to believe he had been the unfortunate victim of a savage bear attack, if not a murder. How much did Amber McRae know, and when did she know it? Was James Edward Davis an unwitting pawn in the scheme, accused of homicide, the ultimate payback for the man who had bedded Garrett's wife?

What if Rick's instincts were wrong? He was driving across an empty desert that was the realm of ruthless cartels that often warred among themselves. Law enforcement was either nonexistent or ruled by the smugglers. What about his family? While Sage's prognosis was promising, she still had not yet beaten cancer. Abby had suffered the excruciating blow of losing her mother, and now her final remaining blood relative was on a reckless mission in a foreign land.

Why was he doing this? What was his motivation? Did he believe that bringing Garrett McRae to justice merited the risk of literally sacrificing life and limb? Perhaps Jack had been right. Rick's close friend and loyal undersheriff was drawing on a wealth of law enforcement experience when he suggested they take a breath and think things through. Jack's sound reasoning was hardly contemplated, submerged beneath Rick's raging river of unbridled fervor. Was it Rick's ego, perhaps? Had his fiery temper been ignited by the fact he'd been duped by the wily bowhunter? The lives of both men had been touched by tragedy that deeply affected both of them. What was Garrett's intent in executing his complex ruse?

Why did all of this feel so … *personal?*

Darkness soon cloaked the desert. Rick followed his high beams along the uneven roadway, his eyelids sagging as exhaustion set in. He shifted in his seat, his entire body aching from hours on the road. Cuidad Obregon was still fifty miles away. He reached for a cup of coffee he had purchased in Tucson, taking a final sip that was cold. He vowed never to complain about Helen's coffee again.

He tossed the cup onto the passenger side floorboard, then looked at the dash to monitor his speed. Raising his eyes, he spotted a large desert tortoise that had wandered onto the roadway. He swerved hard to the left, his tires squealing on the still-warm pavement. His hands clutched the steering wheel like talons, shoulder blades pressed hard against his seat. The vehicle rumbled into a mix of rocks, dirt, and sand, kicking up a storm of dust as he struggled to regain control. The Durango now was bound toward a large cluster of cholla cactus.

Teeth clenched, Rick yanked the wheel hard to right, clipping one side of the large plants and sending a huge burst of sharp spines across his windshield. The right side of the front hood jumped as the right front wheel crashed over something large and hard, possibly a boulder. The vehicle bounded back onto the highway, crossing the right shoulder.

Another explosion of dust. Three more rapid swerves followed, whiplashing Rick's torso back and forth and stinging his ribs. He clamped his eyes shut, wincing in pain. Finally, he managed to regain control, reducing his speed and easing to the side of the road. He could feel the steering wheel tug to the passenger side, the grinding sound of metal heard from beneath the right front fender. His head bobbed up and down as he struggled for breaths.

He stepped out to survey the damage, using his phone to guide him through the darkness. The right front tire was shot, gashed open as though someone had sliced it with a Bowie knife. The rim was a confused mass of crumpled metal. Rick slammed the side of the wheel with the heel of his boot, pausing a beat before doing it again.

He looked back down the roadway. Traffic had been sparse, but the narrow shoulder was no place to change a tire. He followed his headlights further up the side of the road, deciding he could do no additional damage by slowly inching forward. Perhaps there would be a turnoff where he could work safely. He got back into the driver's seat and put the vehicle in gear. The demolished wheel brayed as Rick moved along a mix of asphalt, rock, and sand. After a half mile, he turned onto a narrow, pitted road lined by shrubs and cactus. A small culvert led him to a flat clearing littered with broken beer bottles, empty fast-food bags, and other assorted trash. It would have to do.

Rick opened the rear gate of the Durango and lifted the carpeted panel to find the spare. After removing the lug wrench, he walked to the front of the vehicle and loosened the nuts, hoping that the frame and suspension weren't severely damaged. Straining to turn the wrench, sudden stabs of agony echoed through his rib cage, emptying the air in his lungs. He stood straight up, his arm draped beneath his chest. He drew rapid breaths through his clenched teeth, his eyes trying to blink away the agony as he stared at a night sky ignited with stars.

He caught sight of faint headlights moving toward him. He dropped to one knee and resumed his work, loosening the rest of the nuts and putting the jack in place beneath the frame. As he cranked to raise the jack, the vehicle drew closer, its lights dancing in the darkness as it crept along the rugged sand-swept road. It was a large black SUV, perhaps a Yukon or Tahoe, its tinted windows opaque. He released a long exhale as it slowly passed him.

A high-pitched squeal pierced the air as the night lit up with the bright glow of brake lights. Rick swallowed, his throat dry, when the doors of the vehicle opened. He trained his eyes on the tire in front of him, his heart thumping as he heard the sound of footsteps grinding on crushed rock. He turned his head to see three sets of black military boots, pants tucked inside in the fashion of a soldier. Raising his eyes, he saw the silhouette of a broad-shouldered man in a tight-fitting black T-shirt. His dark eyes glowered above his thick chest, his stomach flat save for the Glock that was tucked beneath his belt.

"*Problemas con el coche, amigo?*" he asked.

Rick didn't reply.

"*Hablas Español?*"

"*Un poquito,*" Rick murmured. He didn't move, his hand still clinging to the lug wrench attached to the jack. He thought of the Colt Python he'd brought with him. It was inside the vehicle, beneath the driver's seat, a million miles away. Exhaustion breeds foolish mistakes.

"What brings you to Mexico, gringo?" the man asked in a thick accent. "And what are you doing on this road?"

"*Sí,* gringo," another one of the men said. "*Eres follando loco?*" That comment brought laughter from the three of them.

"Look, I don't want any trouble," Rick said, looking at them briefly before averting his eyes. "My wife's father is very sick. I'm driving down to check on him."

"Why isn't your wife with you?"

"She … doesn't have a passport."

"Your wife is *mojado?*"

Rick had heard the term before. It literally meant wet, and it referred to someone who had entered the US by swimming across the Rio Grande. "Yes," he said.

The man pulled the Glock from beneath his belt and squatted next to Rick, his face within inches. He had the odor of dried sweat, his breath reeking of smoke and alcohol. His bloodshot eyes slowly widened with displeasure. He pressed his gun against Rick's temple. The muzzle was warm and smelled like fireworks, indicating it had been recently fired. "So tell me, gringo, if you have a señora, why you no speak Español?"

"We haven't been married long," he said softly.

The gun whipped across the side of his forehead, ripping a gash that sent a stream of warm blood down the side of his face. Rick groaned as he tumbled sideways, his face slamming against the ground, his head filling with the smell of dirt and sand.

"You lie, gringo!" the man yelled. Rick rolled onto his side, wrapping his arms around himself. One of the other men stomped twice on the side of his rib cage, robbing air from his lungs and leaving his mouth twitching like a fish out of water.

He heard the sound of the jack being raised and the scraping sound of the wheel being removed. Two of the men dragged Rick's head beneath the sharp edges of the hub. "Okay, gringo, here is your final chance," the first man said. "You need to tell us the truth. Are you DEA?"

"No, I'm not DEA!" he shouted with passion, trying in vain to pull his neck and head out from underneath the car.

"I think you lie, gringo," a second man said.

Rick stared at the hub hovering above his face. All they had to do was kick the jack away and the weight of the SUV would drop on him, crushing his skull and making his face an ideal candidate for a closed casket. That is, if anyone ever found him. He pressed his eyelids together, his brain hearing Abby's voice say, "Just don't die."

The men suddenly loosened their grip. The sharp whoop of a law enforcement vehicle filled the air as he saw red and blue lights illuminate the ground. He heard several voices speaking Spanish.

Rick's eyes squinted from beneath the dark undercarriage of the vehicle. He could see a police SUV roll to a stop twenty yards away. The three men walked toward it, where they were met by an officer. A good sign.

Maybe.

Rick carefully eased himself out from under the wheel hub, watching closely as the clamor of voices continued, gradually growing louder. He heard the words *policia* and *muerte*, the latter word he recognized as *death*. Finally, the three men stormed away, shouting epithets toward the police officer. Rick heard the roar of an engine, followed by a spray of crushed rock ricocheting off the rear panel of his rental.

The officer squatted next to him. "Are you hurt, señor?" he asked in a soft accent. He looked about thirty, his brown face smooth and clean-shaven, eyes sharp and purposeful. A silver crucifix dangled from the open collar of his dark-blue uniform shirt. "Looks like I got here just in time."

"I would agree," Rick said, easing into a sitting position and wiping dust off his shirt. "Were they cartel?"

"Sí," the officer said. "You picked a bad place to change a tire. This road leads to a village that they control."

"It's a fair argument that you just might have saved my life," Rick said with a long exhale. "I guess you must not be too concerned about collecting your pension." He brushed his hand along the side of his forehead, painting his fingers with blood. "How did you get them to back off?"

"Some days are better than others. There is a war going on down here. I can't do much to stop narcos from killing each other, but I can try to protect the civilians. Sometimes they will let me." He smiled, his eyes lighting up. "Lucky for you, I went to high school with two of those guys."

"Lucky for me," Rick murmured.

The officer extended a hand. "Paco Ramos."

"Rick Morrand."

Paco placed a burly forearm under Rick's bicep and helped him to his feet. "Wait here a minute." He walked to his SUV and returned with a bottle of water and white terrycloth towel, which he handed to Rick. "So, tell me, what brings you to Mexico, Rick Morrand? Those three guys swore you were DEA."

Rick uncapped the bottle and took a long swig of water. "Not DEA. But I am law enforcement." He poured water on the cloth and dabbed the blood beginning to cake on the wound above his eye. "I'm the sheriff of Dexter County, Montana."

"Moan-tahn-ya!" Paco exclaimed, the words tumbling gracefully off his tongue. "It is a beautiful place, no?"

"Yes. I can't wait to get back there." He blew out a breath. "Guess I'm not a fan of drug cartels."

"The situation is not ideal," Paco agreed. "But I accept it, only because I have no choice." He reached into the top pocket of his shirt and retrieved a pack of Marlboros, then flipped one of them into his mouth. He offered the pack to Rick, who declined. "I guess you would say the cartels and *policia* coexist," Paco said. "Unfortunately, drugs are Mexico's number-one export. Some say that smuggling saved our economy more than once."

"Drugs help your economy, and our people pay the price."

Paco took a long drag of his cigarette. "Perhaps selling drugs wouldn't be so successful if Americanos didn't have such an appetite for them?"

Rick didn't immediately answer. He was intimately familiar with the appetite of which Paco spoke. "Still, these men down here are criminals," he finally muttered.

"Not all of them. Ordinary citizens work for the drug cartels in order to feed their families. If it weren't for the cartels, a lot of children would starve."

"Mexican children eat, and American kids get hurt," Rick said. He frowned at Paco. "You almost sound like you are defending the drug trade."

"No, *compadre*," he said, wagging his head. "What I am saying is that people will do desperate things when it comes to protecting their families, especially their *niños*. Would you not agree?"

Rick considered Paco's words. It was true he had loved his daughter and would have done anything for her. Rick also believed that Garrett McRae, the man his was tirelessly pursuing, deeply loved his son. Rick released a sigh. "I suppose I would."

Paco flicked his cigarette with his thumb, took another drag, and exhaled into the night air. Darkness had chilled the desert. "Only God is perfect," he said softly. "Men can interpret what is right and wrong. The true answer lies with the Spirit."

The two men stood in silence, reminded of their mortality as they gazed at the countless stars that shimmered across the Sonoran sky. "So tell me, Sheriff," Paco finally said. "Are you down here on official business?"

"I don't know if I would describe it as *official*, Paco," Rick answered. "To be honest, I haven't really gone through the proper channels."

Paco turned toward Rick and lifted an eyebrow. "I see. And what would you say if I asked whether you were carrying a gun?"

Rick hesitated a beat. "I guess I'd say I'd prefer you didn't ask." He turned toward his Mexican counterpart. "Look, Paco, by this time tomorrow, I'll be back in the States. I'd really appreciate it if you would let me finish up my business and head back home."

Paco lifted his hand to his lips and took a long, deep pull from his Marlboro, the bright coal illuminating his gentle eyes. He glanced toward the rear of the Durango. "You got a spare back there, *amigo*?"

"*Sí*," Rick answered with a nod and a grin.

Paco threw down his cigarette and crushed it in the sand. "Let's change your tire, then. It is getting late, Rick Morrand."

CHAPTER 55

Rick headed south on Highway 15 toward Ciudad Obregon, his rented Durango traveling on a spare tire rated for speeds of fifty miles per hour. As he sped along at seventy, he harbored serious doubts whether the spare would make it to Alamos and back up to Tucson.

Ciudad Obregon had a Farmacias Benavides, Mexico's answer to CVS. Rick purchased a tin of Band-Aids, gauze, medical tape, two elastic bandages, ibuprofen, and, most importantly, a small tube of Krazy Glue. He used the glue to pinch and seal the gash on his forehead, a technique he'd heard about from a handsome rodeo cowboy who didn't want facial injuries in the arena to affect his late-night social pursuits. The gauze was for a dirt-caked abrasion he'd discovered on his elbow, while the elastic bandages were wrapped around his ribs, which he was certain he had reinjured.

Deciding it would be best to stay in Ciudad Obregon for the night, Rick found a motel called La Flor del Desierto, translated to mean "The Desert Flower." From the looks of the faded turquoise paint on its crumbling adobe walls, the structure was more akin to a water-starved weed. Rick's room had all the opulence of a prison cell, the seedy double mattress covered with a faded and torn bedspread, the threadbare carpet emitting a dank odor that indicated someone had urinated on it more than once. The entry door appeared to have been forced open multiple times, slivers of light from the parking lot seeping through the splintered wood. Rick hooked the door chain, which was held in place by a single ill-fitting screw.

He tried to reach Sage, but his calls kept getting dropped. He lifted the handset of a phone on the nightstand. It was dead. He texted the words "Will call tomorrow. I love you" into his phone and pushed the Send button, praying that the gods of AT&T might see fit to deliver the missive to his fiancée. Placing his .357 beneath his pillow, he collapsed onto the bed, its rusted mattress springs creaking loudly as he fell asleep fully clothed, one of his boots still touching the floor.

He awoke the next morning and looked at his phone. Sage had texted back. "Where are you???" her message read. Outstanding question, he thought. His mouth was parched, his head throbbing. He'd swear it was a hangover had he not known differently. He rose from the bed and inched toward the bathroom, his palm gingerly caressing his rib cage. Standing in front of a blurred mirror, he peeled the excess Krazy Glue off the wound on his forehead and doused his face with water that smelled of sulfur. The shower provided one solid minute of hot water, for which he was eternally grateful.

Pulling on a pair of jeans and his last clean shirt, he tucked his pistol into the small of his back and walked out to the parking lot, the early morning sun stinging his eyes. His destination was seventy-six miles away.

• • •

The pueblo of Alamos lay nestled in the western foothills of the Sierra Madre, a stepping-stone along the mountain range's lengthy ascent skyward from the sea of Cortez. Once known for the mining of its rich silver and gold deposits, the village eventually evolved into a tourist center, albeit one that was more quaint and less trafficked than some of the larger cities in Mexico. The cobblestone streets were lined with magnificent architecture flavored with both Spanish and indigenous influences that whispered memories of distant grandeur.

As he rolled his wounded rental into the town, Rick decided to commence his search for Garrett McRae by locating the white Silverado that Jesse Lone Wolf had reported stolen. Though the village was small to begin with, Jack Kelly had made it even smaller by identifying a sector from which phone calls were exchanged between burner phones. Rick also possessed the photo of Garrett that was given to him by Amber McRae. While Alamos received a fair share of its visitors from the United States, the sheriff figured it wouldn't be too difficult to track down a gringo who had taken up residence there.

Taking out Garrett's picture from the top pocket of his shirt, Rick's mind trailed to his first visit to the McRae home, when Amber appeared genuinely distraught over the possibility that her husband had been trapped somewhere beneath the uncontrolled fury of the wildland fire roaring across the Crazy Mountains. What did she truly know? Were her displays of emotion authentic, or was that all by design? Driving through the hometown of legendary Mexican film diva Maria Felix, Rick wondered whether he had fallen prey to a gifted actress named Amber McRae.

His phone rang. It was Sage. "Did you receive my text?" he asked hopefully.

"What text?"

"Guess not."

"Where are you?" her voice strained with emotion. "I've been worried sick."

"I'm sorry, Sage. The cell service is a bit sketchy down here." He turned his Durango down another cobblestone street lined with shops, their entrances shaded beneath a long row of small arches that danced gracefully across the tops of spotless white pillars. "I'm in a little town called Alamos. I plan to be home tomorrow at the latest."

"I had this awful dream last night. You were in this place, and you were in some kind of grave danger."

"Just a dream, Sage."

"Are you in any danger?"

"Not at present."

"I just worry."

Sage's voice was threaded with fear and forewarning, her clairvoyance sending a cold shiver through him as he considered his near-fatal encounter with the cartel. When Christine had died, and once again when he lost Chloe, he had found himself trudging through a deep tunnel of darkness in which his life was of little consequence. He had lost purpose, and at times he was without concern whether he lived or died. In listening to Sage's soft voice, he realized how much had changed. He had a future wife and a granddaughter who needed him, now as never before. He needed them as well. They were all he had, and that meant they were everything.

"Please don't worry, Sage," he whispered as he turned another corner past a street sign that read Calle Victoria. "Like I said, I'll be heading back later today."

"Have you found what you are looking for?"

As she spoke, Rick spotted a truck parked on the right side of the street. Though it was shrouded in reddish-brown dust, he could make out that it was a white Chevrolet Silverado.

"I believe I have."

• • •

Rick glanced at a photo of a 2004 Silverado he'd saved on his phone. The truck on Calle Victoria certainly appeared to match. The fact that it had a Sonora license plate did little to dissuade him. Rick figured that Garrett ditched his Montana plates not long after he crossed the border. Finding a new set of plates in Mexico was probably easier than if he'd ordered them on Amazon.

Rick parked the Durango and got out. The street was lined with ornate structures that once served as private residences in a regal era long passed. Some now housed restaurants, mercados, and assorted clothing shops. Toward the end of the street was a two-story hotel, its sign reading "*Hacienda de Majico*," which Rick presumed meant "House of Magic." It was made of sun-dried brick that was painted bright white, the wood trim around the windows the rust-like color of red clay. Heavy arched wooden doors served as its entrance. An exterior stairway curled up one side of the building, leading to a cantina, where soft ranchera music drifted out into the warm open air.

Rick spotted a street vendor, his large wooden cart boasting everything from piñatas to fresh flowers. "*Buenas días, señor*," he said, smiling as he approached.

"*Buenos días*," the man said. His tanned skin was the color of dark leather. He grinned at Rick, exposing yellowish teeth, two of which were rimmed in gold. His face was smooth, save for wispy hairs on his chin, and his eyes watery and bloodshot, either from dust or drink.

"*¿Hablas inglés?*" Rick asked.

"*Un poco.*"

Rick lifted the photo of Garrett McRae from his pocket. "You see this man?" he asked, tapping the photo with his index finger. "He is my nephew."

"Nephew?"

"Sí," Rick answered. He patted his own chest with his palm. "I am uncle."

"Uncle?" the man said. "Sí, sí." He pointed at the photo. "Tu sobrino."

"Sí, mi sobrino," Rick said. He pointed two fingers toward his own eyes. "You see mi sobrino?"

The man looked at the photo again. He tapped a finger on it, his eyes brightening with seeming recognition. He paused for several seconds in contemplation, studying Rick's face with caution. Rick reached into his pocket, peeled off two twenty-dollar bills, and handed them to the vendor.

The man prepared to speak, then hesitated again. He stared at the money in Rick's hand, pushing his mouth to one side as though he'd suddenly lost confidence in his memory. Rick smiled and peeled off two more twenties.

The vendor's eyes trailed up the stairway of the hotel. "La cantina," he said. "Tu sobrino like la cantina."

CHAPTER 56

Rick climbed the sunset-colored terra-cotta stairs, his fingers tracing along the smooth paint of the white mud-brick wall. His breath pounded from his nose like a piston, his heart hammering in anticipation of a face-to-face encounter with Garrett McRae.

He spotted the cantina through a blue-tiled archway bordered on each side by potted palm trees. A bartender wearing a white cotton shirt leaned against a counter that fronted a backlit wall of liquor. No patrons were present, but a half-filled glass rested beside a dark long-neck bottle of beer at the end of the bar.

"*Buenas tardes, amigo,*" Rick said awkwardly as he sat on a padded stool.

"Good afternoon, sir," the man replied with a smile, perhaps assuming that Rick had reached the outer boundaries of his Spanish. "Can I get you a *cerveza?*"

"No," Rick said, shaking his head and smiling. "Do you have a Coke in a bottle? I hear Mexican Coca-Cola is quite good."

"*Mucho azúcar,*" the bartender said with a laugh. "Lots of sugar."

"Perfect."

The bartender put a glass of ice in front of him, a wedge of lime on the rim. He poured the Coke, then set the bottle on the bar. Rick took a long drink. Sweet indeed. The soft, tender voice of a Mexican vocalist came through a pair of speakers mounted in the ceiling. Two fans twirled quietly above. Rick stared through a pair of paned doors leading to a tiled patio, feeling a delicate, warm breeze trickle gracefully through the cantina. He thought of Sage, his stomach churning and heart sinking with every note of the Spanish song. He yearned for her, cursing himself for leaving, vowing to never be away from her again.

"You like this song, señor?" the bartender asked.

Rick nodded. "Yes … I do. It's beautiful."

"It is called *Cuando Calienta el Sol*. It means 'When the sun warms.'"The bartender picked up the bottle and filled Rick's glass to the top. "A man named Javier Solis sang it. He was very popular among the Mexican people. There's no telling how great he might have been. He died very young."

The notes of the soft melody continued to float through the air. Rick looked at the bartender. "How old was he?"

"Thirty-five."

"You sure he's dead?"

The bartender's brow furrowed. "Señor?"

"Never mind."

From the corner of his eye, Rick noticed a man enter the room. He appeared relaxed, although his stride suggested a slight limp. The man was American. He wore a flowered shirt, white cotton slacks, and light-brown leather sandals. His brown hair was thick and nearly shoulder-length, a full beard covering his face. Taking his seat at the end of the bar, he emptied the rest of the bottle into his glass. "*Uno más, Sergio*," he instructed the bartender. He shot a brief glance in Rick's direction and quickly turned away.

Sergio uncapped a Bohemia beer and presented it to the man. "Here you go, Mr. Robert."

Mr. Robert?

Rick fished into his pocket for his phone. He opened his text messages, locating the burner phone's number sent to him by Jack Kelly. Drawing a deep breath, he pressed the Call button. After several moments, he heard the sound of a ring. The man at the end of the bar was drinking his glass of beer. He remained frozen for three rings before he put down his glass and slowly reached into the top pocket of his shirt. He tapped the screen and held the phone to his ear. "Yeah?"

Rick swiveled his stool in the man's direction. "Good afternoon, Garrett," he said into his own phone. "My name is Sheriff Rick Morrand." He picked up his drink and moved two seats closer. Garrett stared at him slack-jawed, slowly returning the phone to his pocket. With his eyes riveted on Rick, he tossed a bill onto the bar, stood, and turned to leave.

Rick placed a loose grip on his bicep. "You know, Garrett, I've traveled a long way. What do you say you sit and visit with me a bit?"

Garrett slid back onto his bar stool and took a long sip of his beer. His expression betrayed a mix of wariness and desperation as he seemingly contemplated a final move. He said nothing.

Rick removed his hat and laid it crown-down on the bar. He roamed Garrett's features. A diet of Mexican food had fattened him. The beard disguised his sharp cheekbones, but the intensity of his eyes matched his photo. "Everyone I have talked to about you has nothing but admiration," Rick said. "From what I can tell, you are a regular model citizen." He sipped his Coke, licking his lips to savor the taste. "I'm trying to figure out why a guy like you would do something like this."

"You know why I did it, Sheriff," Garrett answered in a somber tone.

"Your son?"

"My son."

Rick nodded. "I had a chance to meet Gabe. He seems like a wonderful little boy."

Garrett swallowed, his eyes squinting as his face muscles grew tight. He started to reach for his beer bottle, then withdrew his hand. "Gabe is my everything, Sheriff. When he got injured, I couldn't begin to forgive myself."

"It was an accident," Rick offered. "Not the first time a child has been injured, and it probably won't be the last."

"I don't see it that way. It was my negligence—my *stupidity*—that destroyed that sweet boy's life." He looked at Rick, his eyes glassy. "*Accident?* I'm afraid that's letting me off easy. It was completely my fault."

Rick stirred the ice cubes in his Coke. "So, you figured you needed to find a way to make it right?"

Garrett hiked his brow. "What did I have to lose? Worth a shot, wasn't it? I'm mean, Gabe getting hurt destroyed my family." He gazed out the window of the cantina. "First, Amber and I couldn't talk, and then we *wouldn't* talk. She hated me for what happened, and I can't blame her."

"Is that why she had an affair with Randall Boone?"

Garrett's eyes snapped sharply toward Rick. Perhaps the memory still burned. "That was the rumor. It doesn't matter much anyway. He got his in the end, didn't he?"

Rick cocked his head. "How so?"

Garrett allowed himself a half-smile. "I almost framed him for my *murder*. We had a little scuffle near the campsite. I could've whupped him easily. Instead, I let him break my nose, and I bled like a stuck pig all over him."

"So I've heard," Rick said. He paused a beat, glancing at his soft drink. "How did he manage to get his DNA on your wallet?"

"The night we set up camp, I left my wallet on top of my backpack and asked him to toss it to me. Boone being Boone, he starts rummaging through it before I grabbed it from him." Garrett shook his head in disbelief. "He isn't all that bright."

"The fight explains how your blood got on his shirt," Rick said. "How about all the blood that was found on your belongings? There was a lot of it. In fact, the amount of blood had people convinced that you either died in a bear attack, or maybe Boone gutted you and made it *look* like a bear attack."

Garrett hesitated, perhaps unsure whether he wanted to answer. "I learned phlebotomy as part of my paramedic training, and I had stored up a nice supply of blood that I carried beneath my gear in my pack."

Rick slowly nodded. "So you figured if you soaked your clothes in your blood and placed your rib and leg bones among them, you'd have us convinced."

"I thought it was a good plan," Garrett murmured, his voice colored with defeat.

Rick shifted on his bar stool and studied Garrett's weathered, conflicted face. "Who started the fire?" Rick asked. "Was it you?"

Garrett's forehead crinkled, his expression implying Rick's question was preposterous. "First responders are my brothers and sisters, Sheriff. I would never set a fire that might put them in danger."

"Who was it, then? Boone?"

"That's possible, but I doubt it. I'd heard it started from a downed power line. A lot of kids on that east side of the Crazies like to shoot ravens off the wires. Maybe it was one of them?"

"Were you and Boone friends?"

"We were," Garrett answered, "and then we weren't."

"Boone messing with your wife must have been a hard pill to swallow."

"Like I said before, that was a rumor. I hold no bitterness toward Amber. I haven't been a saint either."

"Are you referring to Meredith Hart?"

Garrett huffed. "Nothing happened between me and Meredith. We were just friends." He drew a deep sigh. "Let's just say Amber and I had a troubled marriage, and I was far from perfect."

Rick sighed, recalling how he had succumbed to temptation when he had burrowed downward into the deep, dark tunnels of alcohol and cocaine. He could barely recall details of his indiscretions, given they had occurred during blackouts. He vowed never to tell Christine, not wanting to hurt her. But she knew. Oh, she *definitely* knew. There was a reason women give birth, he reasoned. They can endure more pain than men. Any kind of pain.

"I assume your wife knew of your plan?"

Garrett shook his head, lips curling downward. "Nope. Not necessarily."

"Not necessarily?"

"I mean, she knew I had a life insurance policy, and I told her what to do if anything happened to me. But as far as her knowing any particular plan—"

"Have you been in contact with her?"

"Not directly," Garrett answered. He glanced at his shiny inexpensive watch, likely purchased locally. "But it's my understanding that she should be across the Mexican border by now."

"Headed where?"

Garrett shot him a wry smile. "C'mon, Sheriff, you know I can't tell you that."

Rick sipped his Coke, wiping his lips with the back of his hand. "Well, I doubt she is coming here. I would imagine you came to this town hoping you could lie low until you could meet up with her. She's headed to one of the larger cities, where arrangements have been made with a doctor who will start stem-cell therapy in an effort to help your son. Am I getting warm?"

Garrett shrugged. "Well, she does have resources to pay for that therapy ..."

"So she *was* in on it?"

"How so? Her husband dies tragically, making her a single mother with a disabled child. Why wouldn't she want to collect on a life insurance policy?"

"You're saying that she knew nothing about this?"

"That's what I'm saying."

"The insurance company she defrauded might not agree."

"Single mother with a disabled child," Garrett repeated. "From a public relations perspective, how did that work out for them last time?"

Rick cocked his head. "You sure seem to know a lot about current events in Montana. I assume you've been communicating with your friend Mr. Lone Wolf?"

"I was until you guys took his phone," Garrett said. "I guess he had quite a start when Boone walked into the Gold Bar with blood all over his shirt. Jesse was sure that son of a bitch had done me in."

"If Jesse was in communication with you, that would make him an accomplice."

Garrett drew a long breath. "I sent Jesse a phone through FedEx from here in Mexico. It's not his fault he answered it."

"He didn't have to keep talking to you."

"Phone records don't say what we talked about."

Rick smiled. Garrett's eyes carried a seductive sparkle. He had an odd, endearing quality that was infectious to men and likely seductive to women. It was no surprise he was well liked—if not revered—by those who knew him well. Had circumstances been different, Rick could see fishing or hunting with him, maybe cracking a beer, if Rick still drank beer.

"How about the truck? The Silverado?"

"It was *stolen*."

Rick placed his elbow on the bar, stroking his lower lip with an index finger. "You got it all figured out, don't you?"

Garrett looked at his half-full beer. This time he drank it. All of it. He tapped two fingers on the bar. "*Uno más, Sergio*," he said. "*Por favor*." Sergio placed a dark-brown bottle in front of Garrett, rivulets of moisture glimmering as they streamed down its sides.

"Look, Sheriff, you and I both know that insurance companies have more money than God," Garrett said. "Insurance companies, banks—remember 'too big to fail'?"

Rick's mind flashed to the stack of medical bills lying on his desk—bills that should have been covered by Sage's insurance, had she not been cancelled. "So that justifies committing fraud?" he asked, but Garrett didn't answer.

Shadows of clouds moved along the whitewashed walls of the mudbrick building across the *avenida*. The wind had picked up, the heavy air now drifting through the window smelling like rain. Rick turned back toward Garrett, eyes narrowed. "Out of curiosity, what made you decide to get a policy with Western Montana Insurance?"

"I'd heard their name before, and so I studied them," Garrett said. "I found out that the guy who started the agency had fallen ill, and his son had taken over. I figured the kid might be green—maybe vulnerable."

"Is that where Lizzie came in?"

Garrett's eyes ignited. "Elizabeth," he said with disgust, practically spitting out her name. His face reddened as he pressed his lips together and stared at his glass. "Lizzie was the name she apparently chose, but to me she's my niece Elizabeth. She wanted to borrow money—said it was for her *tuition*. I offered her an opportunity instead. I figured she could make the acquaintance of the insurance agent—keep an eye on him, maybe even compromise him. She also was supposed to have my back, in case any problems came up."

"What kind of problems?"

"Well, I'd hoped your coroner would look things over and issue a death certificate," Garrett said. "But apparently, he's a bit on the stubborn side."

Rick nodded. "That he is."

"Jesse told me that the coroner in Lupine County is not only a drunk but also a scumbag of sorts. I guess he tried to lure a couple of young Native girls off the res a couple of times, among other things. Not what you'd call a high-character guy." Garrett traced his finger along the rim of his glass of beer. "I figured he might be a little more *flexible*, so I asked Elizabeth to approach him about the death certificate, see what she could work out. It wasn't an accident that I *died* right on the border of Lupine County."

"So Lizzie blackmailed Pernell Crawford? Or bribed him? Which was it?"

"I suppose her plan was to bribe him, but I guess he didn't accept credit terms," Garrett said. "Elizabeth is resourceful—too much so, perhaps." His jaw muscles tensed. "All I know is that the Lupine County coroner issued a death certificate."

Rick lifted his chin. "Do you know where Lizzie is?"

Garrett's nostrils flared, his face contorted with wrath. "I damn sure wish I did," he said. "I don't take too kindly to someone trying to kill my wife."

"Why did you make Lizzie a beneficiary on your policy?"

Garrett wagged his head. "It was a last-minute decision, in case something happened to Amber. She kept urging me to do it, and now I know why. I never actually told her I'd done it, but somehow she found out." He drank from his glass of beer. "I should have never trusted her. She got greedy."

Rick sipped his Coke. The ice had melted. The drink wasn't as sweet. "You grow up in Montana?"

"I did."

"And you were willing to leave forever, never able to come back to your home—or anywhere else in the US for that matter—just to try to help your son?"

Garrett's eyes flared again. "I stole Gabe's life. When he got hurt, doctors couldn't even say how long he might live. He couldn't play with other kids. No hiking. No fishing. No hunting. No high school sports. No girlfriend. No prom. No wife. No kids of his own."

"You don't know whether that's—"

"I *do* know, Sheriff!" Garrett said through gritted teeth, slamming his open palm on the bar. "I took his life away from him—at least, any kind of *normal* life. If he had no life, I had no life." His face crumpled with emotion, his eyelids clenched. He turned toward Rick. "I know about your daughter, Sheriff. I know about Chloe."

Rick's eyes lasered toward him. "What do you mean, you *know* about Chloe?"

"It's why I chose you."

"It's why you *chose* me?"

"I planned every detail of this, Sheriff," he said, his tone intensifying. "I thought it was perfect." He glanced toward Sergio, then lowered his voice just above a whisper. "I even planned for this moment. Right here, right now. I figured that if for some reason my plan didn't work, you might understand."

"Understand what?"

Garrett leaned closer to Rick, eyes pleading, sweat beading on his brow. "C'mon, Sheriff. You mean to tell me that you wouldn't do anything—*anything*—for your daughter to be alive today?"

"How about we leave my daughter out of this?"

"How can we?" Garrett asked. "If anyone understands a father's love of his child, it would be you."

Rick's stomach felt like he had swallowed something still alive. His brain whirled, his vision blurring. No matter how much he resisted, he couldn't seem to stop tailgating Chloe's hearse. He drew a deep breath. "You defrauded an insurance company. You broke the law."

Garrett nodded. "Yes, I broke the *law*, and so you came here looking for *justice*," he said, putting air quotes around the words. He edged ever closer, his breath smelling of malt and hops. "But let me ask you, Sheriff. How do you truly define law and justice?"

Rick swallowed. Images of his loved ones marched through his mind. He thought of the death of Christine, the murder of Chloe, Sage's battle with cancer, Abby forever robbed of her mother. Justice? Not so much.

He considered young Gabriel McRae and a freak occurrence that had destroyed a family. How do such things happen and why? Garrett McRae was a former high school football star. He'd married his childhood sweetheart, was blessed with a son, and was serving his community. In an instant, all of that was snatched from his grasp as though it had never really belonged to him.

Garrett's eyes were fixed on Rick, perhaps petitioning some kind of verdict. Rick threw him a glance before pushing his empty glass toward the bartender. "Let me have another one of those Cokes, Sergio," he said. "I'd also like to see a menu."

Sergio nodded, filled Rick's glass with ice, and placed an open bottle in front of him. He handed Rick a laminated menu, the words *Angel's Restaurante y Cantina* scripted between two clip-art palm trees. Garrett looked at the sheriff, eyes curious and wary.

"You know I'm going to have to report this," Rick said as he casually perused the menu. "Thing is, it would be a shame for me to come all the way down here and not have some authentic Mexican food." He bit the side of his lip. "Chicken enchiladas are what I was thinkin'." He laid down the menu and turned back toward Garrett. "I'm figuring it will take at least an hour or so for these to get cooked up and eaten." He rubbed the stubble on his chin. "Though I'm not all that familiar with Mexico, I understand it's a pretty big place."

Garrett's eyes widened, his expression somewhere between skepticism and disbelief. He rapidly threw two more Mexican bills on the bar and rose from his stool, glimpsing at Sergio as he began to leave. Rick grabbed his arm. "And, Garrett?" he said. "Stop drinkin' so damn much. You have a lot of people who love you."

Garrett nodded and hurried out the door. Rick wondered whether he would ever see him again.

• • •

Two hours later Rick walked down the steps of the cantina, where the street vendor was handing flowers to a tourist. Stuffing folded bills into his shirt pocket, the vendor smiled as Rick approached. "Amigo!" he said. "You find tu sobrino?"

Rick wagged his head. "*Sin suerte*," he said, Spanish for "no luck."

"So sorry, señor," the man said. "I was sure you find him."

"Yeah, me too," Rick murmured. He gazed at bouquets of flowers soaking in buckets of water arranged on three different levels of a green wooden stand. "Tell me, señor—do you have any flowers called tube … tube …"

"Tuberose?" the man shouted. "Sí, señor! I have tuberose. Freshly cut this morning!" He reached into one of the buckets behind him and produced a bouquet. "Beautiful, no? Only twenty dollars!"

Rick studied the bouquet. Water dripped from long vibrant stems that ascended through small white flowers to pinkish-green clusters of buds that had yet to blossom. The fragrance was rich and forceful, almost intoxicating. "Do you have a vase with water?" Rick asked. "I have a long journey."

"Sí, señor!" the man said excitedly. "For you, only ten dollars American!"

"Very kind of you," Rick muttered. He reached into his pocket and handed the vendor thirty American dollars. The man filled a rose-colored vase with water and placed the flowers inside. Rick curled his wrist around the vase, the aroma of the flowers overwhelming him as though they had been sent directly from heaven. He smiled as he envisioned the joy they would bring Sage and Abby upon his return to Montana.

He prayed he could keep them alive.

CHAPTER 57

The bouquet of fresh tuberose Rick purchased from the street vendor in Alamos not only made it back to Riverton but managed to last a full two weeks. Sage admired the flowers each morning, burying her nose into them as she drew a deep breath and filled her senses with their abundant fragrance.

"You sure you still want to honeymoon in Mexico?" he asked her one morning as he sipped a cup of coffee. "Helen told me Hawaii is pretty good."

Sage's forehead crinkled. "When did Helen go to Hawaii?"

"She didn't," Rick answered with a shrug.

A tea kettle whistled on the stove. Sage turned off the burner and poured the steaming water into her cup. She paused in thought for a moment before replacing the kettle. "Are you having second thoughts about Mexico?" she asked as she plunged her tea bag beneath the water.

Rick's mind flashed to his late-night encounter with the narcos who nearly dropped his rental car on his head. "Second thoughts? Me? No," he said flatly. "I just thought you might want some options."

"Are you having second thoughts about anything else?" Sage asked, sipping her tea before placing it on the counter.

Rick stepped closer, pressing his forehead against hers. "None whatsoever." Her eyes were bright and hopeful, her skin regaining its healthy fullness. Another round of chemo was scheduled, but Dr. Tillotson promised it would be far less intrusive.

Sage watched her fingertips toy with a button on Rick's collar. "Did you ever hear anything more about Garrett McRae?" she asked. "I mean, did the FBI extradite him?"

Rick shook his head innocently. "Nothing yet. I'm thinking the Bureau has more pressing concerns in Mexico at the moment."

Sage lifted her head, eyes seeming to gaze into his soul. "That sure is strange. You actually found him, and then he was gone. Flat-out vanished, huh?"

Rick nodded, pressing his lips tightly together. "Flat-out vanished."

She flashed an amused smile. "You are a good man, Rick Morrand."

"Think so?"

"I know so," she answered, luring him into a long kiss.

• • •

Rachel was filling a box of belongings from inside her desk when Spencer approached and handed her an envelope.

"What's this?" she asked. Her eyes were moist, her cheeks smeared with mascara.

"It's a little something I believe you deserve for your service to Western Montana Insurance Company. Go ahead. Open it."

Rachel slid her manicured thumbnail beneath the flap of the envelope and pulled out the check inside. Her chin fell as she stared at it. "This is a lot of money, Spencer."

"Thanks to my father's estate and the sale of this agency, I have a lot of money."

She lunged forward and wrapped her arms around his neck, catching him off guard. He blinked his eyes rapidly and gingerly patted her shoulder blades. After a moment, she pulled away and looked intently into his eyes. "What are you going to do?"

"I'm going back to school," Spencer said without hesitation. "I'm going to become an architect." Rachel tilted her head, smiled warmly, and hugged him again.

The front door of the agency opened. Lorraine's daughter Tilly from the diner walked in, a bright smile glowing from her freckled face. Her red hair danced on her shoulders. She wore a tan suede jacket over a flowered cotton dress that flowed gracefully over the top of her cowgirl boots. "Hi, Tilly," Rachel said. "How can we help you?"

"She's here to see me," Spencer said. "We have a date."

Rachel nodded. She cast a devious glance toward Spencer. He winked at her before following Tilly out the door.

• • •

Lizzie sat in front of the manager of the newest franchise opened by Sundown Beanery, by far the largest coffee chain in the Southwest. He had kept his eyes glued to her resume, apparently incapable of looking at Lizzie for only a few moments before his face would flush.

"So, Lisa, what brings you to Phoenix?" he asked, stealing a split-second glimpse.

"My aunt has fallen gravely ill, and she asked me to help take care of her," Lizzie said. "I assure you that helping her won't interfere with my duties here." She paused a beat, softening her tone. "I do need a job, though, to help with her expenses."

The manager nodded. "I see you listed your previous employers, as well as some references."

"Yes," Lizzie said, smiling confidently. Her references were fictitious humans, of course, but she wasn't concerned. Once a manager met her, they never bothered to call references. In most cases, she was hired on the spot.

"Can you start on Monday?" the manager asked.

"Of course," she said.

• • •

"Gross!"

Rick and Sage interrupted their lengthy kiss. Abby was standing at the edge of the kitchen, her pink nightshirt drooping off her shoulders as she rubbed sleep out of her eyes.

"Abby, doggone it, will you quit doing that?"

His granddaughter ignored him. "Do you really think I might get a horse for my birthday?"

"Good morning, Abby," Sage said.

"What?"

"You think you might say good morning before asking about birthday presents?"

"Sorry—good morning," Abby said, rolling her eyes. "I was just wondering if—"

"You really want a second horse?" Rick asked.

"Absolutely!"

"You sure?"

"Yes!"

Sage glared at Rick, silently mouthing the words, "You're spoiling her!"

"A horse it is, then," Rick said.

"Yes!" Abby screamed as she ran from the room. Sage edged back toward the counter, shaking her head in defeat. Her future husband placed his hand around her waist and tugged her close to him.

Their eyes met and they kissed again.

If you have enjoyed this novel, please consider writing a review. That is the best way to thank an author.

To connect with the author and discover new books, visit www.PeterJRyan.net.

ACKNOWLEDGEMENTS

MY SINCERE APPRECIATION TO my brothers and sisters on the Paradise Valley Fire Department, who have patiently shared their expertise over the past several years. I also am grateful to the members of Park County Search and Rescue, as well as the law enforcement officers I've come to know in Park and Sweet Grass counties. Additional law enforcement insight was provided by Mike Wright, who retired as Master Sergeant after a 30-year career in Washoe County, Nevada, and David Gee, retired four-term sheriff from Hillsborough County, Florida. Medical expertise comes from my nephew, Dr. Casey Cates, and my good friend, Dr. Joseph Nuzzarello. Special thanks to my wife, Derilynn, who provides honest feedback and tireless support as the first person to read my pages.